Praise for *Thicker Than Blood*

"It is rare that a contemporary novel offers the heart-shattering wisdom of Thicker Than Blood. In its portrayals of the always-shifting 'American Identity,' it offers readers insight into how we have perceived the 'American Dream' during the past three generations. Jan English Leary's novel masterfully unfolds the stories of unforgettable characters at the moments when they are making and losing and returning and abandoning all their first assumptions of home and of family."
— Kevin McIlvoy, author of *57 Octaves Below Middle C*, *The Complete History of New Mexico*, *Hyssop*, *Little Peg*, and *The Fifth Station*

"Jan English Leary, a first-rate storyteller, examines the intersection between idealism, the harsh reality of post-racist America, the challenges of adoption and the brutality of family life in general. The journey of parenthood is not for the faint-hearted. I read this novel with great admiration for the writer and vicarious pain for her characters."
— Goldie Goldbloom, author of *The Paperbark Shoe, You Lose These*, and *On Division Street*

"Written with uncommon grace and profound insight, *Thicker Than Blood* is a brave and poignant novel."
— Lynn Sloan, author of *Principles of Navigation, This Far Isn't Far Enough*, and *Midstream*

Praise for *Skating on the Vertical*

"Leary is a truly fine storyteller, and her characters surprise themselves (and us) with realizations that arrive late, but never--we hope, because we care for them--too late."
— Lori Ostlund, author of *The Bigness of the World* and *After the Parade*

"...a lyrical work of art that grabs your heart at every turn."
— Centered on Books

"...in *Skating on the Vertical*, Leary has such feeling for her characters, bringing us into the center of their lives, the conflicts they face, and the emotions they experience as a result. In other words, she makes these characters remarkably, and often heart-rendingly, real."
— Small Press Picks

"Jan English Leary's collection, *Skating on the Vertical and Other Stories* (Fomite) is one that illuminates the vital and pivotal moments in people's lives, in impressively elegant ways."
—Sabotage Reviews

Praise for *Town and Gown*

Jan English Leary's latest novel sweeps the reader into the lives of two women from the same small town as they launch into adulthood. Wanda, a farm girl, marries her high school boyfriend, works at the local bakery, and hopes to someday start a family. Callie, the daughter of a college professor, dreams of bigger adventures far from her overprotective parents and the college town mentality. With writing deeply-rooted in place and character, Leary masterfully immerses us in the lives of these two women as they set out on separate journeys, only to discover the many ways their paths intersect. *Town and Gown* is a moving portrayal of resiliency and second chances, reminding us that while we can't always choose our circumstances, there's power to be found in how we respond.

—Marcie Roman, author of *Journey to the Parallels*

I admire the no-frills, and no-waste, prose Jan English Leary deploys in her novel Town and Gown to narrate the lives of two women growing up–one from the farm and one from the hill–in a college village in the northeast. Despite dread events and bleak prospects that might give Greek drama a run for its money, there is a kind of admirable resilience here, too. Lacking a scintilla of nostalgia, this fast paced and gripping novel does not pine for lost glory days, but instead offers a bracing account of today's small-town America with a subtle but potent feminist slant.

—Charles Lamar Phillips, author of *Estranged* and *Dead South*

This lively, entertaining novel features both deeply felt characters and an engaging plot. It immerses us in the struggles of two young women--one a farmer's daughter, the other a professor's child--as they seek to establish themselves in the world. Through their stories, we see how simple categories, such as the divide between the intellectual and the agrarian, can be limiting, and we come to question easy binaries concerning social status and destiny. The novel also explores the assumptions we make about each other and the kinds of compromises–some big, some small–we all must learn to live with as the inevitable result of creating a life. *Town and Gown* is an empathetic and insightful page turner of a novel, one that I won't soon forget.

—Beth Castrodale, author of *In This Ground*
and *I Mean You No Harm*

Also by Jan English Leary

Thicker Than Blood (novel)

Skating on the Vertical (stories)

Town and Gown

A Novel

Jan English Leary

Fomite
Burlington VT

ISBN-978-1-953236-85-2
Library of Congress Control Number: 2022948687

Fomite
58 Peru Street
Burlington, VT 05401
www.fomitepress.com
09-30-2023

To my families

Prologue

In the Venn Diagram of Shelton (PA) High School, three groups intersect: faculty children, townies, and farmers. The fac brats and townies overlap in classes, athletics, and school activities. The farmers exist on the edges, taking their basic classes—food and nutrition, life skills, metal shop—putting in their time until graduation when, after maybe a stint in the military, they work at a family farm or a factory. Townies go to state schools, if they go to college at all, and many marry people they've known since birth. The professors' kids take AP classes with the ambition of attending top colleges, the Big and Little Ivies or the better state schools like Michigan or Berkeley, which will take them to lives away from their hometown.

PART 1

1

WANDA MACDONALD

In May, the day of her senior prom, while her friends were getting their hair styled and their makeup done, Wanda dressed in black pants, white shirt, and bowtie, then twisted her hair up and held it with pins. She and David Zacek were working a catering job at Brewster College for Alumni Weekend, a reception for rich graduates. Wanda worked as a server and David parked cars. It was good money, paid in cash. They were saving every penny for their wedding one month away.

David picked her up, wearing khakis, a white shirt and tie, looking uncomfortable. "How can anyone wear these things? I can hardly breathe."

"But you look handsome," she said, running her hand along his cheek.

They drove to the college and parked at the far end of the campus. David took his place near the empty field on Cosgrove Road. They agreed to meet when it was over to drive to their spot before going to the post-prom party. "I want to jump you right now," he said. "You look hot dressed like that."

"So, you like it when I dress like a man?"

"What? No." He frowned. "You just look really good."

Wanda kissed him and continued down the road to the Student Center to get her assignment.

The campus was crawling with old men in plastic bowler hats, printed with maroon and white bands saying BREWSTER and their graduation year. Women wore jewel-colored sheaths and sleek, blown-out hair. All the old graduates were men, but at some point, the college had started letting in girls so some of the younger women wore maroon and white ribbons. Wanda tied on an apron and picked up a tray of appetizers to pass out to guests. People grabbed cheese puffs and bacon-wrapped dates, tossing crumpled napkins in the direction of her tray, most of them landing on the grass. Her next tray held Champagne flutes, and she carefully made her way into the crowd, trying not to jostle anyone. She hated these events. Lots of loud, drunk rich people, stuffing their faces. Feeling invisible, she zigged to avoid a man to her left but felt an elbow tip over her tray, sending her entire set of glasses to the ground. The man wiped his sleeve and glared at her as if she'd run into him on purpose. Her wet shirt clung to her chest making her bra show. Mr. Gallagher, her boss, gave her holy hell for the broken glasses and wasted Champagne. She nearly quit on the spot, but they needed the money for two months' rent up front. She swallowed back tears, forced herself to smile at all the jerks, knowing she'd pocket a couple of hundred dollars at the end of the night. The more she learned about rich people, the less she wanted to know.

Since she and David had started working receptions, they'd stopped at a few frat parties after their jobs, but Wanda hated them—the noise, the smells of beer, pot, and puke. College girls were such bitches, looking right past her in her waiter's outfit, clearly not a student. At one party, a girl, totally wasted, hung over the shoulder of a fraternity guy as he carried her up the stairs. If this was college, Wanda wasn't sure she wanted any part of it.

Wanda's family owned a one-hundred-acre dairy farm two miles past the college on Goshen Road. Her brothers, Kenny and Joe, lived nearby with their families and worked with their dad. Mary Sue and Gail, her sisters-in-law, had grown up together in town and now spent their days hanging out with Wanda's mother. Life on a dairy farm was hard, and she admired her parents, but it wasn't the life she wanted.

By the time she reached middle school, the groups had been set: The Honors Kids, the Jocks, the Townies, and finally, the Farmers. The Honors Kids were so full of themselves like they ruled the school. Townies, even the ones who didn't go to college, looked down on the farm kids. She was embarrassed to be at the bottom of the ladder. Stuck out on the farm, she had to ride the bus every morning and afternoon. She'd always imagined that when she grew up, she'd live in town with houses close by and sidewalks where she could walk to the market, the bakery, and the pharmacy, where she could send her kids off to school on foot. Out on the farm, she'd missed that sense of community.

Unlike David, who was in danger of not graduating, Wanda liked school, but since she was in the non-college track, she sat with her friends who didn't care about learning and couldn't wait to graduate. She quickly did her homework and spent the rest of her time reading books from the school library. Historical novels about Scotland and France, places far away and long ago, were her favorites.

This last semester, Mr. Brooks, her Practical Science teacher, suggested she go to college. She was smart. Why not? She told him there was no money and besides, she was getting married. He pointed out that married people also went to college and asked what she wanted to do with her life. She wanted to be with David. That much she knew. However, and she'd never told anyone this, she'd thought of becoming a nurse. At first an LPN, and maybe, eventually, an RN. When she was twelve, after her grandmother had a stroke and moved to the farm, Wanda liked taking care of her, making sure she took her medication on time and got regular exercise. It was her grandmother who suggested Wanda become a nurse. She told Wanda she regretted not going further in school, but no one back then expected a girl to be educated. In the last days of her life, Wanda set up a cot in the room. When it was clear her grandmother had died, Wanda lay down next to her and hugged her, saying goodbye, before going to find her mother.

Lately, the idea of nursing had popped up before darting away again. As graduation and her wedding approached, Wanda particularly missed her grandmother and wished she could share these events with her. She was pretty sure her parents and David wouldn't think it worth the money to go to college. But she was too busy now to think of that.

At the end of the alumni reception, when she'd stuffed all the trash into garbage bags and tossed the empties into recycling, she went to find David, desperate to get out of there, to feel his arms around her even though she was sweaty and stank of sour Champagne.

David was leaning against a car, drinking a beer, talking to his friend, Mosher. She wanted to leave right away, but he said he had to wait until the last car had been claimed. He didn't look a bit tired. "Then," he said, draining his beer and dropping the empty, "we can head to the post-prom party."

Fingering her engagement ring, she leaned over and whispered in his ear, "I thought we were going to have some time together." She nibbled his earlobe. "If we don't leave soon, I'm going home without you."

David slung his arm around her shoulder and nuzzled her, tossing the last set of keys to Mosher. "Listen. We're going to book. See you at Majewski's later, okay?"

"Sure, go ahead," said Mosher, as he flicked his wrist and made the sound of a whip. "*Wuh*-pssh!"

"Yeah," said Wanda, over her shoulder. "You wish."

In the car, she yanked off her tie and let down her hair, opening the window, letting the breeze ruffle her hair and cool her face. She leaned her head on David's shoulder and he steered with one hand out to their spot on Skyview Drive, pulling off the road and bumping down the path between the half-grown stalks. He grabbed the blanket from the back seat and spread it out on the ground before pulling her to him. She unbuckled his belt, he unhooked her bra and peeled down her underpants. Perching on his elbows, he kissed her neck and her breasts as she rose to meet him. When they both came, he flopped down on top of her and they lay there, catching their breath, until he got hard again. The cry he made when he finished was so funny and dear. She loved that she could make him feel that way, every time. Tonight, it was hot, so they lay on the blanket, looking up at the stars, pretending they were in their own bed, married, talking about how many kids they'd have. He wanted four. "No way," she said. "I'm the one who's doing to have to do all the work." Two were plenty.

"I'll help out," he said, gently rubbing her earlobe.

"Sure, you will. They all say that. But your boobs aren't going to sag." He cupped her breast and said he'd love them, saggy or not. They snuggled and he stroked her hair until the air grew cool. Then they dressed and drove to Majewski's barn where the post-prom party was in full swing.

They parked down Cooper Street behind a string of cars and could feel the thump of bass in their bodies as they drew closer. Outside, guys in tee-shirts were smoking cigars and holding red plastic cups as they huddled around the keg. The girls had traded their prom dresses for jeans or shorts, tendrils hanging down from their updos. When they saw David and Wanda, a few of them cheered, "You guys came! All right!" and handed them each a cup of beer. Wanda walked over to a group of girls who were complaining about the rigged Prom Queen vote, how the cool kids were never going to give it to someone outside their clique. One girl, Shelly, her makeup smeared, eyes red-rimmed, said, "Oh, Wanda. It was the *besht* prom ever." But by the look of some of the couples—Andrea Gates screaming at George Szerlip in the corner, Brittany Jones throwing up by the fire pit, prissy Ann Lemond, who couldn't wait to give it up to Sean Fiscetti that night but not remember in the morning—it wasn't the best night for everyone. Still, she'd have liked to see the decorations, to have worn a beautiful gown and danced just once with David under the mirror ball, his arms holding her tight, her face nestled in the curve of his neck, to have a special celebration at the end of all those years in school.

David played beer pong while Wanda stood, nursing her warm beer. Her best friend, Michelle Barnes, wasn't there because her fiancé, Bobby Schneider, who was five years older, had refused to go to a dance with a bunch of kids. She'd made him take her out to a nice dinner at Forento's and buy her a corsage so she could wear her best dress and get her hair done.

Ellen Cambrie came over to her. "Why didn't you and David go to prom?"

"We had a catering job."

"But you'll never get another chance for your Senior prom."

"We're saving money for our wedding."

"That's right. You're getting married. Oh, I'm so jealous."

Wanda said Ellen and Billy would be married before too long, then she signaled to David. She was beat. He saw her but didn't budge. She loved the boy so much it hurt, but when was he going to grow up? She waited for him to finish his game, then he drove her home. In the car, she said she was glad they hadn't spent all that money on the prom. "All I need is to be with you," she said, kissing his ear, then laying her head on his shoulder as she felt herself drift off.

What would it feel like to be married for twenty or thirty years? What would they look like? Would they still be having sex the way they did now? She guessed her parents never did it anymore because they never touched, and her mother picked at her father all the time.

Wanda and David wanted to wait a couple of years before having kids, but Michelle couldn't wait to have a baby. She'd joined Bobby's Life of Christ Church and had stopped having sex with him until their honeymoon. "Poor guy," she said with a wink. "He's going crazy." She'd told Wanda they were going to have as many kids as God would give them. But Michelle was only eighteen. What was the rush?

Although Wanda and David had known each other since kindergarten, she hadn't really paid attention to him until eighth grade, when he'd shot up to six feet and she'd noticed how cute he'd become. At their middle-school graduation party, he asked her to dance, and they rocked from side to side, her hands clammy as she laid her head on his shoulder and closed her eyes, smelling Tictacs on his breath.

That summer, at Joey Parker's cookout, she and David climbed up into the hayloft, and when he leaned over to kiss her, she felt her edges go blurry. For the next couple of weeks, they kissed so much a sore red patch broke out on her chin, and her mother thought she might have impetigo. Wanda made David shave even though his whiskers weren't visible yet.

He played football and Wanda was on the Pep Squad that made signs and decorated lockers for the players on game days. Wanda always centered David's name on her poster and dotted the I with a star. She went to all the games to watch him and when he took the field, she cheered extra loud.

During tenth grade, they started having sex in his grandfather's old Buick. The first time, they didn't use protection, and she spent the next three weeks terrified she might be pregnant. When her period came, she told him they were safe, but he needed to use condoms. He came from a strict Catholic family and didn't like using anything, but her parents would kill her, and probably him, if she got pregnant.

Truthfully though, she'd have continued to sleep with him even if he'd never used condoms because she couldn't resist his skin on hers. She walked around feeling like she was wearing a suit of velvet turned to the inside. The slightest touch turned her on. All day at school, whenever she caught a whiff of Tictacs or his deodorant, she shivered with delight. Although David said he'd never slept with anyone before her, he knew exactly where to touch her until she shuddered.

When David picked her up for a dance or a movie, she'd scoot over and snuggle him as he drove, tickling the back of his neck. "You'll make me crash the car," he'd say. "Don't distract me." When they reached their spot, they'd make out in the front seat for a while, then, if it was cold, he'd lift her and lay her down on the backseat. Because he was so tall, he left the door open, his bare butt and legs sticking outside the car. She told him he was mooning the cows. In warm weather, they spread out a blanket and did it there. Sometimes, they never made it to the movie or dance.

They'd become engaged over Christmas of their senior year. His mother started hinting at holidays together and grandchildren, and before Wanda knew it, she was wearing a ring with a tiny diamond chip—a placeholder until they could afford more—and planning a wedding right after graduation. Her parents were relieved that David had made it official with a ring, although her mother worried that people would think Wanda was beating the stork to the altar. Lately, in the halls at school, Wanda noticed kids checking out her belly for a bulge. Already self-conscious about her weight, she sucked in her stomach and kept walking, her face burning. Not everyone got pregnant before the wedding. Some even went to college or worked at a job before having kids. Were they rushing things getting married right away?

David owed a big project on the Iraq War for his social studies class, and he'd already failed algebra once and was taking it again. She sat with him, helping him organize the magazine and website articles as he tried to write. Finally, she took the scribbled cards and wrote the paper herself. Why didn't he try harder, she wondered? She tried not to worry about that, knowing not everyone was good at school.

During the weeks before their wedding, she and David attended Pre-Cana class at St. Vincent's, but she didn't like lying when they agreed to use natural family planning, and she squirmed at the advice about their (supposedly) future sex life from a man who hadn't even had sex.

David's father, Burt, had pulled strings to get him a job at the foundry over in Granville where he also worked. Wanda had started an after-school job at Howe's Bakery, and they rented a one-bedroom apartment behind the bakery, upstairs from The Barrel, David's hangout place, a bar that never carded. She was eager to put her own touches on their place, to feather the nest. He was glad he didn't need to drive home after a night with the boys.

David just barely graduated. For a while, he hadn't seen the point of a diploma since he was going to work at the foundry, but after the ceremony, he thanked her for kicking his butt.

"You'd be sorry you didn't finish."

"I know. You're always right."

Secretly, she was relieved not to be marrying a high-school dropout.

Michelle threw Wanda a Round-the-Clock shower at Cappelli's with Wanda's high-school friends, her mother, Sandy, and her sisters-in-law, Mary Sue and Gail. Wanda worried that with David's mother Sandy and her mother there, it could turn awkward, that the girls might spill the fact that they'd been doing the deed for a couple of years now. But they all drank just enough that the negligées and the massage oils met with whoops and laughter, even from her mother.

Two nights before the wedding, Mosher hosted a bachelor party where David got wasted because, despite his size, he couldn't handle the hard stuff. At the rehearsal the following evening, he was pale and sweaty and had to sprint up to the church bathroom in the middle of practicing their vows. "Okay," said Wanda, holding a wet cloth to the back of his neck, "You've had your fun. But you have to get it together for tomorrow."

"I know," he said, miserable. "I promise."

That night, it poured, and Wanda woke up several times to look out her bedroom window, watching the sheets of rain, and she stewed about her dress and hair, and whether the wedding would be ruined. As the sky lightened, the rain had slowed to a drizzle, and by nine, the sun was starting to poke through the clouds. The humidity made the air thick and muggy, but at least it wasn't raining.

Her mother made her eat some breakfast even though Wanda's stomach was twisted in a knot, and she worried that food would make her waist cincher too tight. Gail, Mary Sue, and the children arrived to get dressed. Michelle hired Anita from the Beauty Barn to do their hair and nails, her gift to Wanda. Their cousin, Betsy, was in charge of getting her nieces, Leelee and Fawn, into their dresses. The girls fussed at each other. Mary Sue had put three-year-old Leelee in her flower girl dress early, which Wanda knew was a mistake. What if she spilled something on it? Filled with sugar, Leelee raced around in a circle, shrieking. Fawn, who at two was still nursing, poked her mother's breast while Anita teased Gail's hair into an updo. Although Sandy had made Mary Sue's bridesmaid's dress roomy to allow for her growing baby bump, Mary Sue complained that the dress rode up in back and she tugged at the dress as she inspected herself in the mirror. Her poked-out belly button showed through the material.

Wanda's mother and Sandy had coordinated Wanda's colors, fuchsia and rose, for their dresses. Her mother usually didn't wear any makeup, but today, with a touch of mascara and lipstick, she looked younger, pretty. She insisted on the children eating a good breakfast, but Wanda worried they'd get overexcited. And in fact, Leelee wolfed down a cinnamon roll and orange juice and spun around in the middle of the kitchen until she puked on the floor. Mary Sue popped up from her chair to catch the worst of it and sponge off the dress. "Get me a cloth to put on her neck." Leelee was wailing. "Calm down, baby," her mother said.

The flowers arrived and her mother opened the box and passed out the bouquets of daisies, baby's breath, and peonies. She'd given Wanda the ivory fan her grandmother had carried at her high-school graduation, something old and borrowed. That was fine, but to show the fan, the florist hadn't used many flowers, which gave Wanda a stab of disappointment. Her mother fussed that the flowers were already starting to wilt, but Wanda said no one would notice. "Mom, it's not worth getting upset about these small details."

Anita did Wanda's hair in a French twist and surrounded her head with a cloud of hairspray. Gail did her makeup. Mascara always made her eyes water, so Wanda asked for a light touch. "You need something to make your eyes pop," said Gail, aiming the wand at her eye.

"But I have to be able to see," Wanda said.

Wanda felt big and lumpy compared to Michelle, so cute in her tiny, dark pink, tea-length Maid-of-Honor dress. But when she stood up from the makeup chair, Michelle said, "Oh, Wanda, you look so beautiful."

Wanda felt tears rise. Squeezed into her dress, it was hard for her to breathe, and she worried she might faint. Her vision clouded, and she leaned forward, her hands on her knees. Michelle guided her into the powder room off the entryway as Wanda tried to take shallow breaths.

"Hey, slow down. Take a breath. Are you okay?"

Wanda's brow felt hot. Michelle took a washcloth and wetted it, dabbing the back of Wanda's neck. "There. You just take a moment," Michelle said, rubbing her hand in circles on Wanda's back. "It's going to be great. You look wonderful." Wanda nodded, slowing her breathing. "Can I offer a prayer?" asked Michelle.

Wanda nodded even though it felt strange to be standing in a tiny bathroom to pray, but Michelle's voice soothed her. "Dear Lord, hold your child Wanda on this most blessed day." Wanda opened her eyes and closed them again, patting the damp cloth on her temples and the back of her neck. "It's just crazy out there. My dress is too tight." And she thought, are we too young? What are we doing?

"You look perfect."

"I don't know."

"You do. Just take a moment and let God guide you."

Wanda blinked at herself in the mirror. Her cheeks were flushed, but the eyeshadow and mascara made her eyes stand out. This was the right dress, nipping her waist, making it look small. She fluffed her skirt and adjusted her neckline. Feeling a wave of excitement roll through her, she took a breath and smiled at herself, then at Michelle. "I'm ready."

Her father walked into the kitchen in his suit, looking stiff, but when he saw Wanda, his face softened, and he smiled broadly. "Look at you." She fought back tears, waving her hands in front of her eyes. "Well, Mother," her father said, "Let's go get our daughter married." Evelyn gave her a big hug, whispering, "Grandma would have loved to be here." That made Wanda cry, gently patting under her eyes.

As she climbed into the back of her father's car, the hem of her dress slipped into the mud, but she gathered it in her arms, brushed off what she could, and told herself not to worry about small things.

The priest told the congregation that there were those couples who seemed brought together by God. Wanda and David were such a couple. He talked about children, about a long life together. So nervous, afraid she'd forget the words, her voice shook as she said her vows, but when she looked into David's eyes, he anchored her. He grinned at her, winking, and all her doubts melted away. Afterwards, they knelt for the blessing, which went on so long Wanda's knees went numb, and she felt herself sweat and chafe in her dress. At the end of the mass, he helped her to her feet so she wouldn't trip on her hem. All the way down the aisle, she felt as if David were carrying her. As ever, her rock.

At the reception, she slipped into the bathroom to remove her corset so she could breathe. In the mirror, she wiped away a smudge of mascara and patted her stiffly sprayed curls. She stared at her face, her eyes, her cheeks, and thought, this is how I look, married. For the rest of my life.

2

CALLIE MORTON

On a cold Tuesday night in November of her senior year, Callie stood near the concession stand at the hockey rink waiting for her boyfriend, Matt, to shower and get dressed after the game. She stamped her feet, a scarf wrapped around her face, the wet wool and snot chafing her nose. She hated cold weather and found hockey boring, but hockey was Shelton's religion (after Catholicism), and Matt Puchowsky was the Varsity goalie, so she needed to be there to support him. From the rink, they'd go to his brother Jason's house where he'd pound several beers and they'd have sex on the sofa in the basement. When the team won, Matt was always horny and couldn't keep his hands off her and they'd have actual sex. If they lost, as they had tonight, he'd blame himself for letting the goals in and she'd have to cheer him up, ending with her giving him a blowjob, her knees sore from the concrete, her nose full of mildew from the couch. She couldn't wait for the season to be over.

Her best friend Elise's boyfriend, Alex, was also on the team, and had offered her a ride, but Callie said she'd wait for Matt. As the crowd thinned, and the concessions workers pulled down the shutters, she wondered if they'd crossed signals. But he had to know she'd be waiting for him. Besides, he was her ride home.

When Mike Rooney walked out of the locker room, his hair wet, his duffle slung over his shoulder, she asked if he'd seen Matt.

"He left right after the game."

"What? Are you sure?"

"Yeah, I remember seeing him leave. Do you need a ride?"

No, she told him, struggling not to sound upset, she'd call her parents. But that was a lie. She knew her mother would have gone to bed early, and her father didn't drive at night anymore. And since it was a school night, she'd told them she'd be studying at Elise's and would get a ride from her. All they knew was her perfect G.P.A. and were clueless about the rest of her life.

She walked several blocks toward the bus stop in the center of town, shivering, her shoulders hunched, worried that the buses had stopped running for the night. She came upon two Brewster College students, a guy and a girl, standing at the corner, their thumbs raised, hitching. Her parents didn't like her to hitch. Approaching the couple, she asked if she could share a ride with them to the campus. "If there's room," the guy said as he wrapped his arms around his girlfriend and stuffed his bare hands into her jacket pockets as she stuck out her mittened thumb.

A man in an SUV picked them up and they rode to the campus. Callie sat crowded next to the couple who smelled like weed. "Just let us out at the main gate," the guy said. Callie said that was fine for her too.

She climbed out of the car, her feet and hands stiff, and she walked toward her street, a few blocks past the main gates. In the clear sky, the moon was full, the air bracingly cold. Where her street met the main road, she saw Whit Sutter from her class, standing in front of his house. He wore a sweatshirt and jeans but no hat or gloves as he stood looking at the sky.

She stopped. "Aren't you cold?"

"No, I like it like this."

"What are you doing?"

"Looking at the Andromeda Galaxy," he said. He asked why she was out, and she told him she'd been to the hockey game. "Well, bye," he said, turning on his heel and heading toward his house. What a weirdo.

She walked the half-mile to her home, frozen. How could Matt abandon her like that? She'd given up the whole evening when she should have worked on her college applications, just to go to his stupid game. But Matt had already received an athletic scholarship to Penn State and was coasting, so he didn't care what was going on for her. Without her parents knowing, she'd decided to spend her own money to apply to other schools, more prestigious than Brewster, hoping that when she was accepted, they'd be forced to reconsider. Because her parents were older than any of her friends' parents, they were strict and overprotective. They had no idea the pressures on high-school students these days who wanted to get good grades and have a life outside of school.

She slipped in the front door and went up to her room where she texted Matt, asking him why he'd blown her off. Then she opened the computer file with the drafts of the Common App essay. She was weighing which essay to write. One asked to describe an obstacle she'd overcome, another a talent she'd developed, and one that asked her to choose a cause about which she was passionate. Should she even claim an obstacle? It wasn't as if she'd ever faced true adversity. Did old parents who controlled their only child's life count? How about the blinkered vision of a small town? Or a boyfriend who could be a thoughtless asshole? Should she write about some strength? That felt self-centered, and maybe a trap to weed out the narcissists. Should she talk about her town, her school, of how she wanted to move on, to see more of the world than small-town Pennsylvania? Was her parents' opposition to her leaving town enough of an obstacle to write about? And would that signal her as someone to reject since she didn't have parental support? Best to stick with the big issues of global warming or human trafficking. She couldn't ask her parents to read the essays. Elise would help her.

She checked her texts, but Matt hadn't answered. Her parents had refused to buy her a cell phone, so she'd bought a cheap one and kept it on mute when she was at home. Because how could she live without a phone? They still had a land line with dial-up Internet that she used for schoolwork. She'd never told them about Matt because he wasn't in honors classes, so her parents would say he wasn't headed anywhere.

She texted Matt again. *where were you??????* then tried to write more of her essay, but she couldn't concentrate. She texted Elise, but she was probably with Alex and wouldn't be looking at her phone.

She knew about Matt, of course, because he was hot and a Varsity athlete, but she hadn't talked to him until they worked together junior year on a float for the Homecoming Parade. They were charged with painting a banner for the hockey team float. He'd misspelled Spirit as "Sprit" and she'd given him a hard time. But then when she'd dribbled paint on the new sign, he'd teased her. "Spaz much?"

"At least I know how to spell."

"At least I can paint." He took her brush and threatened to paint her nose with it.

"Don't you dare," she said, grabbing his hand, laughing.

The parade, which featured floats from all the teams, took over Main Street and everyone joined in, shouting "Go, Shelton! Beat Granville!" Callie and Elise marched alongside the hockey float toward the parking lot behind the school where, that night, the pep squad built a bonfire and burned an effigy of a Granville Gryphon. Then Elise and Callie met a group at Jeff Parker's garage where they'd painted the hockey float. Matt showed up and hung out with Callie next to the fire. Since she was spending the night at Elise's, he offered to walk with her, and on the way there, he stopped to pull her behind a tree to kiss her. He was funny and sarcastic, and he liked her.

Until Matt, Callie had never hung out with jocks. Now, when any of the athletes saw them together in the halls, they smiled and said hi. At parties, Callie was excited to be seen as someone who could be smart and fun too. "I thought you didn't party," said Maggie, a Varsity cheerleader, "like you'd be studying all the time."

"No way," Callie said, her heart thumping. "That would drive me crazy."

Soon, Callie was making more excuses to her parents about SAT study groups at the Brewster library and extra orchestra rehearsals at school. In her junior year, when she was sure she was one of the last virgins in her class, she and Matt started having sex.

But now, what was going on with him? Why had he blown her off like that? Why didn't he answer her texts? She gave up working on the essay and climbed into bed.

The next day at school, she walked past Matt in the hall, snubbing him, ears buzzing, face burning. At her locker, she punched in her combination and dumped the books she didn't need yet, cradling the ones for her morning classes. Whit Sutter stood a few lockers down, his nose in a book, and she made a point of saying hi to him just so Matt could see her avoid him. Whit blushed and looked at the floor. They stood waiting for Mr. Mitchell to let them into homeroom.

"Hey, Whit," she said. "I couldn't get one of my calc. problems last night. Can you help me?" She pulled the sheet from her book and handed it to him.

He studied the sheet for a moment. "That's easy." He took a pencil and held the paper up to a locker as he scribbled in the margins. When he finished, he gave it to her. The writing was small and cramped, but she saw her mistake.

"Thanks." She stole a glance over her shoulder at Matt, but he wasn't looking her way.

Whit was an off-the-charts genius, a lock for Valedictorian. In class, he sat with his book open, but he spent all class writing in a small notebook. Whenever the teacher called on him, he mumbled something smart, then shrugged and returned to his notes. Hunched over his desk with a short, chewed pencil, he wrote, a gum eraser in one hand, sweeping away the eraser squiggles when they piled up. His hair dangled in his face, and he twirled it, scratching his scalp, breathing loudly through his mouth. If he took a shower and washed his hair more often, he might be presentable. By the end of his junior year, he'd run through all the math and science classes at the high school and was taking courses at Brewster. The only high-school class he had to take besides P.E. was Mrs. Haywood's A.P. English, the same section as Callie.

That left her to vie for Salutatorian with Ed Peak. She had to gut out every single math problem to get an A, but English, French, and history were easy for her. She and Whit had been on parallel paths ever since they were funneled into honors track in middle school. But he wasn't a friend. No way.

Matt texted her during the day. *??????*

She texted back. *!!!!!!!*

She didn't want to get into it with him at school and didn't want to make the first move. Between practice and an away game on Friday, they probably wouldn't run into each other. Let him figure it out.

That night, the house phone rang, and her mother said it was for Callie. "Who is it?" Callie asked.

Her mother shrugged, holding her hand over the receiver. "It's a boy."

Matt would never call on the land line. "Hello?"

"There's this concert at the college on Sunday. They're decent. I could pick you up. That is, if you don't have something else to do."

"Who is this?"

"Whit. Can you go?"

Having no excuse ready, she heard herself say yes, instantly regretting it. He told her he'd pick her up at one. She hung up, her head throbbing. Didn't he know she was Matt's girlfriend? What if people saw them together? And what would they talk about?

Later that night, when Matt finally texted her, he didn't see why she was angry. They hadn't made firm plans to meet after the game. "I just needed to get out of there," he said.

"But what about me? How did you think I was going to get home?"

"We lost. I wasn't thinking about that. I was in a bad mood."

"I had to hitch a ride."

"I let the team down."

"You let *me* down."

He said she was always on his back. She said it was embarrassing to be left there, freezing.

"But I didn't know you were waiting."

"What did you think I'd be doing?" She said, blowing her nose, hearing her voice sound thick.

"You always do this, start crying when things don't go your way."

"That's not fair," she said, feeling her throat close. "You're an asshole." And she hung up.

The week dragged by. She and Whit hadn't spoken since he'd asked her out, but every time she looked in his direction, he was staring at her, which made her stomach twist. Why had she agreed to go out with him? Noticing Callie was in a bad mood, her mother asked what was wrong, but Callie said she was stressed out about college.

"But you're a shoo-in for Brewster."

"I can't let down now, Mom. There's still a lot of work."

On Thursday night, Matt finally called and apologized for being an asshole. They made up and agreed to meet after the game on Friday. This time, the team won, and they bought a six-pack and donuts at the bakery where she saw that girl Wanda from high school who worked there now. How depressing to be trapped in this town, working at that dinky bakery on a Friday night, stuffing herself with junk food. Kill me now, thought Callie. Later, at his brother's house, Matt was still psyched about the win, how he'd flattened to stop the goal. She wanted him to slow down and focus on her, but at least they were back together. "This week has been awful. I missed you."

"It was only a few days."

"Well, it felt longer."

On Sunday, Callie woke up with a headache and cramps, her mouth dry and sticky from partying the night before. She'd planned to sleep in before doing her homework, but then she remembered the concert and wished she could call Whit with an excuse of being sick. She'd told her mother that Whit had asked her to a concert, but she wished she weren't going. Her mother said it would be good for her to branch out and date a nice boy like Whit.

"Eew, Mom, I'm not dating him."

"Well, he's a nice boy."

"No, he's weird. I don't want to talk about it." And she went back to her room and shut the door, lying in bed reading *Song of Solomon* for English class.

At one, the doorbell rang, and her mother answered it. Callie dragged herself down the stairs to find Whit standing on the doormat, pigeon-toed, dressed in a lumberjack cap with flaps, dorky hiking boots, and a scarf tied around his neck. She hadn't heard a car drive up. "How are we getting there?" she asked.

"We're walking."

"But it's cold." She hadn't dressed to be outside that long.

"It's only half a mile."

"Here, Callie," her mother said. "You can borrow my rabbit hat."

"Gross, Mom. I'm not wearing an animal on my head."

"Well, then, wrap up in two scarves and wear warm gloves. You'll be okay once you start walking."

What had she gotten herself into? Did Whit think this was okay? They set off on foot, and she hugged herself against the cold, walking fast as they passed the golf course, the soccer field, and the football field, heading toward the auditorium in the center of campus.

"What's the program?" she asked.

"An opera by Phillip Glass. 'Einstein on the Beach.'"

So boring.

When they arrived at the auditorium, she'd hoped to settle near the back where no one could see them, but he led her to one of the front rows. She didn't want anyone to jump to conclusions about them. But sure enough, Dina Whitney, a faculty wife, approached them with a big smile. "Look at you two opera buffs. Isn't this exciting?" Callie mumbled something and slid into her seat, burying her head in the program, pretending to be interested.

When the singers filed in, Whit started to laugh. Callie looked at him. "What's so funny?"

"I like to see them drop their masks."

"Whatever."

The music was annoyingly repetitive, and she fought to stay awake, but at least she and Whit didn't have to talk during the performance. As he listened, he bobbed his head and hummed along. So embarrassing. She was afraid he'd attract attention and, in fact, the man in front of them turned around and gave him a look. She had cramps, and her eyes were scratchy. She just wanted it all to be over.

As they walked back to her house, and the light was fading, she asked him where he was applying to college. He said he'd continue at Brewster.

"But why? You could get in anywhere."

"I know."

"Don't you want to go somewhere else for college?"

"For grad school, sure. But Brewster is good for now." He didn't ask her about where she wanted to go, so she told him she was hoping for Columbia or Brown. Maybe NYU.

"Yeah, you might get in."

"Why wouldn't I?"

"No, you're smart enough."

At the door, she said goodbye and closed the door, shuddering. To warm up and wash the day off her, she took a hot bath. What a waste of an afternoon.

A couple of days later, her mother met her at the door after school and handed her an envelope, hand-delivered without a stamp, her name written in peacock blue ink. "Is it from Whit?"

"Mom, please. I don't know." The envelope strained to hold its contents. Up in her room, she slit the envelope open and unfolded the thick sheaf of notebook paper. She flipped to the end to see who'd written it, although she knew it was Whit. She started to read.

> *Darling Calliope (Καλλιόπη),*
>
> *How does it feel to be a muse? I've been reading epic poetry to immerse myself in your sphere of influence. Urania would be my muse, but I can't forget*

my Calliope. How could I, when her other role is the muse of memory? I fear I am condemned not to forget you. You've been on my mind since we went to the concert. Maybe writing will help me sort my feelings. I find myself looking at the skies and what do I see? The constellation Orpheus, Calliope's son. So, you see, you're everywhere.

Eew, creepy. She kept reading.

O, Kalliope, "beautiful-voiced," you live up to your name well. I heard you sing in the musical. Your voice is lyrical, your walk is graceful. But you seem sad. And alone. Am I right? You were so quiet the other day. I kept trying to figure out if you are normally like that, keeping your thoughts to yourself, or if you were having a bad time. I'm notoriously bad at reading other people's moods.

I often see you walking by my house. Sometimes, I time it so I can be out front when you go by, but then I lose my nerve and stay inside. I'm a coward. This is my first brave gesture. Next year, if we're both at Brewster, we'll cross paths from time to time. Will you greet me as a friend or will you turn your head?

High school is torture. Brewster is better, but I may not be the kind of person who can fit in. I plan to have my PhD by the time I'm 24 and then do research. Everything else seems meaningless. Maybe that's why I'm drawn to astronomy, to learn what's out there. Speaking of the stars, it's two in the morning and I have to go to bed now.

Callie tried to picture him sitting up late at night writing this thing. After a blank page, she read,

I'm back.

I vacillate between seeing you as an untouchable goddess without a body and as a body I want to bury myself in. Am I just a lustful teenager after all? No, I want something purer, more refined than just animal lust. You're a goddess, perfect in your imperfections.

But what am I?

There is a spider spinning a web between my map and the windowsill. I feel like that spider, edging out onto the precipice, hanging on for dear life, knowing you could swat at me and send me tumbling into the abyss. What's it going to be? Will you turn my hope of pardon into despair?

"Here to rise to life again, dead poetry! Let it, O holy Muses, for I am yours. And here, Calliope, strike a higher key. Accompanying my song with that sweet air which made the wretched Magpies feel a blow that turned all hope of pardon into despair." Dante Purgatorio, Canto 1.1.7 to 12.

At the bottom of the page, there was a drawing of a stick figure on a tightrope over a sea of waves or was it flames? Then his signature, a left-leaning WHIT with a flourish at the end.

Callie tossed the letter aside and lay back on her bed, hugging herself. Why had she read the whole thing? How creepy, knowing his hands had touched this paper, had lingered over what to write to her. What a freak. That weird way he had of smiling when nothing was funny and then frowning the rest of the time. His silly laugh. His dorky way of dressing. His dirty hair and bad skin. What about her made him think she'd like him? Did other people see her like they saw him? Her stomach churned and her mouth watered like before throwing up. Closing her eyes, she took deep breaths to calm her stomach.

Callie had never known what to do with unwanted attention. A colleague of her father's, Professor Mindell, had once cornered her at a faculty Christmas mulled-wine party and had tried to feel her up before she could slip away from him. Rather than tell him to fuck off, she'd let it go on for a minute or so, feeling frozen, his fingers causing jabs of disgust shoot down her neck and into her shoulders. Why couldn't she stand up for herself better? Whit wasn't a perv, just a weirdo, but he creeped her out and this letter was so stalkerish. He must have done research on her name and looked for that quote in *The Inferno*. Who does that in high school?

She had to get out of this town, go to a city where there were different kinds of people, where she could find out who she was and then be that person. This would never happen in Dalton or at Brewster. She pulled out her notes on the application and turned on her computer and started writing the essay on climate change and the urgency of acting now. If we don't act now, it will be too late. Too late. Act now.

3

WANDA

Before Wanda's evening shift at the bakery, she made a meatloaf, mashed potatoes, and mixed vegetables, then ate her meal while reading her book. Preparing a plate for David, she slipped it into the fridge and left a note on the counter for him. His shift at the foundry ended after she started work, less than ideal, but they needed the money from both jobs. She wished they could eat dinner together more often and swore that once they had children, she'd manage her hours to keep a strict family dinnertime. She was trying to put away money to take a class at the community college, but something always came up and she had to dip into the cash drawer: repairs on the car, new work boots for David, but also his video games and beers at The Barrel. It was the only thing about which they disagreed. That and when she was going to get pregnant. They'd only been married a few months. She wanted to get her nursing certificate first. He thought there'd be time for that later, but she knew it would be too hard to juggle school with a baby.

After her supper, she slipped on her work tee-shirt and khakis, grabbed her apron, hair net and jacket, then laced up her gym shoes to start her shift at two. She walked down the stairs and across the alley into the back door of the bakery, past the huge freezer and the ovens, into the store. Maeve stood at the cash register and nodded at Wanda, who stretched a net over her hair, tucking in the stray curls.

Wanda liked the give and take with the customers, many of them people she'd known all her life: friends of her mother's, girls she'd gone to school with, now married, children stopping in for an after-school cookie, parents picking up birthday cakes, lonely old people who liked the personal attention they couldn't get at the SuperSave in town. Wanda didn't like the Brewster students, the stuck-up ones who checked her math or thought she was overcharging them. But this kind of small shop made living in a village special.

Because she and David brought the smells of their jobs home with them, hers sweet and thick, his metallic and sharp, she had a rule that they shower before going to bed. Often, he waited until they could shower together. He shampooed her as she lathered him from head to toe, squeezing his slippery butt before he turned her around, bending her over as she grabbed the towel rack. When the windows steamed and the water ran cold, they toweled each other off, their legs shaky, and headed off to bed.

Because Maeve was on the register, Wanda grabbed a broom and swept around the edges of the display cases. Every day, gum wrappers, donut tissues, and street dirt collected in the corners of the store. She rearranged the milk bottles with MacDonald's Dairy cow logo while Maeve rang up John Panko for his daily order of three Bear Claws. How he stayed so skinny with such a sweet tooth, Wanda didn't know.

Irene showed up at two-twenty, late as usual. "Sorry. One of my kids threw up." Wanda nodded, knowing that raising six kids on her own after her loser husband took off meant she sometimes needed a bit of a slack. Wanda couldn't imagine raising even one child without a man, let alone six.

"It's been slow," Wanda told her. Things always picked up after school and then again right before closing at nine.

She and Irene set about their usual afternoon chores: straightening the six-packs of beer and soda in the cooler, replenishing the boxes of pastry tissues and paper bags, Windexing the glass on the customer side of the display cases, all of that while waiting on customers.

David stopped by at five-thirty to see Wanda before he went upstairs. Her heart sped up a few beats when she saw him framed in the doorway, smiling, his work coveralls dusty, his hair matted down from the hard hat. "Hey, you," she said, leaning over the counter to give him a kiss. He smelled of the foundry and his own sweat, his cheek rough with blond stubble. He flicked her breast lightly with his finger, and she grabbed his hand, laughing. "Not here." But she liked that he wanted to jump her, even in the net that made her hair look like a beaver's tail. "I left you some meatloaf in the fridge."

"Sounds great. Thanks."

"Are you going to The Barrel?"

"Yeah. The Penguins are playing the Bruins, and I'll watch the game with Mosher and Pierce. Come over after your shift." He pulled her in for another kiss.

"Maybe. I'm tired. We'll see."

"Come on, please?" He gave her the sly smile she found hard to resist.

"How about I wait up for you in bed? That sound good?"

"Okay, but if you're asleep, I'm waking you up."

"You'd better." She filched a cinnamon donut with a tissue and handed it to him. He ate it in three bites, then kissed her again, his mouth full of crumbs.

His lips came away tasting of sugar. She wiped them, laughing. "You slob."

He waved on his way out the door, and Wanda watched him go, thinking of them later that night, in bed. She sucked in her breath.

"That boy loves your ass," said Irene.

"Yeah," she said, tucking loose hairs back into the net, her face feeling warm, his smell lingering in her nose. "I know."

Between customers, she and Irene continued their jobs around the bakery. Wanda rearranged the pinwheel cookies, peeling apart the ones that had stuck together, dropping the broken ones into a bag for Irene to take home to her kids. "These stupid cookies always break."

"I keep telling Carlos not to rack them when they're warm, but he don't care."

Even though Mr. Howe instructed them to sell day-old baked goods as fresh, insisting no one could tell the difference, Wanda discounted them because she refused to charge full price for anything not fresh. She knew she was taking a risk, but she couldn't treat the customers unfairly, passing off stale as fresh.

Irene took an order over the phone for a birthday cake for P.J. Donahue, then she grabbed two empty pastry bags. "Wait. Is P.J. a girl or a boy?" A boy, Wanda said, so Irene filled one bag with blue frosting and the other with yellow and handed it to Wanda. Irene wrote *Happy Birthday P.J.* in blue as Wanda piped yellow roses along the edges. They boxed the cake and put it in the refrigerator in back.

Nearing the end of their shift, as Irene took care of the last wave of customers, Wanda wheeled the bucket in from the storage closet, her feet sore, her lower back twingeing, and she lifted the filthy mop and slopped it onto the floor, squeezing the gray water back into the bucket. Then she covered the leftover donuts and cookies with cling wrap, returning the macaroni and potato salads to the big fridge. Mr. Howe didn't want them to start the cleanup until closing time because the wet floor was a safety hazard. However, he didn't pay them after nine, so unless the wanted to work overtime for free, they had to start around eight-forty-five, putting the CAUTION WET FLOOR sign by the door. At eight-fifty-eight, with no one out front, Wanda locked the door and leaned into the deep cooler and sponged the surface, the metal edge digging into her belly, the cool air misting her face. At five after nine, she heard a knock at the door. Outside, that girl, Callie Morton, stood with Matt Puchowsky. He was on Varsity Hockey. Wanda pointed to the clock and mimed, We're closed. Callie shrugged and put her hands together like she was begging.

"Shit," said Irene. "Don't let them in."

Wanda dropped her rag and unlocked the door. "Sorry, we're closed."

"Oh, just one minute, please?" Callie asked. "The game just got out. Overtime." She laughed, but Matt looked impatient. "Can we get some donuts?"

"We closed out the register. And the donuts aren't fresh anymore."

"We don't care. You have a lot left."

"Okay," said Wanda, locking the door behind them, catching

Irene's angry look from the corner of her eye, and headed to the donut display, grabbing a bag and a tissue. "What kind and how many?"

"About six."

"Hurry up," said Matt, heading over to the beer cooler.

"What kind do you want?" asked Wanda.

"You choose."

Wanda picked out two cinnamon, two chocolate, two powdered sugar, and put them into the bag.

Matt dropped a six-pack of Yuengling on the counter.

"I can't sell you that."

"Yes, you can. Come on."

"Do you have I.D.?" she asked, knowing he and Callie were seniors at the high school.

He scowled and reached into his back pocket, flipping open his wallet and holding up a card, obviously a fake, putting his age at 21. Wanda was only 19 herself. But she wasn't in the mood to argue, so she took the $10 bill and tucked it into the drawer. She let them out the front door and they left without a thank you.

"Assholes," said Irene. "You were too nice to them."

Wanda felt tears sting her eyes. Did Callie even remember Wanda? That even though she knew they were under-age, she'd done them a favor? "She was a year behind me in school, but she acted like she'd never seen me before."

"Well, it's clear her shit don't stink."

When they finished the clean-up at nine-twenty, Wanda left again by the back door, hearing the beat of music from the bar, and climbed the stairs to their apartment. If she weren't so tired, she might have joined David at The Barrel, but not tonight. She showered and crawled into bed with her book. Around eleven,

David came home, threw off his clothes, slipping in next to her, kissing her and running his hand up her leg. She turned to him, half asleep, and kissed him back even though he smelled of beer and cigarette smoke. She liked this half-awake sex, which made her feel as if she could float in a dream looking down on them from above. He rolled on top of her, and she rose to meet his mouth, his breath, his smell—throwing off the covers, he turned onto his back, and she straddled him. Yes, yes, you and me. You and me. Feeling a balloon in her belly inflate, rise, and burst as she fell on his chest, squeezing tight.

He stroked her back as she lay on top of him. "Why didn't you come to the bar? I was waiting for you."

"I didn't feel like it. And I didn't want to cramp your style."

"Just what kind of style do you think I might have?"

"I didn't feel like seeing the boys."

He drifted off, and when he snorted, she poked him. "How much did you drink?"

"Just a couple of beers. Mosher was talking about the play-offs, and we got into it. You should have heard him. What an asshole. I bet him—"

"Who won the game?"

"The Penguins in OT. That's why I'm home late."

"I sold some beer to high-school kids after their game."

"Did they win?"

"I didn't ask. I shouldn't have accepted the fake I.D., but I wasn't in the mood to argue."

"It's not a big deal. One six pack."

He fell asleep, and she read for a while, but it still bothered her that she'd been too weak to challenge them.

Ever since their wedding, David had been lobbying for a baby. With three grandchildren, Wanda's parents weren't pressuring her, but David was Sandy and Burt's only chance for a grandchild. Michelle was pregnant and wanted Wanda to have one close in age to hers. But Wanda wasn't ready for a baby yet. They were only nineteen and had been married only five months. She liked her life with David the way it was. And they didn't have money for a baby yet. Wanda knew David wasn't ready either. Why disturb a good thing?

Come January, she hoped to take an introductory bio class at the community college in Granville. It met in the mornings and wouldn't affect her work schedule. Maybe she'd sign up and present it to David as a done deal. That usually worked when he couldn't make up his mind.

A few days later, about an hour after David left for work, he showed up at home, looking awful, his face pale. When she asked if he were sick, he said he'd been laid off. He plopped down on the sofa and grabbed the game remote.

"What happened?"

"They're cutting back. I got the ax."

"Why you?"

"Are you saying I did something?"

"No, of course not."

"They're letting a quarter of the workers go. Last hired, first fired."

"I thought you had job security. Can't your father do something?"

"He doesn't have that kind of power," he said, swiveling and crackling the bones in his neck, a habit that annoyed her. "How am I going to support you?"

"I'm working."

"For minimum wage. That's not enough."

"You'll get another job."

"Where?"

"I don't know. But you'll find something. It'll work out."

"Fuck," he said, holding his head in his hands. Then he picked up the remote again and started a new game.

She sat down next to him and smoothed her hand over his head, giving him a kiss, putting her head on his shoulder as the game pinged and popped.

"Can you take the night off?" he asked.

"I wish I could, but it's too late to find a replacement." She kissed him on the neck and said she'd make him a nice meal. Taking a steak from the freezer, she force-thawed it between two hot pans. She also fried potatoes, opening a bottle of red wine, even having a glass herself before she headed to work. Over the meal, she tried to give him a pep talk, telling him he'd find something. He was a good worker. Lots of places would be glad to hire him. He slumped in his chair, scarfing down the steak and potatoes, chugging his wine and refilling the glass. Then he pushed back his chair, moved to the couch, and started a new game.

"Will you be okay?" she asked, running her hand down his cheek. "I wish I didn't have to go."

"I know," he said, staring at the screen. "I'll probably go to The Barrel."

When she came home, David was still out, and she fell asleep waiting for him. The next morning, she let him sleep in, tiptoeing around so she wouldn't disturb him. She drove to Michelle's and when she said David had been laid off, Michelle said maybe Bobby could hire him. It hadn't occurred to Wanda to ask, so she thanked Michelle and drove home in a good mood. But when she mentioned the job to David, he said, "That guy? No, I don't think so."

"Why not?"

"He's an asshole."

"Well, maybe my dad could use some help on the farm."

"Absolutely not. Work for your dad? With your brothers? No way."

"You can't say no to everything." And she bit her tongue before saying he couldn't exactly be picky. And how were they going to pay for Christmas gifts without a new job?

"It would feel like charity. It's humiliating. I want to find my own job."

"Your father helped you get this one. What's the difference?"

His face flushed, annoyed. He sat with his controller, his thumbs jabbing the buttons, bobbing his head, weaving left and right.

"Have you checked the Internet?"

She heard the dropping sound of a game ending, and he tossed the controller onto the couch.

"I'll figure it out. It just happened yesterday."

"I'm trying to help," feeling her voice grow thin.

"I said I was on it." He began a new game and stared at the screen.

She knew not to push him, that he'd dig in, his pride wounded. Best to give him some space. She set a pan of water on to boil and opened a jar of spaghetti sauce. Before she walked out the door, she gave him a hug, saying she believed in him.

He went to The Barrel and came home saying that Mosher said they might be hiring at the packing plant. "If I get a chauffeur's license, I could drive for them."

"How much does that cost?"

"Don't worry. You're always on me about money. You need to support my plans."

She put a coaster under his beer and went to bed, not crying until she was behind the closed door, realizing that her plans for a course at the community college would have to wait.

That was the last she heard of the chauffeur's license. He spent the next few days playing games and drinking beer. It was like in high school when he shut down and nearly didn't graduate. At the time, she'd been able to encourage him to push on, giving him the nudge to hang in there. This time, he seemed defeated. "You need to believe in yourself," she told him. Instead, he spent money they didn't have on drinking with his high-school buddies. She worried about paying the bills, but she didn't want to add to his stress.

"You just need to keep your eyes and ears open. The right job will turn up. Don't lose hope."

Two days before Christmas, he showed up at the bakery with a big smile, saying he had great news.

"Did you get a job?" she asked. He said he had. "Tell me."

"I enlisted."

A stone dropped in her stomach. "You what?"

"I've been thinking about it for a while, and they'll pay me and train me for a good job."

"You did this without talking to me?"

"You knew I was interested in the Army."

"You mentioned it once in high school and then dropped it."

"They're looking for new recruits. The war will be over before you know it, and I'll come home."

"You don't know that. What were you thinking?"

"This is what I want to do."

"Since when? And you didn't even discuss it with me." Customers were staring at them, so Irene suggested she take her break.

David followed Wanda out the back door into the alley. When he put his arm around her shoulder, she shrugged it off. "Can you get out of it?" she asked.

"No, I signed a contract, and they swore me in. And I don't want to change my mind." The garbage truck was backing up with its annoying beeping. "I thought you'd be relieved."

"Relieved? Are you shitting me?" she said, swiping at her wet cheeks. "It's dangerous."

"They'll train me."

"You could die!"

"That's not going to happen. Things are winding down."

"It's a war. People die in wars. What were you thinking?"

"It's a job, and I needed to make money."

"A job. Not war."

They stood, not speaking. She could hear him breathing, smell his fresh sweat. "I can't even look at you right now." And she ran back into the store.

"What happened?" asked Irene, stroking Wanda's arm.

"David enlisted. Without telling me."

"Oh, sweetie," she said, giving Wanda a hug. "He'll be fine."

"You don't know that."

"You're right. I'm sorry. Of course, you're worried. When does he leave?"

"I have no idea. We didn't get to that."

"The Army is good for some people. Makes boys into men."

"The ones who don't die."

"Don't even say that."

"I feel sick." She pushed through the swinging doors into the back, knelt in front of the toilet, and dry heaved but didn't throw up. Shivering, she splashed water on her face and cupped a handful to drink, staring at the mirror at her pale skin and bloodshot eyes. Rubbing them, she walked back into the store.

David's parents thought he was brave, stepping up like that. His father had missed out on Vietnam (Missed out? Really?) and was proud of him. Sandy thought it might be the best thing for David. Her brothers also supported his choice, but neither of them had volunteered. Did anyone else think this was a terrible, dangerous idea?

When David was unemployed and depressed, their sex life had dropped off. Wanda tried to keep the spark between them alive, but he stayed up late and avoided her. Now that he'd enlisted, he was horny all the time, jumping her as soon as she walked in the door, tired and dirty after work. He'd started working out, doing pushups, arm curls, sit-ups. But now, she'd lost her desire for sex. He could coax her into it, and she went along, but sometimes, in the middle, she'd have a horrifying vision of his death, so she panicked and pushed him away. Usually, she steeled herself to keep going until he finished. During the days, she was full of anger that he'd done this foolish thing and hadn't even talked to her first. And no one except Irene seemed to understand why she was so worried. Michelle got it, but she thought prayer would protect him. Wanda gritted her teeth and went along with the prayers, but nothing took away her worry.

Right before David left for six weeks of Basic Training at Ft. Benning in early January, he put on a full-court press for her to get pregnant. She said there was no way she'd go through a pregnancy alone. Besides, worry about him would be bad for the baby.

"If we have a baby, it means everything will work out."

"That's crazy. What if you die?"

"Don't even say that."

"Don't even say that a baby will make things fine. I want you here, as a part of it, not far away, only seeing the baby through Skype. I can't go through a pregnancy and birth all alone."

"I'll be home by then. Probably."

"How do you know? This is not a reason to have a baby."

"It'll give me something to hope for."

"Am I not enough to hope for?"

"Of course, you are. This would be extra."

"Give me a break." She took her book, closed the bedroom door, and climbed into bed. When she calmed down, she told herself she had to find a way to be as supportive as she could before he left.

She stayed on the Pill, but he didn't know that. She let him think there might be a chance she'd changed her mind. Maybe with that hope, they'd get along and the last couple of weeks would go well. And in fact, they proved to be bittersweet days. She pushed her worry and anger to the back of her mind, making herself savor the time with David. Wanda focused on the good moments between them: sex, lying in bed talking, going on drives, eating Sunday dinner with Sandy and Burt. On the last night, they made love. Earlier in the day, she'd considered skipping her pill and giving nature one chance, but then thought better of it.

Wanda made sandwiches for David and Burt to eat on the drive down to Georgia. David and she took a moment to say goodbye privately, and although she'd told herself not to cry, she lost it when he kissed her goodbye. After they left, she went to bed for the rest of the day with a plastic tumbler of vodka and OJ.

Because she needed something to keep her mind occupied, Wanda had signed up for an intro bio class during the spring session at the community college.

David called her from Ft. Benning, saying he was sore and completely exhausted, but had never felt more excited. "They break you down to build you up. I'm getting so much stronger." She asked if he was getting enough sleep, and he said that when his head hit the pillow, he was out. He didn't like his Sergeant, but that was standard. "They act like assholes, so you'll learn to follow orders. No matter what."

Wanda ordered a used copy of the biology text and felt the same excitement in her stomach she used to have as a girl when she chose her new school supplies. That first day, she ran into Jason Clark, who'd graduated high school that past June, and they decided to carpool together. Because she was married, she felt like an older student. The professor asked why they were in the course, and she said she hoped to become a nurse. It felt good to put it out there. She took notes and found she could keep up. After the first class during which a couple of girls were whispering to each other, she moved to the front of the room so she could listen better. She learned to read the chapter before the lecture to get a leg up on the assignment.

Over the next few weeks, between emails and Skype, she and David kept in regular contact. He sounded happy, tired, but hopeful, more focused and driven than she'd ever seen him. He started using terms like AIT, MOS, OSUT, talking about men in his unit. He talked a lot about himself, which was understandable. Sometimes, he'd ask about her and she said she was fine, missing him. She told him that Michelle had had a girl, that Mosher had started working at a forklift operator.

On her first quiz, she received one of the only A's in the class. The attendance had thinned out. Jason had missed the last few classes, so Wanda now drove herself. Her parents were glad she was doing something to keep busy, but they thought it was just that. She brought her textbook with her to work and highlighted pages when there weren't customers. She made flashcards and flipped through them as she ate her meals. No more TV, no more novels, no wasted time. She allowed herself a vodka and OJ after work, then she took her text and highlighter to bed with her to study before turning out the light. Every morning, she reread the notes from the previous day and on the weekends, she studied. She'd never felt so organized. Her teacher called her out as someone who took the course seriously.

David had decided to stay on at Ft. Benning for his infantry OST and would be done in June. She said she was proud of him and mentioned that she, too, had been working hard and might get an A in her course. "See?" he said. "We're both doing great."

When David finished his OST, Sandy, Burt, and Wanda drove down to Georgia to see the graduation. Wanda's course had finished (with an A) so she was free to take a few days off for the two-day celebration. In the car, Burt drove, and Sandy sat in the passenger seat, talking to Wanda over her shoulder. Wanda had cramps. Bad timing. Unable to read in a moving car, she dozed off and on when she didn't stare out the window at the cars and fields. They spent one night at a motel in Tennessee and insisted that Wanda have her own room, which they paid for. David would be disappointed that Wanda was on her period. Was she? At least she could give him a blow job.

She nearly didn't recognize him with his short hair and deep tan. He seemed taller, his neck and arms noticeably thicker. When he grabbed her into a big hug, whispering that PDA was frowned upon, she kissed him on the neck and breathed in his smell. God, how she'd missed that. Sandy was in tears, saying he looked so handsome, such a man. Burt pumped his hand, his face red from tamping down his own feelings.

In the middle of the energy and the chanting that followed the Commanding Officer's speech, Wanda searched for David in the crowd. He looked so happy, a part of the group. His ability to stick with this hard thing, to be so committed, surprised her. He'd grown. Who was she to say this was a mistake? She was still fearful, but this might be what made him into the man he was meant to be.

David was due to spend some time at home before being deployed to Iraq in August. Back home, he was in a great mood, telling everyone he encountered on the street how they were going to go in and get the job done. In their apartment though, especially in the bedroom, Wanda had forbidden him to talk about the war. "You'll just go to sleep, and I'll be up half the night, worrying."

The night before he left, the family gathered for a barbecue at his parents' house. All his friends from high school came. She looked at him and thought he'd outgrown them all. Had this been the thing he'd needed to find himself? She hoped so.

The day he left, she drank a couple of drinks to steel herself for the goodbye. She kept a brave face, but right before he and Burt set off for Ft. Bragg, after giving him a container of brownies, she kissed him hard and burst into tears. "You get in touch the first chance you have. I'll worry until you do." She watched as they drove away, David's arm waving from the open window, then she ran upstairs and threw herself into bed, hugging his pillow to her. He'd be fine. He had to be.

4

CALLIE

The last month of high school found Callie busy with exams. Whit was Valedictorian, and she finally edged Ed Peak out for Salutatorisitting In addition to Brewster, she'd been accepted by Columbia, Oberlin, and NYU, but her parents were annoyed that she'd done it without telling them, and they shut down any lingering hopes that she could go there. "You get the grades at Brewster to get into grad school and then we'll talk," her father said.

"At least you can look forward to Brewster's year in Lyon," added her mother.

Callie shrugged. At least that meant one year away from Shelton.

Elise was headed for Yale, Zelda for Tufts, and Claire to Oberlin. Callie felt embarrassed to be left behind by all her friends. What did she have to show for all her hard work? She'd have been accepted at Brewster even if she'd been a B student. What point had there been in working for Salutatorian anyway?

It meant having to give a speech, and meeting with Mrs. Foletti and Whit to plan their speeches. She'd ignored Whit since he'd written her that insane letter, figuring he'd get the hint. At the meeting, Mrs. Foletti talked about the importance of setting the right ceremonial tone, and giving an uplifting, inspiring talk. They posed for the local paper and when the issue came out, Callie saw she had a pinched expression and was leaning away from Whit, who gazed at her with a moony look.

Her mother said she was so proud and offered to read versions of her speech. Even though her father had been on her back for years about her grades, micromanaging every class, teacher, and textbook, he didn't have anything to say about her speech. Was he disappointed she hadn't come in first? She wondered if anything would have been enough for him, and she worried he'd interfere with her course choices at Brewster, that she'd never be on her own.

The Senior prom was scheduled for the week before graduation, but Matt dragged his feet about wearing a tux. "It's bullshit."

"I know, but it's our last prom. We can't miss that." At the dance, he sulked, sneaking sips of the flask he'd brought along, but he perked up for the after-prom party when they changed into jeans and tee-shirts and grabbed beers. They found a closet where they had sex and she curled up and fell asleep while he partied until morning.

At graduation, Callie won the French and Creative Writing prizes, and Elise won the History prize. Whit won all the math and science awards and the Rotary Scholarship. Callie gave her speech, which she hoped was inspirational, yet funny enough to show she had a sense of irony. Such a solemn occasion, she'd noted, as if they'd been charged with solving the world's problems by Thanksgiving. "At least take the time to learn about yourself." Introducing Whit as Valedictorian, Mr. Madison, the Principal, talked about him as the most accomplished student ever to graduate from this school, with more college credits to his name than anyone before. Great things were expected of him. Blah, blah. Then in a droning voice, Whit gave his speech, staring at his pages, his hair flattened from the cap. The speech was full of quotes by philosophers and scientists. Everyone rolled their eyes and yawned. Callie looked out into the audience and saw her parents, her mother smiling, and her father nodding off.

After the ceremony, Callie, Elise, and Zelda took off their caps and fluffed up their hair, then unzipped their robes to show their dresses for photos. Matt's mother took photos of Callie and him together, and he posed with one hand around her waist and the other flashing horns in the air, index and pinkie raised. His breath smelled of beer. Callie's parents hadn't brought a camera, so they stood awkwardly to the side, her mother clutching her purse, her father leaning on his cane. Elise, Zelda, and Matt all left with their extended families for cookouts, and Callie went home with her parents to a lunch of chicken salad and rolls, and a cake made from a mix. At the end of the meal, her father stood up, patted his mouth with a napkin and said, "Well, then. I'm off."

"Really, Herbert? Today?" asked her mother.

"Well, yes. I have work." He patted Callie on the shoulder and entered his study, shutting the door. Callie knew he'd been thrown off his schedule by taking time out for the ceremony, and she understood, but it might have been nice if he'd commented on her speech. Her mother said Callie had acquitted herself admirably and that she could hear every word.

"I wish Dad had said something."

"He's very proud. We both are." Well, Callie used to think he was.

That night, Matt picked Callie up to go to the party at The Point. Things had been rocky between them since the prom, but she was determined to have a good time, the last chance everyone would get together as a class. When they arrived, a bonfire crackled, and someone had scored two kegs of beer. As soon as Matt parked the car, he was tackled, literally, by members of the hockey team, who carried him off to wrestle in a squirming mass and do a team chant. Callie poured herself a foamy glass of beer, wandered over to a group of girls camped on logs facing the fire, and sat between Elise and Zelda.

"We'll Skype and we can all get together in Boston or New York," said Zelda, on her way to Tufts.

"I can't believe this is the last time we'll be together after thirteen years," said Claire.

"We have the rest of the summer," said Elise.

"It's not the same," said Zelda. "We won't be together. We won't be classmates anymore."

"And that's a good thing," said Elise, noting it was time to move the fuck on.

"Yes, but this will never happen again."

"There's our reunion," said Sonia.

"That's five years off," said Zelda. "We'll be out of college by then. Who knows where we'll be?"

The East-Coast-bound girls planned to take the Fung Wah bus to New York from Boston. Elise said she'd be in Manhattan all the time from New Haven.

Elise must have noticed that Callie felt left out, so she said, "And when we're home at Thanksgiving, we'll hang out with you."

"Didn't you want to get out of town?" asked Sonia.

"Yeah, but I'll be living in the dorm. No way could I live at home with my parents."

"I'm going to miss my parents so much," said Elise, sniffling.

Callie sat through more crying and sloppy promises to be together forever before standing up, dusting off the seat of her jeans and setting off to find Matt. This party was lame. Lily Dawson, the girlfriend of a hockey player, stood next to the keg, smoking.

"Have you seen Matt?"

Lily laughed and said he was around but was, well, busy.

"What do you mean, 'busy'?"

Lily's eyes darted toward a line of trees. Callie started off in that direction. "Don't go there, Callie. I'm warning you."

Callie skirted the trees and came upon Matt, his back to her, head tipped back, with Angie Track kneeling before him, her head bobbing, his hand on her head.

"Matt?" Callie said, her voice cracking.

"Oh, shit," he said, pushing Angie onto her butt. "Shit." He zipped up and turned around, crossing his arms, backing up. "Hey, Callie."

"Fuck you, Matt."

"It wasn't what you think."

"You liar. Take me home."

"No. I'm not ready to leave yet."

"You're my ride. I want to leave."

"No," he said, walking toward her, reaching for her.

She backed away. He grabbed her arm and she whipped it away. "Don't touch me."

"Come on, Callie. Stop that," and he stepped toward her again.

She shouted, "I hate you! Get away from me!"

"Fine, whatever. I'll leave you the fuck alone." As she walked away, he yelled, "Have a nice life, bitch."

Callie ran down the path toward the bonfire then tripped and fell, scraping her palms. Standing up, she wiped some of the dirt onto her jeans and, crying, stumbled the rest of the way toward the fire. "Can anyone take me home?" No one answered.

She walked over to Elise and asked when they could leave, but Elise said the party was just getting going. Callie told her about Matt and Angie, and Elise said he was an asshole, but she clearly didn't want to leave yet, so Callie knew she was on her own. A group of girls looked at her before going back to their huddle. Matt and Angie had returned to the fire, and the hockey team closed ranks around him. Callie sat on a log, blowing on her stinging palms, wiping her eyes with the back of her hands. She couldn't walk home; it was miles away. She'd wait for Elise, but who knew when she'd be ready to leave? She watched these people, kids she'd known her whole life but whom she felt no connection to anymore. She pulled her knees up close and laid her head on them.

"Are you okay?"

She looked up to see Whit standing over her. "Can you sign my yearbook?" He was wearing khakis and a collared shirt like he was working at a hardware store.

"You brought your yearbook here?"

He nodded, hugging it to his chest. "I didn't get all the signatures I wanted."

"Well, I obviously don't have a pen on me."

"I do." He handed her the book and a pen, warm and sweaty from his hand, and she opened it to the page where she usually signed, a decent photo of her singing her solo in *The Mikado*. She wrote, *Have a great time in college* and handed it back to him, wiping her hand on her pants. He stood next to her, reading what she'd written.

"Can you drive me home?" she asked.

"I rode my bike."

"All the way here? That's nuts."

"I don't drive." He shrugged. "It's not that far." His brow was glistening, and he smelled sweaty.

"But it's dark."

"I have a light."

She put her head down on her knees again, hoping he'd get the hint to leave her alone, but he sat down next to her. "I liked your speech. It was pretty good."

She sighed. "Yours, well, covered a lot."

"I don't know. It wasn't really what I wanted to say."

"I'm not sure anyone was really listening."

"So, are you excited about Brewster?"

"Not really."

"I wanted to talk to you. We never really talked after I sent you that letter."

"I've been really busy."

"I thought you might be mad at me."

"I'm not anything at you."

"We'll see each other on campus next year." She looked at him, his shiny face lit by the fire, his glasses, reflecting the light. "And Matt will be at Penn State. So, if you and he break up, we can do stuff together."

"Oh, my God, are you crazy?" She hauled herself to her feet. "Stop stalking me." He shrank back, hugging himself. "We don't know each other. We aren't friends. I don't want you hanging around me all the time."

He stood, cradling his yearbook, looking at the ground.

"Get a life!" Her voice cracked. "Leave me alone!" Elise came over and took her by the shoulders, giving her a hug. Everyone stared at them.

Whit staggered off, and Elise handed Callie her beer. She took a swig and choked on the fizz. Her nose was stuffed from crying. "Can we please leave now?" Elise said sure and signaled to Alex. Elise told her to forget Matt. He was an asshole and she'd never liked him. Callie could do better.

Callie sat in the back seat of Alex's SUV, leaning against the door because she was sharing it with Claire and Jason, who were sprawled over each other, making out. "Awesome party," said Alex, and Elise agreed. Callie felt a pang of regret over taking out her anger on Whit when she was upset about Matt. But Whit needed to learn not to act like a psycho. It wasn't her fault he was so weird. And she didn't want anyone at Brewster connecting her to him. But because he was a science geek and practically a sophomore, maybe she could avoid him.

At home, lying in bed, she swore off her old friends except Elise, deciding to start from scratch at college. What had she been doing with someone like Matt anyway?

She'd wanted to find a summer job to earn spending money, but her parents insisted she take a French course at the college so she could place into French 303, putting her in better shape for her junior year in Lyon. "You don't want to be with those students from two-bit schools," her father said. She wanted to say that at Columbia, there wouldn't be any of those types, but she didn't.

French 225, Survey of French Literature was going to be taught by Professor Minot, a new instructor her father didn't know. The class would meet in Putnam Hall. Her father's office was on the top floor. As a girl, she used to walk past that building, looking up at the light in his office, wondering how he could spend so much time there. What could be so interesting? She knew how to avoid him on campus, and, since she'd be living in the dorm, something she'd insisted on when they'd denied her the other schools, she could come and go without seeing him.

On the first day of her French class, Callie dressed in jeans and a flowered peasant blouse and walked to campus. The first one to arrive in class, she spent a few anxious moments choosing the right seat at the large wooden table, then she unpacked her textbook, notebook, and pen, wishing she had a laptop like other students. She doodled for a while until a girl with a streak of blue in her hair, wearing a camisole over a black bra and ripped cutoffs, popped her head into the room and nodded in Callie's direction. "I'm Raquel," she said, sitting down next to her. No backpack, book, pens. "You don't look familiar. What year are you?"

"I start in the fall."

"Aren't you just a bit early?"

"I grew up here."

"Eew, what's that like?"

"You know. Boring."

"Well, yeah. Why are you spending the summer taking a course?"

"Why are you?"

"I need to make up credits. This summer, I'm living in Dewey, but then I'll live in Parker. What about you? Tell me you're not going to live at home next year."

"God, no. My father's a professor here. That's enough. We live on Goshen Road."

"I hope he's not one of the professors whose course I dropped."

"Professor Morton? Greek?"

"Do I look like someone who'd take Greek?" Callie admitted she didn't. She wondered what kind of students did take her father's courses. "Is it weird to go to the college where your father teaches?"

"I don't know."

Other students arrived and Raquel introduced Callie to Mathilda and William. "She's a tender freshman. And a fac brat."

"Don't hold that against me," said Callie. When she said her last name, she met blank faces. "Oh, yeah, him," said Mathilda. "I've seen him around." And Callie didn't know what that meant. "He's pretty old, right?" Callie said that was him.

"Why would you choose to go to college so close to home?"

"It's free."

"Good luck with that," said Raquel. "Nothing in life is free."

Right before ten, a man in jeans and a dark navy shirt arrived and dropped a backpack at the end of the table. Callie noticed that instead of a belt, he cinched his pants with a knotted length of rope. He introduced himself as Greg. "None of that Professor Minot bullshit." He reached in his backpack and pulled out a dog-eared text and placed it on the table. "I'm new to this bustling metropolis, having left New York behind. What was I thinking?" Several students snickered. "What I need to know is where to get a decent cup of coffee. I'm dying here." They laughed again and William said there was a café in town. "So, let's get going. French 225. *On y va?* He looked to be in his late twenties and had thick black eyebrows over blue eyes. His hair was curly and had been tamed by gel. He wore wire-rimmed glasses that sat crooked on his face, and when they slipped down his nose, he pushed them up with his middle finger like he was flipping everyone off. He spoke French perfectly, even saying "Euh" instead of "Um." When he smiled, the skin around his eyes pleated, and when he turned to write something on the board, Callie could see he had a spot of white hair that looked as if a drop of bleach had been dropped there.

Callie struggled to take notes as he talked about writers she'd never heard of: Césaire, Glissant, Fanon, Schwarz-Bart, writers not in the text she'd bought, which featured Molière, Racine, and Hugo. Was she in the wrong class? She'd received a 5 on her AP exam in French, but this was way over her head. Maybe she should drop down a level. Greg explained that his specialty was the Négritude Movement, and he was working on a dissertation about Edouard Glissant and Patrick Chamoiseau.

After class, she gathered her courage and approached him. "*Excusez-moi, M. Minot?*"

"Yes? And it's Greg."

"I'm not sure I'm in the right class."

"Why do you think that?"

"I was lost."

"So was everyone. It's my way of weeding out the dregs. Give it a few days."

On the walk home, she gave herself a pep talk. Hang in there. Don't bail so soon. She did the assignment with a dictionary and found it wasn't completely impossible. She worked for two hours to write one page, an *Explication de Texte* of a poem by Glissant. At dinner, she mentioned what she'd been working on, and her father asked when they were going to read the Classics.

"They're all dead white men," she said. "Shouldn't we be exposed to other voices?"

"The canon is the basis for all study."

When she said that she was interested in what was going on in Haiti and Rwanda, he said the class should be about literature, not current events.

A couple of days later, as Greg passed back the papers, he'd written a note. *Viens me voir.* Come see me. Her heart seized. Was he going to make her drop the class?

She approached him at the end of the class, "Was my paper that awful?"

"No, it was pretty good. I just wanted to go over it with you. Can we grab some coffee?"

"Sure. When?"

"Now?"

"Okay." They headed toward the student union, and she struggled to keep up with him in her flip-flops. Her hands shook as she carried her coffee over to a corner table.

"Let me show you a couple of things you need to watch out for."

She was grateful he didn't insist on speaking French outside of class. She felt so tongue-tied around him, even in English. He scowled at the page, adding a few marks.

"I'm sorry my French sucks."

"It doesn't suck. And at least you did the paper." She noticed that Raquel hadn't turned hers in. She felt hot and flustered at each mistake he corrected. "You need to be less apologetic. I'm being hard on you, but that's okay. You won't break, right?"

"I guess not."

"I can tell you're smart. Give me a high-school student who's trying over some fuck-up college student making up credits."

To occupy her hands, she took notes, grateful she had a pen and paper.

When he handed her the marked copy, he sat back. "Are you related to Herbert Morton?"

"He's my father. My parents were pretty old when I was born. And my father is older than my mother." She found herself clicking her pen nervously, so she dropped it and folded her arms.

"Why Brewster? Don't you want to spread your wings a bit?"

"I got into Columbia, Oberlin, and NYU, but Brewster's a good school."

"But it's not Columbia."

She sat back, feeling the blood rush to her face. "So why are you here if you don't think much of it?"

"I have to finish my dissertation, but when I do, I'll get on tenure track at a better school." He frowned at his empty cup. "No offense."

"Sometimes small schools are better than big ones."

"And sometimes they're not. Listen, I can tell you're smart. Just don't settle, okay?" She nodded, both flattered and disconcerted. "Now back to your paper."

In class, Callie stared at Greg as he spoke, watching as he raked his hand through his hair, causing the curls to escape the gel and spring up, untamed. "*Regardez ça,*" he'd say and would repeat a line from Césaire or Glissant, *Ecoutez cette mélodie.*" He had a way of closing his eyes before answering a question as if the question were so interesting it needed to sink in. Callie made a point of commenting at least once every class, although sometimes she knew her points seemed silly and obvious. She found she liked Caribbean literature—the use of rich nature imagery, the fluid borders between life and death, the strong female characters. Callie noticed that Raquel never missed a movie day, but her attendance otherwise was spotty.

Since her break-up with Matt, she'd avoided parties, so she saw less of Elise and Zelda as well. It was easier to walk to the college and see Raquel than to go into town. One Friday, Raquel told Callie about a party at the AD house. "Normally, I avoid frats because they're a bunch of rapists," said Raquel, "but the house is a dorm for the summer while the frat is on probation." Callie said she'd go and told her parents she needed to study late at the library.

The night of the party was hot, so she slipped on a sundress and sandals and tucked ten dollars into her bra. As she walked across the golf course, a short cut she'd been taking to avoid passing by Whit's house, she could hear the thump of music coming from fraternity row. When she arrived and saw a crowd outside, dancing and drinking, she nearly left. But then she found Raquel, William, and Mathilda, who pointed toward the keg. She filled a cup and joined them dancing. Raquel pulled Callie into the middle of the dancing, and Callie whipped her hair around as she jumped, spilling her beer. She took a hit from the bong, kicked off her sandals, and rejoined the dancers. "You go, Callie," said Raquel, whose arm was slung around the shoulders of a girl named Sage, who wore her hair shaved on one side and long on the other.

The two beers she'd drunk had run through her. "Where's the bathroom?" Someone pointed toward the frat house. "First floor, near the back."

Her head was whirling, and she struggled to walk straight, stepping barefoot onto the sticky floor and heading down the hall toward the dining room. The bathroom was occupied so she closed her eyes, leaning her head against the wall. Finally, a guy and a girl stumbled out, surrounded by the smell of weed. In the bathroom, she peed, then splashed water on her face. Looking at herself in the smudged mirror, she saw her hair wild and her face ruddy, but she looked good. She ran her fingers over her face, staring at herself.

On her way toward the front door, she noticed Greg sitting in the sparsely furnished living room talking to the couple from the bathroom, who were passing around a joint. She flopped down on the sofa next to Greg and said, "Hi!"

"Yes, you appear to be," he said, smiling. She laughed and leaned toward him, running her hand along his arm. He studied her. "So, not such a high-school girl after all."

"I didn't think you'd be here," she said.

"I didn't think *you'd* be here."

She was feeling very loose as she accepted the joint from him, thinking about her lips touching the paper where his lips had been.

"I need a beer," she said. "Does anyone want one?" She stood up, stumbled, and Greg held out his hand to steady her.

"Do you need help?"

He put his hand on the small of her back as they walked toward the kitchen. An old refrigerator held cans of Yeungling and PBR. She grabbed two, handed one to him and ran the sweating can along her face. She leaned back against the refrigerator and opened the beer, taking a sip and spilling some on her chin. He wiped off the dribble, then kissed her. She put down her beer, wrapped her arms around his neck, pulling him closer. They kissed for a while, her head twirling with the weirdness of that. Then, smiling at him, running her hands through her hair, she knelt in front of him, reaching for the knotted rope holding up his pants. "Not here," he said, pulling her back into a pantry, shutting the door, and lifting her onto a table. He buried his head under her skirt, pulled down her underpants, and went down on her. Matt had never done this, and she wondered what it would feel like. At first, she felt awkward, but when a wave ran down her legs, she tilted her head back and rode it out until she came, squeezing her legs against his head and shoulders. "See?" he whispered to her as she flopped off the table and into his arms. "You just have to let yourself go. You have it in you." She felt completely wrung out and yet all her nerve endings were fired. She pulled up her underpants, barely able to stand, so she leaned on him. Too shy to look him in the eye, she stood at his side, trying to steady her breathing. "Come see me tomorrow at four," he said. "After office hours."

"Okay." She stumbled out the door, looking for Raquel and her friends, and not finding them, tried to locate her sandals, which were lost as well. She walked home barefoot, the grass soft and dewy, except when she had to cross the pavement to get to her house. The air on her skin felt wonderful though, the heat of the day now cooled. At home, she slipped upstairs and lay in bed on top of her sheet, letting the breeze from the screened window run over her, head spinning, waves of pleasure rippling through her and setting off little surges. Greg was a man, not a boy.

In class the next day, Raquel asked where she'd been. "You just disappeared. Did you bail?"

"Yeah, when I couldn't find you guys, I went home. I was so high."

"You were hilarious."

Throughout the class, Greg didn't make eye contact with her, but she stared at him, her face warm, the blood rushing to her cheeks. Had he changed his mind or was he just being careful? She could barely pay attention to what he was saying, worried that if she showed up at his office later, he'd laugh at her. After class, she went to the library and sat with her book, unable to concentrate, feeling his mouth, letting waves of heat roll off her.

At four, she walked toward Putnam but nearly backed out, afraid she'd misinterpreted what he'd said. If he humiliated her, would she have to drop the class? Would he fail her? And if so, what would she say to her parents? She climbed the stairs and forced her shaking hand to knock. She heard nothing. "It's Callie," she said in a small voice.

The door opened. "Did anyone see you? Lock the door behind you."

She fumbled with the old lock then turned to him. With the lights off, and a window behind him, she couldn't make out his face in the shadows. "Listen," he said. "You've got to be cool about this. You can't tell anyone. Do you understand?" She nodded. "I'm taking a huge risk here."

"No, I promise." Little pings of excitement raced through her belly and down her legs.

He smiled. "What a nice surprise you are. He studied her, and she looked away, embarrassed. "Are you on birth control?"

"Just condoms."

He frowned. "Get something more reliable."

He led her to the couch, pulled down her jeans, and went down on her again. When she was about to come, he put his hand over her mouth. "Ssh. The walls are thin." She nodded. "I'd put on music, but then students would know I'm here and would try to see me."

He stripped, then put on a condom as she ran her fingers through his hair. Naked now, she lay back as he entered her. She'd never taken off all her clothes with Matt and was shy about Greg seeing her body. All that skin contact was overwhelming.

Afterwards, they lay on the scratchy, sat-out couch, his head on her chest as she told herself, this is life, this is how it feels. Bolder now, she stood up and walked over to the window to look at the huge maple tree outside, the one that turned scarlet in the fall. He told her not to stand so close to the window. "No one can see me through the leaves," she said over her shoulder. "I know what it looks like from below."

"I could get into big trouble. Your father could make it very hard for me."

"Trust me. He's in his own world."

"Still, we have to be careful. There are rules about this. I didn't anticipate this happening. I don't do this kind of thing."

He told her she was sexy, that she was old for her age, that the ten-year difference between them didn't matter. Her skin was humming, her legs rubbery, her face chafed. She slipped out of his office and down the back stairs. Her father's office was on the floor above and she knew not to use the elevator. Instead, she took the stairs to the first floor.

As she walked across campus, she wondered if anyone looking at her would know what she'd just been doing. But no one would care if she'd been with a student. She needed to see a doctor for birth control, but she couldn't go to anyone in town. She'd visit Student Health Services to get an IUD.

Her parents seemed pleased that she was enjoying her course and was spending so much time at the library. "See? We knew you'd like Brewster once you started there," her mother said.

She and Greg met during non-office hours, early and late, at times when students were unlikely to show up. Greg said she could bring work and she did, sitting on his ratty couch while he wrote at his desk. But she found it hard to concentrate, and she'd stare at him, hoping to catch his eye. She'd scootch down to the end of the couch and snake her bare foot up his leg, hoping he'd drop his work and jump her. Sometimes it worked; sometimes he was lost in concentration. He was under a lot of pressure to finish his dissertation, from what she could understand, a brilliant study of men in Glissant and Chamoiseau. She went to the library and looked those writers up, feeling guilty for reading a translation, but she wanted to learn what she could on her own. She asked Greg for things to read so she could understand more although she loved that they could barely keep their hands off each other, she had to help him get his work done.

"How is this going to work when I'm a student here?" she asked.

"We'll find a way. You can't take any of my classes, obviously. It will be easier once you live in the dorm, but we can't go there either. But at least you won't have to answer to your parents." He was renting the coach house behind the Mullers' house in the middle of town. Once, she snuck away, walked downtown, and slipped into his apartment to see him, but she couldn't spend the night, and she worried about running into people she knew. So, they continued to meet at his office.

Raquel had missed a bunch of classes and hadn't yet turned in a paper. Callie urged her to get the work done, but Raquel said Greg was boring. "I don't think he's so bad," Callie said, her heart fluttering.

"I'll get the papers done by the end of the session. I have a plan." Callie wondered if this was her usual failed approach. "Don't worry about me." Raquel wondered why Callie hadn't gone to any more parties, but Callie said she was busy, a lame excuse, she knew. She wanted to tell Raquel about Greg, but she didn't dare. She couldn't even tell Elise.

She and Greg maintained the same maneuvers for the rest of the summer session. Once, she opened the door without knocking and found him with a girl going over a paper. Caught up short, she asked if he'd received her paper. "I got it," he said, giving her a sharp look. She left, worried he was angry. Would he break up with her for being a needy girl? She waited until office hours were over, then she texted. When she arrived, he opened the door. "Don't do that again," he said, his face stony.

"Please don't be mad at me."

"You have to remember what I'm risking here."

"I'm sorry. I'll be more careful."

A few days after the summer session ended, Callie told her mother she needed to go to campus for pre-registration and to check out the dorm. She hadn't seen Greg in a couple of days, and it was driving her crazy. She went up to his office and saw his door open, so she stuck her head in. "Hey." His desk was piled with packing boxes. "What are you doing?" she asked, her heart seizing. He motioned for her to close the door.

"Those assholes." He was shoving books haphazardly into an open box. "They reneged on my deal. They said I could have time to work on my dissertation, but then they loaded me up with freshmen courses and committee work. And they said that because I haven't finished it yet, my future here wasn't certain."

"That's not fair. They promised."

"They got their summer out of me. They don't care." He hadn't shaved and his hair was mussed.

"What can you do?"

"I'm out of here, obviously."

A blow to her stomach. "What? You can't do that."

"I have no fucking job."

"Can you stay in town and write? That way we can see each other."

"No, I have to get out of here."

She started to cry. What about them? Where did that leave her? She asked what he was going to do.

"I'm going to Martinique for research."

"Why can't you do it here?"

He said he needed the access to primary sources. She willed him to ask about her, to talk about their future. As he packed, she sat on the couch, crying. Finally, she said, "What am I going to do without you here?"

"Come here." He tossed the extra books off the couch and pulled down her pants. It was fast, and when she came, she burst into tears. Then she lay under him, sniffling, unable to keep from crying. She could smell that he'd been drinking, and she wove her arms around him and buried her face in his neck, breathing him in, feeling his heartbeat against her chest. Their breathing synched and she felt herself drift toward sleep. When she awoke, he was sitting on the arm of the couch, staring at her. "Come with me."

"What?" She said, sitting up. "I can't do that."

"Why not?"

"I have school."

"You don't even want to be here."

"I would if you were here. And my parents are expecting me to go."

"And you're always going to do what your parents want you to do? What about what you want? What about what I want? If you want to be with me, then let's go."

"How can I leave, just like that?"

"We can do anything we want."

"What does that mean, be with you?"

"Come here." He pulled her onto his lap. "Let's get married."

"You don't have to say that."

"I know I don't. But I want to."

"Married?" she said, her voice shaking. "Really?"

"Yes, we love each other. You need to get away from here and your parents to have your own life. You can go to college wherever I get a job. But we'll be together."

"But will I see my parents?"

"Eventually, but now you've got to make a clean break. It's better if you leave before the semester starts. It's better than dropping out. You'll take a year off and travel with me, do your own reading, work on your French. I'll give you books. It'll be your French immersion program."

"My parents will kill me."

"That's why you have to do it and then let them know. You're eighteen, an adult. You don't need their permission. Once we're married, they won't be able to do anything about it. This is your life. Think of it. Martinique for a month and then New York for a while, and we'll spend the rest of the year in Paris."

"What will we do for money?"

"I have some savings. We'll figure that out. You can get a part-time job. Don't put roadblocks ahead of our happiness. This is our chance. You have to jump. And I need you. I can't do this alone."

"I love you so much. But it's scary."

"Anything worth doing is scary."

They decided to leave together by car on move-in day for new freshmen. In the two weeks before then, she pretended to be immersed in packing for college, even letting her father dictate what classes she should take—Intro to Philosophy, third-level French, a Shakespeare class,and one of her own choosing. He mother seemed happy to see them agree on this and said she was glad that Callie was looking forward to Brewster. "You'll still come home for a meal now and then, right?" Callie said she would, but it pained her to tell that lie. What would their lives be like when she was gone?

Little by little, she transferred clothes in her backpack to Greg's place. He'd urged her to pare down her possessions because they'd be on the road a lot. No books. He'd get what she needed. He had a laptop. She would need clothes for warm and cold weather. Her mother had just bought her a new winter coat, so she packed that. In her mother's file box, she found her passport and birth certificate and tucked them away.

The day before Elise left for Yale, Callie went to her house to say goodbye and help her finish packing. She sat in Elise's bedroom, folding clothes from the pile on her bed as Elise debated what to take and what to leave. Elise was obsessing about how many pairs of shoes she'd need. All Callie could think of what how unimportant shoes were, and she nearly confessed to Elise about Greg. But how could she explain the past two months? Would Elise be mad at her both for lying and for bailing on college?

"You'll visit me over mid-semester break, right?" Elise asked. "I can't wait to show you around."

Callie knew that by then, she'd be in New York where they could in fact see each other. "That sounds great. Maybe we can also go to New York, right?"

"Sure. It's close."

"I'm going to miss you so much," said Callie, starting to cry.

Elise hugged Callie. "Best friends, no matter the distance, right?"

"No matter what?"

"Of course." She handed Callie a tissue. "Now, I need to stuff a few more things in." Callie laughed. "You laugh, but you can go home if you forgot something. I have to think ahead."

"I do too."

Finally, the day came. When she left the house that morning, carrying a small duffle, she gave her mother a big hug, lingering, trying not to cry, wondering when she'd see her again. "This is a big day for you," her mother said and offered again to drive her. No need, said Callie. She was almost moved in. "We're very proud of you and know you'll do brilliantly." Callie was wiping her eyes. "I know you wanted to go to Columbia, but I'm selfishly glad we'll have you nearby a bit longer." A sob rose in Callie's throat. "Be sure to stop by your father's office once in a while." Callie nodded, her face burning. "I envy him, being able to see you there."

"Would he even notice?"

"He notices more than you think."

When she said goodbye to her father, he was at his desk, working, as always. "Dad, I'm heading over to campus now."

"Good for you." He looked up at her, his eyes darting over her, then he hunched back over his paper. He was in his zone, and she knew he was eager to get back to work.

"Well, bye, Dad," she said and walked away, wishing she'd made more of the moment. She gulped to keep from crying.

The campus was crawling with new students and their parents settling them into the dorms, signing up for clubs, going to orientation meetings. Callie walked right past them and took her last walk down the hill. When she was a girl, after a huge snowstorm, kids from town would sled down the hill and onto Main Street down below. Callie didn't have a sled because her parents didn't have a clue about winter sports and wouldn't have let her do anything that risky, but she'd borrow a plastic disk from Elise. Despite the heat of this August day, she remembered the chill of the wind on her cheeks, the bump of the plastic under her bottom, and the thrill of hurtling down the hill, swerving out onto the street, as she'd twirl around and come to a stop in a snow drift. Now, she watched the line of backed-up cars, SUVs, and taxis making their way up the hill toward the campus. This life now seemed so far from hers. She'd skipped to adulthood.

Her future with Greg was wide and exciting. She started to jog down the hill, the duffle bumping against her hip, her hair ruffling in the breeze as she headed toward her future, free.

5

WANDA

When officers came to Wanda's door to tell her David had been killed by an IED near Baghdad, she didn't cry right away, worried it might embarrass the nice men. Somehow, she found the breath to give them her parents' number and then the three of them sat, silent, while she struggled to breathe, and they waited for her parents to come rescue her. When she heard her parents open the door, her whole body started to shake. Her mother rushed over to help her into the bedroom, but when she saw the bed she'd shared with David, a scream poured from her, so her mother led her back into the living room, covered the day bed with a quilt, and tucked her in. Her father gave her a sip of water, but she gagged, spitting it back into the glass. Her mother whispered, "I know, baby. I know," as she rubbed Wanda's back.

While Wanda lay curled up, her father made phone calls to family. When David's parents arrived, Sandy collapsed on top of Wanda, sobbing. In the moment, it occurred to Wanda that because David was an only child, his parents would be Wanda's responsibility from then on. Later that afternoon, Gail and Mary Sue brought coffee, Michelle arrived with a cold-cut platter, and

Mr. Howe sent Irene up with a tray of cookies from the bakery. The smell of butter and sugar made Wanda's stomach turn. Irene gave her a crushing hug, stroked her hair, and told her she wasn't alone, that people loved her and would help her out.

Calls came in all day including one from an Army Grief Counselor, giving her details on returning David's body, asking if she were planning a religious or civil ceremony, but it was too much, too soon, too many people crowding their apartment. How was she even certain that David was dead? Maybe it had been a mistake.

Everyone was relying on Wanda to make decisions, but Wanda couldn't think, could barely breathe. Her mother sent Sandy and Burt to the farm with the rest of the family. Decisions could wait until the next day. Michelle offered to stay with her, but Wanda's mother said the fewer people the better. She gave Wanda an Ambien and sat with her, saying she'd sleep in Wanda's bed for the first night or as long as Wanda needed her. Wanda hadn't changed the sheets since David left so she could keep his smell with her, and now she was embarrassed.

The next few days flew by in a blur. They said it would take a couple of days for David to be transported to Dover, then up to a week being prepared and embalmed before going to Pittsburgh, then Shelton, so the family planned a funeral mass for two weeks from then. In the meantime, her mother, Michelle, and her sisters-in-law took turns sitting with Wanda during the day, although she found it exhausting to have them there when she had nothing to say and could barely sit up. Finally, she sent her mother back to the farm and told Michelle she needed time to herself.

The first day alone she couldn't bear to sit still, so she took the car and drove around town, circling the main square, up and down side streets in widening circles, then up past the college where the summer students tossed around Frisbees on the fraternity lawns ambling like cattle in front of her car, making her want to ram them with her bumper. How dare they walk around so carefree? She drove on, past the sports fields where the houses had larger lawns. She drove past the farm and continued along the pasture with the grazing cows and the acres of field corn, half of it harvested, the rest standing tall. Round bales of hay lay on their sides like toppled game pieces on a board made of circular grooves. It was haying season. Life went on, even if hers had ended.

The next day, when out driving past her and David's spot, she pulled off to the side of the road, turning down the dirt path into the space between the fields, half hoping to find him there, waiting for her. She climbed out of the car, walked down the path, then, not finding him, she sank to her knees, digging up stalks of corn, smelling the soil, crumbling clods of dirt between her fingers, then clenched her fists and pounded the ground as she screamed at David, furious with him for throwing away his life and with it, hers.

When she calmed down enough to drive, she got in the car and took the back roads into the village, around the square with the gazebo and the fountain across from St. Vincent's, past the row of shops, the grocery, the pharmacy, the liquor store, the yarn shop. Finally, as the sky started to darken, she drove back to their, now her, apartment, parked the car and climbed the rickety stairs that David kept promising to fix, and poured herself a vodka and OJ and sat in front of the TV until she fell asleep.

Two days before the funeral, the day before his body and coffin were due to be delivered, she sat on the sofa, clicking through the TV channels and saw an ad for life insurance with a retired couple surrounded by their grandchildren. Feeling the walls close in, panic rising in her throat, Wanda poured another slug of vodka into her half-full bottle of OJ and grabbed her keys. She needed a cool place to sit and catch her breath.

She found herself steering the car up the hill, windows lowered, feeling the fresh air roll over her face and neck. She'd planned to bury David's high-school ring at their spot but too exhausted to drive further, she pulled into the college parking lot instead. She sat taking sips of her drink then turned off the car, tucked the bottle in her bag, and staggered toward Bascom Grove, the college nature preserve with pine trees and shade plants and wooden foot bridges that crisscrossed a brook. High school students went there to make out or slip into the underbrush for sex. She and David had gone there a few times before he got his license and the Buick. Wanda found the smell of pine and decaying leaves soothing and craved the cool that descended on her as she as she entered the canopy of trees.

She sat on a wooden bench next to a foot bridge with a plaque in memory of Alice Gould Putnam, 1911-2004. Wanda fished the ring out of her bag, feeling its weight in her hand, the curly grooves around the blue stone. Class of 2005. At the time, David had wanted the ring, but he'd never worn it, and hadn't wanted a wedding ring. Maybe she'd bury the ring there. She let herself cry, taking sips of her drink, sweet but harsh, as it slipped down her throat.

"Are you all right?"

She looked up to see Whit Sutter, a boy who graduated a year after her and David. A brainiac. He often came into the bakery and bought Hermit cookies, the kind old ladies liked—full of raisins, but dry and hard to swallow. Sometimes, she gave him day-old ones for free.

"Yes. Well, no. I'm not all right."

"You were crying."

"I thought I was alone."

"I live right over there. I saw you from my window."

She slipped the ring into her pocket.

"I heard your husband died."

She sighed and a sob caught in her throat.

"So, you're sad, right?"

"What kind of stupid question is that?"

He drew back, his face flushed.

"Sorry, I'm not myself."

He stood there, breathing through his mouth. What did he want?

"Sit if you want."

"I don't know anyone who died in the war," he said, settling next to her. She could smell beer on his breath.

"Well, except David."

"I didn't really know him though."

"I guess not."

They sat for a while as she tipped the bottle up to drink, wiping her nose and mouth with the back of her hand. She felt dizzy.

Finally, he asked, "What are you going to do?"

"I don't know," and she started crying again.

He said he was sorry, and he didn't want to upset her. She said he hadn't, that she cried all the time now.

"That's okay. You can cry if you need to."

She took a deep swallow, feeling the sting of the orange juice. Closing her eyes and shaking her head made everything spin, so she lay her head on his shoulder, breathing his smell, tipping the bottle, spilling, wiping, sticky. Skin, breath, cool breeze, hot wind. David, where are you? Please, baby, where are you? Let me touch you. Swimming, twirling, reaching, falling.

"I'm sorry it was so fast," Whit said. And she opened her eyes, surprised to see him sitting there.

"That's okay."

She tried to stand but sat again and buried her face in her hands, her stomach wobbly, head spinning.

"I'm sorry about your husband."

"Yeah, I'm sorry too." She stood up and staggered back to her car, fumbling with the key, then she sat, trying to clear her head. With shaking hands gripping the wheel, she drove slowly back home. Parking next to the apartment, she sat in the car before getting out and climbing the stairs, her legs thick and slow. She fell onto the sofa, thirsty, unable to get up to fetch a glass of water.

Wanda woke up the next morning on top of the covers, still dressed, her head pounding, her mouth dry and sticky. She couldn't remember anything about the night before except she'd gotten drunk. As she lay there, trying to settle her stomach, she remembered driving, sitting in the Grove, but not how she got home. Was Whit Sutter there or had she dreamed about him? A sour belch rose up, and she swallowed, vowing never to drink and drive again. In fact, she should stop drinking altogether. Although how could she get through the next few days without something to dull her pain?

That afternoon, the coffin arrived, and Burt picked her up to drive to the mortuary. Sandy couldn't bear to see him and had stayed behind. But when it came time for Wanda to view David, she fell apart, saying she couldn't do it, couldn't look at him dead. What if that was all she could remember about him? Burt went in alone, spent a few minutes, then came back, his face pale. He said David looked peaceful, like he was asleep. He hugged Wanda and she felt him tremble with the effort of keeping himself together. That night, she drank herself to sleep.

The day of the funeral, hungover, Wanda pulled on the dress that Michelle had bought for her, which was too tight in the bust, but she managed to zip it up, and she slipped on her black pumps she'd dragged from the back of the closet. Although she felt sick, she needed a drink to get her through the service and burial. Her stomach shaky, she walked up the aisle to the front pew leaning on her father, her brothers standing stiff in their jackets and ties, her sisters-in-law tending to the fussy children, Sandy and Burt on either side of her, Sandy sobbing as she squeezed Wanda's hand until the bones scraped together. Father Gallinski talked about David's bravery, his fight for their freedom, that even though he hadn't fought for long, his sacrifice was noble and would sustain his family. *Go away, leave me alone.* Why did her husband have to be the one to sacrifice his life? She needed him, needed him to keep her from falling apart. What good did his heroism do her? At the end of the service, she ran into the bathroom and threw up. Her mother rubbed her shoulders and gave her a wet paper towel to wipe her mouth, telling her she had family to get her through this.

At the graveside ceremony, she held a folded flag in her lap, and her foot fell asleep, so she stomped it on the ground, her heel sinking into the sod. She was too shaky to stand on her own, so she sat while others dropped soil onto the casket.

She spent the next few days sifting through their wedding album, trying to replace the sight of the coffin with happy images. She looked at a photo of them at the lake, his arm around her and another one at a family pig roast, his head thrown back in laughter, eyes shut, as she looked at him, smiling, a beer in her hand. Her parents wanted her to move back home, but she couldn't leave the home she'd shared with David. Especially now, she had to keep that part of him alive. To leave felt disloyal.

Sandy and Burt continued to include her in their Sunday dinners, but now, the air in their house felt thick with David's absence. They'd hung a huge formal portrait of him in his uniform above the mantel. Every surface in the living room held photos of David over the years. The Army was going to send Wanda his Purple Heart, but she'd promised it to Sandy and Burt, who'd already bought a frame to display it. And they'd displayed a Gold Star in their front window. Wanda hadn't even changed the sheets on her bed yet, but Sandy was decorating. A stupid portrait and medals wouldn't bring David back.

One night at dinner, a few weeks after the funeral, Sandy said, "I just can't get over the fact that if you and David had gotten pregnant, there'd be a child so David would live on and carry the family name." Burt said that Wanda didn't need to hear that kind of talk, and Sandy apologized, starting to cry. Her words stung, and Wanda wondered if they blamed her for this. Had David told them that Wanda wanted to delay a baby? Should she have given in and gotten pregnant?

A week before David was deployed, Wanda had started an Intro Chemistry course at the CC, but all that fell apart when he died. She didn't have the will to catch up or the strength to explain to her professor why she'd gone missing. She knew it was time to get back to work which would get her out of her apartment and keep her from drinking. Because Irene didn't know David well, she could distract Wanda in ways that Michelle and her family couldn't. Everything they said forced David's death in her face. Irene was full of stories about her kids' screw-ups—how Lizzie left a pizza in the toaster oven until it burnt to a shriveled disk and set off the smoke detector, how Charlie lied about partying with friends, but then, reeking of weed and beer, he'd puked his guts out all over the bathroom. Wanda needed those boring everyday stories.

One day at work, a couple of weeks after the funeral, Whit rode up on his bike and parked out front. Seeing him, she broke into a sweat and started to shake, nipping into the back room, grabbing a tray and loading it with fresh donuts.

"Wanda?" Irene said, poking her head through the swinging doors, "Someone's here and he's asking for you."

"Tell him I'm busy," she said, struggling to catch her breath. What was happening?

"I need you out here. There's a line."

"Okay." She pushed through the door. "Yeah?" She forced herself to glance at his dopey face. What did he want?

His glance darted to her, then away. "How are you?"

"Busy. What do you want?" She asked as she wiped off the counter and grabbed a paper bag.

"Two Hermits. No, three."

She took his money, counting out the change, dropping it into his hand rather than touching him, then wiping her hand on her apron. She turned to the next customer. "Mrs. Dooley.

What will it be?" Whit stood to the side, and she made it a point to look busy. When he walked out the door, his smell twisted her stomach.

"Whoa. What was that all about?" asked Irene.

"Oh, him? Some annoying person I went to school with."

"It's not like you to be short with a customer. Are you okay?"

"I'm just having a bad day."

"Oh, sweetie. Some days are just going to be hard."

Whit started showing up regularly at the bakery, and Wanda fought back panic and disgust as he hung around, staring at Wanda as he pretended to decide what he wanted, finally buying his Hermit cookies and a Sprite. Every time he left, she felt sick to her stomach.

So, maybe they'd kissed, a big mistake, but it was in the past. He'd forget about her and they'd both move on.

6

CALLIE

Greg and Callie arrived in Alphabet City on the Lower East Side, where Greg's friend Jean-Michel lived. He was going to spend a sabbatical year in Aix and was staying with his girlfriend until then, so the place was free if they wanted it.

The first morning, they grabbed coffees at a bodega and set off walking across Houston and through Chinatown toward Soho, eating along the way: Chinese dumplings on Eldredge, gelato on Delancey, drinks at a wine bar on Christopher Street. "I could get used to this," she said over a glass of Rioja. "Maybe you'll get a job at Columbia or NYU."

"New York is expensive."

"I can get a job too."

"Let's not get ahead of ourselves. Academic jobs are hard to land."

"You're brilliant. You'll find a great job." He wasn't sure. "Forget Brewster. We'll figure it out."

They met Alana and Steve, friends of Greg's, for dinner at a tapas place in the East Village. Alana was beautiful and smart and next to her, Callie felt like a lump, her tongue frozen. Alana and Steve never spoke to her, as if she weren't even there. As they talked about books and films she didn't know, she leaned her head on Greg's shoulder and drifted off. At the end of the evening, Alana said that Callie was "adorable," which made her face burn. As she and Greg headed toward the subway, she asked him if he'd ever slept with Alana. "Does it matter?" he asked. She was afraid of the answer. "Hey, I'm with *you*, now." He pulled her in for a hug, and she pushed those thoughts aside.

The original plan was to get married at City Hall before flying to Martinique for a combined research trip/honeymoon. But there wasn't enough time to get the license before their trip. Changing the tickets would incur a stiff fee. "I feel married already," Greg said. "That's enough for now, right?"

"Of course," she said, disappointment snagging in her chest. "We're together and that's what counts." Did the legal papers matter as long as she was with Greg? In the back of Jean-Michel's closet, they stashed their warm clothes along with books and other possessions they wouldn't need for the trip. She'd left her desktop computer with her parents and planned to use Greg's laptop. She brought a few paperbacks in English that she could jettison after reading and a French/English dictionary, which she'd need for the French books she planned to read while there.

Before they left town, she texted Elise at Yale.

dont tell anyone im in love its greg my instructor from the summer class my parents dont know yet im so happy!!!!!
Elise texted back.
Where R U? R U OK?
Callie wrote:

Sorry Will tell you more later ILY

She told Greg she needed to let her parents know she was okay. "So they don't worry I've died."

"Don't call. Email."

"No email. They're old school. I'll send them a letter. They'll know it came from New York, but that's all they'll know. What should I say?"

"Tell them the truth, that you're an adult, and it's your life."

She chose a card with a Redon painting of wildflowers, and she wrote,

Dear Mama and Papa,

Please don't worry about me. I've decided to defer college for a year and am traveling. I'm sorry I had to do it this way without telling you, but I know you wouldn't approve. I'm in love with Greg Minot from my course this summer. He loves me and wants me to go to college and I will when he gets a teaching job. He's brilliant and I've never been happier. Brewster would never really be my school. I need to be my own person. I hope you can understand that someday.

I will write more later.

Love,

Callie

Sealing the envelope, she dropped it in the mailbox, her heart pounding, then she started to cry, but Greg reminded her that it was better to be clear and direct. They'd never agree to this, and she needed to break it to them on her own terms. "They'll come around in time," he said. "And if they don't, that's their problem."

"I hate to hurt them."

"This is your life. Our life."

When Greg revealed that they'd be taking short flights from San Juan to Dominica to Martinique, Callie, a nervous flyer, was upset he hadn't warned her. He offered her some Ativan to relax her. After sharing a beer at the airport, she took the pill, which fuzzed her out, so she dozed for the long leg of the trip. By the time they boarded the small plane in Puerto Rico, she sat back, ear buds in place, listening to calm music as Greg stroked her hand and she rested her head on his shoulder.

They arrived in Fort-de-France, Martinique, late that night, the air steamy and dense. Greg grabbed a cab, and they bounced along bumpy, ill-lit roads as she floated in and out of a groggy semi-consciousness, a breeze from the open window, cooling her face.

They were exhausted, so they fell asleep immediately, and she barely focused on the room. The following morning, she woke up to Greg kissing her neck and shoulders, running his hands up the insides of her thighs. It took a moment for her to realize where they were. The air was sweltering, the light filtered through gauzy curtains. After half-awake sex, she rose from the bed, parted the curtains, and opened the windows to the intense light that poured in. As she peered over the balcony, a gecko scrambled up the cracked stucco wall at ear level, startling her.

"Come back to bed," Greg said, and she turned, smiled, and crawled back under the sheet. She kissed him, eyes closed, as he held her.

He wanted to stay in bed all day, but she said she wanted to explore. Besides, she needed coffee. She showered and dressed in a sundress and sandals, slathering on sunscreen. Greg took a shower and when he walked naked into the room, the sight of his butt, his shoulders, his hair slicked back with water, made her want to jump him. He was letting his beard grow out and had a few days of stubble. It tickled, but he said it would smooth out in a day or so. She was still getting used to sharing a bed and bathroom with him, those intimacies of living in close quarters.

They were due to stay in Fort-de-France for two days before heading to Le Diamant, a small fishing village where Greg would settle in to write in earnest. Before they left town, he needed to pick up some books, then they'd have a picnic and explore.

After breakfast, as they emerged from the dark quiet of the hotel lobby, the hectic sounds of the city hit them. They zigzagged through the street markets run by women selling melons, bananas, tomatoes, and breadfruit. Next to them sat displays of fish, glistening in the hot sun. After finding a bunch of tiny bananas they snaked single file on the narrow sidewalk, and they bought a baguette at a *boulangerie* and cheese at a small grocery.

They came upon a covered market where the smells of fruit, flowers, and spices mingled—spiky red and yellow flowers, bright blues, clusters of orange blossoms. The dust of cinnamon, cumin, and turmeric floated in the air, making her sneeze. Everywhere she saw bright madras cloth—reds, pinks, and yellows.

They spotted a stall displaying bottles of a brown liquid with a sign, *Bois Bandé, Redresseur de Zizi.* The saleswoman smiled and beckoned Greg over. "*Eh, Monsieur,*" she said, holding up the bottle. "*Ça fait bander ton zizi. Ta femme, elle aime ça.*"

She raised her index finger at a forty-five-degree angle, laughing. Greg examined a bottle. Callie asked what *bander* meant.

"To get a hard on. It's an aphrodisiac."

"And *zizi?*"

"Cock."

"What's this made of?" asked Callie.

Greg told her it was ground-up tree bark. The woman's accent was hard to understand, but she was clearly flirting with Greg, but he kept his arm around Callie. "*Et toi,*" the woman said, pointing at Callie. "*Les femmes peuvent boire.*"

"*Moi aussi?*" she asked. "Is it safe?"

Greg bought a small bottle and tucked it into their bag, kissing her on top of the head. "Let's give it a try."

As they walked away, she added, "And I learned two new words."

"Now, I want to buy something for you to wear."

He bought her a madras skirt with matching head scarf and the saleswoman tied it for Callie with three points jutting up, showing her heart was taken.

They stopped at the library, a building painted in yellow and orange stripes with ventilated wrought-iron grates, where he checked out some books. At a bookstore, he bought Callie a copy of Césaire's poetry, and he got into a discussion with the bookseller. Callie found a shaded bench out front and sat, fanning herself with the map, leafing through her new book. Without her dictionary, she couldn't make much headway. She guessed at words like *gemmes, putréfactions, trompettes*, but words like *calcanéum, crasse, scintillement, marais* were beyond her. *Les trompettes absurdement bouchées* must mean trumpets absurdly—what? *Bouche* meant mouth, but what was this? She closed the book. Greg wanted her to read this, so she'd make the effort. Her stomach felt sour from the strong coffee and all the fruit she'd eaten, but the breeze cooled her skin. She smiled at people walking by, all Black, no doubt locals. Why not soak up what was around her? Learning by observing. That was as good as reading, right? And to think she could be sitting in a boring freshman orientation right now when life had so much more to teach her.

They arrived at the car rental office, and Greg signed the papers. Callie couldn't manage a stick, so he'd drive, and she'd navigate. Greg turned down the additional GPS in favor of a map, saying they couldn't get lost on such a small island. And wandering was part of the fun.

Greg drove the tiny Renault, snaking along the winding, narrow road leading away from the city, through the gritty out-skirts of town. Signs pointed to Morne Rouge, the bluff below Mt. Pelée, a dormant volcano on the northern end of the island. On the way, they passed banana trees in front of villas owned by rich tourists alongside shacks with rusty corrugated metal roofs where the locals lived. When Callie looked down at the map for more than a few seconds, she felt carsick.

The road was deserted except for an occasional car careening around turns, passing them in the opposite direction. Greg pulled over, let a truck pass, then shoved the gearshift into first, and their car fishtailed onto the road, stirring up a cloud of pebbles and dirt.

They rounded the curves, her hand gripping the door handle. As they drove into the rain forest, a cloud of mist enveloped the car. When the mist cleared, they looked down into a gaping ravine, choked with palm trees and vines. Above them shot craggy walls of rock from which gushed emerald water. She aimed her camera out the window, but the photos looked blurry.

They reached the summit of Morne Rouge, where the trees were scrubby, and they could see the hazy view of the Caribbean in one direction and the cloudy peak of Mont Pelée in the other. Callie found a flat, cleared spot where they set up their picnic of bread, cheese, and fruit. Greg pulled out a bottle of wine and a corkscrew. She drank a soda and sliced cheese on small rounds of bread to feed to Greg. It was perfect, just the two of them away from the rest of the world. After lunch, he lay back and closed his eyes. She crawled over to give him a kiss, and he gathered her up in his arms and settled her next to him. In a minute, he was snoring. She wasn't sleepy, so she peeled off his arm and sat, watching Greg lying on his back, his arm slung over his eyes, letting out little snorts.

She took her camera and walked around the bluff, aiming it at Fort-de-France in the distance. Then she sat back down and watched Greg as he frowned and swiped at his cheek, batting away an insect. She took a couple of pictures of him while he slept.

The wind soon picked up, and the sun gave way to lead-colored clouds which loomed large above them. Tossing the picnic debris into sacks, she jostled Greg. "Wake up."

"Uh huh."

"Greg. Come on." She nudged him in the side. "It's going to rain. Soon."

They made it to the car as a heavy sheet of rain drenched them. They dove into the car and slammed the doors, laughing, wiping the rain from their eyes. "That came up so fast," she said. "Sorry I didn't wake you sooner." Greg started the car and turned on the AC, but it wasn't working, so they fanned themselves as the windows fogged and they waited for the storm to pass before they could drive again. We could take off our wet clothes while we wait, huh?" she said, leaning over to kiss him. She put her hand on his zipper. "*Où est ton zizi?*" She unzipped his pants. "*Oh, voilà ton zizi.*"

"It's a baby word, what mothers say when talking to their little boys."

"How was I supposed to know that?"

"Think about it. *Zizi?*"

"So, why don't you teach me to talk dirty? I'll be a very good student." She kissed his ear. "How *do* you say 'cock'?"

"*La bite.*"

She kissed him on the neck. "How do you say, 'Fuck me'?"

"*Baise-moi.*"

"See? This is the kind of thing teachers should teach. That's useful vocabulary."

"Oh, yeah? That'd go over well in high schools."

"No student would ever miss class."

She peeled off her wet sundress and threw it in the backseat. Then she whispered in his ear, "How do you say, 'I'm going to give you a blow job'?"

"*Je vais te faire la pipe.*"

She leaned over as he cranked down the seat. "*Je vais te faire la pipe.*"

When the storm finally passed, and the sky grew bright again, and all the surfaces shone off the reflected rain, they opened the windows, got dressed, and drove off.

Back in Fort-de-France, she put on her new skirt and blouse and they each drank a *vieux rhum* at the hotel bar before a dinner of conch in a spicy sauce. After a long day in the sun, the rum hit her hard. A music combo started to play, and Callie pulled

Greg up to dance. Feeling loose and drunk, she twirled in her skirt, feeling it rustle around her bare legs before lacing her arms around Greg's neck and swaying with him to the beat. He'd sweated through his shirt, and she ran her fingers through his damp hair as he spun her around until she was dizzy.

Finally, they staggered off, nearly tripping as they climbed the stairs to their room. Greg opened the bottle of *bois bandé* and sprinkled it into a mug of hot water and took a swig. Too bitter, he said, so he added some sugar, then offered her some. She hesitated but took a sip.

The sex was intense and when Callie came, she burst into tears, and Greg rubbed her back as she steadied her breathing. He stayed hard, even after he came, and wanted to do it again, but Callie felt too drunk, so she slipped under the covers and waited for her head to stop whirling. Greg woke her in the middle of the night to make love again, although she was sleepy and still drunk.

In the morning, he wanted to do it again. "This stuff is in-credible," he said. She was hungover and sore but didn't want to disappoint him. She loved not having to sneak around, but was there too much of a good thing? After he came again, she said, "*Je t'aime, je t'aime.*" He was too far gone to talk, but he stroked her hair and kissed her. "*Je t'aime,*" she said, one more time.

The next day, they packed up and drove to Le Diamant, where Greg had rented a bungalow on the beach. It was gorgeous, the water deep blue, the air warm and lazy, the beach white and clean. Le Diamant was an enormous craggy rock surrounded by birds sitting off the coast. The beach was lined with palm trees, but the concierge warned them not to sit under them because of falling coconuts. Callie changed into her bikini and waded into the waves. Greg sat in a chair with a book. She splashed around in the waist-deep water, letting the waves lap over her. She stretched out and floated on her stomach, waiting for the waves to carry her to shore. She stood up and raised her arms over her head when a wave hit her from behind, flipping her over. Her nose took in water, and she panicked, not knowing which end was up. She pulled her head above water, only to be knocked down again by the next wave. She tried to crawl onto the shore, but felt the sand give way beneath her feet. Finally, she felt a wave lift her onto the beach, the water receding, as she lay coughing, her eyes stinging, her throat raw.

"Are you okay?" Greg ran to the beach and helped her up.

"Wave…hit me."

"They're stronger than you'd think." He touched her face. "Uh, oh. You've scraped your chin."

"Ow." It stung, and her torqued back hurt.

Greg wrapped her in a towel, walked her to a chaise, where she curled up, shivering. "Are you going to be okay?" He combed the wet hair out of her eyes and stroked her cheek.

"Yeah. It just threw me."

"You sure?" She nodded. "Just rest."

She looked at him, his hair fluffed from the salt air, his nose reddened from the sun. "I'm fine."

"Good."

They ate langoustines at the hotel and Greg drank two beers and smoked a cigarette. Callie had fruit juice. After lunch, Greg wanted them to nap together. He drank more *bois bandé* and got hard right away. During sex, he was intensely focused on her body and when he came, he let out a huge groan, his eyes squeezed shut. "Greg, people can hear us."

"So what?" He was covered with sweat, eyes closed, breathing heavily. Soon, he fell asleep.

Deciding to explore the village, she dressed and took her bag and floppy hat, heading out to the main road. She passed another hotel then came upon small shacks open to the street with old men sitting outside, the smells of frying fish wafting out, a few children playing in the road. A truck passed, kicking up a cloud of fine dust. On the beach, a small motorboat sat hoisted on blocks, fishing nets draped over the sides. A young girl stood behind a stand selling conch shells painted with island scenes—*lambis 5 euros.*

Callie found a small store that sold cold drinks, chips, cigarettes, and magazines. She bought two tabloids in French: *Voici* and *Oops!* Finally, some easy French. She managed a simple conversation about the price, then she thanked the shop owner. Greg would be pleased that she'd initiated a conversation on her own.

On the way back to their bungalow, a rat scurried between two houses, and a pipe emptied water onto the beach. At the end of the street, she came upon a fence beyond which lay green hills dotted with goats. Storm clouds, dark and billowy, were gathering out over the water. Wanting to avoid another cloudburst, she turned and walked briskly along the road, eager to tell Greg about how she'd gone exploring. Maybe they'd take a walk together before dinner.

When she opened the door to the bungalow, careful not to wake Greg, she found him sitting in bed, smoking. "Where were you?"

"You were sleeping, so I took a walk."

"You didn't leave a note."

"I didn't have paper, and I figured you'd know what I'd done."

"How could I know that?"

"Where else would I go?"

"I was worried."

"I'm sorry." She sat on the bed and took his hand.

He pulled away and stubbed out his cigarette. "Just leave a note. That's all I ask."

"Again, I'm sorry."

She'd been proud of herself for venturing out on her own, but she'd never thought he'd be worried. She put on her bikini and grabbed her Césaire book and the dictionary and went outside. She also brought the bag with the magazines.

The storm clouds had passed, and the sun shone again on the water.

She read a couple of pages of Césaire, but it was slow going and she felt herself nod off. She reached into her bag and pulled out *Voici*. The photos made it easy to follow the story, such as it was.

"What are you reading?" asked Greg, standing behind her.

"It's just for fun." She admitted she needed to work harder on her French but thought this would be a fun break. He took her hand and kissed it, and she put down the magazine and focused on the water and the big rock.

That night at dinner, she asked him about what he was reading. About his plans for his dissertation. Was he finding good sources?

"It takes time. It's a balance between reading and thinking. I'm going to have to sift through a lot of material before I find anything worthwhile."

"That makes sense."

He said he hoped it was enough, that this dissertation would land him a good job. She said he was working in an exciting area. Of course, he'd find a great job.

"Academic politics are fucked up."

"I believe in you. You're brilliant."

"Not brilliant."

"Yes, you are." She smiled at him. "We'll figure it out."

He took a deep slug of his *vieux rhum* and lit a cigarette. "I hope so."

For the next week, they had a routine where they woke up, made love, ate breakfast at the hotel, then returned to the bungalow where Greg sat down to write, and Callie went outside to read or walk along the shore, picking up shells or tracking tiny crabs as they darted in and out of sand holes. She made herself read five pages a day of Césaire, and it was getting easier, then she rewarded herself with a tabloid. She'd become braver with the shopkeeper and the employees of the hotel, ordering in French and exchanging pleasantries. She made sure she let Greg know when she set off to explore. Sometimes, he was hard at work; other times, he was napping, so she tore off a scrap of paper to write a note.

Greg took her out on quiet roads and taught her to drive a stick shift, and after some bucking starts, she got better at it. She didn't miss the Internet so much or the rest of the world outside of what she read in the tabloids. Once or twice a day though, she thought of her parents and wondered if they were worried about her. She considered sending them a postcard but worried they might try to find her. Still, she hoped they weren't too upset. The rest of the time, she loved being on the island, the pace, the smells, the music, the people, the language. She could see them spending more time there, turning brown as dust, learning to cook creole, getting to know native Martinicans, making a place for themselves. This was heaven.

After they'd been there two weeks, out of the blue, Greg announced they were heading back to New York.

"I thought we were staying until the end of the month."

"I can't get any work done here."

"I thought it was going well."

"I've done the research, but the pace is too slow here. I need the energy of New York."

"Okay, if that's what you need." But she realized she'd miss this time when she had him all to herself. What would it be like when they were back where it was so expensive and dirty, and she'd have to find a job? "I'm going to miss it here though."

"It's not real life."

"I don't care where we go. I just want to be with you."

7

WANDA

At first, when Wanda's period didn't come, she thought it was the shock to her body brought by grief. Maybe because she was now a widow, her body was shutting down, making her old before her time.

Smells put her off—butter and sugar at the bakery, milking machines in the barn, a customer's cigar—all made her queasy. She assumed it was a stomach bug, but after she ran to the bathroom several times one day, Irene asked if she could be pregnant.

"Why would you say such a thing?" Wanda asked, wiping her clammy brow, swallowing back the lump in her throat.

"I have six kids. I know the signs."

"How could I be pregnant?"

"Only one way I know of."

Even though her breasts grew tender, and her stomach wouldn't settle, she pushed away the thought of a pregnancy until she couldn't avoid it any longer. David had been gone six, nearly seven, weeks, but she'd had her period since then. That time with Whit happened four weeks ago. She didn't even remember if they did anything, of his being inside her, just the feeling of wetness on her thighs. Was that even sex? How could it be Whit? A smear of wet on her thigh, the smell of his breath. Parts of that night hit her in flashes.

She drove to Walmart and bought a pregnancy test, hoping it would prove her fears wrong. But when she saw the red +, her head started to spin, and she sank to the toilet seat to steady herself. What was she going to do? She couldn't have a baby, not alone, not if it might not be David's. She'd have to get an abortion. But where would she get enough money? What kind of person has sex with a stranger right after her husband dies? What was wrong with her?

She made an appointment at a clinic in Granville. When she opened her calendar to write in the date, a week away, she saw the invitation to the baby dedication ceremony that coming Saturday for Michelle's newborn, Kymberlee Faith. Michelle had asked Wanda to be the godmother months ago, right after David left for Basic Training. Wanda had agreed because it was Michelle and because she'd felt so lonely then. With David's death, she'd completely forgotten her promise. And now, how could she be someone's godmother? How could Wanda stand in a church and agree to be a moral guide to an innocent child when she was about to have an abortion? Michelle's baby deserved better than her. How could she love any child right now? Her chest felt like a burning brick of charcoal inside.

The next day, she drove to Michelle's to tell her she wasn't emotionally ready to take on such a serious commitment. One of Michelle's two sisters could fill that role. Surely, she'd understand that David's death had changed everything. She'd been out of her mind most of the time since he died.

Wanda pulled into Michelle's driveway and parked, then she knocked, announcing herself, and walked toward the sun-splashed great room. Kymberlee Faith whirred around in a mechanical chair that bounced and rocked like a tiny spaceship. Michelle lay on the floor, pumping her arms with her head and legs lifted. The floor was covered with baby equipment—a playpen, a colorful floor mat, rattles, a Diaper Genie, stuffed animals, mobiles, a jogging stroller, and piles of unopened Amazon boxes stacked in the corner.

"Oh, hey, I didn't hear you," Michelle said, popping to her feet and giving Wanda a long hug. "How are you, dear?" she asked, stroking Wanda's cheek. "Here, stretch out," and she pointed to the sectional. Wanda slipped off her shoes, put her feet up, and accepted a glass of iced tea from Michelle who sat down with her back against the opposite arm rest, her knees bent, the soles of her bare feet touching. After her pregnancy, Michelle's belly had snapped back to its former flat shape. Today, she was wearing leggings and a sports bra with no muffin top at all.

"I can't believe you just had a baby," said Wanda, wiping her sweaty hands on her pants. "You're so skinny."

"No, I'm not," she said, scrunching up her face. "I'm all loose."

"You look great."

"You're lying, but that's okay. I've gotta lose two more pounds before the dedication."

Before Wanda could bring up the godmother topic, Kymberlee Faith started to fuss, and Michelle hopped off the couch, lifting her from the bouncy chair, picking a bit of crud from the baby's eye with her pinkie, and wiping it on her leggings. Then she grabbed a bottle from the table and shook it, propped Kymberlee Faith on her lap, and slipped the bottle into the baby's mouth. Michelle had dressed her in a purple dress and pink tights with knitted black Mary Janes covering her feet. Kymberlee Faith had no hair, so to prove she was a girl, Michelle had stretched a sparkly elastic band around her head. "I'm getting her ears pierced right before the dedication. I showed you her dress, right?"

"Yes, it's beautiful." Michelle had paid $200, a ridiculous amount for something the baby would only wear once. But Michelle had the money, it seemed.

Wanda's arms shook as she felt the bundle in her arms and breathed in Kymberlee Faith's baby-powder-and-formula smell. The baby sucked on her bottle, eyes still wet with tears. With her baby acne and sucking blister, she wasn't beautiful. Wanda ran her hand along Kymberlee Faith's pudgy legs. The baby looked at her, eyes not quite focused. Tiny beads of sweat sprang up on her forehead as she sucked noisily, and she clasped her fingers around Wanda's pinkie. Such a strong grip. The touch of Kymberlee Faith's hand set off a rush of heat that washed over Wanda, bringing a flush to her face and tears to her eyes. That smell, the grip, the unfocused eyes seeking hers. That dear child! The baby's eyes closed, and her lips let go of the nipple. As she drifted off, her lips turned up briefly. Wanda found herself weeping and covering her mouth to keep from waking the baby.

Michelle returned, rubbing lotion into her hands. "Oh, Sweetie, let me," she said, reaching for the baby. "I'm sorry. Did holding her make you sad?"

"No, not at all. I'm not sure why I was so emotional for a moment, but I loved feeding her."

"Did she burp?"

"No, she fell asleep."

Michelle gathered her up onto her shoulder, patted her back, and gently placed her back in the bouncy chair. "I know she loves you already. I can see the bond you two have. God has given you to each other. I am so blessed."

Wanda was openly crying now, trying to stop, not to lose it completely.

"I know this doesn't make up for David's loss, but maybe being her godmother is the Lord's way of giving you love when you need it."

Wanda felt the blood rush to her face. No, she thought. *No.* Her arms felt empty, and her pinkie still buzzed faintly from the baby's touch.

Michelle plopped back against the cushions, making a face. "Ow. I'm still sore down there."

"That's a shame."

"Bobby wants to jump my bones, but I just need a little bit longer."

"Tell him that."

"Are you kidding? I want to hang onto my man." She clapped her hand over her mouth. "Oh, I'm sorry. I didn't mean to be hurtful."

"That's okay. I know what you mean. But sex shouldn't hurt."

"I'll get used to it."

"Are you sure you don't want to talk to him about it?"

"God only sends what I can handle." As she sipped from her glass of tea, her diamond solitaire twinkled in the light. "He's looking out for you too."

Wanda stood up, forcing a smile, and said she needed to get going but told Michelle she'd be at the church early on Sunday, as planned. No turning back now.

She started the car and backed out of the driveway and onto the road. She could still feel the flush of warmth from holding the baby. Her chest tightened, and she fought to catch her breath. Not ready to go home yet, she turned right on Grainger Road and headed toward her and David's spot. She'd taken to going there and spending time talking to him. Sometimes, she cried and said she missed him. Sometimes, out of nowhere, her anger bubbled up and she yelled, "Why did you do this to us?" Eventually, she found herself going to talk to him, one-sided conversations where she talked about how she felt, how she was coping without him. She hadn't yet told him about the baby. Did he know? Was he looking down on her? No, she didn't believe in that. But it helped to talk to him.

She parked and took the blanket from the trunk. Fanning it out, she lay on her back and looked at the clouds, then closed her eyes and pictured David beside her, waiting for her to roll into his arms. She grabbed the corner of the blanket and pulled it over her and started to talk. "David, Sweetie. I miss you so much. I miss your arms, your smell." She curled up and wrapped her arms around her knees, cradling her belly. Could she do this alone? Was it a sign that she was meant to keep this baby? That this was her chance to love someone after David? "There's something big I need to tell you." She told him how sad she'd been, how she'd been crazy with grief, how she'd been drinking too much and had done something she hadn't planned. "But now, I think I want to do this. I hope you understand."

She counted the days since David's departure and fixed his last night as the new date of conception. Why not? A wonderful surprise, a sign of life carrying on, a gift she could give to the family. She knew the lie was risky, but she had no choice. She couldn't live with another death after David's.

After rehearsing her story of grief, shock, then joy at the new chance for life, she gathered both sets of parents to tell them. As she said, "I have some wonderful news," she worried her voice would betray her, but if anyone doubted her, they didn't let on. No eyes cocked to the side as they counted the weeks, no frowns of disapproval. Sandy burst into tears and hugged Wanda, and her parents asked if she felt she could do this on her own. But Sandy said she wouldn't be alone. She had family. Telling them sealed her fate. She couldn't back out now, and the more she told the story, she almost came to believe it herself.

At the baby dedication, Wanda stood holding Kymberlee Faith as the pastor talked about the responsibility of raising this child in God's name. Although Wanda felt like a fraud going along with what she didn't believe, she allowed herself to include her unborn baby in those blessings as a measure of extra protection. Just because she didn't believe didn't mean her child should suffer.

Word spread around town and now everyone coming into the store congratulated her. As she started to show, they asked how she was feeling, and she said fine, a bit queasy, but good. This was the right thing to do. It hurt no one. A baby was a good thing to come out of this sad time, a way to make things right. She hoped that was true.

Throughout the fall, whenever Whit made his stop at the bakery, Wanda was careful to cross her arms over her growing middle and worried it was only a matter of time before he'd know as well. And what would he think if he guessed the truth?

Gradually, she allowed herself to imagine what it would be like to have a baby, a tiny thing to cuddle, love, and watch grow. No longer just a widow, but a mother-to-be, she joined the club of women with children and fed on their optimism and good wishes. She continued to talk to David, and gradually, she found herself able to forgive both of them, putting aside her anger and guilt in favor of the belief that this baby would prove to be her hope for the future and maybe even her salvation.

By her third month, Wanda quit her job because she'd developed varicose veins from standing all day long at the bakery. Irene told her she needed to put her feet up. "I had veins from my third kid on, so I sat around home like a queen and made the older kids wait on me."

Her survivor's benefits had started, which gave her some income. Even though she was committed to staying in the apartment she'd shared with David, every time she came upon a reminder of him: a Penguins cap dropping from the closet shelf, a video game peeking out from under the couch, his favorite heavy metal band tee emerging from the bottom of the hamper, grief splashed over her, and her legs buckled, her chest tightened as she gasped for breath. Still, she couldn't throw those things out.

Michelle was already talking about how Wanda should come to her church and meet some of the unattached men.

"David is barely gone. All I can focus on is this baby." She might swear off sex altogether.

"We're thinking of getting pregnant soon," said Michelle.

"Really? Didn't you say you needed a rest?"

She fiddled with her rings. "I don't want to be an old mom. I want all my kids to be close in age."

"But you're only twenty."

"I'll take what God gives me. We're doing rhythm, but it turns out we're really fertile."

"I guess." Wanda knew all it took was one time.

"And our kids can be BFFs. Wouldn't it be great if you had a boy and him and Kymberlee Faith got married? We'd be family."

"Don't marry them off just yet."

"It's fun to think about."

Wanda said they could go to school together, but Michelle said she was going to homeschool her kids. She'd heard about a Christian program that provided all the books and worksheets. "I'm going to run a regular little schoolhouse here. You should join us."

"I need to get this kid born first."

Michelle was worried about Kymberlee Faith's weight. "I'm going to sign her up for dance lessons to get rid of that pudginess."

"Don't you think that's just baby fat?"

"I'm taking no chances," she said, rubbing lotion into the creases of the baby's legs. "It's okay for a boy to be chubby, up to a point, but not a girl."

When Kymberlee Faith finished her bottle, Michelle handed Wanda a cloth for her shoulder and Wanda patted the baby's back until she burped. "Good for you!"

"I tell you. That child likes to eat." Wanda had read somewhere that breast-fed babies don't get overweight like bottle-fed ones could. She didn't tell Michelle she'd decided to breast-feed.

On her way home, the thought of Whit popped into her head, which led to a burning lump in her chest. If the hook-up hadn't made her pregnant, she'd have felt awful about sleeping with another guy, but she might have forgiven herself for the slip. But this child would be a constant reminder of what she'd done. She wanted to be happy about the pregnancy, and she was—a second chance for her—but she also feared that the truth would stand in the way of her loving this child, this innocent child. Would that make her an awful mother? She couldn't tell Michelle, who was so righteous and wouldn't understand how this was something Wanda hadn't planned. Would Michelle judge her or say it was God's will? Would she then say that David's death was God's will? Where would it end? Wanda couldn't listen to that nonsense. But she worried about how stress could affect her unborn child.

Back home, Wanda parked and walked over to the bakery, entering by the front door like a regular customer. When she opened the door, the smells of butter, sugar, and milk, mixed with disinfectant, hit her stomach. She took a few shallow breaths before continuing inside.

Irene stood adding cookies to the display case behind the counter. When she turned and saw Wanda, her face brightened. "Hey, you." She hurried around the counter to give Wanda a hug. "How's it going?" Wanda said fine. She stood back to inspect Wanda's belly, smiling.

"Turn to the side." Wanda smoothed her top and Irene ran her hand over Wanda's bump. "You're carrying low and straight out. I think it's a boy."

"You think?"

"How're your legs and back?"

"Better when I can sit and put them up. Sleeping is getting hard. I just lay there and think too much."

"Then don't do that." She took Wanda's hand and gave it a squeeze. "Well, you look great."

"Thanks. So do you." Irene didn't. She looked tired, and her hair was a weird shade of red.

"I look like shit. Here, have a cookie." Irene grabbed a tissue and opened the case. "What kind do you want?"

"Butter Brickle, please." She reached for her wallet, but Irene waved her off and handed her two cookies.

"I miss you, Sweetie. The time drags when you're not here."

Wanda swallowed. "I miss you too." Could she tell Irene about Whit? Of everyone she knew, Irene would be the last one to judge her. She imagined Irene telling her that having a sweet, innocent baby was all that counted. It didn't matter who the real father was.

"Irene?"

"Yes?"

The bell above the door rang, and Mrs. Daddario hauled her metal cart over the threshold. She wheeled it to the milk cooler, leaned over and hoisted one quart of milk and a pound of butter, then shuffling over the counter, she placed the items there before heading back to the cooler for eggs and a container of macaroni salad. Standing at the counter again, she fumbled in her purse and pulled out a crumpled scrap of paper. "Let me see," she said, scanning the display case of baked goods.

"What can I get for you, Mrs. Daddario?" asked Irene, winking at Wanda because Mrs. Daddario always bought the same things.

"Three hard rolls to start with."

"Okay," Irene said, popping them into a bag. "What else?"

"And a quarter pound of the sharp cheddar, please."

Irene lifted the glass dome covering the cheese wheel and picked up the long knife, setting it in place. "That about right?" she asked before slicing off a wedge and wrapping it in paper.

"How are you, Mrs. Daddario?" asked Wanda.

"The woman looked at Wanda as if she'd just noticed her standing there. "Well, you're showing now, aren't you?"

"I am. Three more months to go." She had four months, but she kept to her story.

"You're not that big. Are you sure it's okay?"

"Now don't go scaring Wanda," said Irene. "I'm sure everything is fine. Every pregnancy's different. I gained twenty pounds with my first and sixty with my last."

"I guess," said Mrs. Daddario, eyeing Wanda's middle before asking how much she owed. Irene handed the bag to the woman, who fiddled with the clasp on her change purse. Wanda's stomach had curdled, and her legs throbbed. She stuffed the second cookie into her mouth and swallowed it in a few bites.

When Mrs. Daddario left, Irene said, "Nosy old bitch."

"That's okay. People are curious."

By then, a man had come in to buy beer, and two teenage girls followed, paying for sodas and a bag of cookies, then someone called to place a cake order. Irene tossed two more cookies into a bag and waved as Wanda left the store. Although she'd planned to put the cookies away for later, Wanda sat on the couch and stole a bite, then another, and within a few minutes, she'd finished them. Could anyone tell she was lying about her due date? Irene didn't seem to suspect anything. Because the doctor didn't know when David died, she'd been honest about her last period, and he'd given her a due date in April. She hoped the baby would come early, not too early, of course, but enough so no one would be tempted to count the weeks and figure things out.

As Thanksgiving approached, Wanda knew it would be a hard day for Sandy and Burt. Usually, they all met at the farm, but this year, Sandy announced she wanted to cook, that she needed to keep busy. She invited Wanda to eat with them, but Wanda's mother got her nose out of joint when Wanda told her. "It's not fair for them to pressure you like that."

"David was their only child. I have to do this."

"They could come here."

Wanda said that wasn't what Sandy wanted, and her mother called Sandy a drama queen. "You lost your husband. You need to be with family."

Wanda said she'd split the meal between the two houses and told her mother she'd be eating light.

But, of course on the day, her mother insisted on loading up her plate. "You're eating for two now," she said, waving off her refusal of more stuffing. "But you always liked my stuffing."

"I have to have some appetite for Sandy's meal."

Wanda could tell everyone was walking on eggs around her to avoid mentioning David. Too little talk about him at the farm and all the Zaceks would talk about at their house. Wanda wished she could have skipped both meals and stayed at home. It was clear her mother was stretching out the meal to make a point. Wanda finally stood up to leave before dessert.

"Oh, do whatever you're going to do. I give up," her mother said, throwing her napkin on the table and crossing her arms.

By the time she was in her car, driving to Sandy and Burt's, heartburn seared her from throat to stomach.

She arrived at their house with the Gold Star banner in the window. It was clear that Sandy had started on the blush wine. Wanda offered to help, but Sandy shooed her out, letting her set the table, but saying she should be resting her feet instead. Sandy managed to burn the rolls and the turkey was dry, which upset her. She'd made David's favorite sweet potatoes with marshmallows that no one else liked and Burt couldn't eat because of his diabetes. Two whole pumpkin pies sat next to the dishes that had barely been touched. "I guess I was thinking of how much David used to eat," she said, crying. "I'm sorry. I'm such a mess today. I need to go lay down." She stood and bumped her shin on the table leg. Burt took her arm and helped her into the bedroom.

While Wanda washed the dishes and covered the leftovers with foil, Burt came back and apologized for Sandy. Wanda said it wasn't necessary.

"As you can see, she's not doing so good."

"I know. It's so hard."

"We're both struggling," he said, opening a beer. "And I try to keep up a positive front for her, but it's hard. I miss him too. It's not like a mother losing her child, but I miss him so much."

"I do too. We all do."

"What I can't say to her is that I feel guilty."

"Why?"

"I should have discouraged him from going. I should have said it was too dangerous."

"I tried, but he wouldn't listen."

"Maybe he thought I expected it of him."

"He knew you loved him and were proud of him."

"But what a goddam waste. I can't say that to her, of course."

Wanda took his hand and squeezed it. "You can say it to me." His eyes turned red, and he cleared his throat before turning his back and walking into the living room.

One snowy day in mid-December, Wanda slipped on her coat and stepped out the door to take a bag of trash to the can at the bottom of the stairs. She'd cleared a narrow path of snow down the steps and was careful to keep her footing.

"Hello." There stood Whit, holding a bakery bag in front of him with both hands. "Where have you been?" he asked, his eyes making brief contact with hers before fixing on the ground. "I haven't seen you at the bakery for a while."

"I quit."

"Why?"

"I'm getting widow's benefits from the government," she said, lapping her coat over her stomach.

"Well, they owe you that at least." Had he noticed her bump? "I saw that article on your husband in the paper." He made no move to leave.

"Yes, they're going to add his name to the plaque in the square."

They stood, not talking. She hugged herself in the cold air, feeling her nose start to run. "How's college?"

"I thought people would be smarter there than in high school." He was crinkling his bag, rocking back and forth on his heels. "But they're not."

"So, you thought we were all stupid?"

"No," he said, shrugging. "I've been thinking about you," he said.

She averted her gaze to the dumpster in the alley, the blue paint peeling, replaced by rust.

"When I didn't see you at the bakery," he continued. "I worried something was wrong. That you were too sad to work."

"No, well, of course I'm sad, but work helped."

"Then why did you quit?"

She'd imagined running into him, and she'd practiced her lie. She patted her stomach. "I have this miracle to keep me going."

His eyes widened, and he took a step back. "Whoa." He looked at his feet.

"Yes, it's been a great distraction."

He was breathing heavily.

"That time in the Grove? I didn't know that I was already pregnant. It happened right before David left." Her face burned. "Kind of a miracle."

"Now, you'll have someone to keep you company."

"Yes, and to remind me of David."

He nodded as he looked at her. "I was afraid I'd forced myself on you when you were grieving."

"It really was nothing." Should she have said that? "Did you ever tell anyone what happened?"

He said he hadn't. "I tried writing you a letter, but I couldn't find the right words. I kept starting, but then I tossed them."

"It's just as well. Really, it wasn't that big a deal." She knew she shouldn't have said that. He'd clearly been a virgin. "Well, I have to go back inside. Take care of yourself. Okay?" He stood there, not saying anything, not leaving. "Listen, it's cold, and I gotta get back inside. Have a good year in college."

"Yeah, okay." He turned and walked away, and she watched his back, her heart pounding. Then she saw he'd left the bag of cookies on the trash can. At least she'd seen him, told her story. She hoped he'd keep the secret. but it was done, and she had to look ahead and make the best of it all.

8

CALLIE

Back at Jean-Michel's place in Alphabet City, they settled in for an extended stay. In the living room, there was a futon, a scarred coffee table, and a sat-out armchair. The windowless bedroom with its lumpy mattress, stained pillows, and threadbare sheets smelled of radiator rust, roach spray, and incense. The water heater only had enough hot water for one shower at a time, but the apartment was free, and it was their first home together. New York was the most exciting city for being in love. They'd given themselves a few days before Greg would start writing again in earnest, using Jean-Michel's carrel at Columbia, and Callie would go looking for a job.

Money was tight, so they walked everywhere, from the Lower East Side to the Upper West Side and back, stopping to share an espresso or to drop a few coins as a token donation at the Metropolitan Museum or to leaf through books Downtown at The Strand. Callie loved that in the space of a few blocks, the city changed dramatically. Although it was September with the leaves starting to change, heat still radiated off the sidewalks, intensifying the smells of garbage and diesel exhaust. Despite that, Callie found the fast pace, the crowds, the energy all exhilarating. Back at their place in the evenings, they cribbed the neighbors' Wi-Fi, Callie made sandwiches or scrambled eggs, and they sat on the futon to watch videos online before heading off to bed.

During the days, Greg took the laptop to Columbia, and Callie scoured the neighborhood looking for a job in a store, a restaurant, any place that would hire her. Finally, she found a server job at a Korean-fusion place in the East Village called Seoul Food, where she worked the dinner shift and was paid under the table. Tips didn't amount to much, but she was grateful for a job. Since she had her days free, she took walks up Third Avenue to 8th Street, over to Washington Square, where she sat with her book of Césaire poetry, reading for a few minutes before closing it in favor of studying the people around her—rich, homeless, immigrants, artists, nannies with babies, crazy people. She made up stories to explain the old woman carrying a baby doll or the man with dreadlocks playing chess. Did the tattooed tweaker with bad skin and the twitchy Wall-Street type screaming into his headset do the same drugs? In this nexus of colleges, she figured she could distinguish an NYU student from a Eugene Lang one or an arty Cooper Union type. If she were at Brewster now, she'd be sitting in some class with students who looked like her, who'd gone from their parents' homes to that Ivory Tower without having had any real experiences.

She missed Elise, who was just a train ride away at Yale. They'd crept back into regular contact via texts, and Callie was working to soothe Elise's hurt feelings that Callie hadn't entrusted her with the secret of Greg. Callie also had written to Raquel at her Brewster email to see if she'd gone back to school. Raquel texted her, saying she'd taken the semester off and was living back near home in Chicago. *Academic Probation*, she'd written, which Callie felt certain was code for flunking out. Callie told her about Greg, nervous that Raquel wouldn't understand.

Damn girl baller move scoring a professor and bailing on college.

Well, Im in love, wrote Callie.

During the days, when not with Greg, guilt about her parents bubbled up. Without telling him, she'd rented a P.O. box and had written again to her parents, just to let them know she was settled back in the U.S. After a week, she received a letter from her mother. Seeing the familiar, slanted writing on the envelope made Callie's heart thump and her fingertips tingle. She could hear her mother's voice as she read:

Dear Callie,

We are relieved to hear from you but worried. Your father is devastated. He had so looked forward to your studying at Brewster. What kind of man would take you away like that? In the meantime, we are at a loss to explain to people what you're doing. Despite this, we both love you. If you choose to give up this delusion, know that you can come back home.

Mother

Callie read the letter, her eyes welling. She'd hoped her mother would be more understanding, but all she could talk about was their embarrassment and their judgment of Greg whom they'd never even met. She wasn't a child. This was her choice. But what did she expect, that they'd be happy for her? They only wanted their version of her life. She tucked the letter into a zipped pocket of her bag and set off walking again.

She cut through Tompkins Park where she watched children with nannies play on the jungle gym, down Third to their apartment on Avenue B. At home, she cracked a window to let out the musty air, and she straightened up, making their bed, sitting down to read before she had to get dressed for work. She'd dipped into their savings to buy clunky non-skid waiter shoes, black pants, and a white shirt, which she washed every night in the sink and hung in the shower to dry.

At the restaurant, she spent the first part of her shift in the sweltering kitchen, cutting julienned slices of daikon radishes, carrots, and ginger, piling them into mounds, her fingers cramped, her back sore from bending over the low counter. After a quick staff meal, the dinner service began, and she waited tables. The heavy tray strained her right arm but after a week or so, she grew stronger and no longer feared dropping the tray. Although she wore her hair up, it always felt damp and never lost the smell of grease, even after being washed. Her armpits chafed and her back hurt from standing the whole shift.

Others on the wait staff included a Serbian painter named Nadia and two aspiring actors, Brody and Kyle, who went on auditions during the days, hoping for a break. The only Korean not in the kitchen was Mi-Jin, a tiny woman with spiky hair. Her boyfriend, Keun, was the head chef. In the first week, she mixed up an order, and because she was rattled, had nearly dropped a tray. Hyoji, the boss, threatened to fire her if she didn't get it together and fast. Nadia said Hyoji was an asshole, and Callie just needed to schmooze the line cooks and she'd be fine.

At the end of every evening, Callie gathered leftovers and headed toward the train. First thing back in the apartment, before she'd let Greg touch her, she stripped off her smelly clothes, popped them in the sink to soak, and took a tepid shower.

Sometimes, Greg waited for her. Sometimes, she'd find him asleep on the futon, beer cans and plates littering the table. Although exhausted, she washed the dishes to keep the roaches and mice away. "Oh, hey. You're home already?" he'd say, waking up. Then they'd head off to bed.

After work each night, Nadia, Brody, and Kyle went to the bar next door for drinks. They always invited Callie, but she said she had to get home. But after coming home to him asleep on the futon several nights in a row, she decided one time to stay for a beer. Her phone had run out of juice, so she couldn't call, but figured Greg would probably be asleep anyway, and she didn't want to wake him.

They bought a pitcher and sat in a booth, where they talked about trying to get gallerists and casting directors to notice them so they could do their real work. Nadia had a second job as the studio assistant of a famous artist whom Callie had never heard of but who was apparently both a genius and an asshole. Brody and Kyle complained that they needed just one chance, and they'd be launched.

Nadia turned to Callie. "What do you do besides being a server?"

"Not much. My fiancé is working on his dissertation, so I'm the one with the job for now."

"Fiancé?" Nadia asked. "How old are you?"

"Eighteen. It happened really fast. He was my professor. You don't choose when you fall in love, right?"

"I guess," said Nadia, her eyebrows raised as she doodled, adding armpit hair to the Bavarian barmaid on the coaster.

"When he gets a teaching job, I'll go to college there and it'll be free."

"Does he support what you want to be?" asked Nadia.

"Yes, of course," she said, feeling her face grow warm. "We'll figure it out."

Later, she headed home on the train, pleasantly buzzed, eager to tell Greg she'd made some friends. She gave a wide berth to a homeless-looking guy sitting next to a puddle of something scary, and it occurred to her that she'd become a lot tougher in the past few weeks.

When she carefully opened the door to their apartment, she found Greg awake in front of the laptop, smoking a joint and drinking a beer. "Where've you been?" he asked. "Your phone went right to voice mail."

"I'm sorry, baby. My phone died."

"You could have borrowed a phone to call me."

"I'm sorry. I thought you'd be asleep, and I didn't want to wake you up."

"I was worried," he said, his voice shaking. "You're usually home by now."

"I know. I didn't mean to worry you."

She curled up next to him on the futon. "I had one beer with my friends." He smelled of weed and sweat. When she kissed his neck, he pulled away.

"I worry when you're out late."

She stood up. "I said I was sorry." She started to collect his dirty dishes and empty cans from the table but shrieked at the sight of a mouse scurrying under the stove.

"Leave that. Come sit with me."

"No," she said. "We can't leave food out. Augh, disgusting."

He took her hand to pull her down next to him, then ran his hand over her hair, massaging the back of her neck. "I imagined the worst."

"Next time, I'll text you."

He buried his face in her neck.

"Wait," she said. "I reek. Let me take a shower first." She jumped up, peeling off her shirt, bra, underwear, and heading toward the bathroom.

"Don't take too long."

She shivered under cold water and lathered herself for a quick shower. How was she supposed to know that he'd still be awake? As she toweled herself off, she reminded herself that this wasn't just about her anymore. With her parents, she'd have asked permission. This was about communication, about sharing a life with someone.

When she crawled into bed, Greg lay on his side, facing the wall, a book propped in front of him. She nestled against his back and gave him a kiss on the nape of his neck. "I'm all clean now," she said, and he rolled over, pulling her to him. Balance, it was all about balance. Give and take. They'd figure it out.

At first, Greg spent weekdays at Columbia and came home excited about his writing. He explained the main thrust of his argument, something no one had written on yet, and Callie nodded, happy to have him share this with her. She felt sheepish about not having finished the book of Césaire's poetry and made herself a goal of at least five pages a day. The price of living with a genius was that she had to play catch-up. But she was delighted to so engaged by his work after the raw deal Brewster had given him.

However, after a few weeks, he took to starting later each morning, grumpy but still insisting it was going well. One afternoon, when he hadn't gone out all day, and she was getting ready for work, she asked, "So, how was writing today?"

"Fine," he said, staring at a movie on the laptop.

"Did you finish that chapter?"

"It doesn't work that way, Callie. It's not a straight-through process."

"I know, but you must know when a chapter's finished, right?"

"It's not formed enough for that. But it's going."

"Hey, did you think to shop?" she asked.

"Callie, come on. First you criticize me for not writing, then you wonder why I haven't shopped." He'd run his fingers through his hair, and it stuck up as if he'd been wracking his brain for ideas.

"I just wondered. I told you we needed milk." He tipped his beer bottle to his mouth and then dropped the empty on the floor with a clunk.

"Never mind," she said, grabbing her bag. "I'll run to the corner."

"Can you pick up more beer and cigarettes?"

She wasn't sure she had enough money. "It seems as if all my wages are going to beer and cigarettes these days." As soon as she said that, she regretted it. He said nothing and stared at his screen.

She swallowed hard. "I'm doing my best, Greg," and she headed toward the door, fighting back tears.

As she pulled the door shut, she heard him say, "So am I."

Wiping her eyes, she walked to the bodega and bought milk, cigarettes, and a six-pack. Then she walked the few blocks to her P.O. box to check her mail. Nothing. She thought about her mother, how she always put her father's work first, how she'd given up her dissertation to follow him to Brewster, how she made sure the house was quiet so he could work even though he didn't seem to acknowledge her. Callie often felt critical of her mother for putting his needs first, for being a doormat, but wasn't that love, putting aside your own needs for the one you love?

As she climbed back up to the third floor, she could hear Charlie Mingus blasting. She opened the door to see Greg dancing around the room, tossing bottles into the trash, pulling the tie on a garbage bag. He apologized, said he'd been in a bad mood about his writing but shouldn't have taken it out on her. As he pulled her into a hug, he swung her around, his hair was damp and combed, and he smelled of soap. He opened two beers and handed her one. He apologized again. "You're the only reason I can write anything."

"It's okay," she said, taking a sip of her beer. "You're entitled to be in a bad mood from time to time."

He led her to the bedroom, and they made love with her half-dressed in her work uniform. Afterwards, he lay, sprawled on the bed, wrapping her in his arms.

"This was a blip," he said. "It's to be expected, right?"

"It's called juggling," she said, as she pulled up her pants and zipped them, straightening her hair. "And, speaking of juggling, I have to go to work." She pantomimed tossing three balls in the air.

He lay on the bed, staring at her. "Hey," he said. "I love you." She said she loved him too.

At work, she had a good shift, bantering with some regular customers, getting decent tips, joking with Brody and Kyle as they negotiated the tight spaces in the kitchen, getting a grudging compliment from Hiroji. Balls in the air; not dropping one.

Back home, before climbing into bed with Greg, asleep with a book, Elise texted about her Freshman Seminar and how smart and intimidating everyone at Yale was. Callie skimmed until she found: *Is Oct break OK for U? Ill stay w/ my cousin @ NYU I cant wait!*

Callie was both nervous and excited to introduce Greg to Elise. Right before leaving to meet Elise at NYU, they quickly had sex and he gave her a hickey, which stung as she washed her face. He stood at the sink, dressed in jeans and a jacket, his hair longer now, the beginnings of a beard with its sprinkling of white.

"You look so handsome," she said, nudging him aside so she could dab concealer on her neck. He kissed her, then wiped a dab of toothpaste from her cheek.

The weather had cooled so she wore a jacket over her sweater. They walked arm in arm along the street, and she cupped his butt, feeling frisky. "Being honest about us really turns me on."

"Oh, yeah?" he said, pulling her close for a kiss.

When Callie saw Elise, a thrill rippled through her. They hugged, jumping up and down. Elise had shaved her head on both sides with a topknot securing the rest of her hair, and now a tiny red stud decorated her nose. "Look at you," said Callie, who pulled her into another hug, smelling her familiar almond lotion, and feeling some extra padding on her hips. "I almost didn't recognize you."

"I can't believe we're both here." They held each other, rocking from side to side.

"What's this?" Callie asked, pointing at the nose stud.

"Do you like it?"

"Sure. You look great."

"So do you. You're so skinny."

When she introduced Greg to Elise, he leaned in and kissed her on both cheeks, saying how glad he was to meet her. Elise looked nervous. Callie felt wonderful to have her two favorite people finally meet. "How's Mexican?" Greg asked as he slung an arm around both of their shoulders. "There's a good place on Houston." Elise said that would be great.

At the restaurant, Greg ordered a pitcher of Dos Equis and served Callie and Elise as they tucked into the chips and guac. Callie asked Elise to fill her in about other members of their class, how they were doing in college. As Elise talked, Callie leaned her head on Greg's shoulder, running her hand along his leg, nuzzling his neck. At one point, she saw Greg sneak a look at his phone. "I'm sorry. This is boring for you. We can talk about this later."

He took a sip of his beer. "No, you've got to catch up."

Elise asked Greg about his dissertation.

"It's a Lacanian analysis of Glissant and Chamoiseau, focusing on the castration of the male in Creole literature."

"Wow, sounds impressive," said Elise.

He said it was a big topic. "Groundbreaking, but as an outsider, white and non-Caribbean, I have an uphill battle against the entrenched establishment."

"Greg is brilliant," said Callie, taking his hand and kissing it. "It's going to be a huge success."

"Don't go overboard. You haven't even read it yet."

"I keep asking you to let me," said Callie, poking a finger into his ribs. He said it wasn't ready for that yet. "Greg and I went to Martinique so he could do research. I just loved it there, the food, the music. It was idyllic."

"What kind of research did you do there?" asked Elise.

"There are sources at the library there that don't exist elsewhere. But mostly, it's a theoretical argument I'm building from primary sources."

"Are you writing it in French or English?" asked Elise.

Callie felt Greg stiffen. "English," she said, jumping in, "because it needs to be accessible to people who don't read French. But he could write it in French if he wanted."

"Obviously," he said, grabbing his beer and emptying it, "I could have written it in French, but this has more possibilities for publication." He refilled his glass and ran his finger along the rim, taming the foam. Elise fingered her nose stud.

When the food arrived, they busied themselves with their fajitas, and Greg signaled for another pitcher. Callie gave Elise a wide, happy smile and asked what she was taking this semester.

"The seminar on Islam, Intro to Psych., a Comp. Lit. course on suicide in fiction, Comparative Religions, and a Poly Sci course." She took a bite of her fajita and chewed, wiping her chin with a new napkin. "I know I'm probably crazy to take five courses my first semester, but I couldn't decide which class to drop. There's still time to drop one if it's too much."

Greg asked her about a professor in the French Department named Robert Gandry, someone who had built a decent reputation despite plagiarizing ideas of his colleagues. "No one trusts him. And he's kind of a gasbag. I'd avoid him if I were you." Elise said she appreciated the tip, but she'd probably be studying Arabic.

Callie was glad that Elise and Greg seemed to be hitting it off, even if Elise was trying a bit too hard. They'd gone through two pitchers of beer, and Callie felt herself slip into a fuzzy blur as she leaned her head on Greg's shoulder.

At the end of the meal, Elise offered to pay for herself, but Greg insisted on treating them both. Callie knew they couldn't afford it, but she thanked Greg for being so patient with all the high-school talk. They set off toward Washington Square again, but because the sidewalk was too narrow for the three of them to walk abreast, Greg led while Callie and Elise followed, arms linked.

Callie suggested that she and Elise meet for breakfast the next day. "We can explore before you have to go back." Elise said that would be great. They walked along 3rd Avenue, past St. Mark's, along 9th Street, heading toward NYU. Elise said she loved this part of the city. She'd never spent much time Downtown before. "We love it," Callie said, "don't we, Greg?" He nodded, blowing smoke out the side of his mouth and raising his thumb in approval. The evening had turned cool, and as they stood out front of the door, she and Elise huddled together for warmth. Callie invited Greg to join them for breakfast, but he needed to write. He gave Elise a two-cheek kiss and then pulled Callie to him, steering her across the street and over toward 3rd Avenue. They walked for a block without talking, Callie feeling full and tipsy, leaning on Greg for support. "I'm sorry we talked so much about home. I haven't seen her since I left."

He gave her a squeeze, and she stumbled. "Are you drunk?"

The beers had hit her harder than she realized. "No, just clumsy. Well, maybe a little." She slung her arm around his waist. "So, what did you think of her?"

"Fine. She'll get her edges rounded at Yale. She's the kind of person they like there."

"But what did you think?"

"She's a nice girl."

"Girl? I'm the same age as she is. Am I a girl?"

He pulled her in for a kiss. "No, you're not a girl." He fondled her breast and pressed his hand between her legs. She laughed, not caring that the old woman standing next to them on the street could see him grope her.

Back at their building, they climbed the stairs, her legs stiff and heavy, as Greg fumbled with the lock. She stumbled in, her head spinning, and they fell onto the bed. Greg pulled her into a hug, and they lay quiet as the room spun, but her neck felt strained in that position, so she slipped out of bed, stripped down, peed, and drank a glass of water. As she stood in the entrance to the bedroom, brushing her teeth, she said, "I'm so glad you finally met." He was lying diagonally across the bed, his arm covering his face. "Hey, scootch over," she said. "I'm getting in." She snuggled in the crook of his armpit, running her finger along his side, tickling him. He brushed her hand away.

"It means so much for you to meet my best friend. We share a childhood. It goes deep."

"True, but you have so much ahead of you. A life bigger than Shelton, Callie. Right?" And he rolled over. In a minute, he started to snore.

She lay in bed, unable to sleep, her head whirling, her thoughts racing. Did being with someone mean you lost touch with your past?

The next morning, Greg left for Columbia, and Callie met Elise at Zucker Bakery on 9th Street. They ordered espresso and chocolate babka and sat at a table by the window. Callie was eager to hear what Elise thought of Greg but hoped Elise would bring him up first. After they'd left her, Elise had stayed out late with her cousin to a party. NYU was different from Yale, she said. No one talked about their courses. They talked about being in New York.

She'd wanted to leave, but her cousin convinced her to stay, and now she was hung over. And she still had a seminar paper to write that was due in a few days. She yawned, rubbing her bloodshot eyes. Her topknot had unfurled into a limp ponytail.

"So, tell me. Have you met any guys yet?" asked Callie.

She shrugged. "There's this guy, Ben, from one of my classes. He lives in Calhoun, which is an advantage. What if we hook up and then it goes badly, and we have to share a bathroom? Or we start going out with someone else? Best to have a bit of physical distance."

"I can't imagine trying to get some dude to like me. I'm so glad that's behind me."

Elise raised her eyebrows and sighed. "Well, at least I have choices."

"I'm sorry. That was rude," said Callie. "I wasn't thinking."

"That's okay."

Callie cut the rest of the babka into two pieces and pushed the plate toward Elise. "I can't believe we're sitting here in New York. It's so great to see you."

They sat for a moment. Elise nodded, yawning, and covered her mouth. Outside the bakery, a taxi stuck in traffic laid on the horn.

"Isn't Greg amazing?"

"Yeah, he's smart, handsome. Those eyes," she said, staring into her tiny cup. "I don't know him well enough to say more."

"But you have an impression, right?"

Elise tore another sugar packet and sprinkled it into her coffee, taking a sip, as she stared out the window, her eyes squeezed shut. "Are you sure you know what you're doing? Giving up on college, even for a great guy. Really?"

She said she didn't expect Elise to understand. It happened so fast. "But I'm happy. Just because our lives are different now doesn't mean you can't try to see that I'm happy."

"But do you really know him?"

"Yes, I really do." She sat back, hugging herself. "And he knows me better than anyone."

"I thought I knew you pretty well."

"I'm sorry I didn't tell you. I just couldn't."

They sat for a moment, picking at the crumbs on their plates. Callie had lost her appetite, and as she lifted her cup for a last sip, the muddy grounds sloshed into her mouth, catching in the back of her throat. She coughed. "What do people say about me not going to Brewster?"

"At first, everyone was pretty shocked. Then they all were involved in college. No one's mentioned you recently."

Callie swallowed. "You can tell them I'm doing great."

"You could tell them yourself."

Callie said it would feel weird to reach out at this point. Elise said Callie would see them all at Thanksgiving.

She hadn't thought about the holidays. Even though her parents weren't big on celebrations, her mother always cooked a turkey with her special dressing. What would she and Greg do this year?

Elise studied her fork, pressing the tines into her finger pads. "Have you talked to your mother?" She dropped the fork and rubbed her hands together.

"No, but my parents know I'm fine."

"They must want to hear your voice."

"I can't do that yet. I had to make a clean break. And Greg couldn't be with me openly at Brewster, particularly after they screwed him over."

"Callie, listen. I'm sorry. I'm only here for a short time. Can we put it aside? I don't want to leave with us feeling tense with each other."

She nodded, blowing her nose on her napkin.

"Can you come to New Haven next time?"

Callie said it depended on her work schedule. She stood up, her legs rubbery. "I need to get some air. Can we take a walk?"

"I should head back to school to work on that paper. I still have a lot of reading to do."

She said she understood, then walked Elise to NYU and gave her a hug. Elise said she wanted Callie to be happy. Callie said she was, but as Elise walked away, Callie felt homesick, not for Shelton, not for her parents, but for a time when she and Elise knew exactly what the other was thinking.

She spent the rest of the day walking from the East Village to Midtown and back, stopping in stores and galleries, still not convinced that things were back to normal between her and Elise. Were they just in different places?

Some days, Greg was in a funk, saying the writing wasn't going well, and he would barely leave the apartment. Then he'd have a few days of smooth writing and he'd be reinvigorated and hopeful and be gone for hours. She learned not to mention his work unless he brought it up first.

A couple of days later though, after a frustrating shift at work where a table of jerks had sent food back and then had left no tip, she came home to find Greg surfing the net leaving bottles and plates covered with leftover food and the sink littered with dirty dishes. When she turned on the overhead light, roaches scattered into the corners. "Fuck!" she said, gathering up his empties. "If you're going to be here all day, why the fuck can't you keep on top of the mess?" She sat down next to him. "I work, you know." Then he slapped her. She recoiled, too shocked to cry.

"Oh, my god, I'm sorry," he said, reaching for her. She stood up and backed away, but he grabbed her hands and pulled her into a tight hug. "I'm so sorry. I don't know what happened. I'm so sorry." He held her in a tight squeeze. "I can't believe I did that." Her face stung, and she tried to steady her breathing, afraid to move for fear he'd hit her again. "I'm having such a hard time, and I snapped. I'm so sorry. I'm worried about my dissertation, if I'll ever finish it. What if I can't get a job? Please, forgive me. You're the only good thing in my life." They sat, and he lay his head in her lap while she stroked his hair until he fell asleep. Then she left him on the futon and spent the rest of the night alone in their bed.

The next day, Greg had left a note for her next to a Starbucks coffee and scone. *Please forgive me. I love you!!!* he wrote. Her cheek felt better, but her bloodshot eyes had dark bags under them. At work, Nadia asked if she were okay. Of course, Callie insisted, tying on an apron and starting in on the vegetable prep. "I'm just tired."

That night, Greg bought her a bodega bouquet, but because they had no vase, he put individual flowers in beer bottles, and she came home to a dozen bottles arranged around the living room. He apologized again for his outburst, telling her how much he loved her, what it meant that she'd stuck by him. He was being so sweet. Maybe this bump in the road had scared him and they were now on a better course. She came to see how much was riding on his getting the dissertation done, how bad he must have felt to act that way.

But a week later, when she asked him an innocent question, not even a criticism, about what he was planning to do about a bill addressed to Jean-Michel, he hit her again, this time twisting her neck, sending a hot rush of pain up into the back of her head. He was drunk. She could smell it, and he was unsteady on his feet, slurring his words. He swore he hadn't meant to hurt her. She was everything to him. He was fucked up. But when she doubted him, he said, it scared him. He was so afraid of losing her, and he couldn't stand that pressure. She stood there, unable to bend her neck as he cried, promising never to hit her again, making it seem as if she'd caused this to happen. She sat as quietly as she could, afraid to set him off. Finally, he staggered off to bed, taking her by the hand. She followed. He was too drunk to get it up, and he fell asleep with her in a tight squeeze.

She lay there, her neck aching, smelling his beer breath and sweat, listening to the blood rushing in her ears. When he started to snore, and she was sure he was sound asleep, she peeled his arm off her, and slipped out of bed, dressing, and throwing clothes into a duffel, her heart pounding, her breathing tight. She closed the door quietly and crept down the stairs and out onto the street.

9

Wanda

In January, when Wanda was in her sixth month, there was a brief thaw then a freeze that covered everything with ice. Wanda kept mostly to her apartment for fear of falling, making do with salads and milks from the bakery. Eating healthy for the baby, no alcohol. One morning, as she sat at breakfast and watched "The Today Show," her mother called to say that a terrible thing had happened. Whit Sutter, that boy whose father taught up at the college. He'd committed suicide in his dorm. Slit his wrists.

"What?" said Wanda, her mother's words thinning, then returning like a boomerang. "That's horrible."

"Did you know him?"

"No," she said, as waves of heat flowed through her. "We weren't in the same class."

"He was up at the college too. They say he was real strange."

"He was real smart."

"Who'd do a thing like that, letting some other kid discover him?"

"Mom? I have to go lay down. I'm not feeling good."

She hung up and dropped into a chair. She was trembling

and when she closed her eyes, she could smell beer and collar dirt, could feel the touch of his chapped lips on her chin. "No!" She shook off her memory, grabbed her glass of juice, half finished, reaching under the counter for vodka, which she hadn't touched in months, pouring a long slug into the juice. She downed the drink, coughing, feeling the rush of sugar and the slap of alcohol. Then she pulled off her nightgown and robe and turned on the shower. She stood under the spray, eyes closed, taking deep breaths, trying to calm herself, to chase away the bad thoughts. But then her vision blurred, and her head felt as if it were tipping backwards. She dropped to her hands and knees, lowering her head, letting the water pelt her back as she reached up to turn off the water, rolling up into a ball, hugging her knees to her belly, waiting for her head to stop spinning. She was cold but didn't move until her stomach turned, and she heaved herself out of the shower and crawled to the toilet. As she vomited, her belly sagged, and her breasts swung heavy with the spasms. Afterwards, she laid her cheek against the cool tiles of the bathroom floor and pulled a towel from the rack to wipe her face and then cover herself up.

No more drinking for her, not while she was pregnant. It was bad for the baby and made her do things she regretted.

For an instant, relief wiggled in her belly that now, no one besides her knew the secret. What a terrible, wicked thought to have. The boy was dead, and she was relieved. What was wrong with her?

What made Whit do this? Why hadn't she sensed anything the day she'd seen him outside the bakery? When he'd seen her stomach, his face had frozen. Did he make the connection and figure out the truth? Was this her fault?

Whit's obituary announced the memorial for Friday at the college chapel. Her mother had asked why she wanted to go to another funeral, especially since she didn't know this boy. Wanda said she knew what the family was going through, and she wanted to pay her respects.

The campus had cleared out for winter break. The ice storm had also shut down the public schools for the past two days, but from her window, Wanda could see a flag flying at half-mast from the high-school tower. She dreaded showing up at the memorial alone, worried that people would wonder why she of all people would choose to be there. But she had to go.

Because she didn't have any maternity dresses, she squeezed into a blue jumper with a blouse that pulled against her belly. And the elastic band of her tights kept slipping below her bump. She drove to the college and parked behind the student union, then made her way carefully toward the chapel, her too-tight boots breaking through the crusty top layer of ice. Her mother had told her to be careful on the ice, and Wanda assured her she would.

David's funeral mass had been celebrated at St. Vincent's, and so many people had come: football teammates, classmates from high school, friends of their parents, David's out-of-town relatives, local Vietnam, Desert Storm, and Iraq War veterans, Sandy and Burt's church friends, Wanda's family, even people Wanda didn't recognize. They filled the church, front to back, every pew. During the long mass she sat, the flag given to her by the Army folded stiffly in her lap. Because the mic worn by the priest distorted his voice, she could barely make out his words. For the condolence line, she was too shattered to stand, so she sat, offering her hand to each person who filed by, voices and faces all a blur.

For Whit, no more than a couple dozen people gathered in the college chapel, men in tweed jackets, women in wool suits or hand-knitted sweaters. A couple of Asian students arrived together, and Wanda wondered if one of them, staying on campus over Christmas, had been the person to discover Whit in the bathroom. There were some kids she recognized from high school sitting together. Not her crowd.

The altar held no coffin, just a few flower arrangements, and slow organ music played. A slender woman with a tight gray perm and a black dress, and a tall, stooped man with a thick head of white hair and a weak chin, made their way to the front row, him guiding her as she walked dazed, like she'd been medicated. Mr. and Mrs. Sutter. Wanda studied them to see what features might show up in her baby. She barely remembered what Whit had looked like. She'd had to check the yearbook to put a face to the rough skin of his hands, the smell of his breath, the sounds he made. She had no memory of the color of his eyes or the texture of his hair or if his teeth were straight or crooked. There she sat, five rows behind his parents, and they had no idea she was carrying their grandchild.

The college president rose and walked to the wooden stand, placing reading glasses on his nose, then unfolding notes in front of him. He said that Whit was a brilliant young man with so much promise. This was an immense tragedy. His mother let out a sob like the cry of a small animal caught in a trap. While still in high school, the president continued, Whit had started taking courses at Brewster and by the time he'd graduated first in his class, he'd earned a full year of college credits with an A average. He was interested in astrophysics, ecology, philosophy, classical piano. Whit's interests ranged from the vast reaches of the universe to the microscopic life of animals and plants. At an early age, he could identify all the flora in Bascom Grove, where he spent many hours exploring. Overtaken by dizziness, Wanda's eyes blurred, so she put her forehead down on the pew in front of her, trying to steady her breathing so she wouldn't faint or get sick.

"We strive to find something we can cling to, but there are no answers here."

Wanda struggled to gather scraps to connect Whit to this baby, to admit to herself this connection, even if it could never be shared. Down the road, what would she see in her child that would remind her of Whit? The way he or she walked or held his head or those things for which she had a passion? Wanda didn't belong here with these people. Did her guilt show? She fought the urge to shout that she hadn't meant to hurt anyone, that she'd been out of her mind with grief, that Whit had been kind to her in her sadness. Instead, she asked silently to be forgiven. Her back ached, and her stomach burned, and she laid her hand on her belly while the baby kicked furiously.

She noticed the couple sitting down the pew from her. The woman wore her hair pulled back in a bun, and next to her sat an old man who'd nodded off and made whistling sounds through his nose. They were Mr. and Mrs. Morton, the parents of that girl, Callie. She was supposed to go to Brewster for college, but instead she ran off with one of her professors, causing a scandal. Wanda thought that Callie probably was one of those people who did exactly what she wanted, no matter who she hurt. Back in school, she'd treated Wanda and her friends like they weren't worth the time of day.

At the end of the service, Wanda struggled to thread her

arm into her coat sleeve. Mrs. Morton scooted over to help her. "There you go," she said.

"Thank you. I've gotten so big, it's hard to do this on my own."

"How are you doing, dear?" she asked, her hand on Wanda's arm.

"Oh, okay, I guess."

"I'm so very sorry for your loss. It must be very painful to attend another memorial after your husband's."

Tears filled Wanda's eyes, and her throat tightened. "I know how it feels, and I thought I should come."

"That's lovely of you." Wanda was surprised the woman knew who she was. She thanked Mrs. Morton and stood to leave. It was kind of her to show sympathy for another family, particularly when they didn't see their daughter much if at all. However, Callie wasn't dead, just gone, living who knew where? But she could still come home. Not like Whit. Or David.

Wanda decided to skip the reception and go over to Michelle's instead. On her way, she thought about the scholarship in Whit's name the college president had mentioned. At least there was that. The only public sign of David, aside from his grave, would be his name engraved among the war dead in the town square. At least someone would benefit from Whit's death. No one was better off because David had died.

At Michelle's, she let herself in to the sounds of wailing. Michelle sat on the couch, wearing ear buds and watching the screen of her phone. Kymberlee Faith lay on her mat, howling. The baby had recently started wearing a helmet to correct the shape of her head, which was flat on one side. Michelle had been upset that her baby was deformed—her word—and hated making her wear that ugly thing. She'd decorated the helmet with stickers and glitter to make it more girly.

Wanda had told her that she'd be fine and anyway, she was a girl and could wear her hair puffy. Michelle had said that Bobby wondered if she'd done something during the pregnancy to cause it. Laying the wrong way. She'd been praying on that.

Today, when Michelle saw Wanda, she removed the ear buds. "Kymberlee Faith hates tummy time, so she cries. I'm sick of it." The baby lay on her stomach fussing, her head wobbling under the weight of the helmet. Michelle plucked her off the floor, removed the helmet, and handed her to Wanda. "And I'm having morning sickness, so I just lay around and try not to puke." She looked as if she'd lost weight with this new pregnancy. Her hair was dyed a lighter shade of blonde and it looked brittle beneath the headband.

Wanda stroked Kymberlee Faith's face, smiling at her. The baby was trying to catch her breath, on the verge of crying again. When Michelle didn't bring up the service, Wanda did.

"Oh, that's right. Was it sad?" She was poking her finger at the screen.

"Yes, of course."

"I'll say a prayer for him." She popped up, grabbing Kymberlee Faith from the mat, her face drawn and tired.

"It sounds as if you're busy."

"No, stay."

"I need to get going." She stood up, gave Kymberlee Faith a kiss and handed her back to Michelle, saying goodbye.

She couldn't go home yet, so she drove to her spot and sat in the car. She wished she could confide in Michelle, but some things were just too big and shameful to confess. Instead, she unburdened herself to David, who couldn't judge her. A life after two deaths. That had to be a good thing. How could bringing a baby into the world be a bad thing? But not telling his parents, was that unforgivable?

Two weeks before her due date, she went into labor at home, her water breaking as she stepped out of the shower. Her parents called Sandy and Burt then drove her to the hospital. Her mother had been pushing for Wanda to be induced since supposedly she was past her due date, but Wanda didn't want to mess with nature and have an obviously premature baby. She'd opted for an epidural, and she'd shooed her mother and Sandy out of the room. "You're both distracting me. Go wait until it's over." Her mother was hurt, but she agreed, her eyes welling. Sandy took her arm and left, saying that the grandmothers would keep each other company. The nurse stayed with Wanda, holding her hand, telling her when to push and when not to. As she bore down, she pictured David's face, eyes locked with hers, urging her on.

David MacDonald Zacek, "Macky," weighed 6 lbs., 2 oz. Wanda feared everyone must know he wasn't David's, that he couldn't be overdue, as she'd claimed. He was skinny with wrinkled skin, a long head, and spiky brown hair. And blue eyes. She couldn't tell whom he resembled, but certainly not David, who was big-boned and blond with meaty hands and wide feet. Macky had dark hair and long, thin fingers and toes. Did she see any of herself in him? So hard to tell. But she fell in love with him on sight.

If anyone suspected the truth, they didn't let on. Maybe David's parents wanted so badly to believe in their one chance for a grandchild that they let logic fly out the window. And who would suspect that Wanda would have sex with anyone but David?

Her mother convinced her to spend a few nights in her old room at the farm, but Macky screamed, and Wanda worried that the stress of trying to keep him quiet would affect her milk, so they returned to the apartment after one night. She placed a crib next to her bed, but then brought him under the covers with her so she could nurse without getting up. Wanda longed for touch, for skin-on-skin contact, the bonding of nursing, the kind of connection she hadn't felt in months. Her milk came in, but Macky startled easily, couldn't latch on, then after spitting up his feeding, he cried for hours. Wanda stumbled around during the day, sleep-deprived, barely able to get dressed or to shower. He nursed a tiny bit at a time, then he'd arch his back and shriek, leaving her breasts sore as bruises, leaking milk. Or if he did nurse, he spat up the milk when she burped him. Michelle had urged her not to nurse. "You don't want a baby hanging off your boob all the time." But Wanda wanted him to have the antibodies to give him the best possible start, and she knew it helped with bonding. Her mother pushed for her to give him formula, but Wanda held out for a few weeks until caving in and giving him a supplementary bottle, which made her milk supply drop. Wanda had wanted the connection of nursing and was sad she couldn't seem to get it right. She walked around holding him as he cried, her eyes bloodshot and stinging, waiting for him to drop off so she could grab a catnap.

Her mother was impatient with Macky's crying and looked at Wanda as if she were the problem. Sandy, on the other hand, had an easy way with him. His crying never bothered her, and she sat staring at him, even when he was red-faced and hot.

One day, when Macky was two weeks old, Sandy showed up and told Wanda to get out of the apartment. He was wailing, hot and red-faced and she was exhausted, having been up in the middle of the night with him. Sandy handed her a gift certificate to the hair salon in town. Wanda was reluctant to leave him, but after a quick shower, Sandy shooed her out the door. "We'll be fine, me and Macky. You need this. You'll feel better." Wanda walked up the street, her heart pounding, stomach in a knot, afraid that Macky would fall apart without her.

But when Tina at the Beauty Barn greeted her and wrapped her in a nylon cape and sat her down at the sink, the warm water on her head and the scalp massage made her feel human for the first time since his birth. She showed Tina and Connie Beacon photos of Macky and Tina put down the hairdryer to say he was the cutest baby. Mrs. Malden asked whom he looked like, and Wanda mumbled something about her grandfather, but she said he was David's little angel.

When she was done, she hurried back home, sweating, worried she'd been gone too long, that Macky would be screaming, only to find him asleep in his crib and Sandy crocheting an afghan for him. "You look great. See? He survived and so did you." Wanda had to agree that she welcomed the break.

Mr. Howe at the bakery told her she could return to work whenever she wanted, but she couldn't imagine leaving Macky for hours at a time. Not yet. She had both mothers for babysitting, when the time came, but not now. Her mother brought her casseroles, more food than she could eat, and Sandy invited her to dinner a couple of times a week.

Eventually, Wanda developed more of a routine, and Macky, now on bottles, was sleeping better at night. She missed the regular touch of another person's skin and had longed for that connection with Macky. Even though he didn't like to be touched, he cried if she left his sight. So, she put him in the chair and watched him, one hand rocking his chair, the other holding a book, waiting for him to lead the way.

Even though Wanda was grateful to Sandy in so many ways, she found it hard to hear Sandy talk about David as a hero, how he'd sacrificed himself for this baby's freedom. "I just wish David could have laid eyes on this angel. He'd have been the best father. You'll tell Macky about him, right?"

"Of course, I will," she said, swallowing her guilt, wondering how it would feel down the road to talk to Macky about David, how keeping the lie going would feel.

David's father couldn't talk about him without his face turning red and tears brimming. This was a man too embarrassed to show emotion, clearly humoring his wife who needed to talk about their son. But it was clear David was always on Burt's mind. Wanda tried to be patient with Sandy, knowing she needed to talk about David, but all Wanda could think was that David had thrown away his life for nothing, and now she had no husband.

The weather warm now, Wanda took to walking into town with Macky in the stroller. She always stopped at the bakery to see Irene, then she'd make her rounds to show him off. Mrs. Cerone at the pharmacy, Mr. Munger at the grocery, girls she'd gone to school with who were starting to have their own babies. She felt a part of the life in Shelton as she never had before. When people asked whom he favored, she mentioned her mother's relatives, people from out of town. "He keeps changing. Sometimes, I see David's side. Sometimes, mine."

"Isn't that the way?"

"I guess," she said, feeling herself shiver. Was this the way it was always going to be, her waiting for people to figure out the truth?

10

CALLIE

Callie ducked into a graffitied doorway littered with empty beer bottles and balled-up take-out bags a block away from her apartment. She texted Nadia, breathless, her fingers shaking. *Can I saty w u? Cant go hoem.* She had no gloves, forgetting them in her rush to leave, so she shoved her hands in her pockets as she walked to an all-night diner on Delancey to wait for Nadia's answer. She ordered a coffee and filled it with creamer and two sugars, the grains spilling out onto the tabletop as her hand shook. Her phone pinged. It was Greg. *I'm so sorry. Please come home.* She turned her phone over on the table. Another message: *I love you. Let's talk.* Where was Nadia? This was her night off, so maybe she was with that guy—Callie forgot his name—but she'd have her phone. Greg again, *Where are you? I'm worried.*

She nursed her coffee, her stomach sour despite the cream and sugar, her neck throbbing, her eyes stinging. She texted Nadia again and this time, got a response. *Not a good time. C U @ work.*

But Callie wouldn't be returning to Seoul Food. Greg would go look for her there. At least she'd just been paid, so she had some cash. What would she do for money when it ran out?

Another text came from Greg. *I love you, but you're scaring me.*

She texted *FUCK YOU LEAVE ME ALONE.* She tossed the phone onto the table and grabbed several napkins, blowing her nose as she gulped to catch her breath. The server, a middle-aged woman, brought the coffee pot to refill her cup and asked if she was okay. Callie's throat muscles had clenched tight so she couldn't talk, and she pointed to her throat. The server patted her on the back and brought her a glass of water. Across the diner, the only other customer, a man, sat hunched over, his fingers twitching as if casting a spell over his plate. He shook his head and rubbed his eyes before staring at Callie. It was two thirty-three. The server returned and asked if Callie needed anything else.

"Thanks. Do you have any Advil?"

"Sorry, no, sweetie. But there's a 24-hour Duane Reade on the corner."

Callie shut her eyes, breathing deeply to steady her pounding head.

Maybe she could go to New Haven to see Elise as she'd been planning to do since the fall. She wouldn't tell Elise the whole story about Greg, but she had no other place to turn. She picked up her phone and texted, *r u up?*

asleep whats going on?

can i come see u?

Elise wrote that Callie should take the train and text when she arrived.

Callie paid for her coffee and headed to Duane Reade. She walked up and down the aisles, slipping a bottle of Advil into her pocket, then standing in front of the gum display, choosing a pack, then paying for it, her heart thumping. Duane Reade wouldn't miss one bottle of Advil.

Outside, she pried open the bottle, dry-swallowed a pill, which stuck in a lump in her throat. Carrying the duffel over her shoulder hurt her neck, so she shifted it from one arm to the other as each grew tired.

When she reached Grand Central, she found that the next train to New Haven didn't leave until six-twelve a.m., and the ticket window was closed. That meant waiting three hours in the waiting room filled with homeless people, all men except for one woman, camped out on the wooden benches with blankets and plastic bags. One person had draped a sheet from head to toe like a cloth over an unused piano. She found one free bench and sat down, wedging her duffle behind her head and pulling her legs up, hugging herself. Snoring and strange muttering sounds surrounded her. Finally at five, the ticket window opened, and she bought a seat for New Haven.

Finally, when the train was boarding, she took her seat, her teeth sticky, her neck a ball of tension, her feet cold, as passengers settled, opened their newspapers, stared at phones or laptops. The trip would take two hours. She set the alarm on her phone and closed her eyes.

At every station, the loudspeaker woke her up—Rye, Greenwich, Cos Cob, Darien. When the ticket taker tapped her on the shoulder, she jumped, her heart beating in her throat and fingers tingling, she reached into her bag for her ticket, which he punched and slipped into the clip on the seat in front of her.

She'd tell Elise she'd decided to give Greg some space so he could write. She didn't want to confirm Elise's doubts about him, and she also didn't want to say out loud that it was truly over between them. And who knew? Maybe they could still patch things up. She needed some time away to think.

When the train arrived in New Haven, Callie caught the bus for the campus. New Haven looked grittier than she'd expected. She found a McDonald's where she bought a coffee and a Dollar Meal, texting Elise to say she'd arrived. Elise answered that she'd forgotten she had a class at nine. *new semester new sked*. But she'd come right afterwards to get her. Callie thought Elise could at least blow off one class under the circumstances, but Elise didn't know how serious this was. Callie had come this far. She could wait a bit longer. So, she sat watching people, almost all of them Black, as she checked her phone, willing the time to pass.

After no contact for several hours, Greg had started texting again. She declined the calls but texted, *need time to think*. His next text said he wanted to work things out with her, to be a better man. Maybe after a few days they could talk. She really wanted her stuff and kept remembering things she'd left behind—her Aran Isle sweater, her opal earrings, her journal.

Finally, after ten, Elise rushed in the door and threw her arms around Callie. It hurt her neck, but she hugged Elise back and started to cry.

"What happened?" asked Elise. "Are you all right?"

Callie lowered her voice. "Can we go to your room first so I can lie down? I didn't sleep at all." Elise took Callie's duffle and they started off for campus. The temperature had dropped, so Callie tucked her bare hands under her armpits and hugged herself. Elise peeled off her own gloves for Callie.

With its Gothic towers and huge trees around blocks of quads, Yale's campus was a city within a city.

"I can lend you some warm things to wear. Here's my scarf," Elise said, wrapping it around Callie's neck. Elise put her arm around Callie, and she greeted other students, shuffling along the sidewalk. Callie felt acutely aware of her grubbiness, knowing she looked bad and smelled worse. She couldn't wait to shower and put on clean clothes.

Since Callie had last seen her, Elise had gained more weight and her chin was dotted with acne. The shaved sides of her head were growing out now and the hair stuck up awkwardly. She still sounded like the old Elise as she pointed out dorms and halls by name, not that Callie cared about random old buildings.

They arrived at Timothy Dwight College, a brick courtyard building with a large tower. They climbed the worn stone steps past a wood-paneled library, up to the fourth floor toward Elise's room. "Kind of like Hogwarts, right?" said Elise. Students in sleep pants and tees, guys with man buns, girls with slept-on hair, nodded at Elise.

"I suppose." A bulletin board held a poster announcing a lecture by a MacArthur Genius Grant recipient, a sign-up sent for volunteers to tutor in New Haven schools, and one for a spring-break trip to Florence.

They headed down a long hall to Elise's room. She opened the door. "You can sleep in my bed." She pointed to the lower bunk. "I'll stay with Ben," she said, smiling. "That's going well."

"What about your roommate?"

"Parvati's almost literally never here. She lives at the library and has a boyfriend in Davenport she's practically engaged to. You might see her for a minute."

Mirror-image desks, bookcases, and dressers flanked the room with a bunk bed in the middle. Callie caught a glimpse of a red and gold felt flag from Shelton High on the left side of the room.

Elise lent her a towel, shampoo, and toothpaste, and Callie headed down the hall toward the bathroom. She found a stall and stripped, draping her clothes over the top, letting the hot water run over her sore neck, washing her hair with Elise's coconut shampoo, and brushing her teeth with a finger.

Back in the room, she slipped on one of Elise's tee-shirts and towel-dried her hair, lying down on the lower bunk, which smelled of Elise's patchouli. Elise handed her a plush purple pillow, which Callie wedged behind her sore neck. Elise pushed aside the other pillows and stretched out at the foot of the bed. "We can go to lunch in a few. But first, tell me what happened."

Callie started by saying that Greg had been a total slob, but then she felt her resolve slip away and found herself talking about their fight. "Maybe I overreacted."

"Overreacted to what?

"We were arguing."

"Okay, and...?"

"And he kind of hit me."

Elise looked shocked. "What?"

"It was an accident."

"He hit you?"

"More a slap than a punch."

"Does that matter?"

"No, but I mean it was an impulse rather than a plan."

"Asshole!"

"It got intense. On both sides."

"Did you hit him?"

"No."

"That's abuse. He hit you. How many times?"

Callie couldn't admit the truth. "I shouldn't have made such a big deal about it."

"Do you hear yourself? Don't defend him." Elise popped up and paced around the room. "This is not okay. I'm glad you left. Have you told your parents?"

"I can't tell them. They hate him and will hate me for running away with him."

"They won't hate you."

When she asked Callie what she wanted to do, Callie said, "I don't know. Maybe stay here until I figure it out?"

Of course, she could, Elise told her.

Callie asked her not to tell Ben, and Elise said she wouldn't. Callie blew her nose, tossing used tissues on the bed next to her. When Elise suggested they go to lunch, Callie realized she hadn't eaten in hours and was starving. Her headache had faded into a dull buzz, but her neck twinged when she turned her head even slightly. They walked to the TD dining hall and ordered grilled cheeses and fries.

"God, I love the food here," said Elise, starting on her fries. "But I'm gaining too much weight." No, she wasn't, Callie lied. Elise shrugged, then started in on Greg again.

Callie said he wasn't a bad guy, really.

"He fucking hit you." A girl at the adjoining table looked up from her book. Elise lowered her voice. "That's not okay. Ever."

"I probably exaggerated it."

Elise said there was no exaggerating being hit. "Come on, Callie."

"I keep remembering things I left behind."

"It's just stuff. You got out, and that's what counts."

Callie said she shouldn't have talked about it, but Elise said it was exactly the thing to do.

"He was stressed. It was an accident."

"Did it only happen once? Which, by the way, is too often."

Callie said it was only once on purpose. "But when he's not angry, he's great."

"Wow. Do you hear yourself?"

"Can we talk about something else, please?"

Elise nodded and sat back, shredding her napkin onto her plate, taking bites of her now cold French fries from under the paper. Callie pushed her half-eaten sandwich over toward Elise.

"Tell me about going home for winter break," Callie said.

"I was so glad to be done with exams. Five courses kicked my butt. I've never had so much work. But it was great to be home and to see everyone."

Callie felt a tug. "Who'd you see?"

Zelda and Claire, of course. Whitney was away skiing. I also saw Jenna. Oh, and Matt." Callie shuddered and made a face. "Claire likes Oberlin, but Zelda is miserable at Tufts and is going to transfer. Remember when she thought she'd die if she didn't get in? And now she hates it. I saw some others at the memorial."

"What memorial?"

"Oh, my God," said Elise, covering her mouth. "You don't know?"

"Know what?" Callie said, her head buzzing. "What happened?"

Elise sighed and leaned forward, taking Callie's hand. "Whit. He died. He killed himself."

"Oh, no." Her vision blurred. "How?"

"He slit his wrists in his dorm bathroom." She sat back in her chair. "I can't believe you didn't know."

"How could I have known?"

"I thought your mother would tell you."

"I haven't heard from her lately." She realized her mother would continue to send letters to her P.O. box in New York and would have no idea that Callie had left town. "When did it happen?"

"A few weeks ago."

"That's terrible."

"He was smart, but so strange," said Elise, who picked up her phone to return a text, and as she did that Callie sat, her stomach twisted, her head aching, thinking about Whit, his moony face, his geeky clothes, his creepy letter. After the text, Elise asked whom Callie was in touch with.

"I tried Zelda and Claire, but all they could talk about was college. I couldn't explain why I'd left with Greg."

"Yeah, I can imagine." She gathered their trays and they stood up to leave. "I can't wait for you to meet Ben. He'll be at dinner tonight."

Callie listened to Elise talk about Ben, how great he was, how smart. Her head was swimming, and her neck ached. And all she could think about was getting some sleep. So tired, she could barely keep her eyes open.

Elise walked Callie back to her room and headed off to class. Callie crawled into bed and pulled the covers over her head, but although she was exhausted, she couldn't sleep. She climbed out of bed and scanned Elise's bookshelf for something to read. She found a text on feminist theory, pulled it out and lay back on the bed. But after a paragraph, her mind began to wander. She reread it, but the writing was so dense and complex. Had her brain turned to mush? Thoughts of Greg and Whit, jumbled, mixed together.

She walked around the room. Over Parvati's desk hung a print of a figure split down the middle, half blue man, half woman with gold skin, standing in front of a goat and a cow. An incense holder with a trail of ash sat on the desk. Parvati's side of the room was neat with books lined up, papers stacked neatly. Elise was such a slob. Sock and pants on the floor, earrings, necklaces, and receipts littered her dresser top. Callie opened a drawer and found a similar tangle—wadded-up underpants, a stretched-out sports bra, a package of almonds, a tube of Monistat. Over her desk, she'd pinned up photos of friends. One showed Elise, Callie, Zelda, and Claire at the Winter Carnival their senior year. In the photo, Callie was laughing, her eyes closed and mouth open. She remembered the winning hockey game and the party afterwards where she and Matt got wasted. Thinking of Matt, she felt a twinge of arousal. Strange. What was that all about? She wondered if he liked college, if he was doing anything besides hockey and partying.

Next to that photo was one of Elise with a guy, probably Ben. Tall, thin with a wispy mustache, he wore a weird lumberjack hat, which made his ears stick out. His arm snaked around Elise, who was leaning her head on his shoulder, her eyes half-shut, grinning. Callie felt a wave of sadness and nostalgia for Greg, remembering cuddling in bed with him, his kissing the back of her neck before she fell asleep. Feeling safe and loved. What happened?

She reached into the drawer and took an Advil from Elise's bottle, then the bag of almonds and opened it, popping a few in her mouth, letting the salt melt on her tongue before biting down on them. She wiped her hands on her tee-shirt and crawled back into bed, hugging the pillow, closing her eyes.

Callie woke to the sound of Elise opening the door, apologizing for waking her up. Callie rubbed her eyes and said she'd had a good nap. Elise explained that she needed to do some reading before dinner. Could they meet at six?

Callie wandered the TD halls, peeking into the library, the study spaces, and the workout room. To think this was just one dorm that was duplicated all over the campus. Yale was Brewster on steroids. As she passed by other students, some of them nodded at her. She wondered if she could pass for a Yale student or if she stood out as someone who didn't belong here. As she walked down the hall, she detected the mingled smells of weed, popcorn, and laundry soap. A girl and guy were having a whispered argument in the corner of the study room while another student slept on the sofa, a book over his face.

At dinner, Elise introduced Callie to Khalil, Amanda, and Drake, Callie realized she needed a story to explain where she'd been that didn't reveal she'd skipped out on college and had followed a man who'd hit her. She decided on a gap year with a trip to Martinique, New York, and then she'd be off to Paris and Madrid. As she spun this story, she shot Elise a glance asking her, please, not to let on what had really happened. Khalil, who was from Pakistan, asked how they knew each other, and Drake, a guy with a bushy head of black curls and stubble, asked which college she'd deferred.

"Columbia."

"Columbia's decent," said Drake. "I thought of going there. Because New York. But then I got into Yale and couldn't turn it down."

"But Callie, you didn't defer Columbia. You turned it down," said Elise.

"Yes, Elise," she said, shooting her a look. "I did. When my parents said I had to save money by going to Brewster. But then, I just couldn't follow their plan."

"Parents always have a plan," said Khalil. "Just travel and enjoy yourself."

They added their own stories about thwarting parental expectations as if they too wished to be on the open road instead of being perfect Yale prodigies. She didn't buy it.

Drake asked if anyone had written the paper for film studies and then they talked about a weird movie where someone cut a woman's eyeball with a razor. Callie knew she wouldn't like it.

At the end of the meal, a tall, thin guy walked up and wrapped his arms around Elise, nuzzling her neck. Ben. Elise lit up when she saw him. She introduced Ben to Callie, and he placed his palms together and gave a slight bow. Then he grabbed a chair and scooted up between Elise and Khalil. Ben again stuck his nose in Elise's neck and tickled her. The others stood up to leave, making plans to meet later at the library, telling Callie it had been good to meet her.

After they left, Ben placed his hand on Callie's arm and asked, "How are you doing?"

"Fine. It's great to see Elise again."

"It's got to be really hard to process the breakup."

Callie looked at Elise, who shrugged. "Sorry. I told Ben a little."

"Well, I don't feel comfortable talking about it here."

"But it might help to talk," Ben said, "to make sense of it."

Callie felt herself start to shake. "I'd rather work it out by myself." She glared at Elsie, who was mashing her soggy bread with a fork.

"I don't know how a man can hit a woman," Ben continued. "Or how a woman would ever go back to a man who hit her."

Callie shut her eyes, her neck throbbing again.

"That's blaming the victim," said Elise. "It's more complicated than that."

"No, it's simple. One's self-preservation instinct needs to kick in. Callie was right to come here. You did the right thing."

Callie could feel her brow sweat. "Can we just change the subject?" She rubbed her eyes, suddenly weary.

"Come on, Ben," said Elise. "Callie doesn't feel comfortable." Ben and Elise stole glances at each other, smiling. He whispered to her, and she laughed, pretending to bat him away. "Callie, Ben and I are going to do some studying. Do you mind going back to my room by yourself? Here's my key card." Callie knew that studying meant fucking in Ben's room. Couldn't she take one night off?

"Yeah, of course. I'll be fine." Elise then said they'd meet in the morning and that if Callie was hungry, she could just swipe Elise's card if she didn't have enough money. Callie felt her face burn. "I just need a good night's sleep."

Elise had taken her laptop with her, so Callie couldn't access the Internet. She crawled into bed and closed her eyes, trying to picture what Greg was doing right then, if he worried about her, if he'd thrown out her stuff. Did he miss her and was he sorry? She hated him, but she missed him, missed the good things. What did Elise see in Ben, that poser? At least Greg was a man.

She woke up to the sounds of someone going through one of the closets, rattling hangers. A girl walked over to the dresser, leaned to one side, and started brushing her long, loose black hair.

"Hey," said Callie.

She turned, startled. "Who the fuck are you?"

"I'm sorry. Callie. Elise's friend from high school. And you're Parvati?"

"Where's Elise?"

"With Ben. I'm staying here for a few days. I hope that's okay with you."

"I wish she'd told me." She was mahogany-skinned with large, wide-set eyes. But clearly not happy to see Callie there.

"Sorry. Elise said you don't spend much time in the room."

"But still. My stuff is here."

Parvati folded her towel and hung it in the closet, straightened the throw rug and tossed some of Elise's discarded underwear onto the lower bunk. Then she grabbed a pile of books and stuffed them into her backpack and headed toward the door without a backward glance at Callie.

"Nice to meet you," Callie said as the door closed.

The next morning, Callie bought a coffee and muffin, then set off walking around the campus. She found a copy of *Pride and Prejudice* in the TD library and back in Elise's room, she folded clothes, reshelved books, trying to be a good guest. At dinner, Ben continued to monopolize Elise's attention, talking about people and things Callie had no knowledge of, and Elise acted all adoring around him. Callie liked Amanda and Khalil. Drake less. He was kind of a poser, but at least he wasn't vying for Elise's attention.

What if she and Greg were really finished? If they were. No, they were. No backsliding. What should she do now? Reapply to Columbia for the following year? Or why not Yale? Get a scholarship? She liked the energy of New Haven, less overwhelming than New York. Maybe she could get a job to pick up some cash.

Back in her room, Elise announced she was going to sleep in the room instead of with Ben. "Cramps."

Elise's period always put her in a crabby mood, and Callie had learned to give her space when that happened. "What should I do?" asked Callie.

"Sleep in Parvati's bed. The sheets are clean." She crawled into the lower bunk.

It was early, and Callie wasn't sleepy. "Can I use your laptop to check my email?"

"Sure. Just don't make too much noise."

"I'll take it down to the Buttery so I won't bother you."

"Thanks."

Callie bought a chocolate chip cookie and a Diet Coke and surfed the net. When she returned to the room at ten, she found a taped-up note. CALLIE SORRY. DO YOU MIND SLEEPING IN THE COMMON ROOM? E. And a winky face. Elise had left a pillow on the floor in front of the door. What the hell? Why didn't they go back to Ben's room? Callie took the pillow and headed toward the common room. A guy with a Comic-Con tee-shirt was sleeping on one of the leather sofas. She lay down on the other one and hugged herself. It was cold and she wished that Elise had at least left her a blanket. The guy snorted a few times, so Callie put the pillow over her head to try to drown out the sound, but that made her face hot. The next morning, having barely slept, she waited until she was sure Elise and Ben had left for class, and she slipped into the room, climbed up onto the top bunk, and closed her eyes. Her neck had kinked from sleeping on the sofa.

Elise returned later that morning. Callie was reading in bed, pillows propping her head. "Oh, good," Elise said. "You got back to sleep."

"I got almost no sleep last night. A guy was snoring, and I was freezing."

"Sorry." Elise stripped off her clothes and leaned over to study her face in the mirror. Her butt had grown wider, and she had some back fat, but her waist was still small. "Hey, listen. What are your plans?"

"For today?"

"No, where are you going from here?"

"I thought I'd figure that out while I'm here."

"I didn't realize this was a long-term thing."

"It's not forever."

"The thing is, I have so much work this semester. I can't do it and keep up a relationship if you're here and I have to help you out all the time."

Callie said she didn't expect that of Elise.

"Is there someone in New York you could stay with?"

"If there were, I wouldn't have come here. And I can't afford to live in New York."

"Well, I have a huge paper due in a week, and I'm completely stressed out about it. And it's hard to focus on Ben when I'm distracted, thinking that you're sitting here alone. It doesn't feel like my room anymore."

Callie figured Ben had been behind this change of heart. "Can I at least have a couple of days to figure it out?"

"It's up to you," she said, but she looked put out. "I have to jump in the shower before class." She stripped naked, wrapped a towel around her and left the room.

Was that a way to treat a friend? Ben had changed her, made her more selfish. Where could she go? All her friends from high school were in college. No one had a job or a place for her to stay. Then she thought of Raquel, who was back home in Chicago. Callie glossed over the messy details and asked Raquel if she could visit her soon. Did she have room?

awesome i live in boys town the cubs pizza come visit!

Why not? thought Callie. A new start. Chicago was cheaper than New York, and she could find a job, maybe even go to school eventually. She was done with the East Coast.

She and Elise didn't speak for the rest of the day. Callie told Elise she would take the train back to New York the next morning and then go on to Chicago, where she had a friend. Elise seemed relieved to be done with her but said they should have one last meal together, just the two of them. They walked to a pizza place near campus. Callie wanted to tell Elise she was nervous about going back to New York to get the bus, but she was afraid Elise would lecture her again and make her feel worse. So, she listened to Elise talk about a party she and Ben were going to that weekend.

The next day, Elise rode with Callie to the train station, and they sat there, having run out of things to say. Callie could tell Elise was relieved to see her go, but there was a moment where they hugged, and both teared up. "Let me know as soon as you get to Chicago, so I won't worry. And don't go back to your old place."

"I won't." But part of her wondered if she could sneak in and recover a few things she'd left behind.

When she arrived in New York, she went first to the Post Office, where she picked up her mail and closed out her box rental. She found a letter from her mother dated two weeks earlier and several advertisements for cable service. In the letter, her mother told her about Whit's death and how it had shaken the whole town. *His poor parents. A dreadful thing.* And she enclosed a check for Callie to use for a flight home. *Please don't give us more reasons to worry.*

Callie stuffed the letter in her pocket and headed to the nearest check-cashing, where she cashed the check. When she was settled in Chicago, she'd write. She couldn't imagine going to Shelton now, even for a short time, and at this point, it was too late for that. It might be all right seeing her mother, who'd at least written to her to say she loved her, but facing her father, seeing his disappointment, she couldn't right now.

Even still, she found herself heading toward her old neighborhood in Alphabet City. Elise had given her a knit cap, and she wore sunglasses as a disguise. Her ears buzzing, head swimming, she inched toward their street and found a doorway where she stood, unseen, and watched the front door. Her bus for Chicago wasn't until six that evening so she had most of the day to kill. Maybe Greg would leave the apartment and she could sneak back in and grab some of her stuff. But after half an hour of standing, cold and bored, her feet freezing, nose running, she decided it wasn't worth the risk. She walked around, past places where she and Greg used to go, and she thought about the things she'd left behind. Some things could be replaced. Others, like her journal, were gone forever. Dirty snowbanks lined the sidewalks. Some blocks were salted; others were icy, so she had to step carefully.

She decided to have one final lunch at Seoul Food. Mi Jin was setting up tables for lunch and said that Nadia would be in later. "Where'd you disappear to? Hyoji was pissed you quit and didn't tell him." Callie didn't explain but said she had to leave town without notice. "Did you get another job?"

"Actually, I'm moving to Chicago. Tonight." And she asked if she could stow her duffle there until later. Mi Jin said she'd hide it in the back.

She ate her bulgogi tacos and paid, then set off walking again. Her neck felt better when she wasn't carrying her duffle, but the cold had made it stiffer. She worried Greg had done permanent damage to her neck.

She walked through Central Park, down 5th Avenue, and then, because she was cold and time was running short, she took the subway to the restaurant, got her duffle, and headed to Port Authority, grabbing a stand-up slice of pizza before boarding the bus, a granola bar and a water stashed in her purse for later.

She found a seat next to the window and put in her ear buds, closing her eyes. A man sat next to her. He smelled of ashes, and when he started talking, she turned toward the window and put her head down, closing her eyes. Finally, he gave up talking and looked at his paper.

As the bus pulled out of the station, and she stared out the window at the buildings and the people, she felt a strange mix of sadness and excitement. She hoped Chicago would be a place where she could take charge and not be dependent on anyone but herself. Once she was settled and had found a job, she'd write to her parents, and they'd have to see that this was the best thing. She tucked her feet up, leaned her head against her duffle, and closed her eyes to sleep.

PART 2

11

WANDA

As long as Macky was little, Wanda didn't want to be tied down to a regular job. Her survivor's benefits kept them afloat, but just barely. She worried about emergencies and how she'd cope. Sandy and Burt had offered to help financially, but Wanda didn't want to accept more than a weekly Sunday dinner with leftovers and occasional gifts for Macky. Was it guilt, pride, or both? She wanted to stay in the apartment so in a few years Macky could walk to school and play on the jungle gym or on the fields. After school, he could go over to a friend's house to play or stop at the bakery for a cookie. Wanda still needed to keep the physical connection to the memories she'd made with David. She'd displayed happy photos of David—in his football uniform, at a picnic with Wanda, on their wedding day—so Macky would have a face to put with the stories she planned to tell him. For now, until he was bigger, and she could afford a place with two bedrooms, this was fine.

One day, when visiting Sandy, Wanda let slip her worry about money and after Wanda once again refused their help, Sandy suggested that she look for house-cleaning jobs in town.

Good money under the table and she could make her own sched-ule. Wanda didn't feel ready to leave Macky yet, but Sandy said they'd all manage. "Evelyn and I can take turns watching him. You're done nursing. He'd barely know you were gone." Wanda liked cleaning, dusting, doing dishes, keeping things straight. Maybe cleaning houses was worth a shot. Wanda's mother was a casual housekeeper, her only rule being that everyone shed shoes in the mudroom before stepping into the kitchen. Otherwise, the rest of the house was a clutter, beds unmade, piles of clothes ev-erywhere. Wanda kept her room neat, her refuge from her messy brothers. On Sandy's computer, she typed up a sheet with tear-off strips and posted them around town, in the market, the pharma-cy, and the café.

She still worried about leaving Macky. At five months, he was hard to put down for a nap, easy to startle, only really com-fortable with her. Of the two grandmothers, she trusted Sandy more than her mother. Sandy doted on Macky, although Wanda had to remind her that Macky didn't like being hugged all the time. Her own mother seemed burdened by him, unable to soothe him, impatient when he cried, and he picked up on her tension. Who'd have figured that a mother of three and grandmother of five would be impatient with a baby?

Sandy got her a job with a bridge-club friend, Sylvia Futral. One of her daughters, Katie, had been in Wanda's class at school and was now married. The Futrals still lived in the house where all six kids had grown up, a big Victorian with gingerbread trim and a wrap-around porch, right up the street from the town center. When she was in high school and stuck out on the farm, Wanda had always fantasized about living in a place like that one day, raising her kids with David.

Katie Futral and Wanda had been friends for about a minute back in 8th grade. Wanda remembered going over to Katie's house after school a few times. In her room, Katie had a big bed with a canopy and a dust ruffle. Photos and posters covered the walls, and a lighted mirror hung over her vanity. But Katie dropped Wanda suddenly and started hanging out with Lucy Lattimore. Clearly, Katie felt she'd traded up to a cooler crowd.

The morning of her first job, Macky woke up with a stuffy nose and she nearly cancelled, but Sandy told her he'd be fine. She dressed in jeans and a tee shirt and tied back her hair, then packed Macky's bag with diapers, bottles, zinc oxide for his bottom, a bulb syringe to suction out his stuffy nose, and a change of clothes. A few hours wouldn't be that bad, she hoped. Sandy promised to call if there was a problem.

She drove past the ice rink to the Zaceks' ranch house on the edge of town. Parking out front, she lifted Macky, asleep in the car seat, and headed to the front door. Wanda handed Sandy the car seat with Macky and his bag. "You go on ahead," said Sandy. "We'll do fine. It's just a cold." Would Macky be frightened to wake up and not find Wanda, particularly since he was sick? She reminded Sandy about his nose bulb and ointment. As she walked back to the car, she fought back tears.

Mrs. Futral wore turquoise capris and matching sweater with a flowered top. She was on her way to the Beauty Barn for a wash and set. Wanda wondered if she should hug Mrs. Futral or keep things professional. It seemed clear Mrs. Futral didn't recognize her, so she was glad she hadn't been familiar. As Mrs. Futral showed her around the house, Wanda mentioned she'd visited before, when she and Katie were in school. "Oh, sure. Wanda." Wanda asked about Katie, and Mrs. Futral said she was married with a baby on the way, but she didn't ask about Wanda or give her condolences about David.

Mrs. Futral wanted the kitchen straightened, the bed changed in the master bedroom, and a general clean-up. She'd be gone about three hours, but Wanda could leave when she was done. She pointed to a $50 bill on the kitchen table. "I figured you'd prefer cash, right?" Wanda thanked her. "Well, bye now," said Mrs. Futral on her way out the door.

Wanda had assumed there'd be cleaning supplies, but all she found was a broom, some paper towels, and an old, half-empty bottle of Pinesol. The kitchen was a mess, the sink full of dishes with dried-on food, and one filthy sponge. Wanda turned on the hot water and squeezed out dishwashing soap to soak the dishes as she pushed dirt around the floor with a broom and dented dustpan. Ant traps lined the kick boards under the cabinets. The counter was covered in a greasy film. Mrs. Futral always dressed well, and to the outside world, she seemed to have high standards, but this didn't fit. It wasn't like she was still busy raising children.

As the dishes soaked, Wanda climbed the curved staircase, stopping to look at the family portraits hung along the wall. Professional photos of the six Futral kids growing up, one of Mrs. Futral in her wedding dress, and a group photo with three generations of Futrals wearing shirts of the same Hawaiian print, a sunset in the background. She identified Mr. and Mrs. Futral's bedroom by the smell of Mrs. Futral's perfume. Stripping off the old, musty sheets, she found a new, unopened queen set, 600-count, Egyptian cotton, periwinkle blue, with a price tag of $150. She shook out the folds and stretched the fitted bottom over the stained mattress pad and layered the top sheet and comforter, then plumped the pillows. When she ran a broom under the bed, dust bunnies rolled out. Clothes lay scattered on the floor, so Wanda picked them up and folded them, placing them on a chair. They also smelled of perfume and some of them needed a wash. She didn't touch Mr. Futral's shirts or pants hanging on the back of a chair next to the bed.

She wondered how Macky was doing with Sandy, and if he felt okay. After finishing the bedroom, she called, but Sandy didn't answer the house phone or her cell. Where could they be? Surely, Sandy would have called if they'd gone to the hospital.

Before heading downstairs, she peeked into Katie's bedroom with the same canopy bed and her name spelled out in pink and purple padded fabric letters on the wall. A photo collage of Katie with friends hung over her desk. Wanda saw part of a sleeve that looked like her old red jacket, peeking out from under another photo. But when she raised the corner of the photo, she saw Lucy Lattimore, her arm around Katie's shoulder, both smiling.

Back in the kitchen, she swiped at the plates and glasses and placed them in the dishwasher. Since there wasn't room for the big pots, Wanda washed them by hand and laid them on towels to dry. She'd planned three hours for the job, since Mrs. Futral had asked for a light clean-up, but this job would take a full day. If Mrs. Futral wanted her to come back, she'd bring her own supplies and would ask for more time. She wished she could have left the house in better shape, but it was the best she could do today. She needed to get back to Macky.

She pocketed the $50 and drove to Sandy's, her chest tight. The musty smells of the Futrals' house lingered in her nose. When she opened the door, she heard nothing. They weren't home. She tried Sandy's cell, but it buzzed from the kitchen table. Had Sandy been in such a hurry she'd forgotten it? Just as she was looking up the number for the Emergency Room, Sandy opened the back door and hoisted Macky's car seat up onto the kitchen island. "Where were you?" Wanda asked, her heart racing. When Macky saw her, he started kicking his feet.

"See, Macky?" said Sandy. "I told you that Mama would be back soon." Wanda's heart fluttered as she lifted him out of the seat, buried her nose in his hair, which smelled like Sandy's lavender soap. Sandy asked how it had gone.

"I called but you didn't answer. I thought something had happened to Macky."

"Sorry. I forgot to take my cell. We took a walk to the cemetery, didn't we?" she said, tweaking Macky's foot in his sleeper pjs. "I wanted to put new flowers on David's grave and to straighten it up."

"You took him outside when he was sick?"

"He was fine. Fresh air is good for him." His cheeks were pink. From fresh air or fever?

It bothered Wanda that Sandy had taken Macky to the cemetery without asking her first. Wanda hoped Sandy hadn't upset him by crying. "Do you think it's a good idea to expose him to cemeteries yet?"

"He didn't know where we were. I just wanted him to be close to his father. I talked to him about David. It helps me and someday, it'll help him."

"I guess, but I wish you'd asked me first." The thought of Macky among all those graves made her angry. What right did Sandy have to do that? Wanda couldn't bring herself to visit the grave, couldn't bear to think about David under ground, couldn't stand to see the things Sandy had told her people left behind, a row of flags, a laminated photo of David in his uniform, a felt pennant from Shelton High, a can of Bud. She preferred to go to their spot to think about David and to talk to him. A place that meant something to both of them. But if it comforted Sandy to keep the flowers fresh, then Wanda could live with that. For now. It was true that Macky wouldn't be affected yet by any of this, but as his mother, she'd have to know when to put her foot down. Someday, Wanda would figure out how to talk to Macky about David, to give him stories. The military stories, this fantasy of a hero, was the last thing she wanted to remember about him.

That night, after putting Macky to bed, she tucked the cash into the kitchen drawer. At moments like this, alone, after Macky was in bed, she thought about how it would be if David hadn't died, or if he'd never gone into the Army. Maybe they'd have a child by now, their child, a different one. But she couldn't visualize a child other than Macky. If she hadn't gotten pregnant, if Macky hadn't existed, would she have been able to survive David's death? Maybe Macky saved her life.

Macky's early fussiness turned into an extreme sensitivity to sounds and smells, making visits to the farm tricky. One day, when he was about eight months old, Wanda was visiting her parents and decided to take a walk, so she put Macky in her front pack and headed outside. She cut through the milking barn toward the path that followed the stone wall next to the big pasture. However, as soon as they entered the barn, Macky started puffing, his eyes shut. She backed out of the barn, and he stopped, but started again when she stepped inside. A few months later, she saw him do the same thing around a strong smell—this time, her uncle Roy's Brut cologne. Roy descended on Macky, eager to hold him, but Macky started puffing again, his face red and pinched. Wanda explained that Macky felt shy around people he didn't see often. That solidified her resolve to limit his contacts to people like Sandy, Burt, and her close family.

By the time Macky was eighteen months old, Wanda could tell he was really smart. Even though he had trouble pronouncing R's and L's, he used words she'd never heard her nieces or nephews say at that age.

One day when he was two and a half, he pointed to a cardboard box and said, "Mott's Apple Juice." At first, Wanda assumed he knew the logo, not the words. But a few days later, he read the word PIZZA on the neon sign outside Fiorno's. When she read books to him, he stopped her when she'd skipped ahead. Soon he sat, one skinny leg crossed over the other, his feet bobbing, as he read to her. She called her mother, excited to report his new skill, but her mother said he'd be better off at his age learning to kick a ball than read a book. True, he wasn't as rough and tumble as his cousins, who spent their time at the farm crawling over piles of dirt and running around poking things with sticks, but that was okay.

When they drove around town, she tested him on his reading (Grocery, Auto Repair, Subway, Package Store, Munger's Fine Foods). One day, when he was about three, she pointed to a sign, but he said he couldn't see it. "Right there," she said, looking over her shoulder at him squinting from his car seat. As she pulled up closer and pointed again, he said, "Oh, yeah. Dwy cweaning." She took him to get his eyes checked and found he was near-sighted. The doctor asked about family history. Her heart thumping, Wanda said no one in her family wore glasses but she didn't know about her husband's side. The little green plastic frame with thick lenses looked out of place on such a little boy, but she was glad he could now see clearly.

Over the next couple of years, Wanda picked up more clients: the Allens, Mrs. Petrelli, the Conways, Lucy Lattimore (now Finelli). Sometimes, she could do two small houses in a morning. No full days until Macky was in school. She planned around Sandy's bridge group and hair appointments, so as not to have to ask her own mother. The money in the drawer grew, and she tried to pretend it wasn't there so it would feel like a lucky surprise. She was saving to buy a computer for classes at the community college and for Macky when he was old enough to use one. For the time being, she used Sandy and Burt's at their house.

Wanda learned more about the way people lived than she bargained for. It amazed her how people kept their secrets hidden from the outside world but didn't mind that the cleaning lady knew. Some clients made an effort to straighten before she came so she could clean rather than pick up and fold. Bathrooms were usually filthy though. Did people have no shame? Bottles of medication left out on the counter for her to put back in the cabinet. She knew which couples shared a bed and who'd settled into separate bedrooms. In houses with cats, the clean-freak owners stocked extra kitty litter and air freshener while the sloppy ones let the cat box overflow with stinky, clumped turds. In the children's rooms, she found food wrappers, cigarettes, or baggies of pot hidden under the mattress. She could guess which boy was secretly gay by the hidden porn, which girl had faced a pregnancy scare, which teenager with an anger problem had punched a hole in the drywall.

Mrs. Allen was a hoarder, her house infested with roaches and mice, stinking garbage, and piles of old magazines. What did she expect Wanda to do with all of that? After Mrs. Allen wouldn't let her throw anything away, she decided not to go back. She learned not to overstep. Mrs. Daddario scolded her for recycling old yogurt containers and glass jars, claiming she wanted to save them for craft projects. And other clients were annoyed if she didn't take the initiative to throw things out. She had to adjust to each household's expectations.

One day, when Macky was three, Wanda had a job scheduled, but Sandy had a last-minute conflict, and Wanda wasn't going to ask her mother, so she brought Macky with her. She packed books and snacks, telling him to sit and read while she worked. Checking on him as she moved from room to room, and seeing he was absorbed, she figured this might work in a pinch. In the living room, at the other end of the house from him, she plugged in the vacuum and started to run it over the carpet. Then she heard Macky shrieking, "Not the woud fing, Mama!" So, she turned off the machine and went into the den to pick him up. At home, she always waited until he was fast asleep and behind a closed door before she vacuumed because he hated the sound. "Sorry, Bud. We can go home soon." Clearly, she couldn't bring him to jobs until he was older. She'd have to find a backup for Sandy. Maybe Michelle, but she had her hands full with three kids and one on the way.

That night, after she put Macky to bed, she sat with her book but couldn't stop worrying about him. Was her mother right? Did Macky have real problems that would make him stand out as weird? Was being smart and unathletic going to make him an outcast? How could she help him? She tried to remember things about Whit in school, but they'd never shared a class, and she'd barely seen him except during awards assemblies, where he was always called up to the stage to receive a prize. She knew nothing about him. Whit's mother could tell her stories from about his childhood, about his medical history, but of course, she could never, ever tell that secret. Would Macky's life be as hard as Whit's?

12

CALLIE

Callie's neck throbbed from sitting up all night during the nineteen-hour bus trip, and she worried Greg had done serious damage when he'd hit her. She'd barely slept because of the cold, her sore neck, and her seat mate's cigarette-and-fart smells.

Too excited to sleep soundly, Callie watched the skyline of Chicago draw closer as the bus followed the highway north from Indiana. When they pulled into the Greyhound station downtown, Callie unkinked her joints and grabbed her backpack from the rack above her head, feeling a deep twinge in her neck. Out on the street, following Raquel's instructions, she found the Red Line and took the train to Addison. She exited next to Wrigley Field, shuttered for the season, and headed toward Raquel's place on Brompton, pleased that she could navigate on her own. Raquel lived in a courtyard building with bars on the windows. Inside, the living room was furnished with a beanbag chair, two plastic lawn chairs, and a wicker trunk for a table with an ashtray, a collection of bongs, and take-out containers on top. Raquel showed Callie where she'd sleep, a walk-in closet with a narrow futon. Coats hung above, but Raquel pushed them to the side to give her room. "It's not much, but at least you'll have privacy."

"No, this'll be fine," said Callie. She couldn't be picky about a free place to crash. What was left of the money her mother had sent her would be enough to survive on for a week if she didn't eat much. "Can I take a shower?"

"Sure," said Raquel, and she pointed to the bathroom, which was tiny and had no shower curtain. "Just put the towel on the floor when you shower," she said. There was only one towel, and the window had a crack, so Callie shivered as she stood under the water. But it did feel good to get clean again.

She joined Raquel, who was sitting on the beanbag chair, texting. "That felt great."

"So," Raquel said, her thumbs tapping, "tell me what happened with Mr. Professor Man."

At first it had been romantic and exciting, she told Raquel. They'd decided to travel so he could do research, but when they returned to New York, he couldn't write, so all he did was sit around and she had to support him. Then he hit her.

"Asshole," she said, laying down her phone. "So, you left. Good."

"I was stupid."

"You were in love and yes maybe stupid. But so what? You're out of that now." But Callie wasn't sure yet that she was.

"I should have gone to Brewster."

"That's the lesson you're taking from this? That you should have caved and done what your parents wanted? No, this is exciting. You can make your own life. You don't need college."

"Tell my parents that."

"Yeah, well, parents." Raquel said her parents wanted her

to live back in Flossmoor with them, but there was no way she'd survive in the suburbs. She'd barely made it out of there alive.

When Callie asked her if there was anything to eat, Raquel said, "I have to walk the dogs, and we can grab something while we're out. You can get a sense of the neighborhood."

"You have dogs?"

"No, I'm a dog walker. A total scam. Good money for a couple of hours a day. Let's go."

She laced up her Doc Martens, put on her coat, and grabbed some plastic bags. Callie zipped herself up and they set off. It had started snowing heavily, and the traffic moved slowly along Halsted Street, where the stores had names like Gay Mart and displayed leather harnesses on mannequins with huge bulges under skimpy briefs. She noticed a billboard for a real estate agent who, it seemed, moonlighted as a drag queen. Or maybe real estate was his side gig. Raquel stomped a path on the uncleared sidewalk, and Callie followed her single file on the narrow groove made by Raquel's boots.

"We can go to this bar called Hydrate tonight. We're meeting my girl Kai and our friend Sacha. Are you up for that?"

"Sure, as long as it doesn't cost too much."

"This is the best neighborhood, except for the sidewalks. Fuck!"

They arrived at a townhouse a few blocks away, and Raquel took out a big ring of keys and ran up the stairs. "Wait here." Callie stood and watched cars drift by, exhaust billowing, then a bus passed, displaying a sign advertising the upcoming Cubs Convention. Cool that the neighborhood offered both baseball and drag shows.

A few minutes later, Raquel emerged with a Corgi on a leash. They walked a couple more blocks and picked up a terrier, Afton, then finally a beagle named Bagel. Raquel wielded the leashes like reins as the dogs wove from side to side, stopping to sniff every yellow ribbon of snow. When they'd all finally squatted and shat, Raquel scooped up the turds into plastic bags and tucked them into snowdrifts rather than looking for a garbage can. Raquel handed Bagel's leash to Callie, and they turned back toward the dogs' homes. Raquel was supposed to walk them for a full thirty minutes but in this snow, no way. She returned them in reverse order.

Back at the apartment, Callie remembered they hadn't stopped for lunch. She made a mental note to buy a loaf of bread and some peanut butter to contribute the next time she went out. Then she lay down for a rest but woke up with a start after a bad dream about Greg. She had to remind herself that she was safe and far away from him. Thinking of him made her neck ache.

Raquel wasn't in the apartment, so she rooted around in the cabinets and opened a box of crackers, bit into one, found it stale, and spat it out. She looked in the refrigerator but only found a bottle of Kombucha and some Chinese take-out that looked iffy. Sitting on the beanbag chair, her stomach growling, she texted Elise to let her know she'd arrived safely. She thought about writing to her parents but wanted to get a job first.

Raquel showed up with a container of ramen for Callie, which she balanced on her knees and devoured. Just what she needed. They sat and talked, and Raquel again mentioned it was going to be so fun hanging out together. Callie agreed, so glad to be in Chicago and not in New York or Shelton. "Oh, God, not Shelton," said Raquel.

That night, they met Raquel's girlfriend, Kai, and Sacha at a bar. Although Callie was exhausted, she stayed through several

Karaoke songs, barely able to keep her head up, but she knew she wanted to be a good sport.

They returned to the apartment at two, and Callie crawled onto her futon and fell asleep, her neck aching, her throat dry. She smelled weed and could hear Raquel, Kai, and Sacha laughing, so she shut the door. Then, when it became too hot and claustrophobic, she opened the door a crack.

The next morning, Callie found Sacha sleeping in the beanbag chair and Raquel's bedroom door shut. Callie crept into the kitchen, where the sink was full of dirty dishes. Mouse turds in the corners made her worry about mice in the closet.

Sacha stirred.

"You're up early."

"Not really, for me. When does Raquel usually get up?"

"Who knows? It depends on what she took the night before."

"Doesn't she have a job?"

"Yeah, so?"

Raquel appeared, looking ragged. "Is there coffee?"

"No, dude," said Sacha. "You forgot to buy some."

"Fuck."

"What are you doing today, Callie?" asked Sacha.

"I need a job. Any suggestions?"

Around ten, she bundled up and walked to the nearby Starbucks, where she picked up an application and a coffee. Then she continued, stopping at every store, asking if they were hiring. She knew most of the managers would throw her application away without looking at it. Finally, by late afternoon, after widening her search area, she found a small gluten-free café called FLOWER looking for someone to make coffee and cover the register. She told the manager, a stocky person named Chris with whiskers and a belly, that she'd worked as a waitress in New York but hadn't been a barista. Chris offered to train her, starting the following day.

Excited to share her news, she walked back to Raquel's, but no one was home. She pulled out a postcard she'd bought at Walgreen's and wrote to her parents, telling them she was in Chicago and had a job and asked them not to worry about her. She didn't mention Greg and included Raquel's address.

After a few days, she'd learned to make recognizable swans, hearts, and trees in latte foam. Because it was on a side street and a block from Starbucks, the café didn't get a lot of customers, but she could read and have free coffee and pastries during her shift.

A week after she wrote to her parents, she received a letter from her mother, filled with questions about why she was in Chicago, what she planned to do there. She renewed her plea for Callie to come home. *Put that chapter behind you.* Callie could start at Brewster in the fall and be back on track again. She mentioned that Callie's father was very worried. But there was no way Callie could go back there, not until she was established, not until she could prove she'd done the right thing not going to Brewster. She couldn't face her parents shoving her failures in her face.

A month since the neck injury and it continued to feel stiff, particularly in the cold. She worried it wasn't getting better. She found a flyer for a massage in Uptown, cheaper than a doctor. She made an appointment and found the place in a storefront on Argyle. A middle-aged Vietnamese woman greeted her. Callie explained about her neck pain. "Whiplash?" the woman asked. Callie said she'd wrenched it slipping on the ice. The woman led her into a dark room. Callie pulled off her boots and lay down while the woman placed a warm towel over her eyes. The atmosphere was tranquil—the low lights, the soft music, the warming oil—so different from the chaos of Raquel's place. As the woman rubbed her fingers up and down the sides of Callie's neck, cradling her head and lifting it, angling it gently from side to side, Callie realized she'd been holding herself protectively for weeks, since Greg. But this woman was gentle, and Callie felt she could trust her. She also realized she hadn't been touched, seriously touched, by anyone since Greg. After the woman finished on her neck, she asked if Callie wanted a foot reflexology massage. Callie said she couldn't afford to pay more, but the woman said she'd do both for the same price. Peeling off her socks, Callie dipped her bare feet into a bucket of warm tea-colored water. Then the woman started kneading Callie's leg from thighs to calves to feet. She massaged one foot at a time, pressing her thumb into the arches, the pads, the joints. When she touched a spot near the arch of her right foot, Callie winced. "You have a womb problem?"

"No, I don't think so. I get bad cramps. Can you tell that from my feet?" She said she could. The woman returned to massaging Callie's heels. Her touch was surprisingly strong. She had isolated a line at the base of Callie's toe. "For the neck." She pressed her fingers into the spot and Callie felt an intense pain and she took small breaths until it faded. At the end of the session though, Callie felt looser, warmer, almost wrung out. "How did you do that?" She asked.

"The foot has points to the body," she said, showing Callie a chart with replicas of the organs nestled inside a drawing of each foot.

"Does it take a long time to learn to do this?" Callie asked. The woman shrugged as she pulled the sheet off the table and turned on the light. Callie blinked, thanked the woman, and gave her a tip. The woman advised her to rub Arnica on her neck every night and to sleep without a pillow.

Out on the street again, she swiveled her head from side to side, then treated herself to a bubble tea and an almond cookie at a Vietnamese bakery.

Over the course of the next few months and into the spring, Callie read about eastern massage, acupuncture, acupressure, Reiki, and the benefits of Tai Chi. She'd seen a flyer about a Tai Chi Meet-Up in the park near Foster. It met on a Wednesday, her regular day off. It was May, and she showed up the following Wednesday to look for the group. On the knoll near the beach, she found several old Asian men and women, a middle-aged white woman in flowing white pajamas, a guy about her age with a ponytail and beard, and a beefy, balding man with tattoos. She placed herself near the instructor and tried her best to follow the others' moves, but there was no verbal instruction. Every time the group changed directions, she had to follow a new person. The moves were fluid and graceful, and even the old people were limber, flexing their knees and crouching low. In comparison, she felt stiff and awkward. But there was something about the slowed-down pace, hands flowing, slow graceful steps, the quiet, everyone moving together without talking, that she found appealing. As they did the forms, the sun rose higher over the lake and birdsong surrounded them. When the group broke up, the pony-tail guy introduced himself as Garrett. "You haven't been here before, have you?"

"Pretty obvious I don't have a clue, huh?"

"No, you'll learn. It takes years to master." He lowered his hands in a gentle, calming gesture. "Be patient with yourself." When he raised his arms to refasten the elastic around his long hair, the curve of his triceps peeked out of the sleeves of his tee-shirt.

He suggested they go for a coffee at a diner, then she found herself back at his place on Winthrop, sharing a joint and fucking him on his dirty sheets. It was the first time she'd been naked with anyone since Greg, and she was surprised at how into it she was. At one point though, Garrett ran both hands along the sides of her neck, and she froze, pushing him off her. She sat up, pulling her knees to her chest. "Don't do that."

"What?" His dazed face framed by tendrils of loose hair.

"My neck is really sensitive."

"Sorry." He rolled over, his skinny butt tensing as he reached for his pipe. He lay on his side and smoked while she dragged on her clothes and slipped out the door, knowing she wouldn't be returning to that group again. Did he think she was crazy, pushing him away like that? What was wrong with her? Had Greg hurt her in more ways than she'd realized?

She'd done research on massage therapy programs in Chicago and found two centers on the North Side that held classes at night, which meant she could keep her café job. She didn't know how she could pay for it. Could she ask her parents to help her? It wasn't college, but it was school. She'd read that they studied anatomy and physiology and it overlapped with some of what she'd studied in A.P. Bio. Her memory was really good, and she had to admit she'd missed studying.

She wrote to her parents and told them about the program,

saying she'd found what she wanted to do, something that would lead to a career. Could they help her out? Her mother wrote back with a plane ticket. *This is not college. We will not support this whim of yours.* Callie decided to hang onto the ticket. She really couldn't stand living at Raquel's anymore, but she didn't have the money to rent her own place. Maybe though, this program would give her a skill that would support her and be fulfilling. That became the goal—to keep her head down, save every penny, and do this on her own.

13

WANDA

The summer before Macky was due to enter kindergarten, he was reading Harry Potter but still wasn't toilet trained. His huge, amazing brain didn't seem to communicate with the rest of his body. Dr. Frogg said that some children took longer than others. Not to worry. Very few kids go off to college in diapers, he'd joked. But she did worry, and lied to her mother and sisters-in-law, saying he was trained. She limited their visits to the farm, making sure he pooped before they left home. But one day at the farm, he did poop, and she snuck into her old bedroom to change him. Her mother found her kneeling on the floor as he stood reading, a book propped next to him.

"What? He's not trained yet?"

"Mom, please," Wanda said. "He mostly is. And I'm trying not to make it a big deal." She wrapped the dirty Pull-up and grabbed a clean one.

"Shame on you, Macky. You aren't a baby."

Macky blinked behind his glasses.

"Mom, stop." She tapped his leg, and he lifted each foot so she could slide his Pull-ups then his shorts over his butt. He

padded into the other room as Wanda rose to her feet, shuddering. "You embarrassed him."

"He should be embarrassed. A five-year-old in diapers."

"Pull-ups."

"Same thing. You're not doing that child any favors."

"I'm doing my best," she said, fighting back tears.

Her mother turned and left the room. Wanda hauled herself
up, shaking, wondering if it were her fault.

But nothing seemed to work. He hated feeling wet or soiled
but couldn't plan ahead. She worried he'd be kept out of kindergarten in the fall. Sandy advised her to take away the Pull-ups,
sit him on the pot right after he ate, and get him up in the middle
of the night to pee. She tried that, but now his mattress and rug
were stained and smelly.

Macky taught himself to read but wasn't toilet-trained, could
talk in full sentences but couldn't dress himself. He could build
an entire advanced Lego set but couldn't run without tripping
over his feet. At times like this, she wished she could ask Mrs.
Sutter if Whit had had similar problems. But she didn't want to
think too much about Macky resembling Whit.

It was August, one of those days when you could feel the change of
season in the air. Wanda's family had gathered for a pig roast. Her
parents, Joe and Kenny with their families, Wanda and Macky.
The men tended the fire pit out behind the house while the women
shucked corn and stuffed deviled eggs as they drank wine coolers
in the kitchen. Wanda had told them she wasn't drinking, but they
gave her a glass anyway. This time, she accepted it, adding seltzer
to weaken it before taking a tiny sip and setting it aside. Leelee
and Fawn, aged ten and nine, sat on the floor braiding friendship

bracelets while Macky lay on the couch, reading *Harry Potter and the Goblet of Fire*. Simon and Luke headed out to the barn. Age six to Simon's seven, Luke idolized his older cousin.

"Go on, now," Wanda said. "It's a beautiful day. Get some air." He dragged himself up from the couch and shuffled out the door, and Wanda allowed herself the thought he might have a good time if he just let himself. As he did every day, he wore his favorite jumping dolphin tee-shirt and fleece shorts with his army cap pulled down, so his ears stuck out.

When the screen door slammed, Gail asked, "What's with the hat?"

"He's attached to it," said Wanda. "I make him remove it for his bath, then he slaps it back on his wet hair. I don't have the heart to take it away from him."

"Yeah, well," said Mary Sue, "I lose my kids' things when they're old and worn out." She waggled her fingers. "They just disappear."

"He doesn't let it out of his sight long enough to do that. He'd notice if it wasn't right by him."

"When Simon had a blanket," Gail said. "And he was sucking his thumb, we told him that he was too old to do that anymore. Kenny was burning brush one day, and we told Simon that the time had come, that big boys don't carry blankets. So, he just threw it on the fire."

"You didn't," said Wanda. "Did he freak out?"

"He was sort of upset, but he got over it. They do. Sometimes, you just need to push them, you know?"

"I can't do that." What a terrible thing to do to a child, make him give up his blanket like that, watching it burn, knowing he'd thrown it on the fire himself.

"Suit yourself," said Gail, "but it works. That hat could end up in the fire pit today if you wanted."

Mary Sue laughed. "Oops. So long, hat."

Wanda's mother was spooning mayonnaise into the bowl of diced potatoes and tilted her head as if to say, "See? I'm right." It hurt that her mother got along better with Gail and Mary Sue than with her and preferred the older grandchildren to Macky.

"Well, that's not going to happen," said Wanda, her heart thumping. Would one of them torch the hat? What would she do then? She took a sip of her drink and gathered up the corn husks, dumping them in a plastic tub. "I'll take these to the compost," she said, an excuse to grab a break.

The compost bin sat between the back door and the vegetable garden. She grabbed a garden fork to stir the husks into the mound of wormy, rotted scraps. Back near the edge of the cleared land, her father and brothers stood next to the fire, surrounded by a cloud of smoke, as they drank beers and poked the wood. She waved to the men and headed down the path toward the pasture to stretch her legs and get a breath of fresh air. However, when she heard screams coming from the milking barn, she broke into a run. Inside the hay loft, Macky dangled, his shorts around his ankles, his cartoon-animal Pull-ups in full view, his legs twisting, as his cousins held him by the arms from above.

"Stop that!" She ran to Macky and grabbed him around the legs. The toe of his shoe caught her square in the throat, and she fell back onto her butt. As she rose to her feet, she croaked, "Let go!" And Macky dropped into her arms, squirming and pounding her with his fists. "Get out of here, both of you! Go!" The boys scampered down the bales and out of the barn.

Macky broke away and ran outside through the open gate and onto the mowed field, his legs and arms pumping. She followed him. When he stopped and crumpled to the ground, rocking, hugging himself, she lowered herself next to him "Hey, Bud." She longed to fold him to her but knew to let him wind down on his own. As his crying slowed, she told him to roll onto his side, and she rubbed gentle figure-eights on his back as he sniffed and hiccupped. She looked at her boy, his brow sweaty, still snuffling, but winding down. How could she send him out into the world if he wasn't even safe with his cousins?

"Come on, Bud," she said, rising to her feet and offering him a hand. "We're going home." He sat up, his nose running, his face smeared with dirt and snot. She helped him blow his nose on the hem of his tee-shirt, then they headed back toward the driveway. "Hop in the car," she said, opening the door for him. He crawled into the back and lay down. "I'll get your book." The boys were now busy digging a hole next to the house. When she headed in their direction, they stole glances at each other. "That was mean," she said to the boys, her voice shaking. "You stay away from him if you can't be nice." They looked at her dully, pretending not to understand.

Back in the kitchen, she grabbed her purse and his book. "Sorry, we can't stay."

"What's wrong?" asked her mother, sitting between Mary Sue and Gail, all with cigarettes.

"Ask Simon and Luke."

"What do you mean?" asked Mary Sue, although she must have seen what happened.

"They ganged up on Macky and were teasing him. They got him up onto the hay bales and then wouldn't let him down."

"I'm sure they were just playing," her mother said. "Come on. Don't spoil the day."

"I won't let him be bullied."

"He's too sensitive," said Gail. "And you baby him."

When she let the screen door slam, her father called to her. "Where're you going?"

"Home!"

She jumped in the car and started the engine, peeling out of the driveway and onto the road, her heart in her throat. She could just see her mother and sisters-in-law blaming her for being too sensitive, getting a laugh out of it. As she crested the hill at the edge of their land, she said, "Dammit, Macky. Why'd you let them do that to you?"

"I don't know," he said, his head barely visible in the back seat.

"I can't be worrying about you getting hurt all the time. You've got to stand up for yourself."

"I'm sorry, Mama," his voice soft, his nose stuffed.

She took a deep breath. "I'm not mad. Sorry." She didn't want him to know how worried she was. "Just a bad day, huh?" She looked in the rear-view window and saw him slumped in his seat, reading again.

She had to get him trained, so she said that the Lego set he wanted for Christmas, the one she'd hoped his grandparents would give him, could be his now if he started using the pot. "You can still wear Pull-ups at night, but you have to start wearing underpants during the day. You just have to." He really wanted the Taj Mahal set, but it cost too much. They settled on a battleship. She dipped into her cash drawer for the money. No wonder she couldn't gather the money for another college course.

She was worried about Macky's school, how he'd get along with the other kids, but she was also excited for him to have a library and be able to do math and science. And she really hoped he'd make at least one friend.

Although he could read and had a big vocabulary, he looked young for his age. He talked on and on about whatever he was interested in—sharks, quartzes, spiders, the Civil War. She wished he could be more rough and tumble while still being her sweet boy. He needed to be with kids his own age and not adults all the time.

Dr. Frogg wanted her to push the calories, but he wasn't there when Macky refused to eat what she served him. She figured it was better to give him what he wanted. So far, she'd followed his vaccine schedule, but she also worried that Michelle might be right that they caused autism, so she'd delayed his last booster shot.

Macky fussed about everything that touched his skin. Once he was finally trained, she let him walk around dangling free at home, a weird sight with his glasses and hat, which was threadbare with its bent visor and frayed edges. He still wore the same size as the year before, but she took him shopping for new school clothes. His tee-shirts had to be soft cotton, and he made her cut the labels off because they bothered his neck. Socks had to lie flat with no seam touching his toes or he'd yank the shoe off and try again. At the store, he agreed on elastic-waisted pants and a few tee-shirts and one sweatshirt.

Wanda was excited for Macky's teacher to see how smart he was. Had she ever taught a child who could read so well at his age? What would he grow up to be? A doctor or a scientist or a professor? He might be a genius. They'd test him to find out. He was still young enough to think she knew everything, but that wouldn't last. He was so much smarter than she was.

"Do you think I'll be able to do experiments?" he asked. "Can I bring my lichens with me? Do you think there'll be a class snake?"

"I don't know. Ask your teacher."

On the first day, he wanted to wear his hat. She told him he could wear it up to the door then put it in his backpack until the end of the day. When he took it off, his hair had dried with a dent around the crown of his head. She wanted to brush it, but he wouldn't let her. His skinny legs stuck out of his new shorts, and he shuffled, pigeon-toed, in his new gym shoes with neon laces. As they crossed the street, weaving through the line of cars heading toward the school, she told him, "I can't wait to hear about your day. I'll be thinking of you all morning." He clung to her hand, and he seemed so small, particularly when she saw other bigger and sturdier children. He froze at the entrance, putting his hands over his ears. "Macky? Look at me." She lifted his chin. "You'll have a great time. Just listen to the teacher and have fun. I love you." He nodded and walked into the building. It was sad to drop him off at school, the first big step in his leaving her one day, when she'd have to face being alone. But she had years before that happened.

That morning, as she ran the sweeper over the stained, wall-to-wall carpet at the Holtzmans', she wondered how Macky was doing. Today, as usual, she missed David and saved up stories to tell him later. But if David had lived, she wouldn't have Macky. What a thought. She couldn't imagine life without Macky, but then again, she couldn't have imagined life without David.

At eleven-thirty, Wanda drove home and joined the group of kindergarten mothers gathered out front. They were all girls she'd gone to school with, but none of them, including Mary Sue, were real friends. It was like high school cliques all over again. If not for Michelle and David, she'd never have survived growing up. She wished Michelle weren't homeschooling her own kids.

She walked up to Tara Novicki, who married David's cousin Rick. Tara asked if Macky was going to play soccer.

"No, that's not his thing. He's more of a reader."

"Huh," said Tara and she looked over Wanda's shoulder, waved at another mother, and walked away.

The door opened and a line of kids followed Ms. Gannon. At the end of the line, Macky appeared, and her heart started beating hard. When he saw her, he broke into a grin and ran to her. She threw her arms around him. "How was it?"

"Good." His hair stuck up in the back and she itched to smooth it. He unzipped his backpack and grabbed his hat, plunking it back on his head.

On the way home, she asked him about the day, what he'd done, what his favorite thing was. He said he'd read a book. "Did you meet other kids?"

"There are twenty of us."

He reported that the classroom had one hundred-seventy-one books, but only a few chapter books. "We sat on the triangle on the rug, and Ms. Gannon told us where to sit. We're supposed to watch her the whole time. We had a snack, but I only ate the graham cracker. I told her I don't like milk, and she asked if I am lactose intolerant, and if I am, you have to let her know. I said no, I just don't like it. She said I should drink it then, but I left it on the table. I'm done talking about it now. Can I go read?"

Back home, she asked if he'd hung out with Luke at all. No, Luke played soccer with some kids. Macky had already stripped naked and was lying on the daybed, his legs spread as he touched himself. "Hey, Macky, that's for private. Not in front of me. Or anyone else, okay?"

"Uh huh." He rolled over on his side, his legs bent, as he sneaked his hand between his legs.

She heated rice and added some tofu, which he didn't love, but she wanted him to eat some protein. "Lunch. Go wash your hands."

For the first week, they had the same routine. She dropped him off, did a half-day cleaning job, and was back in time to pick him up. Every day, she asked him about school, and he gave short answers. The more she pushed, the more he resisted, so she backed off. He would only talk about what he had read. Once he landed on an interest, he never stopped talking about it. "Macky, sweet boy, I'm so glad you love lichens, and you've told me a bunch. But that's all I need to know right now, okay?"

On Tuesday of the second week, he said he had a headache and wanted to stay home. "What's going on, huh? Did you stay up late, reading?"

"No, I'm sick."

"Did something happen at school yesterday?"

"No."

"Then, let's get going."

"I'm sick."

She felt his forehead. "You don't have a temperature."

"My glands are swollen."

She felt them. Nothing. "Get up, you'll feel better." He sleep-walked through getting dressed and eating breakfast.

When they reached the front door of the school, Wanda noticed a group of boys about his age, huddled together, looking in their direction. As Macky passed them, they swiveled their heads and laughed. One of them darted his eyes toward her and stopped laughing. Wanda's heart sank. Macky ducked his head and hauled open the door, slipping inside.

As she cleaned that morning, she wondered if he was sick after all or if it was something else.

When she picked him up, she noticed his glasses were taped at the temple. He also had a scratch on his nose. "What happened?" she asked.

"I fell."

"Macky, what happened today?" He wouldn't make eye contact.

"A first grader told me to run, and he chased me, and I fell."

"Who was it?" He told her. Mike Chapelle's kid. Mike had been a bully too, back in the day.

"Did you tell your teacher?"

"She taped my glasses."

"But did you tell her about the boy chasing you?"

"No."

"I think I need to call her."

"No! Don't call her. It was fine. It was an accident."

"Are you sure? Maybe I should talk to his mother."

"No! Don't do that."

"Macky, look at me." His eyes met hers briefly, then returned to his book. "If something happened, would you tell your teacher?"

"Yes, but nothing happened."

"You sure?"

"Yes. Can I read now?" He rolled over, cradling his stuffed

rabbit, a favorite from an early age which he'd dug out of the bottom of his toy box. He'd also returned to sucking his index finger.

The next day, he was groggy and said he didn't feel like eating. He wanted to take his rabbit to school, but Wanda said no. She nearly gave in, thinking he might need it, but knew it would be awful if anyone saw it.

A few days later, Wanda had just mopped the kitchen floor at the Barbers' house out on Stanhope Road when her phone rang. It was Mrs. Preston, the school principal. There'd been an incident at school. Could Wanda come pick Macky up?

"What happened?"

"He was wearing a hat, which is against school rules, and a couple of children started playing with it, and Macky became very upset. It spiraled out of control."

"Is he okay?"

"He's in the nurse's office, resting."

"But is he hurt?"

"No, but Ms. Gannon thought he should sit out the rest of the morning."

"All this was because of a hat?"

"Hats are not proper school attire."

"I know. I told him that, but he loves it. He wears it all the time."

"Kindergarten is where children start to learn the difference between home and school. What if every child brought something from home? A stuffed animal or a blanket? That's for home, not for school."

"I'll make sure he knows."

"The problem is that it led to a reaction that was over the top."

"What happened?"

"He ran out onto the field and wouldn't let anyone near him, not even his teacher. He was crying and he wet his pants."

Oh, Macky. "He has a clean set of clothes, right?"

"Of course, but for today, he needs to go home. And I'd like you to come in for a meeting. Are you free tomorrow at nine?"

"Yes, I'll be right there." She wrote a quick note to Susan Barber, saying she'd had an emergency and would come back later to finish the job.

At the nurse's office, she found Macky lying on the cot in the back room, rocking from side to side, sucking on his finger. "Macky," she said, sitting down next to him. "What happened, buddy?" He had his hat pressed against his nose and he started mumbling into it. "I can't hear you. Take your finger out of your mouth."

"They stole my hat and started throwing it around." His eyes focused over her shoulder.

She scooted the chair closer. "I'm so sorry. Did you ask them to give it back?"

"I did, but Luke said I was faggy for wearing it." He started rocking again, hugging the hat, which was caked with mud.

"That was not a nice word to use. But maybe you need to leave the hat at home."

"No, I like its smell."

"I know, but the other kids made fun of you, and your teacher said it wasn't allowed." She reached for his hat and his backpack. "Let's get you home."

He sat up, wearing his back-up set of clothes, an old pair of red sweatpants with a patch on the knee, and a stained tee-shirt. The nurse handed her a bag with his wet clothes. "Feel better,"

Macky." She gave him a panda sticker and patted his shoulder. He shrugged off her hand and walked out the door. Wanda thanked the nurse and joined Macky in the hall, guiding him past a group of kids who whispered as they walked by. Wanda glared at them.

Before climbing the stairs back at home, she took the hat and slapped it against the wooden railing to get rid of the clods of dirt. She made lunch, and he read all afternoon in the sunlight streaming onto the daybed, the hat back on his head, finger back in his mouth. She didn't tell him about her upcoming meeting with the principal. That night, after he fell asleep, she lifted his hat off his head and rinsed it out in the sink, rolled it in a towel, and dried it with her hairdryer before placing it next to him in bed. Had she made a mistake in trusting him to leave the hat in his backpack? Was Mary Sue right, that she should just get rid of it on her own? The hat was really important to him. Lately, he'd been reading about the Army and had started asking questions about David, usually right after seeing Sandy and Burt. Wanda avoided talking about the war, about how David died, instead telling him about memories from school, from the football team, about his love of sports. She said David had wanted to be a soldier, that he wanted to serve, but she wouldn't talk about how she thought it was a mistake. At some point, Macky would press her for more details. Sandy had given the hat to Macky, a kid-sized version of what soldiers wore. It was a troubling reminder for her, but she tried not to let her mind go there.

She felt guilty continuing the myth of David as his father, but it was as important for her as it was for Macky to see him that way. It was a way of keeping David's memory alive while also pushing the secret of Whit to the background. If she told enough stories about David, then maybe they'd be true somehow. Would she ever tell Macky the truth? As long as Sandy and Burt were alive, she couldn't bear to break their hearts. Maybe one day she could tell him, but then would he hate her for hiding the truth all that time?

The next day, she dropped Macky off at school. He clutched his backpack, head lowered, and steamed through the crowd of kids out front of the school. "See you later, Macky."

She hung around until the mothers all left, then she entered the building and headed down the hall toward the principal's office with the same hollow stomachache she'd felt as a first-grader when she and Michelle had been sent there after breaking all the crayons in half so they could share them, which had seemed like a good idea at the time. The hall smelled the same as it had in her day—poster paint, graham crackers, and waxy milk cartons.

In the office, she found Mrs. Preston, Ms. Gannon, and a woman she hadn't met before, Ms. Filogrado, the school psychologist. They sat in a circle. The psychologist held a yellow pad of paper to take notes. Wanda wiped her sweaty palms on her sweater and crossed her arms.

"Mrs. Zacek," said the principal, "thank you for coming in on such short notice. I've been wanting to talk to you. I hope Macky is feeling better today."

Wanda said he was.

"This is not the first time he'd had some difficulty with other children, and frankly, we're concerned about him."

"What do you mean?" asked Wanda, who'd been hoping for an apology.

"He's had a difficult time fitting in so far this year."

"He's shy. It's only been a couple of weeks."

"True, but there are red flags."

"Oh?"

"Does he have friends outside of school?" asked Ms. Filogrado, taking notes.

"Not yet, but I'm hoping that'll happen this year."

Ms. Gannon said, "We're concerned that he puts himself at risk by his behavior."

"What do you mean?"

"There's no excuse for children teasing others," said the principal, "but some children create a situation where that's more likely to happen. Macky is a sweet boy."

"Thank you."

"But," the teacher continued, "he can also be blunt in ways that put people off." She looked angry, her eyebrows pinched. Was it possible she didn't like him? "He talks a lot during triangle time, bringing up facts the others aren't interested in."

"He tends to go on when he likes something."

"And he's sometimes rude. He told one boy he smelled bad."

"He is very sensitive to smells, but he shouldn't do that."

"And he refused to paint a picture."

"He doesn't like getting his hands messy."

"If it were up to him, he'd read all day." Ms. Gannon made air quotes when she said 'read.'

"He loves reading. And he's not faking. He can read really good."

"But kindergarten is more about his psycho-social development than it is about reading. I want him to fit in, to learn the kinds of things he needs to know in life."

Her head started to throb. "I'm sorry. I don't really understand. Isn't reading something he'll need in life?"

"Yes, but for instance, do you hold him to standards at home?" asked the psychologist.

"Of course, I do," said Wanda, hearing her voice shake.

"Sometimes," added the principal, "parents give in too easily to their children with all the best intentions, of course, but that can lead to enabling him." She nodded at the psychologist. "We know it's hard being a single mother. But sometimes parents, particularly single parents, have a hard time setting boundaries."

"I do my best. I'm sorry he's having a hard time." Her mother would say he just needed a spanking now and then.

"You must understand. He's a sweet, but very demanding, child who requires more than his share of my attention," said Ms. Gannon. "It's not fair to the others."

"Be assured, Mrs. Zacek," said Ms. Filogrado," that we want the best for Macky."

Wanda's stomach was churning, and it was hard taking everything in. "But I thought that because he's so smart—"

"He may be advanced in some areas," said the principal, "but behind in others. This is the time to focus on what he needs."

At the end of the meeting, she stood up. "I'm sorry he's having problems. I'll do my best and will talk to him." She stumbled out the door and held back her tears until she reached the street. Were they right that she was too loose with him? She should go back to the Barbers' and finish the job, but all she wanted was to go home and have a drink. No, she'd worked too hard to give in now. Besides, what would they think at the school if she showed up in an hour, smelling of beer? That would confirm the worst suspicions about her. In the mirror, her face looked blotchy and red from crying. She blew her nose and blotted her eyes before pouring a drink of water and picked up the phone to call Michelle. She could hear Michelle's kids in the background, and she asked how Michelle managed all her kids when Wanda couldn't even raise one without messing up. She told Michelle about Macky melting down at school and how the principal had said she was too easy on him.

"That's not right. Mean, wicked children."

"Mama?" Wanda could hear Kymberlee Faith's voice.

"That's good, baby," said Michelle. "Now go practice your letters." Kymberlee Faith was a year older than Macky, and she wasn't reading at all yet.

"You know what I think," said Michelle.

"I can't homeschool him."

"Why not? I'm doing it, and I was no student," she said, laughing.

"I have to work. And the books are expensive."

"We can lend you the books. I have crates of them. Come to our homeschooling moms' group and meet some of them. Macky'll do great."

Wanda didn't mention that Macky was way beyond any of her books. "But I don't go to your church."

"That doesn't matter. It's for sharing stories about homeschooling. We're meeting tomorrow. Come see what you think."

"Are you sure?"

"We'd be blessed to have you."

She hadn't really considered homeschooling Macky. How could she do it? She wasn't a teacher. How could she manage all his classes? And they'd get harder each year.

That evening, she sat with Macky at supper. Tonight, she let him read while he ate, and she watched him as he stared at the page, his food mostly untouched.

"Macky?"

He looked up through smudged glasses. She asked for them and wiped the lenses before placing them back on his face, running her finger along the curve of his ear. "How can you see to read when your glasses are so dirty?"

He shrugged.

"What do you like about school?"

"I like that there are lots of books, and I like the sun coming in the window when it's rug time. I like the sand table. And the rocking chair by the bookshelves."

"That sounds real nice." She watched him turn a page. "What don't you like?"

He looked at her warily.

"Go on. Tell me. I know you had a hard time with some kids. What really happened?"

"They took my hat and threw it over my head so I couldn't reach it, and they said they were going to flush it down the toilet."

"Tell me. Was Luke one of those kids?"

"Yeah."

She could picture Luke's brush of hair and his husky voice as he egged the others on. How she wished Macky weren't related to him.

"They said I couldn't play with them, but I didn't even want to. My teacher said we had to play outside. And she wouldn't let me bring my book."

"I'm so sorry those boys were mean. That's not right. But Ms. Gannon also says that sometimes you don't want to do what the group is doing."

"I don't like singing. It hurts my ears."

"Sometimes you need to go along when you're in a group. You could maybe sit quietly and think your own thoughts."

"I wanted to read, but Ms. Gannon said I couldn't. And then when I tried to talk during triangle time, she said I was talking too much."

"She probably wanted you to listen to others too."

"But I had things to say."

"Macky, I'm real proud that you're such a good reader and are so smart, but I also want you to learn how to get along in school."

"I don't like school."

That broke her heart. "Macky, you don't mean that, do you?"

"My teacher said I can't understand the books I'm reading. She says I'm faking it. And being braggy. But I read some of the book out loud to her, then she told me to sit down and be quiet and to stop sucking my finger. She said that children who suck their fingers can't read. But she's wrong because I can read, and I suck my finger."

"You have to try to break that habit, particularly at school. If kids see that, they might make fun of you. It's not fair, but it happens."

He put his head on the table and pulled the brim of his cap over his face. "Can we stop talking about this now?"

The following morning, she gave Macky a pep talk before dropping off at school. He looked unhappy but resigned. Then she drove to Michelle's. The mothers' group gathered in the Great Room, eight mothers and eighteen kids, aged toddler to twelve, she guessed. Michelle asked why she hadn't brought Macky along, and Wanda said she needed to decide before taking him out of school.

Michelle sent all but the very youngest to the basement rec room to play while the mothers had their meeting. They helped themselves to sweet tea, coffee, and cookies as they settled on the sectional and on folding chairs arranged in a square. Michelle led them in a prayer: "God, look over us today as we attempt to do your work and to raise our beautiful children in your name, according to your teachings. We ask a special blessing for Wanda. Help her make the righteous decision for her beautiful son, Macky." Wanda felt strangely moved and blinked back tears. She didn't buy into religion, but it felt good to be appreciated and cared for.

The women were all members of Michelle's church, and Wanda knew some of them from school. One of them, Cheryl Crane, had been wild in high school, dropping out pregnant in the 11th grade. She eventually married Herbie Cowen and had three more kids. Maybe the church had helped her straighten out.

Rather than a meeting, it was more of a social club for stay-at-home moms. They went around the circle and talked about Christian values and the importance of being with their children during the day to instill these values in them. They mentioned flexibility and letting each child follow his or her bliss, how the public school had lost the moral code it had once taught, how children there were ill-behaved and lacked direction. And of course, with such large classes, children could be lost in the shuffle. They talked about choice and nurturing, and how this group was like a big family, how it was a myth that homeschooled kids were antisocial or weird. And there was plenty of time to do things together, take hikes, make projects, read Bible stories, be a family.

Finally, the meeting ended, and Wanda thanked Michelle. "Everyone seems real nice."

"We would be blessed to have you join us," Michelle said at the front door. Wanda waved from her car. "I'll let you know. Thanks, again."

On the way home, she knew Michelle would be disappointed, but there was no way she could see Macky sitting around while others colored pictures of Jesus and read watered-down Bible stories. It was one thing to go to church on occasion, but mixing school and God wasn't for them.

That night, she went online and read about homeschooling and found a list of famous people who'd been homeschooled—Condoleeza Rice, Albert Einstein, Alan Alda as well as some Olympic athletes. It wasn't just Evangelical kids who won spelling bees and didn't believe in science. She found links to the state curriculum and saw that they'd send her materials. Maybe this could work.

She walked into the bedroom and sat down next to Macky on the bed. "Hey, what would you think about having our own homeschool, just the two of us?"

He put down his book. "I wouldn't go to school?"

"I could get the books and you'd do the work at home. Or at the library. And you could study nature outside and we could do projects. You could learn everything there is to know about lichens."

"I'm interested in trilobites now."

"Okay, then."

"And I wouldn't have to go back to Ms. Gannon's class?"

"Not if you don't want to. But it has to be a decision."

He chewed on his finger, staring across the room.

"But I don't want you to be lonely."

"You'll be here, Mama. Except when you're working. I can stay with Gramma Sandy and Grandpa Burt."

She figured they'd be happy to see more of him. "But we'll also work on getting you some friends."

He didn't answer. She wasn't sure if he even wanted friends, if he had any idea what that might mean. But putting him back in that school where he was miserable, where he was misunderstood and mistreated. She just couldn't do it.

She sent him in to brush his teeth, and she picked up clothes he'd dropped on the floor and folded them, laying them on the dresser. He popped back into bed, and she tucked him in, kissing him on top of the head, handing him his hat. "You can wear your hat all day if you want." Then she closed the door and pulled back her covers on the daybed, looking out the window toward the school, hoping she was making the right decision. Tomorrow, she'd go to the office and withdraw Macky from school. He'd show them. This felt right.

Lying in her bed, she realized she'd made this big decision without talking it over with David. She didn't know what he'd think, but she hoped he'd approve. Did that mean she was finally taking charge?

She got out of bed and opened the door to the bedroom as quietly as she could and watched Macky, now asleep, sprawled on the bed, the book by his side, his knees bent. Because of his allergies, he snored, a ragged sound that always surprised her by its deepness. Pulling back the covers, she slipped into bed next to him, not touching, but close enough to watch his face in the light from the open door. His lips were moving. He was dreaming, a good dream by the looks of it. She could smell his toothpaste breath coming toward her in puffs. Oh Macky. She closed her eyes and matched her breathing to his, knowing that whoever woke up first would see the other, close by, ready to meet what the day would bring.

14

CALLIE

By winter, Callie had finished the academic portion of the Pacific Arts Massage program and was doing practicums in preparation for her licensing exams in the spring. In the program, she'd made two friends, Ping and Olga, the three of them dedicated to the practice, unlike the New-Age types who'd dropped out after realizing massage therapy involved serious science and not just incense and oils. Ping was Chinese-American from California and Olga had been a massage therapist in Russia, but she'd had to redo the program to be licensed in the US. Callie had also moved out of Raquel's closet and into a sublet owned by Ping's cousin Xiao Jin. In exchange for watering the plants and keeping the place clean, she could stay for free. She'd kept her parents at arm's length, writing to them about her program, knowing they weren't happy, knowing her mother would never mention her courses in her letters, but she wanted them to know she was fine.

One night in February, she invited Ping and Olga over for wine and pizza so they could see each other and compare notes. Three more months before the licensing exam and they could start practicing for real, either at a hospital, a gym, or a spa.

When Ping and Olga arrived, Callie poured wine and dished out slices of pizza. As they perched on the sofa, Olga admired the apartment, eyeing the furniture, clearly assessing its value. "I'm so lucky," said Callie. "I mean, I can't even afford a crappy studio on my own. I just had to get out. I was literally sleeping in a closet."

"You are joking," said Olga.

"No, I am not. A nightmare."

"How often do you see Xiao Jin?" asked Ping.

"Almost never. Interns practically live at the hospital, and when she's here, she sleeps and is gone before I get up. It works for now, but I can't wait to get a job and find my own place."

"I need to make more money," said Olga. "I cannot believe I was forced to spend time studying material I already knew."

"I know," said Ping. "Frustrating. But you'll soon have more clients than you can handle." Ping added that she was worried she'd messed up one of her practicums. "This guy in his fifties with some neck tension failed to tell me in the intake that he'd had chemo. When I started doing petrissage on his back, he yelled at me and said I'd pressed too close to where his tumor had been. He never told me! But I should have asked."

"You're too hard on yourself," said Callie. "I'm sure it went better than that. Don't you think that Mr. Yeung gives you challenging cases because he knows you can do them?"

Ping had great instincts and could problem-solve. Olga was experienced and knowledgeable, but her strong accent made it hard for her to communicate without sounding brusque. She was the one who could give Callie practical advice. Callie's practicums had gone well. She liked working on clients—a young woman with whiplash, an old man with lumbar compression, and a child with Muscular Dystrophy. The academic work had been interesting and challenging, but now that she was actually called upon to figure out a plan for a client, she loved putting the pieces together.

When Callie reached for another piece of pizza, she knocked over her glass of red wine onto the sofa. "Oh, fuck!" She popped up and ran into the kitchen for a wad of paper towels. "Xiao Jin is going to kill me."

"Do you have any sparkling water?" asked Ping. "And bring some salt."

Callie grabbed a bottle and the salt and Ping sprinkled water on the spot and shook a handful of salt over the stain. The red wine had soaked into the floral print of the sofa. Callie was sweating, her heart pounding.

"Let it sit and you'll be fine," said Ping. "Trust me."

After that was done, Ping asked Olga about her young son and how he was doing in school, but Callie was jangled and distracted and couldn't focus. When they left, she checked the spot but knew she wouldn't be able to tell until the morning if the trick had worked. What if Xiao Jin kicked her out? She didn't have enough money yet for a security deposit and first month's rent for a new place. How quickly everything could go south.

The next morning, she brushed the salt off the sofa and found the stain had vanished. A relief. She was due to work at the café before an afternoon practicum. It was sunny and unusually warm for February, and she set out for the bus stop. She loved her neighborhood, Andersonville, with its cafés, restaurants, and bookstores, and she looked forward to a time when she didn't have to be so careful about money.

When she'd first started the program, she pored over her textbook with the drawings of red muscles, the strands feeding into tendons and ligaments, cushioning the skeleton. How beautiful and complex was the human body. She pictured her own injured neck with its tiny tears and why, because the neck had to work full time supporting her head, it had taken so long for her muscles to heal.

Many of the terms came from Greek, which always made her think of her father. She collected beautiful names for awful conditions—hematemesis (vomiting blood), menorrhagia (heavy periods), and dysphagia (difficulty swallowing). She wished her father could see her using Greek, not as literature, but for science. For a while, in her letters home, she'd told her parents she was studying anatomy and physiology, but her mother never commented on her studies, and her father never wrote more than a scribbled line, so Callie decided not to write anymore about the program until she was licensed and had a job.

Now, five months in, she found herself diagnosing the skeletal problems of people she encountered walking around on the streets—the girl with scoliosis, the man with the swayback and locked knees, the old woman whose rounded shoulders and humped back signaled osteoporosis. The man at the deli straining to lift a box over his head mostly likely had rotator cuff tears. At the café, she saw what hunching all day over a computer did to the upper back and neck. She felt like an x-ray machine peering beneath the skin to detect problems.

She walked past the Starbucks at the corner of Berwyn and Clark, looked in and saw Malcolm, a guy she'd slept with a few times, earbuds trailing from his head as he frowned at his laptop. So, this was where he now hung out since they'd broken up. She ducked her head and walked past the café, making a note not to go there in the future.

What had she been thinking? A philosophy grad student? Really? Those Ivory Tower types. Emotionally stunted like Greg. Recently, she'd googled Greg and found that he was tutoring for Stanley Kaplan doing SAT prep. Had he chosen that job for its unending supply of eighteen-year-olds, eager to admire him?

As she stood waiting for the bus, her phone rang. It was her parents' number. Strange. She and her parents rarely talked on the phone. The door swooshed open, and she swiped her bus pass, found a seat, and answered. "Hello?"

"Callie, dear," her mother said, her voice shaky. "I have bad news. It's your father."

"What happened?"

"He died this morning."

"Oh, no. How?"

"A stroke."

"Oh, Momma." Her vision blurred. "A stroke? How?" A woman with overstuffed grocery bags sat next to her. "I can't believe it." She was crying, her head turned toward the grimy window.

"I decided no service. Just a reception at the house. Would you come home?"

Home. "When is it?"

"Thursday at two."

"I can't believe he's gone," she said, realizing she hadn't seen him in almost two years. "I can use that ticket."

"I have so much to do."

"I'm just taking this in."

"The reception is at two. You'll be there?"

"Yes, I'll figure it out." She felt her throat tighten. "Mom, I wish I were there now."

"I do too. Goodbye."

She sat, her nose fogging the window, remembering the last time she saw her father, the day she left with Greg. He hadn't realized it was goodbye, and she was afraid to hug him for fear that it would tip her hand, so she acted as if it were just any day. He hadn't even looked up from his reading when she'd popped her head in the door of his study to say she was going over to the campus. He looked old and frail sitting there at his desk, patting his prosthetic eye with a handkerchief because his eye watered. Now she wished she had given him a hug.

Why hadn't she made the effort to go home at least once? Her mother had repeatedly urged her to come and had sent her an open-ended ticket, but Callie was too ashamed to face them. And the longer she stayed away, the harder it became. She'd always thought there'd be time to make up with her parents. Once she had a career and could show them she was on solid footing, maybe they'd accept that she'd done the right thing for herself in the long run. Her father had been in his fifties when she was born, so he'd always seemed old to her, particularly compared to the fathers of her friends. Somehow though, she'd never really thought of his dying. And now it was too late to make peace.

She nearly missed her stop at Grace but then vaulted out of her seat toward the front of the bus. The driver had to reopen the door for her. She thanked him and stumbled out onto the street. She made arrangements at the café to take a few days off, but Mr. Yeung refused to let her reschedule her Wednesday practicum on such short notice and still allow her to graduate on time.

She pleaded with him, but he wouldn't budge. So, she decided to fly home on Thursday morning and arrive before the reception and then stay until Sunday to help her mother out. She hoped her mother would understand. There'd be more time for the two of them to talk after the reception. It was the best she could do. Then she tried to text Ping to ask her to take in her mail, but her hands were shaking so much she kept making mistakes.

Back at her apartment, as she threw clothes into a duffle, she wondered what it would feel like to go home again, to see only her mother, to sleep in her old bed. She could smell her father's pipe tobacco, see his messy head of white hair, hear him clear his throat. Who would she see in town? She texted Elise to let her know, hoping, but not counting, on her taking time to come home. The same with Zelda at Tufts. Besides Whit, only two other classmates had gone to Brewster, but they weren't friends and would have no reason to show up. There was no one among the townies or farmers whom she wanted to see. All her close friends had moved away.

On Thursday, she dressed in a black knit top and skirt, flew home, wondering, as she sat in the plane, what stories had circulated around Shelton when she and Greg disappeared. What had her mother told her own friends to explain Callie's absence? What did her mother say now that they were back in touch? That Callie was in school, that she was on a path to a career? Or did she avoid talking about Callie altogether? Was it hard for them—it must have been—to explain her absence? Her mother had made that clear, but it always felt more about her judgment and embarrassment than concern for Callie. How had Callie not seen that until now?

She caught a cab at the airport, arriving an hour before the reception, terrified of seeing her mother again. But when Callie caught sight of her, looking exhausted and old, her skin pale, her eyes swollen, Callie melted. Her mother's lips trembled when she saw Callie and opened her arms. Callie walked into a hug. "Mama, I'm so sorry. I wish I'd been here to see him."

Her mother hugged her hard and said she was so glad to see her. Callie let the hug last, listening to her mother's stuffy nose and choked sobs. Her mother felt so thin and small. Was that new?

Callie walked around, taking everything in. The dining room furniture had been moved toward the walls and the table was covered with a cloth, trays, and a coffee urn. In the front parlor, she spotted a hospital bed, folded up, and detected the lingering smell of disinfectant and rubbing alcohol. Back in the dining room, she asked, "Mom? Why were you using a hospital bed for Dad?"

"Your father couldn't climb stairs anymore, so he was sleeping in here."

"How long had he been doing that?"

"Since the first stroke."

"First stroke? He had more than one?"

"Well, yes." She was nesting spoons on the tablecloth. "He'd been sick for a while."

"Why am I just hearing about this now? Why didn't you tell me when it happened?"

"Would that have made a difference? You know we wanted you to come home."

"If I'd known he was sick, I'd have come home."

Her mother trained her watery eyes on Callie. "I've been coping with a lot here, and I made it very clear we wanted to see you. Besides, you and your father had barely spoken since you left, and I didn't want to subject him to turmoil that would make him worse."

"Seeing me would cause turmoil? It might have given us a chance to make peace. Or at least to try to clear the air."

"I could not take that chance. It could have been a disaster."

"We'll never know. I'll never see him again." She stood there, eyes stinging, swallowing back her anger and hurt. And her guilt.

The doorbell rang, and her mother turned to answer it while Callie wiped her eyes and pulled herself together. A young woman with blond curly hair entered and threw her arms around her mother. "Mrs. Morton, I'm so sorry." Her mother put her head on the woman's shoulder and wept. "Of course, it's so hard." The woman was about Callie's age and looked vaguely familiar.

The woman looked over. "Oh, Callie, you're here."

"Of course, I'm here." A warm flush flooded her face.

The woman rushed toward her and gave her a big hug as well.

"Callie?" Her mother said. "You remember Wanda." Her mother was smiling now, having perked up for company.

"Sure, of course," but she really didn't know this person. She backed away from the clinch, the smell of Wanda's soap lingering.

"Wanda is going to help with the food and clean-up." Wanda put her arm around Callie's mother's waist and gave her a squeeze. Who was this?

"I'll stay out of your way." Wanda had brought a casserole covered with foil that she took out of a bag. Callie's mother thanked her and said she loved that dish. Wanda carried it into the kitchen.

Their argument interrupted, Callie hadn't yet finished telling her mother how hurt she was, but now with that woman in the house, and the guests due to arrive, all she could do was whisper, "Mom, we need to talk more about this."

"Not now. Later."

Fighting back tears of anger and hurt, Callie couldn't bear to stand at the door with her mother, acting as it they were getting along, so she busied herself behind the drink table, putting out cups and saucers. Her face felt flushed, her legs wobbly, and she watched her mother receive hugs from friends as they filed in. Many of the people she recognized from the college—professors and their spouses, a couple of women from her mother's book club, Mr. Cooper from the pharmacy. There was no one her age except this Wanda. Elise's parents arrived and said Elise wanted to send her love, but Callie wondered why Elise hadn't called Callie herself. Well, she had sent a short text. Callie forced herself to face the guests as they approached her, offering their condolences, and she welcomed having a task that would give her something to do and say.

When Whit's parents arrived, Mr. Sutter lingered near the door talking to Mr. Winfred, but Mrs. Sutter, tall and thin, her gray hair tightly curled, headed right toward Callie, giving her a faint smile. Reaching the table, she took Callie's hand in her cool palm and said she was sorry for their loss. "What an intellect. Everyone respected him." Callie thanked her and offered to pour her a cup. Mrs. Sutter chose a tea bag and held up her cup. Callie's hands shook as she poured the water.

"Mrs. Sutter, I haven't seen you, and I should have written. I am so sorry about Whit. Just so sorry."

Mrs. Sutter's eyes misted, and her mouth tightened. "Thank you, dear." She put her cookie and tea down on the table. The teacup rattled in its saucer. "I miss him a lot."

"I'm sure you do."

"He always had such nice things to say about you. In his own unique way, of course. He was very shy around girls."

Callie wondered if she knew he'd had a crush on her. "He was so smart. Way smarter than anyone in our grade. I couldn't begin to keep up with him. He always helped me with my math."

"Math was his first language. Talking to girls was a lot harder for him."

Callie struggled to think of something more to say. "Well, he was just so smart." Why was it so hard to form words? Her mouth felt frozen, her jaws ached from the effort to speak.

"I wish smart had been enough."

Callie felt her face burn as she remembered yelling at Whit at the bonfire after graduation, watching him slunk away, humiliated, clutching his yearbook.

"But today is about your father," the woman said, patting Callie's hand. "He will be missed," she said before heading back toward her husband.

Mr. Gooden from the Classics Department walked up to the table. When Callie handed him a cup of coffee, he said, "So, I see you're back from your *Rumspringa*."

Her scalp contracted. "Excuse me?"

"Are you done with your wandering and ready to go back to school now?"

"I *am* in school."

"Oh, where?"

"I've been studying massage therapy in Chicago. I'm about to get my license."

He raised his eyebrows, sniffed, and took another cookie before walking away, pipe smell wafting after him. Feeling faint, she ducked into the kitchen and splashed sulphury water on her face. Wanda was peeling cling film from a tray of cookies. "How're you holding up?" she asked.

Unable to face her or anyone else, Callie slipped into her father's study and shut the door behind her. The smell of old books and dust made her nose stuff up. The desk was piled with yellowed papers and manila folders. The chair and the same crocheted afghan slung over it, and the mahogany sleigh bed was covered with needlework throw pillows stitched by her mother over the years. When she was growing up, her father worked in his office every night after dinner and well after she went up to bed. The next morning, he'd be working there, prompting Callie to believe he'd slept on the sleigh bed. Today, she almost expected to find him sitting behind his desk avoiding his own guests, hiding behind the comfort of his books.

Callie loved this room with its floor-to-ceiling shelves of books, their smell, their feel. Her mother tried to keep her out of there, even when her father wasn't home. "Flimmits," was how young Callie understood "Off Limits" at the time. But that made the study all the more tempting. Sometimes, she'd sneak in, curl up under the afghan, tucking it around her feet, sinking back into the pillows, a book resting on her knees. Always so focused on his work, her father never seemed to notice her there. It was their time though, the two of them, to read silently together. Once, her mother came in and attempted to shoo Callie out. Her father looked up and said, "Oh, she can stay."

"As long as you're not disturbing your father."

They didn't talk, but she loved this time together with him, just the two of them.

Today, she opened her father's Greek dictionary sitting on his desk, hoping to find words she could recognize, but aside from making out single letters of the alphabet, she couldn't read any of the words. It's not as if she could understand Greek. When she put the book on his desk, she found a manilla folder with the name Callie on it. Opening it, she found a number of papers—crayon drawings of cats she'd made as a little girl, a scratched photo of her on a swing, a dried flower, a card she drew for him for Father's Day, a copy of her graduation speech where he'd added edits but also had written Good Point! in the margins (none of which he'd showed to her), and finally, an article on the benefits of massage which he'd highlighted. She burst into tears, hugging the folder to her as she rocked.

Her father had been so angry when she left, so disappointed that she ran out on Brewster in such a deceitful way. During her phone calls with her mother, he rarely got on the line and even then didn't say much. She figured he was too angry, and that she wouldn't have the words to explain herself. But maybe he'd wanted to talk, but her mother had stood in the way, so they never did. She could have been the bridge to bring them together. Had she been jealous of Callie's connection to her father and stood in the way of their making peace?

She sat for a while, steadying her breathing, wiping her eyes, wishing she could slip out of the study and out the front door. Knowing her eyes were red and swollen, she didn't want to see anyone. As she poked her head out of the study door, she heard Wanda at the front door. "I'll come on Tuesday as usual. Are you going to be all right?" Her mother said something Callie couldn't make out. She touched Wanda's cheek and smiled.

When her mother saw Callie, she sat down, patting the cushion next to her. "Where were you? People were asking."

"I just couldn't face them." Callie sat down on the other side of the room.

"I needed you, but you were off by yourself."

"Does it even matter that I was here?" She said, standing up, her voice shaking as she drew the cloth from the table and shook it out.

"Yes, of course. This was your chance to honor your father."

"Isn't it too late for that? You didn't give me a chance to see him before he died. So, you only wanted me here so you could prove to your friends that I'd show up?"

"I should have told you. I regret that. But you cut us out of your life."

"I would have come home if I'd known."

"I asked you to come, but then I realized you wouldn't be able to help me."

"Well, you never gave me the chance to show you."

"Callie, I can't do this now. I'm exhausted. Can we talk more in the morning?"

"Okay, fine." She refused to look up and stared at the paisley pattern in the rug between her feet. Her mother sat for a moment, blowing her nose and crying. Then she sighed, pulled herself to her feet, and went upstairs. To make sure her mother was in her room for the night, Callie pulled the furniture back into place, dropped the tablecloth on top of the washing machine, and started the dishwasher before she also climbed the stairs.

Except for scattered papers and misaligned books, her bedroom looked just as it had when she was living at home—the same chenille bedspread, lamp, bookshelf, bulletin board with ribbons and photos. On her dresser sat her jewel box with a charm bracelet, a plastic snap arm cuff, and a pair of gold earrings from her mother she'd left behind. She pocketed the earrings. A jumble of papers littered her desk, her high-school notebooks piled on top. No clues to be found there in her above-board life. Then she remembered her journal, where she'd vented for two years about her parents but had forgotten in her haste to take. She lifted the mattress, breathless, afraid her mother had found it and read her private thoughts. But there it was, where she'd left it, untouched. Fingers trembling, she opened the book, thumbing through the early entries. It was painful now to read her longing, her desperation to leave Shelton and her parents' control.

I CAN'T BELIEVE MY PARENTS WON'T LET ME APPLY TO COLUMBIA OR NYU. SO UNFAIR. I'VE WORKED SO HARD AND NOW I CAN'T GO WHERE I WANT. I HAVE TO BE IN A CITY. I'M DYING HERE.

MATT AND I WENT TO HIS BROTHER'S HOUSE AND WE HUNG OUT IN HIS BASEMENT. I LOVE BEING WITH HIM. I WISH WE'D GOTTEN TOGETHER EARLIER. EVERY TIME I THINK OF HIM I PRACTICALLY HAVE AN O.

I CAN'T FIGURE MATT OUT. HE'S SO EMO ABOUT HOCKEY. BUT DID I DO SOMETHING WRONG?

Then there was a long, painful entry about the party where she found him being blown by that skank. Then Greg entered the scene, and her mood improved. She talked about how smart he was and how she wished he'd notice her. She also started writing entries in French, as if her parents couldn't crack that code.

G. EST MERVEILLEUX. MAIS IL PENSE QUE JE SUIS UNE JEUNE FILLE.

It was painful to read her complete faith in a future with him.
JE L'AIME IL M'AIME!

Feeling suddenly weary, she peeled back the covers of her bed and slipped between the stale-smelling sheets. Looking out the window at the still, bare branches of the elm, she picked up the journal and started to read again. The entries from the summer became more cryptic, but she could see the plans for their escape. The last entry in the journal, written the day before they were due to leave, said *LE JOUR DE MA LIBERTÉ.* What a fool she'd been. She rarely thought about Greg anymore, shaking off memories when they popped up, but being in the room where she'd spent so much time longing for him brought back an intense wave of feelings. No wonder she'd been so eager to get out of this house. Greg had seemed like her way out.

The next morning, she found her mother reading at the kitchen table. She poured a tea and sat down too, opening the paper, and reading the front page. After a while, she asked her mother what she could do to help and offered to finish putting linens and silver away. For the rest of the day and the next, she found ways to keep busy and separate from her mother. Sitting eating leftovers from the reception, they barely spoke. It was just too hard to know what to say that wouldn't start their argument up again. What was the point of that? The following day, Sunday, she was due to leave. Her mother offered to drive her to the airport, but she'd already ordered a cab. She stood at the door, knowing she should comfort her mother, but feeling it nearly impossible to do so. She gave her a quick hug and then took her bag to the cab. At least she was on her way back home again.

PART 3

15

WANDA

Wanda hadn't slept well, worried about Macky's breathing. He was working on his two front teeth, which always made him cough and wheeze. In addition, a recurrence of croup had sent him to the ER yesterday. They'd had a busy Easter. First, there was the egg hunt at Sandy and Burt's, then a big family dinner at the farm. Macky had been wheezing some but had seemed fine. After the long day though and the dry air from the wood stove, he could barely breathe when they got home. He tended to have croup in the cold, dry air of winter, but this was April. A freak dip in the temperature made her father fire up the stove again. Macky went to bed early but woke up at eight with a tight wheeze and hoarse bark. Wanda turned on the shower to steam his chest, but it didn't work. His lips were blue, and he couldn't catch his breath, so she panicked and called 911, and they sent the EMTs. Benny Carbo was on duty. He greeted Macky, "Hey, Mack the Knife! Lookin' sharp, huh?" Macky lay under the covers, clutching a book, but not reading. She worried he'd have a panic attack on top of the croup, and then he'd be in real trouble. She was so relieved to see them start him on a nebulizer, but Benny thought he needed to go to the ER. Somehow, they settled him in the ambulance without Macky resisting. This was how Wanda knew he was really sick. Usually, when anyone came at him unexpectedly, he'd freak out. This time he let them lift him into the ambulance. His eyes though, round and scared, told her he was terrified. In the ambulance, her own heart racing, she told him he was going to be fine.

Wanda and Benny had known each other in school. He was Kenny's age and had married Connie Butler. They'd had two girls, but then they'd split up and she'd kept the kids in the house, and he'd moved to an apartment out behind the high school. About a year ago, Benny had asked Wanda out to dinner. He'd talked about his marriage and his girls, and she'd told him about losing David and how Macky had saved her. He was nice, but he had a gut and thinning hair, and she really didn't want to get involved with a divorced guy. Besides, she had to put Macky first. He asked her out again, but she kept saying she was busy until he stopped calling.

At the ER, the doctor on call said that Macky was stable, but they put him in a room with the nebulizer to wait for his oxygen levels to return to normal. However, when Macky started to feel better, he fought off the nurse when she tried to place the nebulizer over his face again, and Wanda had to lean in. "Look at me. Breathe. Slow down. The nurse needs to do this."

"He's six, right?" the nurse asked. "Is he Special Needs?"

"Of course not," she said, insulted. "He's very smart." She could feel her pulse race when the nurse spoke to him like he was simple-minded. "He understands you," Wanda said. "He just doesn't like being touched without being asked."

"Well, I have to touch him so maybe you could explain." Wanda convinced Macky to let her put the air machine close to his nose. The nurse held it up for short bursts of air, removing it and then giving him some more. Macky squeezed his eyes shut and let her do it.

As the nurse set the mask aside, she asked, "Is he up to date with his vaccinations?"

Wanda said he was, but she'd let the booster timeline lapse. Michelle didn't vaccinate her children and warned Wanda not to let doctors put that poison into Macky. At first, Wanda had done what Dr. Frogg asked because at that point, he was headed for public school. But now that he was being homeschooled, she thought maybe they'd take a break. Was it too late though? Had he developed autism? She certainly wasn't going to tell this nurse anything.

"You don't want him to get measles," the nurse said. "We're seeing more cases. The MMR is the one you want to get."

"We'll be fine," Wanda said, but the nurse pursed her lips and clearly found Wanda and Macky difficult.

After a couple of hours, Macky was breathing more deeply, and his oxygen levels had returned to normal. Wanda called Michelle for a ride back home. She checked on him several times during the night, afraid to leave him alone too long.

Ordinarily, she'd have left Macky with Sandy when she had a cleaning job, but today, she wanted to keep an eye on him. She'd let him sleep until right before they had to leave for Mrs. Morton's.

She cut up chicken and potatoes and put them in the slow cooker for supper that night. Those were the only things he'd eat for supper these days. He'd pitch a fit if he saw even a sprig of parsley. For his breakfast, she sprayed the skillet with Pam to scramble him an egg. And she popped a slice of wheat bread into the toaster and grabbed the oat milk from the fridge. He still hated dairy and anyway, she didn't want to make him more congested.

Pouring herself a mug of coffee, she opened the door to the bedroom. "Macky, sweetie, time to get up." He groaned and burrowed his head under the covers, his book lying next to him. She suspected he'd read late into the night. It was a struggle for her to get him to put down his book and go to sleep. If it were up to him, he'd read all night. Sometimes, Sandy came over to watch him, or Wanda delivered him to her house in his PJ's. Would it have been easier if he'd had a regular schedule in public school or would each morning be a battle?

"Macky? We're due at Mrs. Morton's in twenty minutes. I need you to get up."

A muffled voice said, "I am."

"I can tell you're laying in bed. Come on."

"Can't I just stay home? Can Grandma Sandy come over?"

"She's busy today, and I want to watch your breathing. And I'm not supposed to leave you alone until you're older." Although Wanda knew he wouldn't do anything dangerous, he'd just read all morning, she couldn't take the risk.

Wanda wished he had a naughty streak, getting into mischief with friends, coming home dirty and exhausted, keeping secrets from her about what he'd been up to, but Macky spent all his time with her when he wasn't with Sandy and Burt. They did school in the afternoons, and she made sure he got exercise, a nature walk or a run around the park. No books allowed. He needed time to be a kid. Michelle's children were sweet but not in his league. And so churchy. Luke and Simon were mean as snakes and his girl cousins annoyed him. Homeschooling didn't help him find friends. She wished he could find one shy, smart kid like him.

Macky stumbled into the kitchen with an open book, and he sat down, resting his head on his hand, pushing his smudged glasses up on his nose. Wanda would ask him if she could give them a swipe before they left. "How do you feel?" He shrugged. She set down the egg and toast and poured him a glass of oat milk. He made a face. "Eat, but don't read. There's not time."

But she knew she'd have to watch to make sure he didn't dump the expensive milk down the sink. "Five minutes and we're out of here." Too much pushing and he dug in his heels. A hard balance to strike.

The other day, when checking the browser history on the computer, she saw that Macky had been researching the Iraq War, particularly battles in Diyala Province, where David had been killed. When Macky was three, she'd explained to him that before he was born, David had died in the war. She knew that Sandy often talked to Macky about his father, but Wanda was careful not to call him that, just David or her husband, carefully threading the needle between truth and a lie. She wanted Macky to know David was important and people loved him. Wanda usually waited for Macky to ask questions, which she answered truthfully but without much detail. She knew that one day, he would ask her a question where she'd have to tell the truth. Until then, she'd keep the myth of David-as-father alive. How would she ever tell him there were two fathers, his real one, who killed himself, and the other who was also dead? How could a child ever understand that? Lately, Macky had been asking about what David liked to do, what he did for work, what his favorite books were. (David was definitely not a book person.) When she talked about David, she said he was strong and kind and brave, and he liked to play football and video games. She said they'd grown up together, and she missed him. Was it too late to tell the truth and would Macky hate her for it? She barely knew anything about Whit, only what she could see in Macky— his intelligence, his curiosity, his brown hair, his bad eyes. What else might show up? His awkwardness, his depression?

So far, Macky hadn't shown any interest in sports, the gloves and bats Sandy and Burt gave him sitting unused in the closet. She hadn't had the heart to donate David's video games to the church rummage sale. After nearly seven years, they were probably too old now.

"Macky, we're off." She told him he could brush his teeth later. He showed up in sweatpants and a tee-shirt, his hair un-combed, his eyes crusty with sleep. Without thinking, she reached to touch his head, but he ducked. She didn't take it personally. As a little guy, he hadn't liked being held, wriggling out of her arms after a short cuddle. Even now, he stripped naked every chance he got, as if clothes hurt his skin. She'd learned to leave a space between them, even as she itched to run her hand over his, to pull him onto her lap, to stroke his hair, his back, to smell his scalp. At these moments, she missed David's touch, skin touching skin, the smell, the warmth.

On the way to Mrs. Morton's, Wanda asked Macky what he was reading. He said it was a book on physics. "Above my head," she said.

"You could understand it if you wanted to, Mom," he said, returning to the book.

Wanda liked homeschooling Macky, enjoyed thinking up projects for him, letting him run with his own ideas. He loved science, math, and reading. Wanda loved reading too, although she read mysteries and historical fiction. She also liked science, but he was on another level altogether. She let him use the Internet two hours a day; the rest of the time, he read or did experiments. He'd run through the first few years of the state's homeschooling curriculum in a few months. Now he was doing sixth-grade work. At this rate, he'd finish high school by the time he was thirteen, if not sooner. What would they do then? Would he go to college at that age? He could get a scholarship to Brewster and live at home. But was he meant for bigger things, a life beyond Shelton, a life away from her? Would he leave her behind, his dull, average mom?

She pulled into the driveway at Mrs. Morton's, and Macky hopped out of the backseat as she retrieved her bucket of cleaning supplies from the trunk. Usually, Mrs. Morton opened the door for her, but not today. Wanda knocked, but no one answered. She rang the bell. Finally, she pushed open the door, stuck her head inside, and called, "Mrs. Morton? It's Wanda and Macky." No answer.

This was strange. Mrs. Morton always had a list of tasks for her to do. And if Macky was with her, she'd offer him a ginger snap, which he'd take and stuff into his pocket, where it would end up a gloppy mess in the wash.

Wanda nudged Macky into the living room and told him to sit tight and read. He backed into a faded armchair and kicked off his shoes.

In the kitchen, sardine and tuna cans littered the counter. The garbage overflowed and smelled of rotten fish. Mrs. Morton must not have washed a dish or taken out the trash since Wanda was there a week ago. She wasn't a great housekeeper, but she'd never left a mess like this before.

Worried now, Wanda walked to the foyer and called up the stairs. "Mrs. Morton?" She thought she heard a sound but couldn't be sure. She climbed the stairs and stood outside Mrs. Morton's bedroom, where the door stood ajar. She knocked lightly. "Mrs. Morton? Do you need any help?"

A faint voice said, "I'm fine," but Wanda could smell something sour.

"Mrs. Morton? I'm coming in, okay?"

"Oh, dear. I'm not decent."

"I don't mind. I just want to make sure you're all right."

Mrs. Morton sat in bed, naked, a soiled nightgown and underpants on the floor. Her long, thin hair fell loose and stringy around her shoulders. The smell made Wanda's stomach rise.

"What are you doing here?" asked the woman, clutching the sheet to her bare chest, her bony shoulders hunched. "I said I wasn't decent."

"I thought you might need help."

"Go back downstairs," she said, her voice weak. "Don't look at me."

"Mrs. Morton, it's just an accident. I've seen worse. Believe me. I'm going to draw a bath and you can get cleaned up."

"I take showers. Just let me do it myself."

"You might fall."

"Don't tell me what to do. You're here to clean."

"And this is a cleaning job. You need some help. Please." She reached for Mrs. Morton, who batted at her, but she was so weak, she barely made contact. Wanda took her wrist as gently as she could and looked straight into the woman's face to see if her pupils were the same size or her mouth was crooked. "I'm a lot stronger than you are. I've done my share of cleaning up after people. You have to let me do this. Just sit tight." Mrs. Morton muttered to herself but didn't move. "Stay in bed." Wanda hurried into the bathroom down the hall and turned on the water for a bath, grabbing the biggest, least threadbare towel she could find.

Back in the bedroom, she opened the window and turned on a table fan, aiming it toward the outside. "I'll catch a chill," said Mrs. Morton.

"I have to air out the room good. I'll close it after you've had your bath. Sorry you're cold. The bath will warm you up." She wrapped the towel around Mrs. Morton's shoulders and let it cover her as she helped her stand. The woman's back and chest were dotted with age spots, and the skin on her upper arms hung slack. Although she was thin, her belly sagged, a pouch of skin above thin pubic hair. The room smelled like a cage.

"Where is Herbert?" Mrs. Morton's husband, gone now for years.

"Do you know what day it is?" asked Wanda.

"What kind of question is that?" Mrs. Morton asked, looking at her bedside clock.

"I'm concerned you've been sick and have been laying in bed all this time."

"Lying, not laying."

"Has this kind of thing happened before?" Wanda was helping her take shaky, stiff steps toward the bathroom. She could feel her narrow shoulders and bony arms through the terry cloth. Clearly, Mrs. Morton hadn't been eating properly.

"I'm fine. It was just a stupid accident."

Wanda lowered the toilet seat and backed Mrs. Morton onto it. Wanda knelt to test the water temperature, and Mrs. Morton perched on the seat, shivering, hugging the towel around her. Wanda found a sliver of soap, then stood and helped her into the bath after first wiping off the worst of the mess with a wet washcloth. She noticed that the woman's skin was red and inflamed in several places, and that her legs had grown skinny.

"Ma'am, your skin is broken out, and it'll get infected if I don't clean you up good." She sponged carefully. "Has a doctor seen these sores?"

"I don't need a doctor," she said, wheezing. "I just need to get clean and dressed."

"Should I call someone who can look in on you?"

"I've been living by myself for a while now. I don't need a nursemaid."

"There's no shame in getting some help. Where's your daughter?"

"Callie lives in Chicago, and she's very busy. I don't need help."

"She'll want to pay you a visit."

"Don't meddle in my family's business."

After the bath, Wanda set her again on the seat as she dabbed antibiotic cream on the sore areas, then covered them with ancient Band-Aids that barely stuck. "That'll have to do for now." She walked Mrs. Morton back into the bedroom and sat her in a chair before closing the window. Then she found a clean nightgown in the dresser and helped her into it, putting clean sheets on the bed. She plumped the pillows and settled Mrs. Morton under the covers. "There. You get some rest, and I'll bring you something to eat in a bit."

"If it's not too much trouble."

"Not at all."

She went downstairs to try to locate an address book and found Macky reading, his finger up a nostril.

"Hey, Bud, sorry this is taking so long. You okay?"

"Yeah, he said and wiped his hand on his pants.

"Okay." She sifted through the mess of papers on the kitchen table. Mrs. Morton stored business cards and notes under a placemat. Once, Wanda had put them in a separate pile and then she'd had to listen to a lecture about not throwing away important papers. Today, she gathered the cards and flipped through, finding one for a Dr. Kellogg, a neurologist, with an upcoming appointment inked on the front. Did Mrs. Morton have Parkinson's or maybe a stroke? Should she call an ambulance?

Wanda wondered how to get in touch with her daughter in Chicago. That girl hadn't lived in Shelton since she ran off with the teacher from the college. The only time she'd seen Callie since then was after her father died. At the reception, Callie hadn't helped her mother out at all, hiding away most of the time in her father's study. True, she was in mourning, but so was her mother. When Wanda had tried to be nice, Callie had snapped at her. Why didn't she pay better attention to her mother? Maybe some bad blood between them? Still, daughters, especially only children, had obligations, no matter what.

What Wanda remembered of Callie from high school wasn't positive. Wanda graduated a year ahead of her, so they were never in classes together and they didn't run with the same crowds. Callie hung out with the honor students. Come to think of it, she and Whit must have been in the same classes. She remembered seeing Callie every day on the school bus, but they never sat together. Callie used to come to the bakery when Wanda was working there, but they barely talked. What a stuck-up brat.

Next, Wanda tackled the mess of books on the shelf next to the kitchen table and found the address book, full of brittle pages covered in tiny, neat writing. Many entries had been crossed out, with new addresses added. She looked under M and found Calliope. There was a PO box in New York City, then a couple of addresses in Chicago.

Wanda used Mrs. Morton's old rotary phone to dial the number. No answer, but she got the machine. *This is Callie Morton at Ravenswood Health Club. If you want to make a massage appointment, please leave your name and number. Namaste.*

"Callie, this is Wanda Zacek. Remember? I clean for your mother? When I got here today, she wasn't doing so good. She's not eating regular, and she seemed kind of fuzzy and out of it. Can you give me a call?" She left her cell number.

In the living room, Macky lay on his belly, his knees bent, feet crossed at the ankles, as he lined up lead soldiers, knocking them down, one by one. "I told you not to touch anything that's not yours."

"I finished my book." He clicked two soldiers together.

"Go outside but put your coat on. If you start wheezing, come back inside. I'll be done soon."

He slipped out the front door and headed into the side yard. She called Dr. Kellogg's office and got their machine. She'd try again later. But there were limits to what she could or should do. This was something for Callie to figure out.

She'd do a surface cleaning and come back later in the week to finish.

He returned a few minutes later, having found a broken bird shell and some rocks, asking when they could go home.

"If I find you a book, would you sit down and read until I'm done?" She stepped over to the shelf, pulled out a copy of *Oliver Twist*, and handed it to Macky. He studied the spine, sniffed and opened it. Give that child a book, from the age of three, and he'd read it.

She checked in on Mrs. Morton, who was sleeping, her breathing ragged but not labored, then she returned to the kitchen. She opened the refrigerator and threw out the worst of the spoiled food, rinsed the fish tins, tossed them into recycling, and wiped down the counter. Next week, she'd bring a casserole. Now at least the house smelled better. Someone else would have to take over for Mrs. Morton.

At ten, she called Dr. Kellogg's office. The receptionist said she'd relay the message to the doctor, but she couldn't reveal anything because of HIPAA unless she had Power of Attorney. "But we have a cancellation next week. Can you bring her in then?"

"I'm not her caregiver. I clean her house. I'm trying to get in touch with her daughter, but she lives out of state."

"Have the daughter call us."

"Again, I'm not family. I just work for her."

"That's the best I can do. You could call Adult Protective Services." Wanda said she was hoping the daughter would call soon.

Wanda made a tray with canned chicken noodle soup, crackers, and kippers and took it upstairs. Mrs. Morton was asleep, but when she put the tray down, she stirred. Wanda said she'd brought her some lunch and she should eat to keep her strength up. "I'll check in on you later this week. Can I pick up anything at the store for you?" She lightly touched the woman's forehead to check for a fever. She felt a bit warm, but Wanda couldn't tell for sure. "I hate to leave you if you need help."

"I'll be fine. Thank you, dear." She lifted her spoon, her hand shaking, and took a sip of the soup. Then she nodded and smiled. Wanda went back downstairs.

Mrs. Morton hadn't left the usual cash for Wanda on the kitchen table, and Wanda couldn't ask for it, especially since she hadn't finished the job. She'd come back the next day and maybe the money would be there.

"Macky, we're leaving in a few minutes." Engrossed now in the book, he said nothing. "Macky?"

"I'm almost done with this chapter."

"You can read it again if you want to come along."

"Can I bring it home?"

"No. It's not yours. Put a bookmark in and let's go." She went upstairs to say goodbye, but found Mrs. Morton slumped over, breathing shallowly. When she couldn't wake her up, she called 911 and asked for the EMTs.

For the second time in two days, she'd see Benny. In fact, he said, "Hey, Wanda, you stalkin' me?"

"No," she said, embarrassed. "Of course not." He laughed and patted her arm as he and the other EMT headed up the stairs.

As they carried Mrs. Morton on the stretcher to the ambulance, Wanda tried to shield Macky's view, but he'd seen her anyway. "Did Mrs. Morton have a heart attack? Is she going to die?" Wanda told him no, then he asked if he'd almost died when the EMTs had come for him. Of course not, she said, trying to distract him, but he broke away and ran to the door to watch them hoist the gurney into the van. She grabbed Macky's hand and pulled him back. His breathing was rapid and shallow, heading toward a panic attack, so she led him into the kitchen, grabbed a paper bag, and held it up to his mouth. "Here. Breathe into this."

Benny had shown her this trick in the ambulance. Macky batted her away.

"Come on. It'll help."

"No!"

When the ambulance pulled onto the street and started its siren, Macky jammed his hands over his ears, squeezed his eyes shut, and started panting hoarsely, his chest heaving. She tried again to place the bag over his mouth, but he swiped at her, gouging her cheek with a fingernail. Without thinking, she swatted him on the butt. "Don't do that!" And she plunked him down and forced the bag over his mouth. He struggled, his eyes wide and terrified. She'd never spanked him before.

"Macky, I'm so sorry. I shouldn't have hit you."

He broke away and ran to the window, falling to the floor and hugging himself.

"Please, baby."

His voice sounded shredded and raspy. She knelt beside him, her cheek stinging, close enough to feel the heat from his body, but not touching him. She patted her cheek, and her finger came away with a streak of blood. "Please, baby. Breathe slow." His lips were blue, his face pale. She wondered if she'd need to call the paramedics back. Would they even come? Should she just drive him there? Leaning over him, she gently placed the bag near his mouth. "Slow, slow," and she kept her voice as calm as she could. "I'm so sorry, baby." His panting eventually slowed to normal breaths, he unclenched his fists and lay on his back as he rocked from side to side. She was ashamed she'd acted like her mother, smacking the fight right out of him.

On the way home, Wanda wondered if she'd done the right thing, sending Mrs. Morton to the ER. What would they do if no one could reach Callie? Or if Callie refused to help? As difficult as Wanda's mother could be sometimes, Wanda would never abandon her.

She examined her cheek in the mirror and saw dried blood around a long, thin welt. Macky sat limply in the back seat, clutching his science book, looking out the window. At home, she settled him on the sofa with a blanket, the laptop, a glass of water, and some animal crackers. He stuffed a couple of cookies into his mouth and started pecking at the keys, back in his element. "Hey," she said. "Why don't you read for a while and then we can walk into town?" He nodded.

She slipped into the bedroom and shut the door and tried Callie's number again. This time, she answered. Wanda wasn't sure whether Callie was relieved or angry to get the call. She seemed preoccupied by her work. "I need to talk to her doctor," Callie said. "It's really hard to get away now." Well, at least Wanda had made the contact. This wasn't her responsibility.

In the bathroom, Wanda wetted a washcloth and cleaned the scrape, then dabbed on concealer to cover the welt. Still revved, she started dusting the apartment, taking everything out of the kitchen cabinets, spraying the shelves, restocking the dishes and glasses in neat rows.

This made two breathing emergencies in two days. Was there something really wrong with him? She shouldn't have spanked him.

At two, Macky was buried in a new book and didn't want to stop, but she told him he could bring it with him, and they could sit in the park after her errand. Reluctantly, he rolled off the couch, grabbed his jacket and cap, and slipped on his shoes.

The sun warmed their faces as they walked up the street toward the center of town. On the way, Macky's questions started up again. "Did my dad die right away or did they have to take him in an ambulance?" "Why did they put IEDs in the ground?" "How did the Army know where you lived?"

"Macky, do you think about this kind of thing a lot?"

"Sometimes. I ask Grandma Sandy questions, but she gets upset."

"Well, it makes her sad to think about him dying."

"She likes to talk about him, just not how he died."

"You can understand that. She wants to remember the good things."

"Am I like him?"

"You are a good, kind person, and so was he. But to me, you're you. There's only one Macky."

"Do I look like him?" He stopped, turned his face to her with his pale skin and spiky hair and gap in his upper teeth where one jagged tooth was coming in crooked. "Whose genes do I have?"

She hesitated for a moment. "Well, you have blue eyes and so were David's." What were Whit's? "But mine are brown." She pushed the tops of her ears forward. "You do have Poppa's ears though."

"Grandma Sandy says I remind her of my dad."

She felt a twinge in her stomach. "I'm sure you can help her remember him." Dammit, Sandy, indulging her grief at Macky's expense. Wanda felt protective of him. But then she couldn't blame Sandy for missing her son, and people saw what they needed to see. However, Macky had started to ask tougher questions, making her skirt the truth in new ways. How much longer could she do that?

When they reached the Rite-Aid, he dug in his heels saying he wanted to wait for her on the bench out front. Normally, she wouldn't leave him alone, an unattended kid in the middle of town, but she didn't want to set him off again. "Okay but sit tight and just read."

In the store, she grabbed a box of Band-Aids and antibiotic ointment for Mrs. Morton and stood in line behind Mona Faxton who chatted with Barbara, the cashier, about the weather and her cat with no sense that anyone was in line. Through the window, Wanda spotted a woman sitting on the bench talking to Macky. Mrs. Sutter. Whit's mother. An electric charge ran down her fingers. She reached for the display case to steady herself. When Mona finally shut her change purse, gathered her bags, and left, Wanda paid and hurried outside. "I was just inside for a moment."

"Hello, Wanda. Macky and I were just having a nice chat."

So, she knew his name. Did she already know it?

"Oh, dear, Wanda. What happened to your face?" Wanda covered her cheek, saying it was nothing, just a mishap with an overhanging branch. Macky shot her a guilty look.

"What are you reading, Macky?" asked Mrs. Sutter.

He held up his book. "A biography of Abraham Lincoln."

"My, that's pretty advanced. You can understand all of this?"

He looked at Wanda, frowning.

"Oh, he can," said Wanda. "I'm homeschooling him, but I can barely keep up. We're at the library all the time."

"You know," Mrs. Sutter said, "I have a lot of books that used to belong to my son. Maybe you'd like to come take some of them?"

"No, that's very nice of you, but we couldn't."

"Mom, please?"

"Macky, don't push. That's a very generous offer. We'll think about it." But she had no intention of accepting any of Whit's books. Or allowing his mother to give Macky gifts.

"I'm happy to do this for such a good reader." She was smiling at him, and Wanda wondered if she was thinking about Whit.

"Well, it was so nice to see you again, Mrs. Sutter. Macky, we should get going now."

Mrs. Sutter added, "I've been meaning to ask you if you had a slot in your schedule to clean for me. Agatha Morton speaks so highly of you."

Wanda told her that Mrs. Morton had gone to the hospital with the EMTs, that she and Macky had been there when they'd taken her. She didn't know if she'd gone home or was staying. Mrs. Sutter thanked her for letting her know. Then Macky told her he'd also ridden in the ambulance a few days earlier, so he knew she was going to be all right. Mrs. Sutter hoped he was feeling better.

"About cleaning," said Wanda, who had no desire to step into Whit's house, "right now, I'm booked real solid, and I have to leave time for Macky's homeschooling."

"Mom, you have time. I do all the work by myself."

"Macky, that's enough from you." She tapped his elbow and said they needed to head home.

"Well, let me know if your schedule opens up."

"I will." Wanda told Macky to say goodbye. On the walk, her face felt flushed, making her cheek throb. She'd been dreading this meeting with Mrs. Sutter ever since Macky was a baby. She knew they'd eventually cross paths but never thought Mrs. Sutter would talk to Macky alone. Did she see something in him that reminded her of Whit? And as he grew older, would the resemblance be obvious?

All the way home, Macky pestered her about the books. Why couldn't they go look? The books would help him with his projects. She said that Mrs. Sutter was just being kind, and he didn't need to clutter up their place with more stuff. "And when I say enough is enough, you need to drop it. Okay?"

"I'm sorry, Mom." They walked another block, not talking. Then he said, "I just really wanted to look at those books."

"I know, buddy." And she said, wondering if she'd dodged a bullet or was facing a new battle on the horizon.

16

CALLIE

During her nine o'clock massage with Mel, a seventy-six man with sciatica and moles scattered all over his back, Callie heard her phone ping in her locker. She'd forgotten to silence it before the session. While Mel was changing back into his gym clothes, Callie grabbed her phone and glanced at the screen, seeing a voicemail from her mother's phone. She wasn't in the mood to talk to her mother now. Since her father's death, nothing had been resolved between them. Her pulse fluttered as she scheduled Mel for an appointment the following week. "Your magic hands always help with the pain," he said, winking at her. Despite his osteoporotic hump and ear hair, he considered himself a ladies' man. He was harmless though, and she was fond of him, so she told him to keep up the good work with the home exercises.

She removed the sheets and tossed them into the bin and stretched clean ones over the table. Then because Mel left behind an old-man musk, she turned up the air filter and sprayed some persimmon essence. Her next client, Jessica, was sitting in the waiting room, talking on her cell against spa rules. Callie should remind her again to make calls elsewhere. Jessica's posture was excellent, but she had hypermobility and that, along with years of abuse to her body, had resulted in a torn hip labrum and frayed rotator cuffs. Callie had seen this kind of injury before, particularly in former competitive gymnasts like Jessica.

As she waited for Jessica to undress, Callie walked to the window in the waiting room and looked out. The slow, blue street-cleaning truck glided down the side of the street, swerving around a parked car. She thought of the Zamboni back home that smoothed the ice between periods of hockey games. Her mother's message had come in at nine-forty-eight Chicago time. She'd check the message during lunch. Maybe.

During the massage, as Jessica talked, Callie tried countering her nervous energy by pitching her own voice softer, telling Jessica she needed to concentrate on socket rotation. "Is there pain when I move your arm back like this?" Jessica answered, then started in again on some story that Callie tuned out. She kneaded the tension in Jessica's upper trapezius, careful not to press too hard and stress the tendons. "Now, it might help to take deep breaths as I work this area." She slowed her own breathing to tame her thoughts. This allowed her to lose herself in the massage, to get into a meditative rhythm that anchored her.

At the end of the session, Callie said they needed to wind up because she had an appointment. Jessica left and said she'd be back next week. Callie loved her clients but needed to keep time limits and enforce physical and personal boundaries.

Callie's appointment was actually a Zumba class. Today, she needed to work off her stress before tackling the voice mail. The instructor, Valentina did everything—salsa, merengue, cambia—in double time.

On her way up to the studio though, she saw Allan, who beckoned her into his office. Fresh from his morning workout, he wore shorts and a tee and grabbed a towel to wipe off his arms and neck. When he ushered her into his office, she ran her hand along his arm and said, "I just got a voice mail from my *mother*."

"Have a seat," he said, sitting behind his desk and motioning to the chair across from him.

"What's going on?" she asked, fearing he'd say they needed to be more discreet about their affair because he was still technically married. At work, they'd been very careful, communicating via cryptic texts to schedule "staff meetings."

"Callie," he said, "there's been a complaint filed against you."

"What? Who?"

He held a sheet of paper. "Jerry Wall." A client she'd seen a few times.

"Really? What did he say?"

"He says you injured his neck and now has severe nerve pain."

"He came to me with a cervical strain, and I worked on him, but I was very careful. I always am with necks. But he didn't do any of the things I suggested between sessions. He still sleeps on three pillows and hunches over his iPad. I told him it would take time and he needed to be patient."

"He claims you were unprofessional," and Allan read the statement from Jerry accusing her of dismissing his pain as minor, then pulling roughly on his neck.

"I didn't do that. And besides, he was inappropriate with me. A couple of weeks ago, he was on his back, and when I leaned over him, he said, 'Mmm, nice breasts.' I told him I wouldn't put up with that kind of behavior. If he did it again, I'd end the session." She felt her cheeks redden. "The guy's a total creep."

"Why do you think he'd make the complaint now?"

"I don't know. He seemed pleased when he left."

"I'm sure that's true, but we have to investigate."

"How can you investigate? It's not as if you have a tape of our sessions. It's his word against mine." She looked out the window, digging her knuckles into her clenched stomach. "Maybe this is retaliation because I didn't like his boob comment. I should have reported him."

"Are you sure you did everything by the book?"

"Yes, Allan. Don't you believe me?" She asked, blinking back the sting of tears.

"I do, but he's threatening to sue the club."

"Well, what can I say? I can't prove when he sustained the injury. How can I prove I didn't make it worse?"

"We'll just have to see what comes of it. Just make sure you're extra careful now, okay?" She sat watching him frown at the computer, and she willed him to look at her. After a moment when she knew she couldn't avoid crying, she left his office. Now it was too late to make the Zumba class. Shit. She was furious about the complaint, her first ever. Her clients always came back, and they recommended her to friends. Because she had more business than she could handle, she was booked weeks in advance.

She'd wanted Allan to console her, to assure her that her job was safe, and most of all that he loved her. Instead, he'd let a complaint by a disgruntled asshole affect him.

Back in the studio, as she placed her phone in the drawer, it rang again, this time with the name Zacek and a Shelton area code. "Hello?"

"Callie? This is Wanda Zacek. Used to be MacDonald?"

"Yes, sure, Wanda." Her mother had hired her to help with the dishes at her father's memorial. How odd that she'd call.

"I left you a message earlier from your mother's phone."

"Is Mom okay? I was working and couldn't pick up."

"She's not feeling so good. She was kind of out of it this morning. I don't think it's life-threatening. The EMTs took her to the Emergency Room."

"Oh?" She felt her legs go weak, so she sat down.

"As you probably know, I clean for her once a week. When me and my son came today, she wasn't up, which is very unusual, and I found her in bed, and she had, well, soiled herself."

"Oh, no."

"And she was kind of in and out and wasn't making sense. She could answer some questions though. Benny, the EMT, do you remember Benny Carbo?" Callie didn't. "Well, he said it probably wasn't a stroke, but she should be checked out."

"Okay."

"I changed the sheets and cleaned her up good and put ointment on her sores."

"She has sores?"

"Yes, and I noticed she hadn't been eating good and the kitchen was a real mess."

Callie's brain slowed down, the words spilling over her too fast. "What kind of mess?"

"Oh, I cleaned that up too."

"I appreciate it. I don't understand what could be wrong with her."

"Do you think you'll come to town?"

"I need to talk to her doctor first."

She said goodbye and hung up, her head buzzing. What should she do? With the complaint, it was a terrible time to get away. And when she wasn't working, she wasn't earning. Maybe it wasn't that serious, and the doctors could advise her over the phone. Did her mother really need her to drop everything and come home? What did Wanda know anyway? She'd call the hospital to find out what was going on.

Callie reached the nurse assigned to her mother. Her mother had a nasty UTI that she'd neglected and was now on an IV antibiotic to knock it out. Her mental status was very muddled, but that was common with such infections, particularly in old people. The nurse asked if she had a caregiver or if there were plans in place for more support. No, said Callie, feeling a headache grip her scalp. Was that necessary yet?

Off the phone, she wondered how she was going to deal with her mother long distance if she needed more care. There must be someone who could look after her. Maybe Wanda did that kind of thing and was calling Callie for that reason. She probably needed the extra money. Then Callie wondered how much it would cost and how she could arrange this without going to Shelton herself.

She looked into flights, but last-minute ones were expensive, so she decided to take a few days off and drive there herself, stay just long enough to get her mother settled with a caregiver, if necessary, and then return. Or maybe it was just a UTI, and when it cleared up, she'd be fine on her own. She hadn't been given the chance to see her father before he died, so she knew that she had to go to Shelton, even if her mother wasn't that sick. She wouldn't forgive herself otherwise. But it wasn't a good time.

On her phone, she looked for Wanda on Facebook and found a page with a blurry photo of a baby and a post about supporting the troops and an inspirational quote about living one's best life, but nothing in the past year. No photos of Wanda herself, just the baby and a maple tree at peak fall color. She was one of those townies who married her high-school sweetheart, had a bunch of kids, and never left.

When she told Allan she needed to fly east to help her mother, he wondered if this was the moment to leave, given the complaint. "I have no choice. This is my mother, Allan." He said she should let all her clients know. "Obviously, I'll do that," she said, her head pounding. For the rest of the day, between sessions, she made calls, telling her clients she had a family emergency. Predictably, some were annoyed at the inconvenience. "I'll make it up to you," she told them, feeling awful about leaving them in the lurch.

She set out the next morning for the eight-hour drive, planning to reach Shelton by the afternoon. As she drove along the Ohio Turnpike toward Pennsylvania, she thought about Allan and how they'd left things. He hadn't been all that supportive about the complaint, and she wished he hadn't been so distracted. What was that all about? He said he'd call her to see how her mother was doing, and he wished her good luck, drawing her into a kiss behind the closed office door. But what she'd really wanted was for him to offer to go with her, even if she said no. It would have meant everything to know he'd do that for her.

As a lover, he was eager, yet patient, the best sex she'd had since the early days with Greg. Better because she trusted him. She massaged his tense muscles. Usually, when a guy heard she knew massage and expected her to work on him for free, she resented it. But with Allan, that didn't matter.

His thighs were like iron, his shoulders sculpted. At forty-two, he took care of himself, he worked out every day, he ran marathons. She learned that if he didn't work out, he was grouchy. That he had unusually tight IT bands and had torn his ACL playing soccer in high school. He had a scar on his leg from the repair and another scar from an appendectomy. He was allergic to shellfish, he hated chocolate, and he was working on getting out of his dead marriage.

Because he'd developed shin splints from running, she was giving him myofascial massage to break up the adhesions. He'd arrive, shut the door, and press her against the wall, kissing her, slipping his hand inside her yoga pants. Then he'd lie on his back as she slowly pressed her knuckles firmly up his shins, feeling the knots release. Then she'd steal a kiss on his knee, one on his calf, another on his inner thigh, his hand stroking her back, cupping her butt when she walked past him.

He promised they'd be together soon, but getting out of his marriage was complicated, particularly because of his six-year-old daughter, Agnes. Callie had been patient for nearly three years now. Her friends at the club, Brigitte and Lacey, had no idea about her and Allan. Ping knew and thought she was in the danger zone, but Callie was sure they were heading toward being together. But were they? She wondered what this all meant, if he was cooling to her, letting this complaint serve as a wedge between them. Had he been looking for a way to bail?

At a turnpike stop near Cleveland, she texted him to say she was halfway there. *I wish I didnt have to do this.* Then, she added, *I miss you,* knowing it was risky to text anything personal.

In the seven years since she'd left home, she'd resolved most of the shame about disappointing her parents about college, the embarrassment of being the girl who everyone in town knew had run away for love. For sex. That was years ago. But she still hadn't been able to get past the anger at her mother for depriving her of the chance to see her father before he died. Yes, she had her own guilt in the matter, but her mother knew her father was sick, and she didn't. But even that, she'd shoved to the back of her mind. She had her life in Chicago, a career, friends, a man she loved. No one in Shelton knew her anymore. And there was no one in town she had any interest in seeing. She'd go there, do her business, then leave. Why then did she feel so unsettled?

In Shelton, clots of snow hid in shady spots, and the air smelled wet and dense, a chill that would last well into May. Then one day, summer heat would arrive and bake off the dampness until the first hint of fall brought it back again.

She drove past the skeletons of new houses being built on the outskirts of town, through the center of the village, past the high school, the cemetery, the hockey rink, and up the hill toward the campus. So many confusing, mixed memories.

When she caught sight of her childhood home, the red bricks, the birdbath under the elm out front, the ruffled eyelet curtains in the bedroom windows, she felt a little flip in her stomach, the excitement of returning home again, but with it came a sense of dread.

The front door had been left unlocked. Walking inside, she felt the stillness of the house, the palpable absence of her parents. But the smells of lemon soap, old books, furniture polish, and hard water brought back her childhood. The same threadbare sofa, faded wing chairs, the same rickety tray table with framed photos of Callie over the years. The photos, taken during school events—a play, graduation, honor society induction, all showed Callie happy. On the sofa sat a tote with a half-finished, rolled-up needlepoint canvas sticking out. Next to the chair was a pair of smudged reading glasses with a safety pin holding the rim to the temple. A library book sat next to a magnifying glass. She dropped her bag in the living room and headed into the kitchen. The refrigerator held nothing edible—a tin of kippers, half-eaten, a withered lemon, a plastic-wrapped ceramic bowl with fat-clogged chicken soup, a tub of cottage cheese. She poured a glass of water and was reminded of its horrible taste and sulphury smell. Next to the sink sat a mug that Callie had decorated for Mother's Day one year. Now, with its handle broken, it held a rusted Brillo pad.

When she was a girl, Callie and her mother used to bake cookies, and because Callie was too short to reach the counter, her mother brought out a low stepstool for her to stand on. They made gingersnaps, and she let Callie measure out the spices on small spoons. That's how she learned her fractions: 1/2 c. sugar, 1/4 t. ginger, 1/8 t. cinnamon. She'd stand looking through the glass oven door as the dough spread and darkened and the kitchen filled with the aroma. Now, the stool sat in the corner with a pile of newspapers on it, the kitchen smelling of oatmeal and tuna. And that awful water, which left white streaks on glasses and wouldn't let shampoo lather. Her mother drank big glasses without ice, calling it bracing, the iron good for her blood. How Callie couldn't wait to get away from that awful water.

Visiting hours would be over soon, so she climbed back in the car and drove down the hill toward the hospital in Granville. Along the way, the flow of the familiar sights—St. Vincent's, the pharmacy—was interrupted by changes—a painted gingerbread porch added to the McMillans' place, and a ranch house with a paved-over front yard advertising a dentist's office.

When she walked into the hospital room, she didn't recognize her mother at first. Her hair was loose, for one thing, and she looked frail and disheveled. Her mouth drooped open, sending a deep shiver through Callie. "Mom?" When her mother turned to look at Callie, it took her a few seconds to register who this was in her room.

"Callie," she said, her eyes rimmed in red. "You came."

"Of course, Mom. How are you?"

"Am I dying? Is that why you're here?"

"Of course not, but you're sick, and I wanted to be here."

Her mother looked around as if she didn't know where she was. Her hands lay on the covers, the veins purple and prominent. Callie knew she should give her mother a kiss. Instead, she leaned in for a quick hug. Her mother smelled of antiseptic soap.

"I was worried," said Callie, "but they said it's an infection, and they're treating it."

"I just don't know why your father hasn't come yet. But he gets so caught up in his work."

"Mom? You know Dad died, right?"

Her face crumpled, and she shook her head. "Of course, I knew that." She fumbled with the covers and fussed with her ID band, trying to pull it off.

"I drove in from Chicago."

"By yourself?"

"Yes, Mom. Of course, by myself."

"I'm not sure why they're keeping me here."

"Well, they need to make sure your infection is gone."

"Wanda came to visit me this morning. She has been so sweet to me."

"She's the one who called me."

"She has the dearest little boy, Macky."

"I haven't met him yet."

"Smart as a whip."

Poor kid, thought Callie. He had no hope living in Shelton with a housecleaner for a mom. But I'm here now, Mom, she wanted to say. I came all this way.

Her mother was grasping at the air in front of her as if she was trying to catch a moth.

"What are you trying to do, Mom?"

"What?"

Her mother seemed floaty, not focused. A nurse entered to take her temperature and to check her pulse.

Callie said, "She seems confused."

"That's the UTI."

"So, she should be okay once the infection is cleared up?"

The nurse motioned for Callie to follow her into the hall. "There may be some dementia. Have you seen any changes in her lately?"

Callie didn't tell the nurse she had no idea what her mother's health had been like these past several years. Instead, she asked when she could talk to the doctor.

The nurse sighed, used to people going over her head. "He'll be in tomorrow. You can try back then."

"When would be a good time?" Callie dreaded the thought of spending all day with her mother waiting for answers. What would they talk about?

The nurse said there was no telling when he'd make his rounds and she asked if Callie had Power of Attorney. When Callie said they'd never talked about that kind of thing, the nurse said the social worker would walk her through the steps and procedures.

Callie told her mother she'd be back in the morning, but because she was drowsy, Callie wasn't sure if her mother had heard her. As she walked to her car, her head ached, and her eyes were burning. She'd have to get more done tomorrow if she was going to be out of there in a couple of days.

On the drive back to Shelton, she swung into McDonald's and wolfed down a cheeseburger and fries without really tasting them. How was she going to cope with her mother's needs now? And when could she get back to her life in Chicago? She texted Allan to say things with her mother had become more complicated. She needed to hear his voice.

Back at the house, she was too wired to sleep, so she walked around, inspecting the other rooms except for her father's study, which she couldn't face. It seemed clear to her that her mother lived principally in the bedroom, the kitchen, and the living room. The other rooms seemed neglected, shabby in a way she hadn't remembered.

Since she'd last been home, her mother had taken to using Callie's bedroom as storage. The bed was covered with folded piles of her father's suits and his moth-eaten sweaters, smelling of his pipe tobacco. A wave of sadness whooshed over her to smell his clothes. As a teenager, she'd disliked his gross, stinky pipe, but now, she buried her face in his old jacket and breathed, holding the smell in her lungs. Why hadn't her mother donated those items to rummage or just thrown them out, ratty as they were? She gathered up the loose clothes and started placing them in neat piles, but then, when the piles collapsed, she tossed the rest on the floor.

She checked her phone. No text from Allan. He was home now and couldn't text as easily. She'd call him tomorrow during work hours when he was at the club and would be free to talk.

Turning out the light, she rolled over and tried to fall asleep. But being at home, smelling the familiar smells of the house, feeling herself a little girl again, all she could think about was her mother and what she'd be called on to do now.

17

WANDA AND CALLIE

Two days after Easter, Wanda dropped Macky off at Sandy's because she had a cleaning job. Ruth Kiernan wanted her to vacuum and use ammonia, and Wanda was afraid the noise and strong smells would set Macky off again. Then she planned to swing by to see Mrs. Morton at the hospital where children weren't allowed to visit.

Macky shuffled up the walk with a backpack full of books. Wanda said she needed a couple of minutes alone with Grandma Sandy. Wanda wanted to tell her about Macky's croup, that he was sensitive to sounds and smells now. She didn't want Sandy to hear about the EMTs from Macky. Who was she protecting? Sandy or herself?

Every time Wanda walked into the living room, she had to steel herself against the gloom, the closed curtains all day, the only light aimed at the portrait of David. She hated that photo. That pose wasn't him, and his uniform brought up too many dark feelings. Wanda always tried to keep it together for Macky. She couldn't afford to let her sadness take over.

Today, fronds from Palm Sunday fanned out from behind the picture frame. The house smelled of Sandy's vegan sugar cookies, the kind Macky actually liked. He'd refused to eat any of the candy from the Easter basket she'd made for him but based on the wrappers left around the living room, Sandy had been dipping into it herself. Taking one cookie with her coffee, Wanda said she could only stay for a minute. Sandy ate two in the kitchen and put four on her plate. Since David died, she'd put on a lot of weight. Today, her stomach pushed against her knit top and spilled over the top of her pants. She'd turned to food for comfort, but with Burt's diabetes, they had no business eating so much sugar. Macky was the one joy in their lives, and Wanda didn't want to deny them contact with him, but she worried that they were trying to re-create David in Macky, refusing to accept that he wasn't at all interested in sports or that he didn't like David's favorite foods from childhood. Did their grief blind them to their grandchild?

Wanda told Sandy about the EMTs and asked her to make sure Macky had a quiet morning.

"An ambulance? He couldn't breathe? Why didn't you tell me earlier?"

Wanda said it was croup made worse by anxiety, and so it was important to keep things calm. "Just let him read or go online. As long as it's quiet time." She looked at the framed Purple Heart propped on the mantel. "And please, if you don't mind, just for a while, don't talk to him about David's time in the Army."

"Why not?"

"He's been reading about the war and asking questions that churn him up."

"That's not fair," said Sandy, her eyes welling. "Macky wants to hear stories about him. Are you telling me I can't talk to Macky about his father?" She grabbed another cookie and took a big bite. "How could you say that?" she asked, her mouth full.

"I'm not asking you to deny David. Ever." She watched Sandy try to swallow while crying, then hiccupping and grabbing a tissue. "Just maybe don't talk about the war for a while?"

"Well, I don't know what you mean, but I guess I'll just shut up and keep my thoughts to myself." She broke apart a cookie, picking up the crumbs with her fingertips and licking them.

"I'm sorry," Wanda said. "I didn't mean to upset you. It's just for a short time until he's not so focused on war and death. He's only six, no matter how smart he is. I want him to have happy thoughts about David. Maybe stories about his childhood?" She hugged Sandy, feeling her mother-in-law's damp cheek against hers. "I'm sorry. See you around three, okay?" She let herself out the door, taking a deep breath of fresh air, feeling guilty about wanting to escape.

On her way to the Kiernans', she wondered if she'd been too tough on Sandy. No, it had to be said, hard as it was for Sandy to hear. As Macky's mother, she needed to support him out in the world.

During the job, she threw herself into the task, welcoming the roar of the vacuum. The deep tang of the ammonia made her feel woozy, but cleansed. The dirtier the job, the better she enjoyed it, scrubbing until each surface sparkled.

After finishing, she drove to the hospital and found Mrs. Morton weak, but with healthier color than the day before.

"Aren't you lovely to visit," Mrs. Morton said. "But how did you know to find me here?"

"I was at your house when the EMTs came, remember?" Mrs. Morton looked confused. "I can see you're doing much better today." She decided not to ask if Callie was coming. "Is there anything I can get for you? I bought you some new Band-Aids, but I could make a casserole."

"That's very sweet of you, but I don't eat a lot. Just having you visit is so nice." They sat for a few minutes, but Mrs. Morton seemed tired, so Wanda left and said she'd visit again. On her way to pick up Macky, she swore she'd smooth things over with Sandy.

✳ ✳ ✳

On Wednesday, Callie's first morning back in Shelton, she sat in her mother's kitchen drinking tea made from a stale bag of Lipton Orange Pekoe. The only coffee in the house was instant, so Callie added beans to her shopping list, just enough to tide her over for the few days she'd be there. She texted Allan. *Seeing my mom today no answers yet.* When she didn't hear from him right away, she figured he must be in a meeting. Then she answered texts from clients, all impatient to reschedule, telling them she couldn't slot in anything until she knew when she'd return. She wondered what would come of the complaint. Would Allan sort it out in her absence? This couldn't be a worse time to be away. On the same sheet as her grocery list, she wrote down questions to ask the doctor about her mother, hoping she'd run into him today, wishing the nurse had been more helpful. She couldn't bear spending the whole day in her mother's claustrophobic room. What would they talk about? Her mother didn't seem up to much conversation, and it could take hours to find anyone to give her answers. The sooner she got them, the sooner she could return to her job and her life. It all felt just so complicated right row. Would it be rude to bring along a book?

The breakfast nook, surrounded by shelves, looked exactly as it had when she was growing up—the clock radio with the cloudy plastic cover, her mother's Japanese Netsuke figurines, her father's chipped mug, the same faded plaid placemats and threadbare napkins. Every day before school, her parents sat at the table reading the paper as Callie gathered her books and homework and stuffed them into her backpack. Although Callie never had an appetite in the morning, her mother always tried to make her eat something solid like oatmeal or eggs. Even now, the smell of eggs nauseated her. Coffee first thing, then a midmorning snack was all she could stomach. The only change to the kitchen was the accumulation of clutter—slips of paper on the table, newspapers piled on the floor, plastic yogurt containers stacked next to them.

She heard the front door open. Still in her yoga pants and sleep tee, she peeked around the door frame. "Hello?" There stood Wanda with a little boy wearing glasses and a cap.

"Oh, hi, Callie. I saw the Illinois plate and figured it was you." She held up a Rite-Aid bag. "Sorry to barge in. I just wanted to drop off some things for when your mom comes home. How is she today?"

"I haven't gone there yet today. When I arrived yesterday, she was pretty out of it. She has a urinary tract infection."

"I know. I visited yesterday too. Poor thing."

Was Wanda trying to one-up her by getting there first?

"So," said Wanda, setting the bag down on the counter. "You haven't been there yet today?"

"No," Callie said, feeling blood rush to her face. "I just woke up. I'm going there soon to talk to her doctor. They thought he'd be in later. No sense going too early."

"I guess." She ducked her head into the living room. "Macky, come here. I went to school with this lady. She's Mrs. Morton's daughter, Miss Morton."

"You can call me Callie. Hey, Macky." The boy, skinny and in need of a haircut, wore a cap shoved down on his head, making his ears stick out. "I can clear out of here if you want to clean."

"No, I have another job this morning," Wanda said, placing her hand on the boy's head. He shrugged her off. "Me and Macky are just passing by."

"That's right. You said that already." She pointed to the pile of newspapers near the back door. "I see that Mom has let her housekeeping slip a bit." She shouldn't have said that. Wanda looked insulted.

"It's her house. I only clean where she lets me. It's not my job to tell her how to live."

"That's true." She looked at the boy. "Don't you have school today?"

"I'm homeschooled," he muttered into his open book.

Of course. Wanda was probably one of those Christian anti-government types. "That must be a challenge."

"We do great, don't we, Macky?" Wanda said as she walked past Callie, picked up the mug and plate and took them to the sink.

"I can do that."

"It's no problem. And I like to keep ahead of the ants." She rinsed the dishes and put them on the drying rack.

Callie wanted to get dressed, but she worried Wanda would think she'd left the dishes for her to wash. "So, you live in town?"

"Near the elementary school. I married David right after graduation."

"That's right."

"But I'm a widow. David died in Iraq when I was pregnant."

"Oh, I'm so sorry."

"You didn't know that?" said Macky, back in the doorway. "It was in the paper. Everybody knew. Why didn't you know?"

"Macky, come on," said Wanda motioning for him back into the living room.

"I didn't know," said Callie. "I've been away. No one told me." Why was she justifying herself to a child?

"And why would you?" said Wanda, hanging the rag up on the faucet. "It's not like you ever come back here."

"I'd have known if my mother had told me." She watched as Wanda grabbed a broom and swept crumbs into a dustpan, dumping them into the trash. Then she washed her hands. "Again, I'm so sorry this happened to you."

"Well, that was seven years ago." She folded the dish towel and laid in on the counter. "Are you staying in town for a while?"

"I don't know. I have clients back in Chicago I have to see."

"Well, you'll want to make sure your mother's okay."

"I'm doing that, but it's not easy being away from work."

Wanda had picked up the broom again and was swiping at the corners. She was the type who could never sit still, always on the go. Macky was leaning against the doorframe, reading his book.

"And you were here when the EMTs came, right?"

"Yeah, I made the call."

"A lot of drama for a UTI." There'd be a huge ambulance bill, not that Wanda cared how much that would cost her mother.

"It could have been more serious. She couldn't even stand up on her own. I had to make the decision."

Callie watched Wanda putter around the kitchen. Why was she even there? "Well, she's going to be fine."

"I'm sure. Give her my best, please." Wanda called to Macky, took the bag of trash, and left with him through the back door. Callie felt the blood banging in her temples. Who was Wanda to question how Callie dealt with her mother?

Wanda had been a year ahead of Callie in school, but now she looked a lot older than twenty-six. Her hips had spread, her hair was dry and frizzy. Callie tried to summon distinct memories of Wanda, but all she could come up with were glimpses of her on the school bus, in the cafeteria, and later, working in the bakery. Wanda hadn't left much of an impression.

Up in her old bedroom, Callie pulled out a box of books from the closet and found the 2005 yearbook. She turned to Wanda MacDonald's senior portrait: poufy, big hair, an awkward, closed-mouth smile. The only thing listed next to her picture was Pep Club. That figured. Farm kids weren't usually involved in extracurriculars. Maybe she had chores or maybe she just wasn't into school. Then Callie looked up David Zacek. Him she remembered. Handsome with a broad smile, a player on the football team all four years. Wanda and he seemed like an odd match. She wondered what David saw in her besides sex. Sad for Wanda and her son that he'd died so young. What a life, stuck in this small town with no husband, no education past high school, and a child to raise on her own. David and Whit. Two people she'd known in high school who'd died.

An hour later, Callie found her mother sleeping, a tray of food untouched on the table. Callie could hear the roommate's TV tuned to a news program. Although her mother's cheeks were sunken and her face thin, lying with her head propped gave her a double chin. Callie flashed on an early memory of one night going into her parents' room with a stomachache. Her mother lay in bed, reading. She looked over the top of her glasses and asked, "Callie, are you all right?" just before Callie threw up on the floor. Her mother tossed her book, jumped out of bed, and told Callie not to worry as she led her to the bathroom. Then she helped her into a clean nightgown, brought her a glass of ginger ale, and tucked her back into her own bed, sitting on the side of the mattress, stroking her hair until she fell asleep.

A while later, she heard a knock and hoped for the doctor. Instead, it was Mrs. Sutter, her hair grayer than Callie had remembered it but in the same tightly coiled style she'd worn for years.

"Hello, Mrs. Sutter." Callie stood up and the woman gave her a hug. "Thank you for coming."

"Please, it's Janine. How's your mother?"

"She was very confused yesterday. It's a urinary tract infection, so they're giving her antibiotics. She's been sleeping since I got here. I'll know more when I've talked to her doctor, but no one can tell me when he might come by."

"Dear Agatha." She patted the foot of the bed. "I had no idea she was here, but I ran into Wanda Zacek yesterday, and she told me."

"I'm sorry. I should have let you know, but it came on quickly, and I just got into town yesterday. Should I wake her up?"

"No, let her sleep."

Callie pulled up a chair for Janine, and they sat on opposite sides of the bed.

"So, tell me," Janine asked, "how's your life in Chicago? Your mother says you studied massage."

"She did?"

"Yes, she's so proud of you."

"Huh." She had no idea what her mother might have been telling people about her.

"Agatha and I spend a lot of time together. We're in the same book club, and we do our volunteering at the Historical Society. We keep busy." She fiddled with her keys in her lap. "It helps," she said, her voice husky.

Callie said that was true, but what she really wanted to ask was what her mother had told Janine. Had she ever talked to anyone about their troubles?

Callie's mother stirred. "What?" And she opened her eyes.

"Agatha," said Janine. "How are you, dear?"

"Oh, Janine, am I late?"

"No, you're right on time." She ran her hand along Agatha's arm. "I'm enjoying sitting here with Callie."

"Hey, Mom, I've been waiting here to see your doctor."

"He's a nice young man." She reached for her friend's hand. "Where is Herbert?"

"Oh, dear. I'm so sorry." Callie and she exchanged glances. "Herbert's gone, but he'd be here if he could."

"Oh, yes, of course." She sighed, tugged on her blanket, and rubbed her eyes.

"Callie and I are having a lovely talk."

Her mother looked at Callie blankly. "Did Wanda come with you?"

"Of course not. I came alone. And I visited you yesterday. Don't you remember?" She felt her face grow warm. "And I've been here already for an hour." Weary, she asked, "How are you feeling today?"

"I just don't know why I'm here. And I can't sleep. All that beeping. When can I go home?"

Janine said, "I think they want to treat the infection first. Can I bring you something on my next visit?"

"I have nothing to read."

"I can lend you the novel I just finished. It's a retelling of *Cymbelline*. I didn't love it, but you might find something to admire. You're so clever." She stood up. "I should go now and let you two have some time together." Callie felt a surge of panic to be left alone again with her mother. Janine gave Agatha and Callie hugs before walking out the door.

Callie had nothing to say, so she encouraged her mother to eat breakfast before they took the tray away. She spooned a bite of eggs into her mother's mouth, then held up the cup. Sitting close to her, listening to her swallow, watching a dab of rubbery egg stuck to her lower lip, turned Callie's stomach. Closing her eyes, she held her breath, then peeked at her phone to check the time and to see if she'd received any messages.

When the nurse arrived to check her mother's vitals, Callie asked when the doctor might stop in, but the nurse said he'd done his rounds early and had left. "Any sense of how long she's going to be here?" Callie asked.

The nurse attached an oximeter to her mother's finger. "You'll have to ask the doctor." At the beep, the nurse unclamped the monitor and left.

Callie mentioned to her mother that she had a lot of massage clients now, more than she could handle, but Callie wasn't sure if her mother registered what she'd said. She talked about her new apartment and how she now had room to take some of her old books with her when she went back.

"Are you leaving for Chicago already?" Her mother asked, frowning.

"No, Mom, of course not," she said. "I want to make sure you're all right."

Her mother sighed, which Callie took as disapproval. Callie stood up, saying she'd be back later after some errands. A day wasted without answers from anyone in charge. Shit. Her head felt hollow, and she couldn't wait to get out of that room.

On the way to town, she stopped at a market in Granville rather than risk seeing someone she knew. Back in Shelton, she drove around the square, up past Matt's brother's house, down the street where Greg rented the coach house, and out Route 9 past the Connors' barn where she and her friends used to party. On Main Street, crocuses had popped up, and the trees were just starting to leaf. She saw Mrs. Grassi out raking her flowerbeds. An appliquéd banner with the Easter Bunny flew from her porch, and the plaster duck in her yard wore a raincoat and slicker. Callie wondered if any of her friends had moved back to town after college. Teddy Scott and Monica Futral had gone to Brewster, but Callie figured they'd escaped to larger towns after graduation. Elise was in law school at Yale, and Zelda was doing med school in Boston, but they were so busy, all they ever had time for was a quick text. She'd lost touch with everyone else. The only people her age in town were ones like Wanda who'd never imagined a life beyond Shelton.

Driving by the high school made her think of Mr. Moriarty, her A.P. European History teacher, senior year. He'd written her recs for college applications. Later, he'd consoled her when her parents had forced her to go to Brewster. In her yearbook, he'd written, *College is what you make of it. You'll do great no matter where you go.* She assumed he was still teaching. Did he know that even though she hadn't gone to college, she'd done well for herself?

She turned into the school parking lot next to the football field, then walked up the path and skirted the building, entering through the front door. After showing her ID to the security guard, she slung a lanyard with a xerox of her license photo around her neck. Then she walked down the deserted hallway, past the gym, the orchestra room, and the cafeteria, where early lunch had started. Coming upon the wall of awards with years of hockey trophies, she found her name on the 2006 plaque for National Honor Society. Posters for the upcoming school musical *Into the Woods* and Pep Club signs for that weekend's games lined the bulletin boards. She continued past the administration offices and toward her old homeroom. The bell rang and the halls filled with students and the clatters and slamming of lockers, the smells of the hallway—gum, sweat, and cigarettes. Now, weaving among the students, peeking over their head into the classrooms, she felt old. She headed toward Mr. Moriarty's classroom, hoping to catch him between classes. Arriving at his room, she saw him, heavier, his hair thinner, standing at the board. A rush of excitement ran through her as she watched him greet the next group in his jovial manner. She willed him to look her way, to break into a surprised smile, maybe even say, "Well, Callie Morton, come on in and say hello," but he turned, and a student shut the door, leaving Callie alone in the hall.

Turning down another corridor, she headed past the guidance counselor's office. Mrs. Foletti sat in a meeting with a girl and her parents. The same faded college pennants from her time decorated the bulletin board—Brewster, Carnegie Mellon, Cornell, Hamilton, Lehigh, Penn State. She slipped past and ducked out the back door, hearing the alarm sound as she jogged to her car.

Taking the short route home, she crested the hill and turned into the campus, where she saw Justice For Trayvon signs poking up from the main quad lawn. Several students, mostly Black, a few white, were stapling flyers to the message boards and taping them to sidewalks. Across the street from the quad, a group of frat boys, all white, played Hacky Sack on the Chi Psi house lawn. Some things never changed. She felt a woozy drop in her gut remembering the party where she'd hooked up with Greg.

She parked and walked across the quad, past the library and the science buildings and the dining hall, the dorms, the art center with a scaffolding out front and workmen milling around. At the far end of the quad stood Putnam Hall. The huge elm tree that used to shade the building had been cut down. How sad. A scarred stump remained and had been painted and plastered with announcements. She looked up at her father's office window on the top floor then, below it, in the corner, the window that had been Greg's. She remembered standing naked at that window, feeling bold and sexy, knowing that the leaves shielded her, giving her and Greg their own private place. Under glaring fluorescent lights in a first-floor classroom, a professor stood giving a lecture. A student walked past her, vaping, leaving a trail of pungent flowery smoke behind him. Her phone pinged. A text from Allan. *When are you coming back?* She wasn't sure how to interpret that. Did he miss her or was he, as her boss, pressing her to return to work? She texted, *Soon I hope how are you?* She reached her car and, having nowhere else to go, drove back toward her parents' house.

✳ ✳ ✳

Thursday, after running errands with Macky, Wanda was heading home to pick up the container of soup she'd made for Mrs. Morton. She'd show Callie what it meant to step up and be the better person, even if she didn't know that's what Wanda was doing. At the intersection near home, Wanda waited through a

280

green light while a school bus, full of kindergarteners on their way home after the morning, made the turn onto Main. Seeing Callie in person yesterday had thrown her, sending her right back to high school.

At the beginning of Wanda's senior year, Mr. Perrin, her Language Arts teacher, had encouraged her to branch out, to do something besides schoolwork. He asked her what she felt strongly about, and she mentioned how the funds had been cut for football fan buses. "Why not write an opinion piece about that for the school paper?" he'd suggested. "Maybe they'll print it."

"I'm not a writer."

"Someone has to write the articles. Why not you?" So, Wanda had gone home and written, *Fan support is important to the team. Spirit helps our teams put out the extra push towards victory.* She did it mostly for Mr. Perrin, but also for David. From the bleachers during games, she kept her eyes on him the whole time, even when he sat on the bench. When he came off the bench, he always looked up into the stands to find her, and she waved back and screamed, "Go, David!" When she finished the article, she printed it out and put it in her notebook.

The following day after school, she brought Michelle along for moral support, and they headed to the newspaper room. There she found Zelda Fletcher, Josh Roth, and Callie sitting around a big table, talking. They looked up, clearly wondering why she was there. Wanda felt her voice shake, and she said she'd written an article for the paper. Could she leave it with them in case they wanted to use it? Callie said she'd look at it, but the paper usually only accepted articles submitted electronically. She held the paper by the corner as if it were dirty. "If there's room. It's pretty late for the next issue." Wanda thanked them and turned to go, out of breath, glad that she'd taken a risk. But as soon as she left the room, she heard laughing. When she ducked her head back inside, she saw Callie drop the paper onto the table and shake her head. Her ears ringing, Wanda headed outside to the bus with Michelle behind her. Why hadn't she just let well enough alone?

When the paper came out a week later, she didn't pick up a copy, but during lunch, Michelle ran up to her, excited. "Look! They put it in." Wanda flipped through and found it, cut by half, and sandwiched between two ads on the back page. But it didn't matter anymore. Wanda had learned not to go where she wasn't welcome. What was it about Callie? Her laugh, the way she tossed her head, knowing everyone was watching her? That fake, I'm-so-cool attitude still rubbed Wanda the wrong way. When she and that professor ran off together, it'd been a big scandal and people seemed shocked, but Wanda wasn't. Callie didn't care who she hurt. And now, when her mother needed her and was all alone, Callie could barely bother to show up. And today, she'd expected Wanda to clean up after her like a servant. And why wasn't she at the hospital anyway? If it were her mother or Sandy, Wanda would have spent the night in the room. What kind of daughter was Callie?

Back at home, she made Macky lunch then slipped into the bedroom and closed the door, dialing Michelle's number. "Do you remember Callie Morton?"

"Sort of," Michelle said. "Why?"

"She's back in town. Her mother's sick."

"Poor Mrs. Morton."

"Yeah, well. Her daughter. Still the same stuck-up B-word we knew in school."

"Did we know her?"

"We took the same bus. I'd see her around. She still has a real attitude. Like she's better than everyone else."

"I remember her now. She got into trouble with that teacher. I feel bad for her."

"Why do you feel bad for her? She's not suffering."

"Do you want her to suffer?"

Yes, she thought. "No, I don't mean that. But she's just so full of herself. Do you remember that time she made fun of me about the article I wrote for the paper?"

"No, I don't remember that. Sorry. I'll pray for them."

"That's nice, but Callie doesn't deserve your prayers."

"Everybody deserves prayers."

Whatever.

Even if Michelle didn't remember, why couldn't she support Wanda and not be all righteous and forgiving? Wanda wished Michelle could just once enjoy a good bitch-bashing like she did back in school.

She took the Tupperware of soup out of the refrigerator and told Macky to grab a book because they were going up to Mrs. Morton's.

✳ ✳ ✳

Thursday morning, Callie arrived at the hospital early and this time managed to catch Dr. Singh as he swung by her mother's room.

"You're doing a lot better, Mrs. Morton," he said, checking her chart, but not making eye contact with either of them. Dazed, but smiling, her mother looked at him, a man in charge.

"When can she be released?" asked Callie.

"That, we don't know yet." He was typing notes on a laptop. "Have you talked to the social worker yet?" he asked.

"No. Why do I need to see a social worker?"

"She's been assigned to the case. I'll tell her you're here," he said on his way out of the room.

Her mother started complaining about the noise and the food. Callie said she was working to get her home as soon as she could. "Neither of us wants this to last much longer." Her mother seemed clearer, less addled, if more annoyed. The antibiotics must be working.

A while later, a woman with a suit and a short silver bob arrived. "Hello, Mrs. Morton, Ms. Morton. My name is Sylvia Patrón. I'm assigned to your mother's case." She turned to Callie. "Can you and I have a chat in the lounge?" Callie told her mother she'd be right back, and she followed the woman down the hall.

They sat and Ms. Patrón opened a file. "The infection is clearing up. Good. Tomorrow, we're going to assess your mother's needs and make a recommendation about a living situation."

"Is this about discharging her?"

"Well, there are things to discuss first."

"Such as?"

"Can she return home and live independently? Does she need in-home care, or should she move to assisted living?"

Callie's vision blurred. "She's been fine living alone since my father died. This was just an infection, right? They said the confusion would be temporary."

"Yes, that's true for the UTI, but the doctor is now concerned about her overall cognitive state. We'll assess to what extent your mother is in the position to make decisions about her own care."

"She's only sixty-five."

"That's right, but it's not too early for signs of dementia to show up. The doctor is concerned there might be underlying dementia that was made worse by the infection. Have you seen a change in her lately?"

Callie felt the blood rush to her face. "I haven't been here in a while, but she always seems fine on the phone."

"Of course, we all have busy lives. When parents need extra help, it's a challenge. But that's why I'm here, to help you come up with options from here on out."

"I don't know what that would mean. Or how much it would cost."

"It varies widely. Do you have Financial or Medical Power of Attorney?"

"No, we've never talked about that kind of thing."

"You're not the first adult child who's had to face this situation. First things first. Here're some pamphlets to look over," she said, handing them to Callie. "They lay out various options of support for your mother, depending on your needs and finances. I'm not allowed to give specific recommendations, but I'm here to help with the transition."

"Wait. Is this necessary? Can't we just see how it goes at home? Does she have anything to say about this?"

"Of course. Your mother is still decisional, but she may need help, and she may not want it. You'll need to start strategizing. Often, in these situations, an adult child must steer the ship." Standing up, she shook Callie's hand and gave her a business card before walking off down the hall.

This couldn't be happening. There had to be a mistake. She had no idea where to start and what to do or if she should trust the doctor and social worker. Her mother could be fine in a day or so and she could go back to living as she had up to then. Someone didn't just start having dementia. Shaken, she walked back to her mother's room and said she had to run some errands and she'd be back later that afternoon. "When?" her mother asked.

"I don't know, Mom. Later." And she hurried to the elevator, her chest tight, her thoughts muddled.

Sitting in her car in the parking lot, she texted Allan, asking him to call her. He answered that he was in a meeting and would call when he was free.

On the drive back to Shelton, she struggled to slow down and pay attention to traffic. As she passed the nursing home on the outskirts of town, she saw an old woman sitting out front in a wheelchair, her head bowed forward, an aide standing a few feet away, smoking a cigarette.

She was heading into the center of town when Allan called. Pulling over in front of the hardware store, she answered.

"How's your mother?" he asked.

"Better, but not better. They're telling me she might have to get live-in help. Or move. I don't know what to do."

"What will that mean?"

"I don't know. This was all sprung on me."

"You'll figure it out. When are you coming back?"

"I can't even think about that until I know what's happening here. Believe me. I'd be gone now if I could."

"Okay," he said, sounding distracted.

"Are you on your computer?"

"I'm listening, but it's been a busy morning."

"I don't know how long I'll have to stay. Can I trust this doctor? I just don't know what to do."

"What shall I tell people here? I've got to deal with Jerry Walls."

She wanted him to reassure her, to tell her that everything would work out, that he had her back. But he didn't, and she couldn't ask him.

"Do you need money?" he asked.

"No, thanks," she said. "I can manage." But she couldn't. Not for long. She only had a thin cushion of savings.

"Did you ask the doctor to explain what he meant?"

"No, Allan, I didn't do that. He passed me off to a social worker. I'm up to my ears in shit here."

"Do what you have to do."

"And what would that be?"

"Don't get mad at me, Callie. I'm just trying to listen."

"Sorry. I'm completely overwhelmed."

"Hey, someone just showed up for a meeting. Gotta go. Bye."

She put down her phone and burst into tears. What she wanted was for him to drop everything and fly out to help her, but he was never going to do that. He wouldn't even delay a meeting for a few minutes to comfort her. Allan had seemed more worried about when she was coming back to work than how she felt. She had so many questions and she needed his advice. Did her mother really need that much support? Was there enough money for that? Would she have to come back to supervise her mother's care? What would that mean for her job and her life?

Back at the house, she saw a car in the driveway. No, not Wanda, please. She considered driving away, but then where would she go? Why was Wanda there all the time anyway, working extra days to soak her mother for more money? Callie sat in the car for a moment, collecting herself before going inside.

In the living room, she found the boy slumped in a chair, reading, his hat pulled down low, his shoes untied. When she said hello, he didn't answer. She was halfway up the stairs when Wanda called to her. "How's Mom today?"

"Better. Hard to say. I don't know."

Wanda stood at the bottom of the stairs, a broom in her hand. "Well, at least they're treating the infection."

Callie sighed, "Well, there's more to it than that."

"Oh? What do you mean?"

"They think she may not be able to live alone anymore."

"Oh, dear. Poor thing."

Exhausted, she just wanted to lie down.

Wanda asked what she was going to do. Would she get an aide, or would she move?

"I have no idea."

"I think—."

"This is my problem to figure out."

Wanda's cheeks flushed.

"I'm sorry. It's been a really bad day," and she headed toward her room.

Wanda called up the stairs. "Do you want some tea?"

"No, I need to lie down. I have a headache."

"Anything I can do, let me know."

"Okay," said Callie at her bedroom door.

"I'm only trying to help." She told Callie it was her regular day to clean, and she figured Callie wouldn't be home. When Callie told her she needn't finish, Wanda said it wouldn't be long and then they'd leave. She started whacking the broom against the risers as she swept the wooden stairs.

Just go away. Callie lay, curled on her bed, eyes squeezed shut.

Callie could now hear Wanda banging around in the kitchen. She was too jangled to sleep, knowing they were in the house. So, she sat up and wandered back downstairs again. When she asked Macky what book he was reading, he mumbled, "*Oliver Twist.*"

"Pretty big book. You can read that?" He shrugged. "Hey, I think that's my copy from high school." He looked at her warily. "No, you can keep it if you want."

Wanda stuck her head in from the kitchen, "Macky, we're out of here in a few minutes. Be ready soon."

Callie followed her into the kitchen and said, "Listen, I'm sorry. I didn't mean to be short with you. This has been really hard on me."

"I'm sure." She was spraying the counter with Windex.

"There's just a lot of pressure on me. I need to get back home. I have clients waiting, depending on me."

"Hmm," said Wanda as she stowed the spray under the sink.

"Please, I know you want to help, but let me deal with my mother. I'm taking care of things."

Wanda studied her. "Are you?"

Callie felt her scalp contract. "Excuse me?"

"Nothing." She lifted a garbage bag out of the can, tugging on the plastic strings. Then she passed by Callie and headed to the powder room under the stairs.

Callie followed her, ducking her head into the small room. "What did you say?"

Wanda washed her hands, then grabbing a towel, she turned to Callie. "I do more for your mother than you do. You didn't even know how she was. I'm the one who checks on her each week. I found her," she said, lowering her voice, "laying in her own mess."

"I didn't ask you to take care of my mother."

"Someone had to." She frowned at the mirror, combing her hair with her fingertips.

Callie wanted to slap her fat face. "Why are you here? Mom isn't even home. Don't you have another house to clean?" Callie could smell the coconut soap and see sweat beading in Wanda's hairline.

"Listen," Wanda said, breathing heavily. "I'm sorry you're having a hard time, but it's also hard to watch you ignore your mother." She pushed past Callie and walked into the front parlor. Callie followed.

"I'm not ignoring her. And it's not your business."

"At least I step up when I'm needed."

"You have no idea about my life. I step up for lots of people."

Wanda straightened the pillows, plumping them angrily. Then she turned and walked over to Callie, winded, her eyes blazing. "Tell me the truth. Did you even know who I was when I called you the other day?"

"What?"

"That first phone call. Did you remember me? Because I did see you at your father's memorial."

"But we didn't really know each other in school. So what if I didn't remember you right away?"

"I knew who you were."

"Okay, but not everyone has the same memories. And we didn't have any of the same classes."

"But we rode the school bus together every day for years. You used to come into the bakery when I was working. It's a small town."

"What's this about? That I didn't remember you instantly? I've had a lot on my mind."

"I know a lot about you. You were in all those clubs and the plays."

"So?"

"Your group looked down on me and my friends. You called us the farmers."

"I never did that."

"Come on. You and the honors group. So stuck-up. Clearly, you haven't changed." She wiped her sweaty upper lip and straightened a throw rug with her foot.

"Wow." Wanda clearly held a grudge. "High school was years ago. Time to move on."

Wanda stepped back, color rising to her cheeks. "Nothing's changed. Your mother needs you and you can barely give her the time of day."

"That's between me and my mother. And what connection does that have to you and high school? This is just weird."

"You know what they say about you?"

She sighed. "Do I even care?"

"Everyone knew about you running off with that teacher."

"That was years ago. And my business. And so what?"

"Couldn't wait to get out of town, huh?"

"Pretty much." And look what happens when you stay in town.

"Well, family is important, even if you move away. You can't leave them behind."

"You don't know me or my family."

"I know enough."

"Well, what have you done with your life, staying here, never leaving?"

"I'm raising a child. On my own. You just give massages to rich people. That's hardly life and death."

"Wow. You have no idea what I do. Don't you think it's just as hard to leave home and start over from scratch?"

"Not necessarily."

"Who are you to judge me? You clean houses for people who'd rather not do it themselves."

"Listen, I need to finish here, then we'll be out of your way. Won't you be glad?"

"Good. Fine. I'll leave you alone." She walked into the foyer and stood in front of a framed lithograph of Odysseus reaching home to find Penelope, and she took deep breaths to calm herself as she studied the details of the picture.

❋ ❋ ❋

Wanda looked at Callie's face, her upturned chin, dark circles under her eyes, pleased to see a booger sticking out of her nostril. She told Wanda she needed to finish and get out of there, and Callie said that would be great. But instead of going upstairs, she stood in the entryway. It made Wanda nervous to have Callie so close by. She needed to finish up and get out of there. She shouldn't have said that thing about high school, but what kind of nerve did Callie have to treat Wanda as if she were nothing? She made people's lives easier. She was making a life for her son. How dare she?

The last thing to do was to dust the front parlor so she grabbed a rag from her bucket. Every surface was covered with silver frames holding photos of Callie dancing, Callie playing the cello, Callie in her cap and gown, Callie in a play, her arm thrown to the side, her mouth wide open. Callie, Callie, Callie. Blah, blah, blah. It was a pain to dust in there because she had to pick up each frame, dust it, dust the table, and put it back in the same place. She was tempted to leave them for next time, but that was just the kind of thing Mrs. Morton would notice and complain about, and she didn't need that right now. Wanda wanted the house to look perfect for when she came home.

Wanda picked one photo up, wiped the glass, removing smudges. It showed Callie in her cap and gown, getting an award, her head tilted, as if she were pretending to be humble. For me? Really? But clearly it was just another award she knew she deserved. As Wanda poked the glass with her cloth-covered finger to wipe the smirk off Callie's face. The frame slipped out of her hand and clattered onto the bare wood floor. When she bent over to pick up the pieces, pain shot up her back, The glass had splintered, a cobweb of cracks spilling out from the center of Callie's face, like a bullseye.

"Oh, great," Callie said, standing in the doorway.

"I'm sorry. It slipped," Wanda said, picking up shards. "I'll replace the glass."

Callie took the frame, frowned at it, sighing angrily.

"I said I was sorry."

She heard Macky calling her from the living room. "What happened?"

"Why don't you leave and stop doing damage so I can have some peace?"

Wanda stood up slowly because of her back. "What's your problem with me? What did I ever do to you?"

"You never did anything. You are *literally* not on my mind at all. *Ever.*" Her face looked so cold, her mouth turned down, ugly.

Wanda's eyes blurred for an instant, a film covering them. "Wow, you are such a bitch."

Callie's eyes widened and her mouth dropped open. "*I'm* a bitch? Fine. Get out of here. Just go!"

"Oh, yeah. We're *out* of here." Wanda said, tossing rags and polish into her cleaning bucket, "You can just clean up the mess if that's what you want."

"Stop!" Macky stood in the doorway, his hands over his ears, his eyes squeezed shut.

"Oh, Macky," Wanda took him aside, lowering her voice. "Sorry. We were just talking."

"No. Yelling." He was wheezing, his breath raspy. He yanked his arm from hers and ran into the living room where he fell onto the floor, his chest heaving, his breathing shallow, hugging himself. Wanda ran after him and crouched down, feeling sharp pain in her back.

"What's wrong?" asked Callie.

Wanda leaned down close to his face, but he pushed her away, shrieking, beating his fists against her.

"Is he okay?" asked Callie.

"Quiet." She was leaning over him, trying to get him to look her in the eyes.

"Can I help?"

"No!" She turned to him. "Slow down, Macky. Please. Breathe." It hurt her back to get down on the floor. "Come on, sweetie, slow, slow. I shouldn't have shouted." Macky was on his back, hammering his feet on the floor, wheezing. She turned to Callie. "Go get me a paper bag." Callie ran into the kitchen. "By the back door." Macky was hysterical. She tried to fend off his kicks, but he landed the heel of his shoe right on her breast. She yelped but forced herself to lean in, guarding her chest from his feet. "Come on, Macky."

Callie returned with a bag. "Open it." Callie shook it and handed it to her. "Come on, baby. Breathe into this."

✳ ✳ ✳

Callie watched Wanda try to calm her son without touching him. She was crying, which made it worse, and the boy was flailing and kicking, his face bright red. He landed blows without her stopping him. He needed help, falling apart so quickly, going from quietly reading to a complete tantrum. Clearly, Wanda was afraid to be firm with him.

"Let me try something," Callie said.

"You don't know how. I've got this."

"I think I can help."

Wanda ignored her and kept asking Macky to please calm down, breathe, as if that would do anything.

When he kicked her, Wanda yelped and fell back, clutching her breast.

Callie said she wanted to do something. "Catch your breath."

She sat behind Macky and said, "Macky, I'm going to give you a big hug." She put her legs on either side of him and wrapped her arms around his chest. He bucked and kicked and howled, but she held firm. He was hot and sweaty and smelled like dirty hair. Arching his back, he rammed his head into her mouth, sending a searing pain through her front teeth. She tasted blood and felt her lip go numb, but she held on, counting to herself, her eyes shut.

Wanda pulled on Callie's arm. "What are you doing?"

Callie whispered to him, "Shh, Macky, shh," as she tried to maintain a calm firmness.

"That won't work," Wanda said. "He has to run down on his own."

As she held him, feeling his skinny arms quiver, his screams shredding her ears. I'm stronger than you, she thought, determined.

He was like a trapped animal, strengthened by his panic. I'm stronger than you. Her arms strained as he struggled, but slowly, his resistance weakened, and she continued her hold. When she thought it was safe, she told Wanda to take over, to hug him from behind as she had.

"What?"

"Yes, take my place. Hold him like I did." Wanda crawled over and reached her arms around Macky while Callie scooted down by his feet. "Don't let go." She slipped off his shoes and tossed them. He scissored his legs, but she grabbed his feet so he couldn't kick her. "Ssh, Macky, ssh. I'm giving you a massage. I'll bet you've never had one of those. That's it. Just breathe." Then as she held his feet with one hand, she started with the other to massage his leg up the shin, from calf to thigh, up and down, rotating the foot, kneading the sole. Then she switched legs and started on the other one.

"Let me call the EMTs," said Wanda.

"No, this should work." She squeezed her hand around his skinny calf. "Hey, Macky, up, up to your knee, down, down to your toes. And around goes your foot. And back up again." Macky's lips were quivering, his body rigid. For a kid with floppy muscles, he was surprisingly strong.

Wanda placed her mouth right next to his ear, crooning to him. "Baby, try to relax."

"That's it. Reassure him, but don't let go." They worked together, Wanda holding him, Callie tapping and rubbing and slowly, Macky gradually gave up his fight until his body grew limp. Wrung out, he now allowed Callie to flex his feet, to bend his knees, to rotate his legs in the hip sockets. Despite his precocious reading and intelligence, he looked smaller and younger than six. She'd seen him walk. His gait was awkward, his muscles hypotonic.

Wanda was scared but had risen to the challenge. Callie could hear Wanda try to force calm into her voice, trying to soothe Macky. How scary these episodes must be. But she clearly loved this odd little boy.

Macky lay on his back, humming, on the verge of sleep, and Callie sat back on her heels, shaking out her tired arms.

Wanda was covered with sweat, her hair wild, her face mottled with red blotches. "How did you know to do that?" Wanda asked, running her hand over Macky's head. "Your lip is cut. Are you all right?"

She felt her swollen lip with her tongue. "His head banged against my mouth, but I'm fine."

"Let me get you ice." She pulled herself to her feet, breathing heavily. It looked as if she had bad knees. "Would you like a glass of water?"

"I guess. But don't you hate the taste of the water here?"

"Yeah, it's awful," said Wanda. "Smells like rotten eggs."

"You should try washing your hair. No lather."

"Yeah, I know."

Callie joined her in the kitchen where Wanda opened the refrigerator, grabbed a bottle of cranberry juice and poured each of them a glass. When Callie took a sip, the juice stung her lip.

"I can't believe you could get him to calm down," said Wanda. "He hates being touched."

"It doesn't make total sense, but sometimes a firm hug is less scary than a light touch. Kids like him sometimes do well with deep massage. Anything softer tickles and makes them feel overwhelmed."

"Kids like him?"

"He's really sensitive, right?"

"Yes."

"Sounds? Smells?"

"Uh huh."

"This has happened before?"

"Yes. And it's gotten worse." Her voice caught in her throat. "He had croup the other day and couldn't breathe, so the EMTs came."

"That must have been scary."

"I thought it was my fault."

"No, you didn't cause this. He's wired this way."

"Is there something wrong with him?"

"He just feels things more than most kids do. You're a good mom. I can tell. And he can get help."

They sat down at the kitchen table, and Callie pushed the slips of paper to the side. Wanda started to straighten them, but Callie told her to sit, to catch her breath. She sat back, closed her eyes, and drank her juice.

"I'm sorry," Wanda said, "for getting so angry at you. And for saying your job wasn't important."

"No, I'm sorry. I've been in a terrible mood. This has been so hard."

"I'm sure," said Wanda, straightening the fringe of the place-mat. "Your mom is going to be okay. You'll figure it out."

"I hope so."

Wanda stood up, walked over, and peeked around the corner, reporting that Macky was still out like a light.

"It has to wear him out completely. And you, too."

She nodded, fighting back tears. "I'm sorry I said you were a bitch in high school."

"Well, I probably was. I hate to think how self-centered I was back then."

"And I'm sorry I said you don't want to help your mother."

"I'm not doing a very good job of it. We don't get along."

"It's hard with mothers and daughters." She said her mother was critical of how she was raising Macky. "She's really hard on him. Not like she is with the other grandkids."

"That's too bad. He's a good kid. So smart."

She thanked Callie then asked what she had to do next for her mother.

"I don't know. And I don't live here and have no idea how to find help for her."

"I can help you. I know some homecare workers."

"Thanks, you've been a big help already. There's just so much going on right now and this came at a bad time."

"Is there ever a good time?"

"I need to be in better touch with her."

"It's not easy," said Wanda. "Do you mind if we stay until he wakes up?"

"Of course. Stay as long as you want," said Callie, pushing back her chair and walking to the window, where she looked out at the bare branches of the maple tree out front which, in a month, would leaf out and shade the front yard for the summer. Then in the fall, the leaves would turn red, drop, and the cycle would start all over again.

✻ ✻ ✻

Wanda watched Callie stare out the window and heard her sigh. What was she thinking about? Her mother? Or was she eager for Wanda and Macky to leave so she could be alone? Wanda felt sad to think that Callie had no family except her mother who was now old and sick. How hard to be torn between Shelton and Chicago. Seeing how strong Callie had been, holding Macky and getting him to settle, she wondered why Callie had made the effort when she didn't have to. Getting down on the floor and rolling around with a child in the middle of a tantrum. Who does that? Was there more to Callie than she realized?

Wanda asked, "Can I tell you something?"

"Sure. What?"

"Let me get some coffee. Want some?" She didn't. Wanda poured a cup and sat down. "I have to say it, or I'll lose my nerve."

"Only if you want to tell me." Callie put her phone down and sat back in her chair. "Take your time."

Wanda took a deep breath. "It happened right after David died."

18

WANDA AND CALLIE

"Really?" Callie asked, clearly taken aback. "Whit? How?"

"It just happened." She flashed on Whit that night, groaning in her ear. "I had to tell someone." Blood was whooshing in her ears, and her eyes stung.

"Why me?"

"I don't know, but I thought you'd understand. You've made your own mistakes. And you don't live here. You won't be spreading it around town."

"You haven't told anyone?"

"Just David." Callie raised her eyebrows. "I talk to him sometimes. But I needed to say it to someone in person."

"Are you sure he's the father?" Wanda nodded. "Do you think anyone suspects?"

"I was sure someone would spot the resemblance to Whit, especially since Macky is so smart and, well," she said pointing to herself, "but no one has. I can see it, though."

"Why would anyone suspect?"

"Maybe they won't, but I keep feeling I should tell the Sutters. I owe it to them."

"Why do you owe them?"

"They're his grandparents. And he's the only grandchild they'll ever have. But first, I need to tell David's parents. And it's going to kill them."

"I get that it's going to be hard," she said. "Maybe they'll surprise you."

"You don't know them, but I can't live with this any longer. And I have to do it soon or I'll lose my nerve." Wanda asked Callie when she was going back to Chicago.

"In a few days." Her phone beeped and she flipped it over with the screen facing up.

"I'm sorry," said Wanda. "I shouldn't have burdened you with this right now with all you have going on with your mom."

"No," she said, silencing her phone, "that's okay." But it wasn't really.

"Any chance you could stay with Macky while I go talk to David's parents? I can't bring him along, obviously. I'd take him to my mother's, but I'm afraid I'll blurt out the truth. And he likes you. Usually, he won't let a new person get close to him."

"Okay, I can do that. When?"

"How about tomorrow morning?"

"Uh, sure. Get it over with."

❊ ❊ ❊

Callie arrived the following morning to hang out with Macky. She said she hadn't realized there was an apartment so close to the bakery and said if she lived there, she'd have gained a ton. Wanda sucked in her stomach and said she didn't think about it much anymore. As if Callie had ever had to worry about her weight.

"Well, I'm off. Macky, you do what Callie says."

"We'll be fine," Callie said and whispered, "Good Luck."

On her way over to the Zaceks', Wanda felt frozen with fear. When she pulled into the driveway, she sat in the car, weighing whether she could back out and leave before they saw her. But Sandy poked her head out the front door. "Hi. You didn't bring Macky?"

"I need to talk to you," Wanda said. She couldn't turn back now.

"What's wrong. Is he okay?"

"He's fine. Is Burt home?"

"Yes. Come in. Burt! Wanda's here." They entered the living room where Burt was watching TV. Sandy told him to shut it off.

Wanda glanced at the portrait of David staring at her from the frame. Her heart was thumping, and she declined Sandy's offer of coffee. She sat across from them and wiped her palms on her knees. "This is so hard."

"What, honey?" said Sandy. "Just tell us."

"You know I loved David so much. I still love him."

"Of course," said Sandy, her voice soft. "We don't doubt that for a moment."

"After he died, I was devastated. Out of my mind with grief."

Burt's slung his arm around Sandy, and she laid her head on his shoulder.

"The day before the service, when we had to go to the funeral home to see the casket, it was so horrible. That evening, I couldn't stay one more minute in the apartment without him, so I drove to a place where I could be alone. I was crying and thinking about him when this person came up. And he was nice to me. I don't know how it happened…"

"Yes?"

Her throat closed, and she tried to swallow. "We did something."

"What did you do?" Sandy said, her face expectant, not yet understanding.

"It was only once." She looked down, took a deep breath, the blood whooshing in her ears. "Then I was pregnant. And I knew…"

"Wait. You mean Macky?"

Wanda nodded.

Sandy let out a long moan, her head in her hands, then she heaved herself up and lunged at Wanda, slapping her, "You slut!"

Burt held her as she strained against him. "Sandy, honey, don't."

He led her back to the sofa. "The day before his funeral?" she said, her voice thin and hoarse. "Then you sat there in the *church* and acted like you were upset?"

"I was destroyed."

"Yeah, I can see that. You couldn't even wait until he was buried to go find someone else." She swiped at her eyes, then glared at Wanda. "You've killed David all over again. And now you've taken Macky from us."

"No, Macky is still yours. Don't hold that against him."

"Get out of here. I can't look at you."

"Please, I'm so sorry to hurt you. I just thought you should know the truth."

"No, get out!"

"Sandy, ssh," said Burt, patting her back. "Please."

She broke away and staggered down the hall. Wanda could hear her gagging in the powder room. Wanda sat, her face burning from the sting of Sandy's slap, her hands icy. Why had she confessed? Now, she'd made everything worse.

Burt followed Sandy down the hall and tried to get her to open the door. Wanda glanced at the portrait of David and felt his stare. She wanted to run but couldn't move. After a couple of minutes, Burt returned to the living room, looking flushed and shaken. Wanda worried either one of them could have a heart attack.

"Please, Burt. Don't punish Macky for what I did."

"Who is it?"

"It doesn't matter. He's not in the picture."

"Has Macky met him?"

"No."

"How can we believe anything you say?"

"Well, it's the truth."

"What does Macky know?"

"Nothing. I'll tell him someday."

"Does he have to know? How does the truth help him? Or any of us?" His eyes were puffy. "Won't it make him feel strange around us?"

"No, he loves you. Please. I don't have to come here any-more, but please don't cut him out."

"When he finds out he'll hate you. And you'll deserve it."

"I have to live with that."

He stood leaning on his recliner, breathing heavily. "I need to go tend to Sandy."

She gathered her bag and stumbled to the door, looking back at the portrait and the gold star in the window. Sitting in her car, shivering, she waited for her hands to stop shaking before she felt safe to drive. And she wondered if she'd done the right thing. Had she been selfish? Should she have just kept the secret? But then she thought of the Sutters and what it would mean to them to know that they had a grandchild. She started the car and drove, heading toward the spot where she could talk to David. She pulled over, cut the engine, laid her head on the steering wheel, and started to sob. When she'd worn herself out, she sat up and told David she knew she had to accept whatever blame was thrown at her. She only hoped that Macky wouldn't hate her when he found out. She couldn't bear to lose him too.

✳ ✳ ✳

Macky sat, his eyes riveted on his screen, and Callie asked if he'd like a cookie from the bakery. He said he'd rather have bread, so she nipped downstairs and bought a loaf of sourdough and took it back upstairs. Then she sliced off two pieces and put them in the toaster before slathering them with butter. But he told her, annoyed as if she should know, that he hated butter and wanted it plain. She cut one for him and ate the two buttered slices herself as she scrolled through her emails. Her phone pinged and she read a message from Maxine, a client with cervical pain, who asked when she was coming back. *This is all taking longer than I'd planned I'll certainly be back next week so sorry.*

She looked around the apartment for something to read, but all Wanda had on her shelf were historical romances. Callie wasn't that bored. Wanda had furnished the apartment with flowered curtains and matching tablecloth. Seeing only one bedroom, she hoped Macky and Wanda didn't sleep in the same bed. In the living room she found a wedding photo of David and Wanda and another of him in his football uniform. Did Wanda have the right idea, to pick someone from her local pool? But then, was it even more devastating to lose her one and only love? At least she had Macky.

306

She studied him, his messy hair, his heavy glasses, his two-finger typing. She couldn't imagine giving birth as young as Wanda had. Callie liked kids, but they seemed far in the future. She imagined being a cool stepmom to Allan's daughter, Agnes, but if he didn't want more children, would being a stepmother be enough for her? They'd talked only once by phone since she'd left Chicago and had texted back and forth. She wanted to blame his wife for making it hard for him to communicate, but she also knew he could have called her if he'd really wanted to. What was she doing, counting on him?

She sat down again. "Hey, Macky, what are you reading?" He was so focused; she wasn't sure he'd heard her.

"An article on arachnids," he said, his eyes on the screen.

"For school?"

"No, it's my own work."

"How's school?

"It's easy. I'm way ahead."

"Do you miss going to school every day?

"No."

"What about friends?"

He shrugged. "I'm fine. I hang out with my mom. And my grandparents."

"But don't you want friends your own age?"

"Not really."

She studied him as he pecked away.

He looked at her. "What?"

"Just watching you concentrate."

He shook his head and peered at his screen again. After a minute, he asked, "How do you know so much about massage?"

"Like you, I studied hard. Muscles, tendons, ligaments. It's really interesting." He was back to typing. "Did that massage help you?"

He leaned forward, squinting at the screen, and she realized she'd embarrassed him. Stupid of her to remind him of his meltdown. She had a lot to learn about kids.

Then she picked up her phone to research agencies for home healthcare for her mother. She wanted a live-in person, but maybe two part-time people made more sense. This all depended on her mother agreeing to this, and Callie didn't know how she was going to pull that off. Her mother had no idea how complicated this was to arrange. Wanda had mentioned some local women who might be less expensive. Was that safe? All this had given Callie a headache. As soon as Wanda returned, she'd head to the hospital to try to convince her mother to accept the inevitable. She'd be patient, but firm, stressing safety. But now it was getting late, and she was exhausted. Maybe she'd go tomorrow morning when they'd both be fresh.

Finally, at around eleven, Wanda came back, her face blotchy, eyes red. She motioned Callie outside and told her that it had been horrible, that Sandy had slapped her and called her a slut. Callie asked if she regretted telling them, and Wanda said she didn't know. She looked exhausted. "I'm going to go lay down. Thanks so much for staying with Macky. I'm so worried this is going to turn his grandparents against him." She started to cry. Callie wasn't sure if she should hug her, but then Wanda threw her arms around Callie and gathered her into a tight grasp. Callie patted Wanda on the back, smelling her sweat and shampoo. "I admire you. This is very tough. But you're facing it."

"I don't know. But it's too late now to undo the damage."

On her way to the hospital, Callie thought about how much courage it must have taken for Wanda to tell the truth after all this time. Who knew the right thing to do, not knowing if she was making it better or a whole lot worse? How does someone untangle a big, knotted mess?

When she walked into the room, she found her mother sitting up in a chair, her hair neatly pinned into a bun. When she saw Callie, her face brightened. "Oh, there you are. I was hoping you'd be able to find me."

"Well, I do know where you've been these past couple of days."

"I know that. I'm just happy to see you."

Really? thought Callie. "How do you feel?"

"Much better." And Callie thought she looked more lucid. "The doctor says I can go home in a day or so."

"About that," she said sitting on the bed next to the chair. "Yes, it'll be great to go home. But the doctors think you're going to need some extra help at home."

"Oh, no. I'll be fine."

"You weren't in good shape living alone."

"I was fine until I got sick."

"Everyone thinks you should have someone stay with you. At least for a while."

"Someone living in my house? I don't want that."

"Mom, I can't be worrying about you from 700 miles away."

"But I'm so much better now."

"Yes, and we want to keep it that way."

"Wanda can check on me."

"That's not her job."

"Such a lot of fuss. Can't you just stay a bit longer?"

Callie felt a flutter in her gut. "No, I have to get back to work."

Her mother said nothing, clearly displeased. Callie felt the pressure on her to cave and let her mother have her own way.

Her mother looked up and said, "I guess I have no choice." To see her mother frail and weak but accepting, making it easier for Callie but harder for herself, Callie felt her anger start to give way to a fear of losing her, something she hadn't really considered before.

"Mom, this will be good. She can keep the place neat and fix meals for you. Let her pamper you."

"So much fuss."

"I'll visit."

She teared up. "I am so touched that you came all this way just to see how I am."

"Of course, Mom."

"You're my girl. I'm sorry to be so much trouble. I know you're busy. I don't know what I'd do without you."

And Callie found herself choked up. "I love you, Mama."

"Of course, dear. I love you too. I wish your father could see you now. He was so proud of you."

Regret sloshed through her. She swallowed hard. "I am so sorry I ran off like I did. That was a terrible thing to do to you both." Her eyes stung, and she wiped them with the back of her hand.

"You had to find your way."

"I'm sorry I didn't make up with Papa while I could."

"You know, I should have helped. I thought I was protecting him. But he did love you and knew you loved him."

Callie rose and gave her mother a long hug, letting herself cry, saying she was sorry, so sorry.

"I knew you'd come back some day."

Callie sat with her mother, and for the first time in ages, she didn't feel like running away. The important thing was that her mother could stay in her house, that she'd see to it that there was someone who would help but not intrude. And Callie would visit now, whenever she could. "It's still home." She said she had to go back to Chicago for a while, but she'd come back as soon as she could.

✳ ✳ ✳

Later that week, Wanda decided to talk to the Sutters. Telling them would be less awful than it had been with Sandy and Burt, but Wanda steeled herself against their reaction. What if they were angry that she'd denied them access to Macky for six years? Would it bring up their grief about Whit? Would they reject Macky, making him the target of their anger when she was the one who deserved it?

Instead, they were thrilled. "It all makes sense now," Janine said. "I thought I was drawn to him because he was so smart, like Whit, now I know it's a deeper bond. He's part of Whit." She took her husband's hand and raised it to her lips. Alden looked at her, his eyes red-rimmed and glassy.

Wanda asked them not to tell anyone yet, acknowledging that was a very hard thing to ask of them. David's parents were hurt and angry, and Macky didn't know yet. "Ideally, he'd know first, but he's just so young. I couldn't wait any longer though to tell the truth." And she apologized again for keeping it from them for so long.

Janine asked if they could see Macky. Could they give him gifts? Have a relationship with him? Janine said they could accept Macky not knowing yet who they were as long as they could spend time with him. And Wanda was grateful for that but worried they'd slip up and reveal the truth.

"I'd always hoped he'd grow up and meet a girl and get married, but over the years, I stopped hoping for that. It just didn't seem

311

like Whit. We'd wondered if he was gay and would have accepted it if he were, but he had such a hard time with any kind of close relationship. We just wanted him to be happy." And she broke down, crying.

"I'm sorry this brings up bad memories for you."

"No, it's both wonderful and sad," said Alden. "A chance for us. But something we can't share with Whit." He looked at his wife, his hands trembling.

Wanda didn't admit that Whit might have known he was the father, that she'd feared it might have been a factor in his suicide, the thing that tipped him over the edge. She imagined he must have been paralyzed at the thought.

They offered to help Wanda financially, but she said she and Macky were fine. She hadn't told them for that reason. It was overdue, but now it felt right. Janine asked what he should call them, and Wanda said that for now, Mr. and Mrs. Sutter, but in time, that could change. Wanda considered him a lucky boy to have six grandparents who loved him.

On her way home, she felt a weight had been lifted, but then, the complications started to dawn on her. Would the adults keep the secret from Macky? Should she tell him now rather than later to avoid his learning by accident? What would the reaction be when the news made its way through town? Would Macky be shunned? Would she be labeled a bad person? Would Sandy and Burt ever speak to her again? Wanda thought of Macky and worried that down the road, he'd miss out on love too.

❆ ❆ ❆

Callie hired Lena Falk, a friend of Wanda's, in her fifties and divorced, looking to earn some money. She'd done homecare work before and agreed to move in to one of the bedrooms. Callie rushed to put all the pieces in place, but she needed to get back to Chicago. She had her clients, but she also had to deal with the complaint. And she missed her friends and her apartment. She bought her mother a new robe and slippers and bought her new books and set up a radio in her bedroom, then worried they were peace offerings to salve her conscience. "I'll be back soon. I promise."

Her mother was subdued, relieved to be home but worried that her privacy would be ruined, making an effort but not happy about the arrangement. When it was time for Callie to say good-bye, it was surprisingly hard to leave. Guilt? Nostalgia? Worry? She hugged her mother, breathing in her lotion smell, then looked back at Lena tending to her mother as she swallowed a big lump in her throat. Why was it so hard to leave?

On the drive back to Chicago, she had plenty of time to think about Allan, the complaint filed against her, her future at the spa, and what she really wanted from life. Halfway back to Chicago, she pulled into a thruway stop, called Allan, and broke up with him. "I just can't sleep with my married boss anymore." When he argued that he was about to leave his wife, that she had to be patient, she said, "It's only one of the reasons. We can talk when I get back." What she didn't tell him is that she'd decided to quit her job. She'd open her own private practice. It was time to take charge of her life.

Even though she hadn't been gone all that long, returning to her apartment felt like she'd been away on a long trip. The familiar smells of coffee grounds and oranges greeted her along with eucalyptus, which Ping had brought and put in a vase. Ping had taken good care of the plants in her absence, and had even replenished her refrigerator with fruit, bread, and a bottle of wine. Callie fixed herself a sandwich and sat in the window with a glass of wine and looked at people out on the street walking dogs, carrying grocery totes, parking cars, jogging. Her neighborhood. Home. But she also felt pulled in another direction, her other home. She called Shelton, and Lena answered but handed the phone to her mother, who sounded chipper, full of bland details about her day. Callie said she missed her but would be back soon. Relieved to be in Chicago but worried about her mother.

The next day, she'd packed her schedule with clients but knew to stretch before and after to avoid strained muscles. She slipped in early and went straight to her studio to avoid seeing Allan. It was great to reconnect with her clients—Jessica, Maxine, Mel, Stanley. Some asked about her mother, some tried to guilt her about leaving them in the lurch, but she didn't let them faze her. She had to resist their chattiness and regain her focus. She relied on her routines—setting the lights, the music, laying out the clean sheets, lining up the bottles of lotion, warming her hands.

When Allan had called her the night she returned, she'd told him she needed to move on professionally, to open her own studio. Was this about the complaint? he asked. No, she knew she hadn't done anything wrong. This was the right thing to do. What she didn't tell him is that she'd already talked to Bethany, Lacey, Ping, and Olga about starting a business together, renting a small space. She hoped to take clients with her, but she could build a practice without having to answer to a boss, particularly one with whom she was sleeping but who didn't care about her.

She'd also decided to spend more time in Shelton. If there were five of them in the practice, she could spend three weeks a month in Chicago, working with clients, and one week in Shelton, seeing her mother. And she could seek new clients in Shelton. It wasn't forever, but it was a way to do her work while also keeping tabs on her mother. That's all she had time for now.

✳ ✳ ✳

Although Wanda had vowed to keep the circle tight, she found herself telling her mother. But although her mother seemed sympathetic, nothing changed in her criticisms of Macky.

She wouldn't tell Michelle. Not yet. Michelle would either judge her or make a point of talking about God's forgiveness, and Wanda didn't need or want that.

One day, she had the strong impulse to call Benny. She made up a pretense, asking him advice relating to elder care for a friend. But really, she just needed to figure out how he'd see her if he knew the truth. Maybe in time, she'd tell him too.

315

19

Wanda and Callie

On Columbus Day, when both Wanda and Macky had a day off from school, they drove up the hill toward the Sutters' house so he could choose books from Whit's room to keep. Janine had been asking Wanda for months to go in and clear out his room before they put the house on the market. Because of Alden's Parkinson's, he and Janine needed to downsize. Wanda and Macky could take what they wanted, and Janine would donate the rest to Goodwill. It was now or never.

Wanda had been dreading this day for a long time, but since the Sutters had been so incredibly generous after learning they were Macky's grandparents, it was time to get over her fear. And she couldn't deny them the pleasure of spoiling Macky, particularly after all the time they'd lost with him. At first, when they'd offered to pay for Macky's tuition at the brand-new school for gifted children in Granville, Wanda had refused, feeling they couldn't take the money. Besides, she'd told them, he'd had a bad start in public school. But Janine had said it was money that would have gone to Whit eventually, and now they wanted it to help Macky. What better use than helping educate their grandson? Finally, when Wanda admitted to herself that Macky had outgrown homeschooling, she agreed, worried though that he might have the same social problems and be asked to leave. But so far, he seemed to like Greenwood well enough. At least they surrounded him with other smart children. Macky hadn't once balked at going or asked where the money had come from. She'd hinted that the Sutters were very fond of him and wanted to help him. Little hints about who they were, dropped here and there, would eventually lead to her telling him some, if not all, of the truth. His going to school full-time meant she could start taking courses again at the CC to work on her nursing certificate.

They pulled into the driveway behind a car where Callie sat, her head bent over her phone. Wanda tapped on the window and Callie lowered it. "Have you been waiting long?" Wanda asked.

"No, I'm just doing work texts. Hey, Macky. How's it going?"

He could barely see around the tower of empty boxes. Wanda saw him make eye contact with Callie, then look away, but even that brief connection showed he liked her. "Mrs. Sutter said I could have as many books as I want."

"Within reason," Wanda reminded him.

"What if there are a lot I really need? I can store them under my bed. Or maybe at Grandma Sandy's."

"We'll figure it out." She was glad to see him so excited. "How's your mom?"

"Okay. Annoyed at me but resigned to having a caregiver stay with her. Lena's so good with my mother, getting her up moving, keeping her clean. I have little effect on my mother, but she'll do what Lena wants."

"It's easier when it's not family. If you saw me with my mother, you'd see a different story." Learning the truth about Macky only gave her mother one more reason not to accept him.

"Oh, I know that," said Callie. "And she's safe in her home so I don't worry so much when I'm away." Callie said she'd be in town all week. She'd picked up local massage clients and would be seeing them at her mother's house.

"We can go visit her in a day or so if you think she'd like that."

"That's great. She loves you and Macky."

She stepped out of the car and the three of them stood looking at the Sutters' house, a dark brick two-story deeply shaded by fir trees. A carpet of needles lay on the bare yard. The Sutters should have the trees trimmed to bring in some sunlight and allow grass to grow before putting the house on the market. Wanda patted Callie on the back, and the three of them walked up the brick path to the door.

Janine gave both Wanda and Callie hugs, then she stuck her hand out to Macky. "How are you today?" Wanda nodded to him, and he shook her hand formally. Wanda was grateful to Janine for her restraint in not hugging him.

"Where're the books?" he asked, as the boxes toppled over into the foyer.

"You be patient, now," said Wanda.

"I don't blame you one bit," said Janine, leading them toward the kitchen. "First though, can I get you both some coffee? And a glass of milk for you?"

"I told you already, I don't drink milk."

"Macky, say 'no, thank you,'" said Wanda.

"That's right," said Janine. "I keep forgetting that. Whit always liked milk—well, I have fresh coffee cake." She turned to Wanda. "Is that okay?"

She poured three mugs, handed plates to Callie and the cake to Wanda. They headed into the living room where her husband sat in his reading chair, a pile of books on both sides. Parkinson's had made his voice weak and his hands shaky, but he could still read. He put down his book, nodding stiffly. "I fear I can no longer stand when ladies enter the room."

"Oh, no need for that," said Callie.

Alden stared at Macky with a slight smile, and Wanda wondered if he saw Whit in her boy.

They sat in chairs facing a coffee table. Wanda balanced her mug and took a slice of cake, but she was nervous and could barely swallow. She washed it down with coffee. Macky picked out a walnut, making a face, and set his plate on the table, swinging his legs, bouncing on the chair.

❄ ❄ ❄

Callie noted how hard Janine was trying with Macky. When Janine looked at him, her eyes misted, but she seemed genuinely happy to see him. Macky didn't reciprocate her warmth, but Janine clearly knew not to crowd him. Macky always had questions for Callie about anatomy and her massage practice. What a smart, quirky kid. How brave of Wanda to face the rippling repercussions of the truth.

Callie picked up a framed photo of Whit from an end table, one of those posed school portraits that are always awkward, but more so with Whit. He wore thick glasses, and his hair stuck out in tufts. Clearly, he'd been instructed to smile, but he clenched his teeth in a snaggley grimace. In high school, Whit still had that smile and no clue how to connect to anyone.

"I remember Whit at this age. This must have been about fourth grade, right? Mrs. Reynolds' class?"

"Yes," said Janine, after swallowing a bite. No matter how hard I tried to make his hair look presentable for picture day, he managed to look as if he'd been rolling around in the attic." She put her plate down and sighed. "But he was so sweet. That was a happy time for him. At least I'd like to think so." Her eyes reddened, and she cleared her throat, looking over at her husband.

Callie glanced at Wanda who was trying to get Macky not to fidget. "I think that was the same year we did the school science fair. I grew crystals. Pretty basic. But Whit did that elaborate, detailed map of the cosmos. Most of the other parents did their kids' projects for them. All those paper mâché volcanoes and projects downloaded from the Internet. My parents made me do everything myself, which I now appreciate, but at the time, I was embarrassed to sit there with my dorky crystals while everyone was oohing and aching over the exploding volcanos and the skeleton. But I remember you came over to my desk and asked me how I grew each crystal like I was an authority. That was so kind of you."

"Of course, dear. I knew you'd done the work yourself."

Callie asked Wanda, "What about you? Do you remember your project?"

"I never did one. I guess they thought we weren't smart enough."

Callie felt her face redden. "That's not true," but she stopped, knowing Wanda might be right. "Just as well. It made me cynical."

Janine turned to Macky. "Speaking of projects, how's it going at Greenwood?"

"Fine," he said scratching his nose.

"Tell Mrs. Sutter about the team project you're doing."

He stared out the window, bouncing.

"They work in teams," Wanda said, "going between independent learning and group work." She patted his knee and continued.

"It's been really good. Greenwood encourages him to move ahead, but they also want him to work on social skills and physical activity."

"Kinetic wellness," groaned Macky.

"Oh," said Janine. "Is that fun?"

He shrugged. "Not really."

"But Greenwood has been great, and he's met some nice boys," said Wanda. "What a difference from the local school."

Callie wondered how well Macky liked Greenwood.

Macky asked when he could see the books.

✳ ✳ ✳

"Well then," Janine said. "Let's do it," and Macky popped to his feet, stacked the empty boxes again and headed to the stairs. Wanda took the top one off his pile, and she headed up behind the three of them. On the wall along the stairs, Wanda spotted a photo of Whit standing in front of a huge telescope, his father next to him, their arms folded across their chests. Seeing the resemblances to Macky—head tilted, chin lifted, nearly made her miss a step. That little boy. The way he stood tall, mirroring his father. What would Macky think to learn he was part of them, part of their blood? Her chest tightened and, feeling faint, she reached out for the banister and forced herself up one step at a time, her head pounding.

She joined them at the end of the hall in front of a closed door. Janine handed Callie a roll of garbage bags. "I'm not going in with you. It's too painful. I've said goodbye to the room."

"Why is it painful?" asked Macky.

"Macky, don't ask personal questions."

"I don't mind, and I'm sorry to inflict this on you." She looked to Wanda for permission to continue. Wanda nodded, trusting her

321

to go only so far. "This was my son's room. But he died." Macky stood still, looking at the floor, but the wheels were turning. "But I wanted to give his books to someone who likes science. You're a lot like him."

Wanda's heart seized.

"Because you like the same things," she continued. "You're both smart."

"How did he die?" asked Macky.

"Macky, no," said Wanda, leaning over and whispered to him, her hand on his shoulder.

"That's okay," said Janine. "It's an understandable question."

"No, you have to learn not to ask rude questions."

"Why is it rude?"

"Should we just go home and forget about the books altogether?" He shook his head and tears sprang to his eyes. "Then you have to work on being more patient and polite." But she knew it was exactly the question that would come to mind. But not yet. Who Whit was, how he died, how could she ever explain? That he didn't want to live anymore? Let her boy be unaware a bit longer and never learn the whole truth. "Good, remember, you can take what you want, but only what can fit in three boxes. So, pack carefully."

"Maybe thinner books so I can get more?"

"That's a thought. But pick the ones you really want."

Janine repeated that as far as she was concerned, he could take the whole lot of them.

Wanda shook her head. "No room for that. You need to choose."

Janine was struggling to keep her composure, so Wanda nudged Macky toward the door. "Go on in and get started." Then she gave Janine a big hug, feeling her shudder.

"I'm sorry I can't help you."

"That's why we're here," said Callie. "We'll do a good job."

Wanda followed Callie into the room, her head thumping, her breathing shallow. The sun shone through the windows and dust floated in the stale air. She worried it might cause Macky to wheeze, but the room was neat, the single bed made up, books orderly on the shelves. Clearly, Janine had been in here at some point to straighten and probably look for answers. If there were any.

Wanda had cleaned bedrooms of many teenaged boys, but this one had no music posters, no piles of clothes or video games, no sports hats, no clutter of any kind. On the wall over the desk hung a map of the world which looked like a flattened orange peel with some of the continents wide and others tall and skinny. On a shelf next to the desk sat a row of dictionaries, textbooks in physics and chemistry and astronomy. A mug held chewed pencils and pens. On the bed sat three sealed boxes with the Brewster logo and the name SUTTER scrawled on the side. His computer sat on the desk.

Wanda fought back panic at seeing things that Whit had touched, in a room where he'd breathed, where he'd taken off the clothes he'd worn the night Macky was made. Had he also been drunk that night? Had it been his first sex? Months later, when he'd seen her pregnant, did he know she was lying that David was the father? Would she have told him the truth if he'd asked her directly?

She hadn't admitted to anyone that she'd been drunk that night or that Whit had seen her pregnant. That she worried it might have been one of the reasons he'd done it.

Out of the window, there was the sweeping back yard leading to the edge of Bascom Grove about 100 yards away. Next to the bed a telescope stood aimed out the window. Did Whit spy on people from his room? She'd always assumed he'd been outside that night, heard her crying, and had come to check. But what if he'd been sitting there, looking through the telescope, waiting for someone? Her stomach rose at the memory of his breath and his dirty hair. Feeling faint, she sat on the bed, but then popped up, her head spinning, sensing his presence next to her on the mattress. Macky stood across the room, pulling books off shelves, making piles, reading the titles that made no sense to her. "Hey, Mom. Wow, this is great."

Wanda took shallow breaths, shutting her eyes and thinking of cool air, of an open field. No backing out now. She had to push on.

"Are you okay?" asked Callie, unspooling a couple of garbage bags. She darted her eyes to Macky. "Do you want to talk?"

"No, let's do this." She sat at the desk for a moment as Macky continued his search.

"Why don't you do the closet," said Callie, "and I'll sort through these boxes and his desk?" She handed Wanda a plastic bag. Wanda took the slick plastic in her sweaty hands. She shook open the bag.

Trapped smells of collar dirt, sweat, and dust flooded her nose when she opened the closet door. Turning on the overhead light, she thought it looked like an old man's things—a rod with shirts and pants hanging, sweaters folded in piles on the shelf above and shoes neatly paired on the floor. Each Oxford and plaid shirt hung buttoned to the top. No jeans, no tee-shirts. Just khakis. David used to drop everything into dirty wads on the floor, and, hating a mess, she'd gather them up and toss everything into the hamper rather than get into it with him. Today, she unbuttoned each shirt, folded it, placing it into the open bag. She sniffed the sweaters, inspecting for moth holes, and threw them in as well. A couple of tweed jackets needed cleaning but would be fine to donate. At the far end of the rod, hung his high-school graduation gown with the yellow honors sash draped around the neck. He kept that? Should she give it to Janine or would it make her too sad? She put it aside to decide on later. On the floor, she found a pair of bicycling shoes, a pair of thick-soled winter boots, and a pair of black dress shoes. Also, a new-looking tennis racket. She separated everything into trash or Goodwill donations, filling the bags. With the closet newly cleared, a pencil drawing became visible on the back wall—a door with a knob, like an opening to a secret passageway. Had Whit imagined disappearing into the wall, escaping into another world? Janine would certainly have the room painted before listing the house. A fresh coat of paint would take away the sadness. No wonder Janine hadn't been able to clear it out. Wanda felt it was important for her to help with this. Hard enough for her, but impossible for Whit's mother. Macky, his head bent over a book, turned the pages, and laughed at something he'd read. A shiver ran through her along with a rush of love for her boy.

Callie knew it must be incredibly intense for Wanda to confront Whit's private things and to think about the person who'd lived in this room. Maybe Callie should have taken the clothes and left the papers to Wanda. Callie hadn't meant to imply that she was the book person and Wanda the house cleaner. But Wanda was working her way through the closet while Macky was in heaven flipping through every book.

She decided to start with the boxes from the college. Whit had been on winter break but had used his ID to slip back into the dorm where he slit his wrists in the dorm bathroom and was found by an international student staying on campus for the break. Horrible. Someone had clearly tossed the contents of his dorm room into boxes to give to the Sutters. She figured Janine and Alden just couldn't face what was in them, even after all this time. Janine had confided to Wanda and Callie that Whit had hated living in the dorm, even after his roommate moved out and he had a single. He couldn't stand sharing a bathroom and found the dorm too noisy for sleep. He'd started spending more nights back home, but the Sutters had held the line, telling him dorm life was part of the college experience. "But maybe it was too much for him," Janine had said. "We knew he was struggling, but we hoped it would get better. I have to live with that fact. We mistook his depression for homesickness."

"You couldn't have known," Callie had said. "Some kids can't wait to leave home. Some can't bring themselves to leave."

"I'll always wonder if we should have let him stay here," Janine had said, her voice husky.

Callie unsealed the first box and started sifting through the papers, making a pile to recycle, another for the Sutters to keep. Whit had enrolled in 300-level physics, math, and chemistry courses. She flipped through spiral notebooks with his tiny handwriting, pages of notes and calculations that were way above her head. His writing reminded her of the creepy letter he'd written, spilling his heart out on pages and pages on thin, crinkly paper. After twenty or so pages of class notes, his writing became sketchier, and he'd started doodling in the margins, stars and rockets, before scratching them out. She put that notebook in a pile to decide on later. Then she came upon a chemistry lab report with a big red C- scrawled on it and a note from Professor Flicker. *I expected better from you. Come see me during office hours.* Holes in the paper looked as if they'd been made by a pen stabbing the page with the words **FUCK** and **IDIOT** written in bold letters. She continued to sort through the box. A textbook still in its plastic cover and a letter from the Dean saying that Whit's advisor was concerned about him and urged him to get in touch with Student Health for an appointment. A tube of acne medication, an unfilled prescription for Wellbutrin, a stuffed dinosaur, a copy of *Bullfinch's Mythology*. At the bottom of the pile was his copy of *The Sheltonian*. She flipped through it and saw only a couple of inscriptions, including the *Good luck in college* she'd scrawled that night at the kegger when she'd yelled at him. The memory burned in her chest. She'd been upset, sure, but he didn't deserve to be screamed at. The way he shrank before her, clutching his stupid yearbook. And how she'd relished flattening him.

Macky kept asking Wanda if he could have just one more book. "Please? I've run out of boxes."

"Fine! Whatever," Wanda said. "Just stop talking so much. Go ask Mrs. Sutter for some paper bags. And give us a moment of peace, please without constant chatter, will you?"

He jumped up and scampered out the door. Wanda sighed and shook her head.

"You okay?"

Wanda sighed and nodded.

"This is so sad," said Callie, still flipping through the yearbook.

"What is?"

"Looking at his yearbook. Almost no one signed it."

"That's not a big deal for some people."

"I think it was for him. He asked me to sign his and we were at a party, and I was in a terrible mood, so I just went off on him. I was so mean."

"I'm sure you weren't."

"No, I was. I screamed at him."

Wanda sat at the desk and started to weep, swiping at her eyes. Callie handed her a tissue. "I'm sorry. Did I upset you?"

"He knew. I told him it was David's baby, but I think he knew."

"But you had to say that."

"I was scared. But it was selfish."

Callie said it wouldn't have helped him to know. What would he have done, offered to marry her? No way.

"Do you think that was why he did it?" she asked, her voice choked and thin.

"No, I don't." She reached for Wanda, hugging her. "He was really unhappy, not just about that. Who knows what he was think-ing?" And she handed Wanda the lab report and the note from the Dean. She sat reading them, sniffing, her breath coming in gulps.

"Poor Whit," said Wanda.

"He was unraveling. Who knows what made him to it? But it sounds as if he was really, seriously depressed." She showed Wanda the empty bottle of antidepressants dated months before he and Wanda had hooked up.

Wanda looked at the door, half open, to make sure Macky wasn't there. "I'm so worried," she whispered, "that this will happen to Macky someday."

Callie leaned in and rubbed Wanda's shoulder. "Hey, listen, Macky is half you. And he's learning from you. You can't allow yourself to believe he's headed in the same direction. He is not the same person."

"I worry all the time..."

Macky burst into the room with a pile of folded grocery bags, giddy, out of breath. "Mom, can I fill these up, please?" Wanda stood up, patting at her eyes, and said yes, but they needed to push on. She headed to the dresser and Callie next tackled the desk.

In the drawer, Callie found ribbons Whit had won in academic contests. She put them aside for Janine and Alden along with a photo he'd saved of a dog, essays he'd written in high school, the Rotary Scholarship plaque, the yearbook. Maybe Janine hadn't been able to imagine keeping these things when she first searched the room, but she'd probably value them now. Wanda added the graduation gown and Callie agreed they should have it as well.

The desktop computer sat there, covered with a layer of dust. Could there be anything disturbing to the Sutters on it? But since only Whit had the log-in code, anything upsetting would be safe until it could be wiped clean. She put it aside to ask Janine about. That and the telescope.

Wanda stripped the bed and put the linens in a bag. Then she took down the map and folded it, adding it to the box for the Sutters. They worked steadily, silently, as the bags filled and his possessions were divided. Finally, when everything had been taken off the shelves and the bed and the walls, and they'd made three piles: keep, donate, and toss, they called the job done. Wanda gave Callie a hug, whispering that she couldn't have done this without her. Macky had filled all his boxes and four bags and was eager to go home and figure out where to put his books. "We need to talk to Mrs. Sutter for a bit. First you thank her, then you can go wait in the car and look at your books." Carrying Macky's boxes and bags to the car took a couple of trips. Then, with one last look at the room, Wanda said goodbye and she went downstairs again.

Janine was sitting on an ottoman next to Alden's chair, and they were talking quietly. When Wanda said they were done, Janine beckoned them into the room.

"How was it?" She asked, giving each of them a hug, trying not to cry.

"Sad," said Wanda, "but I think we worked well together."

Callie handed her a box. "We took the liberty of gathering some of Whit's things that you might want to have."

"Oh," she said, "that's lovely." She looked at her husband. "Right, Alden?" He nodded and cleared his throat. She put the box on the floor next to her and patted it.

"We weren't sure what to do about the telescope and his computer," said Wanda.

"Why don't you keep them? I'd rather Macky have them than Goodwill."

"Oh, but we've taken so much already."

"I'd really like it if Macky took them. If you can manage that."

Wanda had no room for the telescope, and she really didn't want a computer that they couldn't get into, one that might prove troubling if they did gain access to it, but she said sure, they'd take them. How generous.

"This was a huge thing to ask of you, Wanda. I know it was hard. But it means so much to us. I just couldn't do it by myself, and I didn't want a stranger going through his things. I won't forget this kindness."

Alden said they could now say goodbye to the house. Janine took his hand and nodded.

"You've been so kind to me and Macky."

"And Callie, you had your hands full with your mother and all your driving back and forth. Thank you so much for taking this time to help."

"Of course." She gave Callie a plant to take to her mother, something to give her some cheer, she hoped. Callie thanked her.

In the car on the way home, Macky chattered, trying to decide which book he would read first. He opened one and was flipping through the pages. He grew quiet, reading, then after a moment or so, he asked, "Mom, how *did* Whit die?"

She looked in the rearview mirror at him in the back seat, his face, serious. He wasn't going to let it rest at just a quick brush off. "Macky, you know that sometimes, people die even when they're young."

"Yes, but why?"

"I think he was depressed. And he couldn't live any longer."

"Didn't he try harder to be alive?"

"Oh, baby. I think he did try, but it was too hard, I think. I'm afraid he was really sad."

"Was David sad like that?"

"No, that was different. He died because of the war. He was around guns and bombs." Her words caught in her throat. "Does this make you sad?"

"No, I just wondered." He looked at his book again.

She studied him, his head bent over the book. "Macky, I love you and think you're such a great boy."

"I know."

"And I know you have a different kind of family than a lot

of kids since it's just the two of us. Anytime you want to ask me questions about that, you can. Okay?"

"Okay." He sat for a moment. "I do have a question."

"What is it?" she asked, bracing herself.

"Where should I put my telescope?"

"That, we'll have to figure out. Maybe at the farm where you have a wide view of the sky? You can't see much from our place."

"Sounds good." Then he added, "Mom? This was a good day."

"Yes, Bud, a good day."

✳ ✳ ✳

As Callie drove back to her mother's place, she thought about the Sutters and their love for Whit, how he'd been their little boy, and they'd dreamed of a good future for him. Maybe they didn't see him as strange. Did they understand him? Probably not, but they loved him. What would it feel like to be blindly in love with a child? Would she ever feel that for her own child someday? She hoped so.

For years, she'd been fighting against the strands pulling her back to Shelton, had fought against her parents' expectations, their judgments, now her mother's needs. But she had to admit they wanted the best for her even though it wasn't always what she wanted.

She admired Wanda, but she also worried that Wanda was heading into a time when Macky would outgrow her, that he'd learn the truth and hate her for it. Or maybe he'd just see that she'd done her best.

Pulling into the driveway, she brought the plant with her. Inside, Lena was doing the dishes. She said her mother was taking a nap but would get up soon and would have a tray of food. Callie offered to take the tray up to her. "I haven't seen her all day. How's she doing?"

"Fine, she was a little muddled in the morning, but she's good now. I gave her a nice bath and she likes those lavender beads."

Callie put the plant on the tray and carried it upstairs. Her mother was sitting in a chair by the window, her glasses on her nose, a book open in front of her. When she saw Callie, she said, "Where were you all day?"

"I was helping Wanda at the Sutters' house."

"Doing what?"

She stopped herself from saying, "I already told you, Mom," but repeated that they needed some help packing up their house for the move.

"I wish you'd take some of your clothes and books from the room too. I've been meaning to get in there and clear out old things."

Callie didn't want her stuff from childhood but also didn't want her mother going through her room. Right now, the last thing she could think about was sorting through old junk. "I'll get to it, Mom." She held up the tray. "Lena made a snack for you."

"Oh, I don't like those crackers."

"Well, that's what Lena prepared for you."

"She knows I don't like that."

"Then you might just take them and not eat them. But not complain."

"I don't complain."

She gave her mother the plant from Janine. Her mother looked at it and put it aside. "Ooh. My legs keep cramping." She lifted one foot and flexed her thin ankle.

"Would you like me to massage your feet?"

"They're just tired."

"But I could rub them."

"That won't help."

"It might."

She knelt on the floor in front of her mother's chair and lifted a foot onto her lap, removing the slipper. Her mother's bare feet were dry and flaky, and her toenails needed trimming. Callie felt a bit sick. "You have a bunion."

"I've had it forever. Nothing I can do about it but just wear slippers." Callie touched it gently, and her mother winced. "Be careful."

"I'm so sorry. I'll be gentle. I promise." She started to rub light circles along the arch, flexing the foot, testing its mobility. At first, her mother was tense and held her foot rigid, but as Callie continued, her mother sat back in her chair and let Callie add lotion, cradling the foot, pointing, flexing it, warming the skin. Then she worked on the other one before sliding the slippers on again and placing each foot on the floor. Her mother had drifted off to sleep. Callie stood and placed the tray on the ottoman, covered her mother with an afghan and left the room.

20

WANDA AND CALLIE

On Thanksgiving Day, Macky dug in his heels, refusing to go to the farm. He hated the food, his cousins were loud and mean, it was stupid, no one would miss him. Wanda said it would hurt Nana and Pop's feelings if he didn't come and yes, he would be missed. But Macky couldn't care less about that. Finally, to avoid a struggle, she offered two full days of unrestricted Internet and his choice of clothes to wear and book to bring along to the farm. A bribe, but she'd found that trading one thing he liked for something she wanted worked. Another trade—if he brushed his teeth, he wouldn't have to eat everything he was served. "Say no, thank you, but be polite." She suggested it might be better this year. "Just make an effort." She did worry about whether her mother would shame him about his eating. Some things never changed. Maybe Wanda could make sure he got an extra roll or two as she scooped his vegetables onto her plate.

Benny arrived at two forty-five, wearing a sweater and khakis with two six-packs of Bud. He'd put on aftershave, which she liked but Macky hated, and hoped Macky wouldn't pitch a fit. Benny gave her a kiss and greeted Macky, now dressed in his army hat and tee-shirt and dawdling in front of his screen. "Hey ya. How's it going?" Macky grunted, and Wanda rolled her eyes at Benny.

Benny offered to carry her sweet potato casserole to the car. "No, I've got it," and she told Macky they were leaving. "Now." He'd been given a five-minute, then a four-minute warning. "Macky, by the time I count to five…" She'd learned that technique from his teacher, and it seemed to work. Short-term goals with consequences if he didn't do what she asked. He dragged himself up, shrugged on his coat and headed for the door.

On the way up to the farm, Macky opened the car window, letting in cold air, so Wanda asked him to shut it. He left it cracked a hair, and she could hear him doing his deep breathing, which he did when anxious. Benny turned around and asked him what he was reading. Macky mumbled something she couldn't hear. Benny looked at Wanda and winked. Thank God he was so even-tempered. Nothing ever seemed to bother him. He could usually nudge Macky into talking about his current interest, even though Benny never had a clue what he was talking about.

She parked in the circle drive behind Kenny's SUV and Joe's truck. The snow hadn't started to fall yet, but she could smell it in the air. The sun heading down the sky would soon drop behind the hills. Benny carried the casserole, a grocery bag with the beers slung over his shoulder. Macky followed behind, his coat unzipped, his shoelaces dragging.

"We're here." Her sisters-in-law were already in the kitchen, and even though they'd agreed on three o'clock, her mother would still be annoyed that she hadn't arrived early like Mary Sue and Gail. She placed the casserole on the island while Benny gave the women hugs and opened the refrigerator to stow the beers. Gail said to put them in the spillover fridge in the garage. He headed out there as Wanda put on an apron and asked her mother what she should do. Handing Wanda the potato masher, her mother said to warm up the milk first before adding it. "I know, Mom."

Benny returned to the kitchen with a beer and offered to help, something no man in that house ever did. Evelyn thanked him but said he should head on into the family room with the other guys. Football blared from the huge TV, and Wanda's father, brothers, and nephews sat draped over the sectional, staring at the game, stuffing their faces with chips and cheese. Macky climbed onto one of the kitchen stools and opened his book, but his grandmother told him to go join his cousins. He groaned and Wanda shot him a look as he slipped out of the room. Wanda hoped Luke and Simon would be nice to Macky for once.

"So, Wanda, how's it going with Benny?" asked Mary Sue.

"Good," she said, steam from the potatoes misting her cheeks.

"Has he done any CPR on you?" asked Gail, winking as she and Mary Sue laughed.

"Come on, stop. It's good. Complicated because he has his kids part-time, and I have Macky."

"Oh, yeah, I can see that." She leaned into whisking the gravy. "Why isn't he with his kids today?

"Connie has them. They alternate holidays."

"If he can deal with Macky," said Mary Sue, "he's a keeper."

Wanda swallowed the dig.

"At least Benny knows what he's in for," said Gail.

She wasn't worried about Benny, but she did wonder how his girls would take to Macky.

"Actually, they get along great," Wanda said, but caught a look between her sisters-in-law. Wanda could say plenty of things about their kids, no models for good behavior.

Her mother dropped a hot tray of cheese puffs onto the island. "Plate these apps," she said, barking like a drill sergeant.

"I'll do it." Wanda burned her finger on the first one, then grabbed a spatula and lifted a puff onto the plate. The smell of melted cheese and butter made Wanda's stomach grumble.

"I hope Macky doesn't make a fuss about eating."

"Don't worry, Mom. He'll be fine."

The constant criticisms of Macky wore Wanda out. She took a deep breath. Her brow prickled with sweat, and she wiped it with the back of her hand. Then she took a sip of wine and a warm flush rose to her cheeks. Although she almost never drank anymore, she'd allowed herself one glass today to calm her jitters.

The doorbell rang, and Wanda grabbed a towel to wipe her hands, but Mary Sue reached the door first. It was Janine and Alden, her wearing a skirt, him a tweed jacket. Had her mother not told them it was a casual gathering? Maybe this was their casual. She wasn't sure how much her brothers and sisters-in-law knew about their connection to Wanda and Macky. She only hoped that if they did, they'd have some kindness toward Macky and not spill the secret. She'd been laying the groundwork for telling him the truth, preparing to reveal the facts, most of them, but it had to be done gently.

Wanda's mother approached and gave Janine a hug, which pleased Wanda. "Welcome. We're a rowdy bunch. I hope we aren't too much for you." Janine said that she'd been looking forward to a big, boisterous Thanksgiving for a change. Alden looked wary as he sized up the men and boys drinking beers, sodas, and scarfing down chips. Janine handed her hostess a bottle of wine, and Evelyn thanked them. "Well, come on in and get settled. Would you like a drink?"

Wanda asked Benny where Macky was. He didn't know. She went looking for him and found him in her old room, on the bed, nose in his book. "There you are. It's rude to hide in here."

"I don't like football, and it's too loud to read out there. You said I could read. You said so."

"I know, but you also have to spend time out among people. And Mr. and Mrs. Sutter are here, and they'd like to see you."

"I'll be there in a minute."

"No, now, Bud." She stared until he dragged himself off the bed and scraped his feet, glaring at her as he slipped past her and out the door. She steered him over to the Sutters, who still stood awkwardly near the entryway. Luckily, Macky had brought one of the books from Whit's room, so when he held it up for them to see, Janine's face lit up as she leaned over to look at the page. Then he took his book and plunked down in the space where two sofas met, shoving his fingers in his ears.

Luke and Simon were tossing cheese curls at each other, but most of them fell on Macky. Luke said something to him that Wanda didn't hear but he frowned and pulled his feet up under him. Nasty kids. Please, Macky, keep it together.

Wanda asked that someone give Alden a place to sit. When neither boy moved, Kenny blasted Simon, "Hey, move your butt. And stop wasting food." Simon scowled and plunked himself down a few inches over. "Please, sit down." Alden lowered himself onto orange crumbs left by the boys. Her father stood up, offering to grab him a beer.

Wanda's nieces, Leelee and Fawn, drifted by, and Wanda smelled gum mixed with a hint of cigarette smoke. They walked right past the kitchen without offering to help. Mary Sue and Gail didn't seem to care as they chopped, stirred, and plated, all while smoking. Wanda bit her tongue. Leelee was now eleven but looked fourteen with breasts, a short skirt, and a skimpy little top. She looked like Joe but was built like Gail. Was that mascara? Fawn, her shadow at age ten, was skinny as a pole with long legs like Kenny, but Mary Sue's straight brown hair. Braces sparkled in her mouth, and she looked awkward now but would be very pretty someday. Wanda figured they'd both be a handful in high school. Like their moms. And their dads. But their mothers could at least make the girls help with the meal—set the table, pour drinks, pass out apps. No wonder they were such brats.

Her mother asked her to start placing dishes on the table, and Janine offered to help her. The big table had been extended to its full length, and a smaller one stood next to it. Adults and kids separated, which meant Macky would be stuck with his cousins. As she placed the trivets around evenly, she counted and found fourteen places at the adult table and five at the children's. Nineteen? She counted off in her head: her parents, her brothers and their families, the Sutters, Callie and her mother, Wanda, Benny, Macky and came to seventeen. She headed into the kitchen and asked, "Who else is coming besides Callie and her mom?" Gail and Mary Sue shot glances at each other as the doorbell rang again.

Her mother grabbed a dishtowel. "I'll get it." She opened the door and said, "I'm so glad you came!" Wanda followed her and found Sandy and Burt standing at the open door. A shock ran through her, and she wondered if she could escape out the back door. For months, since the day Sandy slapped her and called her a slut, she'd only seen them through the car window when she dropped Macky off. And now her mother ambushed Wanda by inviting them? Her face burned as if freshly slapped. Glancing over at Benny for help, she saw him talking to Alden.

Evelyn put her arm around Sandy. "We are so glad to see you." Wanda stood frozen to the spot, wishing to be invisible. But when Sandy saw Wanda, she lurched forward, pulling her daughter-in-law into a hug. "Wanda, Sweetie." Wanda, her arms pinned to her sides, allowed herself to be hugged. When she realized Sandy meant it, that there was no trick, she leaned into Sandy, both of them crying. Wanda whispered, "I'm so sorry." Sandy patted her back and said she was sorry too.

Sandy pulled away, wiped her eyes, winding a tress of Wanda's hair behind her ear. "Oh, my." She took a deep breath and let it out. "Now, where's Macky?"

Wanda called Macky's name, but because he had his ears plugged, he didn't hear her. Benny nudged him and pointed. Macky closed his book and headed over, a worried look on his face, clearly noting the tears. With his newly sprouted front teeth, he looked older than he had even a month ago. Sandy hugged him and he squirmed out of her grasp. Burt reached into his jacket and pulled out a $10 bill and handed it to Macky, patting him on the shoulder. Macky took the money and studied it. "What do you say?" asked Wanda, and he thanked them, looking at the bill but not them. Gail brought a glass of wine to Sandy and a beer to Burt. Sandy drank half of it in one swallow. Burt wandered over to perch on the arm of the sofa next to Wanda's father. They shook hands and Burt reached for some cheese curls.

Wanda looked at Benny and saw he was waiting for a sign from her. When she nodded, he stood up and wound his way over to them. Her voice shaking, Wanda introduced Benny to Sandy, but Sandy said she already knew him and greeted him coolly, but graciously. Did Sandy think Benny was Macky's father? She'd have to ask her mother if she'd said anything to them. It melted her heart to see how kindly Benny treated them, how he did his best to put them at ease. He was telling them a memory of watching David play football back in high school, how he'd been the best athlete the school had seen in years.

Wanda headed into the kitchen and pulled her mother into the pantry. "Why didn't you tell me you'd invited Sandy and Burt?"

"I figured you both needed a safe place to meet again. A place where no one would make a scene."

"But what if there'd been one?"

"I figured that if they came, it would mean that Sandy wanted to make up. And if she didn't, they'd stay home."

"You should have let me know you were doing this." Her voice shook, and she was sweating.

"And then you'd have been a wreck and might have been disappointed."

"My heart is still beating so hard. What a shock."

"Well, the worst is over. The ice is broken."

"We'll see. Please don't do that again. I don't like surprises."

"Oh, relax. I did you a favor." She patted Wanda on the shoulder. "You're welcome."

They returned to the kitchen where Mary Sue was topping off Sandy's wine and pouring more for herself.

Could her mother be right, that this was the push they needed? Or was Sandy only acting nice because they were around others? Would she turn on Wanda when the anger and hurt bubbled up again? At every turn, Wanda discovered new wrinkles in this family drama. How to incorporate Benny? How to protect the Zaceks from the fact that Macky had another set of grandparents, not just in the town, but in the room? Were they in store for more hurt and anger? After all this time, was she incapable of hoping for a good outcome? Okay, maybe she'd allow herself one more glass of wine, just for today. She looked at Macky with his six grandparents, her parents, her brothers and their families, and folded into that group now, Benny. Would there come a time when he'd bring his daughters too, adding them to this complicated mix, this group of people she loved despite its messiness? Her family.

On Thanksgiving morning, Callie woke knowing her entire day would be devoted to helping her mother bathe and get ready for the MacDonalds' dinner, then transporting her there and watching to make sure she didn't choke or have an accident. Nice of Wanda's parents to invite them, but it would have been a lot simpler to eat a quiet dinner together. She'd given the caregiver Wednesday night through Saturday morning off so Lena could spend time with her own family. Callie was determined to treat Lena well and keep her happy so she wouldn't quit, knowing how hard it was to manage her mother 24/7. But maybe this was more than Callie could handle by herself. After Lena left, her mother regressed, becoming needy and fragile, micromanaging everything Callie did, complaining that Lena did it better. Wednesday night, she struggled to settle her mother down to bed. Thanksgiving morning, her mother had awakened in a cranky mood, claiming she hadn't slept a wink, which wasn't true. In the kitchen, her mother stared, waiting for Callie to mess up buttering toast and pouring coffee. "Mom, I know how to make toast."

After breakfast, she gave her mother a bath. Seeing her mother fully naked for the first time in memory—they'd never been a family comfortable with nudity—she was startled by her mother's extreme thinness and loss of muscle mass. And her skin was so fragile, Callie knew had to use a very light touch so as not to bruise or abrade her skin. Lena did a wonderful job of keeping her mother clean, and Callie was grateful for that. She knew how quickly hygiene fell apart if unattended.

When she found the right temperature and lowered her mother into the bath, the warm water melted away her mother's resistance. "Ah, that's lovely," she sighed. As Callie squeezed soapy water over her back, her mother, eyes closed, hummed a German tune that Callie knew from her own childhood. Callie joined in, and it was a good moment. She'd have liked it to last longer, but the water was cooling, and she wanted her mother to rest before they had to leave. When she offered her arm, her mother panicked. "Be careful! Don't let me fall!"

"Just trust me." She wrapped her mother in a robe and they made their way down the hall and into her mother's room. Callie helped her into a chair and tucked a blanket around her legs. Then she sat down in the kitchen with a book to give herself some respite.

It had been a busy few days. She'd arrived the previous Sunday and in anticipation of Lena's absence had squeezed her four Shelton massage clients into one day. On Tuesday morning, she'd gone to see Elise, who was getting married that weekend at the Episcopal Church. She and Callie hadn't seen each other in person for years, but since Callie's father died, they'd returned to texts, so they were up to speed with each other's lives. Elise had just graduated from Yale Law, where her fiancé, Garrett, had been a year ahead of her. They both had jobs at top firms in Manhattan.

At first, Callie was hurt that Elise hadn't asked her to be in the wedding party but knew that Elise had friends from college and law school to ask. A few days before the wedding, she visited Elise at her parents' house, admired her huge solitaire engagement ring and Vera Wang dress, looked at the piles of gifts (finding her own gift, an artisan wooden bowl stuck behind an espresso maker), listened to Elise and her mother bicker, hearing Elise talk about Garrett's family from Greenwich, wondering who this person was who used to be her best friend. Elise had given her the option of inviting a Plus One to the wedding, but Callie had no one she wanted to invite, no one whom she knew well enough to subject to the long drive and the days with her mother.

"Maybe you'll meet someone new at the wedding," suggested Elise.

"I'm not looking for that right now," said Callie. "And I have my mother to take care of. It'll be so much fun at the wedding. I can't wait. You're going to be beautiful. Just take time to relax if you can."

On her way back to her mother's house, she felt strangely empty. In some ways, seeing Elise felt as if they'd never been apart, two friends who shared a childhood full of confidences. But in other ways, they'd moved along wildly different paths. Elise was status-conscious and success-driven, but she'd always been Type A. Callie wondered what the hurry was to get married at the same time she was launching her career. But Elise always had a plan, even back in high school—Ivy League, then law school. Now it was a handsome, preferably rich, husband, partner track, house in Park Slope, two kids in private school, vacations in Tuscany and Cabo. She'd been the one to kick Callie into gear and aim beyond Brewster. Would Callie have found her way on her own anyway? In the past year of visiting her mother, she'd come to realize that Shelton had its charms.

A life there wasn't wasted, not what she wanted for herself, but always a part of her. Then it occurred to her that when her mother died, she'd have no reason to come back. Her throat tightened to think of her mother dying, but would she actually miss having Shelton in her life?

At two, she dressed and then laid out her mother's clothes: skirt, blouse, cardigan, knee-high stockings, shoes. She'd already packed a bag with extra Depends, her mother's medications, and a small blanket in case the MacDonalds' house felt chilly.

As she knelt to help her mother with her stockings, she wondered why her mother had aged so poorly. Every day at the spa, Callie worked on people a lot older than her mother, and they were in much better shape. They did weight training, yoga, and Aqua Zumba. But her mother had always seemed old to Callie, even when she was young. "Mom, I'm concerned about your lack of strength. You need to find a way to get some exercise."

"Do you talk to your massage people like that?"

"They usually listen to me because they know it's for their own good."

"Well, you're awfully bossy."

"Believe me, if I thought bossing you around would work, I'd do it."

"You're so harsh."

"Oh, you think this is harsh?"

Her mother didn't cooperate with Callie's efforts to dress her, sitting limply, not lifting her arms or feet. Callie had to step back and not physically force her mother into her clothes. Taking a deep breath, she helped her mother stand as she zipped up her skirt, then sat her back down again. Then it occurred to Callie that her mother was probably anxious, worried about how she'd fare in a big group, whether she'd have the stamina to make it through the meal. "You know, Mom. It'll be fine. It was so nice of the MacDonalds to invite us. Janine will be there. And you'll get to see Wanda and Macky."

"She's such a good girl. Raising that boy all by herself."

"Yes, Mom, she's pretty much a saint." She heard the sarcasm in her voice, but she appreciated Wanda's strengths.

Despite starting early, she hadn't planned the time right. She hated, really hated, being late and now they were definitely that. Callie helped her mother down the front steps and into the car, slowly, her mother's walker dragging along the gravel. One of the tennis balls had fallen off its leg, and Callie was afraid it would scratch the floors. Then her mother remembered the box of candy she'd meant to bring, and Callie had to run back inside to find it. On the drive to the MacDonalds', her mother fussed, and Callie tried to tune her out, but she worried as well. What if her mother choked or had an accident and needed changing or just collapsed from over exertion? But everyone there would have to know her mother needed some extra time and attention.

They arrived and parked out on the street because the driveway was full of vehicles. She'd never been to the farm before but had driven past the house with the big barns and the fields stretching out for acres. The barns were now silhouetted black against the setting sun, the house brightly lit where inside the picture window, she could see a group milling around. They were so late. Helping her mother out of the car, handing her the walker, they headed slowly up the driveway to the front stoop. Then Callie guided her up the two steps, her mother wheezing heavily.

Evelyn opened the door. "Sorry we're late," said Callie.

"No, you're right on time," she said and stood to let them pass through, patting Callie's mother on the shoulder and winking at Callie.

Inside, the voices, the bustle of bodies, the TV, were a big contrast from the quiet of her mother's house. She helped her mother off with her coat and eased her into a chair. When she scanned the room, she saw members of Wanda's family as well as the Sutters. Then she saw Burt and Sandy Zacek. Whose idea was that?

Wanda came over to give Callie's mother a hug. Callie took Wanda aside and asked her why the Zaceks were there.

"A surprise," Wanda said, sighing, "planned by my mother."

"Holy shit. What did you do when you saw them?"

"I about fainted. I'm still recovering."

"The Sutters and the Zaceks in the same room? That's the perfect storm."

"So far, no drama. I'm just about holding it together." She picked up her glass of wine and took a sip.

"What can I do to help? Should I talk to Sandy, keep her occupied?"

"Yes, and I'll get your mother an appetizer."

"And some water. In case she starts to choke?"

"Oh, yeah, right."

Callie introduced herself to Sandy, who was hanging out in the kitchen. Of course, Sandy remembered Callie, she said, her speech mushy. Burt was watching TV with the men. No sign of tension yet. Callie glanced over and saw her mother talking to Janine. Then she looked for Macky and saw him squeezed onto the sofa between his cousins, looking like he needed rescuing.

Evelyn called everyone to the tables.

"Hey, Macky," Callie said. "Do you want to sit next to me?"

"Yeah, okay." She'd rejoined her mother to guide her to the table and pointed to the empty chair on her left.

"No, Macky," said Evelyn to Macky, who'd plunked down next to Callie. "You're at the kids' table."

Macky groaned, slumping down in his chair.

"No argument, young man."

Wanda took him aside, whispering to him, and he shook his head. She took his chin in her hand and looked him straight in the eyes. He shrugged and nodded, dragging himself over to his seat with his cousins.

Because of the mismatched chairs, heads sat comically high or low, one person perched on a stool, another's chin just clearing the tabletop. Evelyn and Jack took opposite ends of the long table, and couples sat next to each other, down the sides. Kenny brought a six-pack to the table, and Mary Sue whispered to him angrily, saying he'd had enough. Gail hoisted a gallon of milk, pouring glasses for the boys, but Macky said she should know he was lactose intolerant. Callie helped her mother into her chair and scooted it in, attempted to tie a bib around her neck, which her mother batted away. Jack plugged in the electric knife and held it over the turkey, but Evelyn said that before that, she wanted everyone to go around the table and say what they were thankful for. Simon had already bitten into a roll, so Luke punched him in the arm, and Simon spat the wad of chewed roll in his face. Gail stood up and warned the boys that if they didn't behave, they'd be sorry. The girls laughed, and Simon gave Luke the finger. Macky shut his eyes and took deep breaths, shaking his head. Evelyn said she was so happy that the whole family, everyone, could be together. Janine thanked them for including her and Alden this year. Benny raised a can of beer to Evelyn and all the women for preparing such a feast. Callie also said it was lovely they were included since they weren't family. "You are too family," said Wanda. She looked at the Zaceks. Sandy started crying again, and Burt put his arm around her.

Macky's hand shot up, saying he wanted to tell them what he was thankful for. Wanda held her breath and Evelyn told him to take his cap off at the table. He frowned, removed it, and stood up.

"I am thankful for the species that are not extinct like the Tree Lobster and the Pygmy Tarter, the Nocturnal Gracilidris Ant, the Peccary—"

"Pecker," said Luke, snorting into his hand.

"Luke, enough," said his father.

"Okay, then," said Evelyn, nodding to her husband to start carving.

"I'm not done," said Macky.

Callie nodded to him, Janine beamed, Sandy propped her head on her chin, her eyes drooping.

"There's more. The Arakan Forest Turtle, Goblin Shark,"His grandmother glared at Wanda to do something. She tried to catch his eye.

"The New Guina Big-Eared Bat, the Kashmir Musk Deer, the Laotian Rock Rat,"

"Eew," said Fawn, then Leelee said it too. Benny started to clap and said it was an awesome list, Wanda walked over and took Macky's arm as he continued. Finally, he said he was done.

"Okay, then," said Wanda. "Shall we eat now?"

Acknowledgments

Many thanks to:

Donna Bister and Marc Estrin of Fomite Press for dedicating themselves to creating beautiful books and supporting writers

Julie Justicz, Arlene Brimer Mailing, Mary Beth Shaffer, and Lynn Sloan, members of Writers' Bridge, for patiently reading chapters of this book over several years, always meeting me where I was and helping me find my way forward

Beth Castrodale, Marcie Friedman, Rachel Hall (thanks for the title), Ann Leone, Charles Lamar Phillips, and Bonnie Seebold for reading drafts and offering great support

The Pen-City Writers for reminding me that writing can be an expression of hope in the most hopeless circumstances

The Ragdale Foundation for giving me a room of my own and a fireplace during the polar vortex

Fred Shafer for providing an enduring influence on my writing

David English for sharing my love of books and my parents for inspiring that love

James and William Leary for being most impressive men and excellent shelter companions during the pandemic

John Leary always, for being you. (And for the beautiful cover art)

Fomite

Writing a review on social media sites for readers will help the progress of independent publishing. To submit a review, go to the book page on any of the sites and follow the links for reviews. Books from independent presses rely on reader-to-reader communications.

For more information or to order any of our books, visit:
http://www.fomitepress.com/our-books.html

More novels and novellas from Fomite...

J
Joshua Amses — *During This, Our Nadir*
Joshua Amses — *Ghats*
Joshua Amses — *Raven or Crow*
Joshua Amses — *The Moment Before an Injury*
Charles Bell — *The Married Land*
Charles Bell — *The Half Gods*
Jaysinh Birjepatel — *Nothing Beside Remains*
Jaysinh Birjepatel — *The Good Muslim of Jackson Heights*
David Borofka — *The End of Good Intnetions*
David Brizer — *The Secret Doctrine of V. H. Rand*
David Brizer — *Victor Rand*
L. M Brown — *Hinterland*
Paula Closson Buck — *Summer on the Cold War Planet*
L.enny Cavallaro — *Paganini Agitato*
Dan Chodorkoff — *Loisaida*
Dan Chodorkoff — *Sugaring Down*
David Adams Cleveland — *Time's Betrayal*
Paul Cody— *Sphyxia*
Jaimee Wriston Colbert — *Vanishing Acts*
Roger Coleman — *Skywreck Afternoons*
Stephen Downes — *The Hands of Pianists*
Marc Estrin — *Hyde*
Marc Estrin — *Kafka's Roach*
Marc Estrin — *Proceedings of the Hebrew Free Burial Society*
Marc Estrin — *Speckled Vanities*
Marc Estrin — *The Annotated Nose*
Marc Estrin — *The Penseés of Alan Krieger*
Zdravka Evtimova — *Asylum for Men and Dogs*
Zdravka Evtimova — *In the Town of Joy and Peace*
Zdravka Evtimova — *Sinfonia Bulgarica*
Zdravka Evtimova — *You Can Smile on Wednesdays*
Daniel Forbes — *Derail This Train Wreck*

Fomite

Peter Fortunato — *Carnevale*
Greg Guma — *Dons of Time*
Ramsey Hanhan – *Fugitive Dreams*
Richard Hawley — *The Three Lives of Jonathan Force*
Lamar Herrin — *Father Figure*
Michael Horner — *Damage Control*
Ron Jacobs — *All the Sinners Saints*
Ron Jacobs — *Short Order Frame Up*
Ron Jacobs — *The Co-conspirator's Tale*
Scott Archer Jones — *A Rising Tide of People Swept Away*
Scott Archer Jones — *And Throw Away the Skins*
Julie Justicz — *Conch Pearl*
Julie Justicz — *Degrees of Difficulty*
Maggie Kast — *A Free Unsullied Land*
Darrell Kastin — *Shadowboxing with Bukowski*
Coleen Kearon — *#triggerwarning*
Coleen Kearon — *Feminist on Fire*
Jan English Leary — *Thicker Than Blood*
Jan English Leary — *Town and Gown*
Diane Lefer — *Confessions of a Carnivore*
Diane Lefer — *Out of Place*
Rob Lenihan — *Born Speaking Lies*
Cynthia Newberry Martin — *The Art of Her Life*
Colin McGinnis — *Roadman*
Douglas W. Milliken — *Our Shadows' Voice*
Ilan Mochari — *Zinsky the Obscure*
Peter Nash — *In the Place Where We Thought We Stood*
Peter Nash — *Parsimony*
Peter Nash — *The Least of It*
Peter Nash — *The Perfection of Things*
George Ovitt — *Stillpoint*
George Ovitt — *Tribunal*
Gregory Papadoyiannis — *The Baby Jazz*
Pelham — *The Walking Poor*
Christopher Peterson — *Madman*
Andy Potok — *My Father's Keeper*
Frederick Ramey — *Comes A Time*
Howard Rappaport — *Arnold and Igor*
Joseph Rathgeber — *Mixedbloods*
Kathryn Roberts — *Companion Plants*
Robert Rosenberg — *Isles of the Blind*
Fred Russell — *Rafi's World*
Ron Savage — *Voyeur in Tangier*
David Schein — *The Adoption*

Fomite

Charles Simpson — *Uncertain Harvest*
Lynn Sloan — *Midstream*
Lynn Sloan — *Principles of Navigation*
L.E. Smith — *The Consequence of Gesture*
L.E. Smith — *Travers' Inferno*
L.E. Smith — *Untimely RIPped*
Robert Sommer — *A Great Fullness*
Caitlin Hamilton Summie — *Geographies of the Heart*
Tom Walker — *A Day in the Life*
Susan V. Weiss —*My God, What Have We Done?*
Peter M. Wheelwright — *As It Is on Earth*
Peter M. Wheelwright — *The Door-Man*
Suzie Wizowaty — *The Return of Jason Green*